HOUSE
OF SPIES

Daniel Silva is the award-winning, number one *New York Times*
bestselling author of twenty novels, including *The Unlikely Spy*,
The Confessor, *A Death in Vienna*, *The Messenger*, *Moscow Rules*, *The
Rembrandt Affair*, *The English Girl* and *The Black Widow*. His books
are published in more than thirty countries and are bestsellers
around the world. He lives in Florida with his wife, CNN Special
Correspondent Jamie Gangel, and their two children, Lily and
Nicholas.

www.danielsilvabooks.com

D0235155

DANIEL SILVA

HOUSE OF SPIES

HarperCollins*Publishers*

HarperCollins*Publishers*
1 London Bridge Street
London SE1 9GF

www.harpercollins.co.uk

This paperback edition 2018
1

First published in Great Britain by HarperCollins*Publishers* 2017

First published in the United States of America by Harper,
an imprint of HarperCollins*Publishers* 2017

Copyright © Daniel Silva 2017

Daniel Silva asserts the moral right to
be identified as the author of this work

A catalogue record for this book
is available from the British Library

ISBN: 978-0-00-810476-4 (B-format PB)
ISBN: 978-0-00-810477-1 (A-format PB)

Map by Nick Springer, copyright © 2017 Springer Cartographics LLC

Printed and bound in Great Britain by
CPI Group (UK) Ltd, Croydon, CR0 4YY

Once again, for my wife, Jamie, and my children, Nicholas and Lily

Beware the fury of a patient man.

—JOHN DRYDEN, *Absalom and Achitophel*

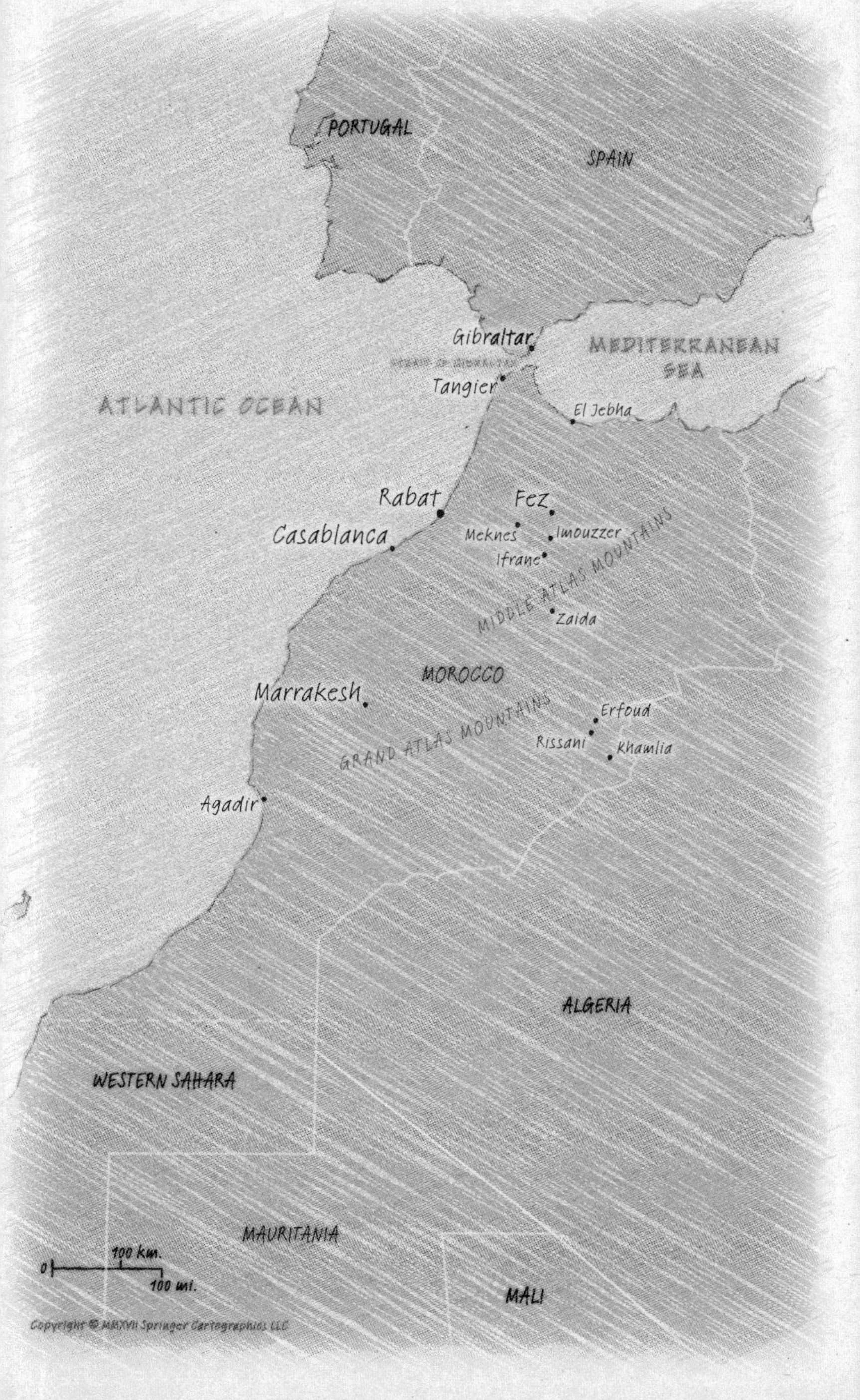
PORTUGAL
SPAIN
Gibraltar
MEDITERRANEAN SEA
Tangier
ATLANTIC OCEAN
El Jebha
Rabat
Fez
Casablanca
Meknes
Imouzzer
Ifrane
MIDDLE ATLAS MOUNTAINS
Zaida
MOROCCO
Marrakesh
Erfoud
GRAND ATLAS MOUNTAINS
Rissani
Khamlia
Agadir
ALGERIA
WESTERN SAHARA
MAURITANIA
0
100 km.
100 mi.
MALI
Copyright © MMXVII Springer Cartographics LLC

Part One

THE LOOSE THREAD

KING SAUL BOULEVARD, TEL AVIV

For something so unprecedented, so fraught with institutional risk, it was all handled with a minimum of fuss. And quietly, too. That was the remarkable thing about it, the operational silence with which it was carried out. Yes, there had been the dramatic announcement broadcast live to the nation, and the splashy first Cabinet meeting, and the lavish party at Ari Shamron's lakeside villa in Tiberias where all the friends and collaborators from his remarkable past—the spymasters, the politicians, the Vatican priests, the London art dealers, even an inveterate art thief from Paris—had come to wish him well. But otherwise it came to pass with scarcely a ripple. One day Uzi Navot was seated behind his large smoked-glass desk in the chief's office, and the next, Gabriel was in his place. Absent Navot's modern desk, mind you, for glass wasn't Gabriel's style.

Wood was more to his liking. Very old wood. And paintings, of course; he learned quickly he could not spend twelve hours a day in a room without paintings. He hung one or two of his own, unsigned, and several by his mother, who had been one of the most prominent Israeli artists of her day. He even hung a large abstract canvas by his first wife, Leah, which she had painted when they were students together at the Bezalel Academy of Art and Design in Jerusalem. Late in the day, a visitor to the executive floor might hear a bit of opera—*La Bohème* was a particular favorite—leaking from his door. The music could mean only one thing. Gabriel Allon, the prince of fire, the angel of vengeance, the chosen son of Ari Shamron, had finally assumed his rightful place as chief of Israel's secret intelligence service.

But his predecessor did not go far. In fact, Uzi Navot moved just across the foyer, to an office that in the building's original configuration had been Shamron's fortified little lair. Never before had a departing chief remained under the same roof as his successor. It was a violation of one of the most sacred principles of the Office, which mandated a clearing away of the brush every few years, a tilling of the soil. True, there were some former chiefs who kept their hand in the game. They wandered into King Saul Boulevard from time to time, swapped war stories, dispensed unheeded advice, and generally made a nuisance of themselves. And then, of course, there was Shamron, the eternal one, the burning bush. Shamron had built the Office from the ground up, in his own image. He had given the service its identity, its very language, and considered it his divine right to meddle in its affairs as he saw fit. It was Shamron who had awarded Navot the job as chief—and Shamron who, when the time had finally come, had taken it away.

But it was Gabriel who insisted Navot remain, with all the perquisites he had enjoyed in his previous incarnation. They shared the same secretary—the formidable Orit, known inside King Saul Boulevard as the Iron Dome for her ability to shoot down unwanted visitors—and Navot retained the use of his official car and a full complement of bodyguards, which provoked a bit of grumbling in the Knesset but was generally accepted as necessary to keep the peace. His exact title was rather vague, but that was typical of the Office. They were liars by trade. They spoke the truth only among themselves. To everyone else—their wives, their children, the citizens they were sworn to protect—they hid behind a cloak of deception.

When their respective doors were open, which was usually the case, Gabriel and Navot could see one another across the foyer. They spoke early each morning by secure phone, lunched together—sometimes in the staff dining room, sometimes alone in Gabriel's office—and spent a few minutes of quiet time in the evening, accompanied by Gabriel's opera, which Navot, despite his sophisticated Viennese lineage, detested. Navot had no appreciation for music, and the visual arts bored him. Otherwise, he and Gabriel were in complete agreement on all matters, at least those that involved the Office and the security of the State of Israel. Navot had fought for and won access to Gabriel's ear anytime he wanted it, and he insisted on being present at all important gatherings of the senior staff. Usually, he maintained a sphinxlike silence, with his thick arms folded across his wrestler's chest and an inscrutable expression on his face. But occasionally he would finish one of Gabriel's sentences for him, as if to make it clear to everyone in the room that, as the Americans were fond of saying, there was no daylight between them. They were like Boaz and Jachin, the twin pillars that stood at the entrance of the First Temple of Jerusalem, and anyone who even thought about playing one against the other would pay a heavy price. Gabriel was the people's chief, but he was still the chief and he would not tolerate intrigue in his court.

Not that any was likely, for the other officers who comprised his senior staff were thick as thieves. All were drawn from Barak, the elite team that had carried out some of the most storied operations in the history of a storied service. For years they had worked from a cramped subterranean set of rooms that had once been used as a dumping ground for old furniture and equipment. Now they occupied a chain of offices stretching from Gabriel's door. Even Eli Lavon, one of Israel's most prominent biblical archaeologists, had agreed to forsake his teaching position at Hebrew University and return to full-time Office employment. Nominally, Lavon oversaw the watchers, pickpockets, and those who specialized in planting listening devices and hidden cameras. In truth, Gabriel used him in any way he saw fit. The finest physical surveillance artist the Office ever produced, Lavon had been looking over Gabriel's shoulder since the days of Operation Wrath of God. His little hutch, with its shards of pottery and ancient coins and tools, was the place where Gabriel often went for a few minutes of quiet. Lavon had never been much of a talker. Like Gabriel, he did his best work in the dark, and without a sound.

A few of the old hands questioned whether it was wise for Gabriel to load up the executive suite with so many loyalists and relics from his glorious past. For the most part, however, they kept their concerns to themselves. No director general—other than Shamron, of course—had ever assumed control of the Office with more experience or goodwill. Gabriel had been playing the game longer than anyone in the business, and along the way he had collected an extraordinary array of friends and accomplices. The British prime minister owed his career to him; the pope, his life. Even so, he was not the sort of fellow to shamelessly collect on an old debt. The truly powerful man, said Shamron, never had to ask for a favor.

But he had enemies, too. Enemies who had destroyed his first wife and who had tried to destroy his second as well. Enemies in Moscow and Tehran who viewed him as the only thing standing in the way of their ambitions. For now, they had been dealt with, but doubtless they would be back. So, too, would the man with whom he had last done battle. Indeed, it was this man who occupied the top spot on the new director general's to-do list. The Office computers had assigned him a randomly generated code name. But behind the cipher-protected doors of King Saul Boulevard, Gabriel and the new leaders of the Office referred to him by the grandiose nom de guerre he had given himself. *Saladin* . . . They spoke of him with respect and even a trace of foreboding. He was coming for them. It was only a matter of time.

There was a photograph making the rounds of like-minded intelligence services. It had been snapped by an asset of the CIA in the Paraguayan town of Ciudad del Este, which was located in the notorious Tri-Border Area, or Triple Frontier, of South America. It showed a man, large, solidly built, Arab in appearance, drinking coffee at an outdoor café, accompanied by a certain Lebanese trader suspected of having ties to the global jihadist movement. The camera angle was such that it rendered facial-recognition software ineffective. But Gabriel, who was blessed with one of the finest pairs of eyes in the trade, was confident the man was Saladin. He had seen Saladin in person, in the lobby of the Four Seasons Hotel in Washington, D.C., two days before the worst terrorist attack on the American homeland since 9/11. Gabriel knew how Saladin looked, how he smelled, how the air reacted when he entered or left a room. And he knew how Saladin walked. Like his namesake, he moved with a pronounced limp, the result of a shrapnel wound that had been crudely tended to in a house of many rooms and courts near Mosul in northern Iraq. The limp was now his calling card. A man's physical appearance could be changed in many ways. Hair could be cut or dyed, a face could be altered with plastic surgery. But a limp like Saladin's was forever.

How he managed to escape from America was a matter of intense debate, and all subsequent efforts to locate him had failed. Reports had him variously in Asunción, Santiago, and Buenos Aires. There was even a rumor he'd found sanctuary in Bariloche, the Argentine ski resort so beloved by fugitive Nazi war criminals. Gabriel dismissed the idea out of hand. Still, he was willing to entertain the notion that Saladin was hiding somewhere in plain sight. Wherever he was, he was planning his next move. Of that, Gabriel was certain.

The recent attack on Washington, with its ruined buildings and monuments and catastrophic death toll, had established Saladin as the new face of Islamic terror. But what would be his encore? The American president, in one of his final interviews before leaving office, declared that Saladin was incapable of another large-scale operation, that the U.S. military response had left his once-formidable network in tatters. Saladin had responded by ordering a suicide bomber to detonate himself outside the U.S. Embassy in Cairo. Small beer, countered the White House. Limited casualties, no Americans among the dead. The desperate act of a man on his way out.

Perhaps, but there were other attacks as well. Saladin had struck Turkey virtually at will—weddings, buses, public squares, Istanbul's busy airport—and his adherents in Western Europe, those who spoke his name with something like religious fervor, had carried out a series of lone-wolf attacks that had left a trail of death across France, Belgium, and Germany. But something big was coming, something coordinated, a terror spectacular to rival the calamity he had inflicted on Washington.

But where? Another attack on America seemed unlikely. Surely, said the experts, lightning would not strike the same place twice. In the end, the city Saladin chose for his curtain call came as a surprise to no one, especially those who battled terrorists for a living. Despite his penchant for secrecy, Saladin loved the stage. And where better to find a stage than the West End of London.

Perhaps it was true, thought Julian Isherwood as he watched torrents of windblown rain tumbling from a black sky. Perhaps the planet was broken after all. A hurricane in London, and in the middle of February at that. Tall and somewhat precarious in comportment, Isherwood was not naturally built for such conditions. At present, he was sheltering in the doorway of Wilton's Restaurant in Jermyn Street, a spot he knew well. He pushed up the sleeve of his mackintosh and frowned at his wristwatch. The time was 7:40; he was running late. He searched the street for a taxi. There was not one in sight.

From the bar at Wilton's there came a trickle of halfhearted laughter, followed by the booming baritone voice of none other than tubby Oliver Dimbleby. Wilton's was now the primary watering hole for a small band of Old Master art dealers who plied their trade in the narrow streets of St. James's. Green's Restaurant and Oyster Bar in Duke Street had once been their favorite haunt, but Green's had been forced to close its doors owing to a dispute with the company that managed the Queen's immense portfolio of London real estate. It was symptomatic of the changes that had swept through the neighborhood and the London art world as a whole. Old Masters were deeply out of fashion. The collectors of today, the instant global billionaires who made their fortunes with social media and iPhone apps, were only interested in Modern works. Even the Impressionists were becoming passé. Isherwood had sold just two paintings since the New Year. Both were middle-market works, school of so-and-so, manner of such-and-such. Oliver Dimbleby hadn't sold anything in six months. Neither had Roddy Hutchinson, who was widely regarded as the most unscrupulous dealer in all of London. But each evening they huddled at the bar of Wilton's and assured themselves that soon the storm would pass. Julian Isherwood feared otherwise, never more so than at that moment.

He had seen troubled times before. His English scale, devoutly English wardrobe, and backbone-of-England surname concealed the fact that he was not, at least not technically, English at all. British by nationality and passport, yes, but German by birth, French by upbringing, and Jewish by religion. Only a handful of trusted friends knew that Isherwood had staggered into London as a child refugee in 1942 after being carried across the snowbound Pyrenees by a pair of Basque shepherds. Or that his father, the renowned Paris art dealer Samuel Isakowitz, had been murdered at the Sobibor death camp along with Isherwood's mother. Though Isherwood had carefully guarded the secrets of his past, the story of his dramatic escape from Nazi-occupied Europe had reached the ears of Israel's secret intelligence service. And in the mid-1970s, during a wave of Palestinian terrorist attacks against Israeli targets in Europe, he had been recruited as a *sayan*, a volunteer helper. Isherwood had but one assignment—to assist in building and maintaining the operational cover of an art restorer and assassin named Gabriel Allon. Lately, their careers had proceeded in decidedly different directions. Gabriel was now the chief of Israeli intelligence, one of the most powerful spies in the world. And Isherwood? He was standing in the doorway of Wilton's Restaurant in Jermyn Street, battered by the west wind, slightly drunk, waiting for a taxi that would never come.

He checked his watch a second time. It was now 7:43. Having no umbrella in his possession, he raised his old leather satchel over his head and waded over to Piccadilly, where after a wait of five sodden minutes he tipped gratefully into the back of a taxi. He gave the driver an approximate address—he was too embarrassed to say the name of his true destination—and anxiously monitored the time as the taxi crawled toward Piccadilly Circus. There it turned into Shaftesbury Avenue, arriving at Charing Cross Road at the stroke of eight. Isherwood was now officially late for his reservation.

He supposed he ought to call and say he was delayed, but there was a good chance the establishment in question would give away his table. It had taken a month of begging and bribery to obtain it in the first place; Isherwood wasn't about to risk it now with a panicked phone call. Besides, with a bit of luck, Fiona was already there. It was one of the things Isherwood liked best about Fiona, she was prompt. He also liked her blond hair, blue eyes, long legs, and her age, which was thirty-six. In fact, at that moment, he could think of nothing he disliked about Fiona Gardner, which was why he had expended much valuable time and effort securing a reservation in a restaurant where ordinarily he would never set foot.

Another five minutes slipped away before the taxi finally deposited Isherwood outside St. Martin's Theatre, the permanent home of Agatha Christie's *The Mousetrap*. Quickly, he crossed West Street to the entrance of the famed Ivy, his true destination. The maître d' informed him that Miss Gardner had not yet arrived and that by some miracle his table was still available. Isherwood surrendered his mackintosh to the coat check girl and was shown to a banquette overlooking Litchfield Street.

Alone, he stared disapprovingly at his reflection in the window. With his Savile Row suit, crimson necktie, and plentiful gray locks, he cut a rather elegant if dubious figure, a look he described as dignified depravity. Still, there was no denying he had reached the age that estate planners refer to as "the autumn of his years." No, he thought gloomily, he was *old*. Far too old to be pursuing the likes of Fiona Gardner. How many others had there been? The art students, the junior curators, the receptionists, the pretty young girls who took telephone bids at Christie's and Sotheby's. Isherwood was no sportsman; he had loved them all. He believed in love, as he believed in art. Love at first sight. Love everlasting. Love until death do us part. The problem was, he had never truly found it.

All at once he thought of a recent afternoon in Venice, a corner table in Harry's Bar, a Bellini, *Gabriel* . . . He had told Isherwood it was not too late, that there was still time for him to marry and have a child or two. The ragged face in the glass begged to differ. He was well past his expiration date, he thought. He would die alone, childless, and with no wife other than his gallery.

He made another check of the time. Eight fifteen. Now it was Fiona who was late. It wasn't like her. He dug his mobile from the breast pocket of his suit and saw that he had received a text message. SORRY JULIAN BUT I'M AFRAID I WON'T BE ABLE TO . . . He stopped reading. He supposed it was for the best. It would spare him a broken heart. More important, it would prevent him from making a damn fool of himself yet again.

He returned the mobile to his pocket and considered his options. He could stay and dine alone, or he could leave. He chose the second; one didn't dine alone at the Ivy. Rising, he collected his raincoat and with a mumbled apology to the maître d' went quickly into the street, just as a white Ford Transit van was braking to a halt outside St. Martin's Theatre. The driver emerged instantly, dressed in a bulky woolen peacoat and holding something that looked like a gun. It was not any gun, thought Isherwood, it was a weapon of war. Four more men were now clambering out of the van's rear cargo compartment, each wearing a heavy coat, each holding the same type of combat assault rifle. Isherwood could scarcely believe what he was seeing. It looked like a scene from a movie. A movie he had seen before, in Paris and in Washington.

The five men moved calmly toward the doors of the theater in a tight fighting unit. Isherwood heard the splintering of wood, followed by gunshots. Then, a few seconds later, came the first screams, muffled, distant. They were the screams of Isherwood's nightmares. Again he thought of Gabriel and wondered what he would do in a situation like this. He would charge headlong into the theater and save as many lives as possible. But Isherwood hadn't Gabriel's skills or his courage. He was no hero. In fact, he was quite the other thing.

The nightmarish screams were growing louder. Isherwood dug his mobile phone from his pocket, dialed 999, and reported that St. Martin's Theatre was under terrorist attack. Then he spun round and stared at the landmark restaurant he had just departed. Its well-heeled customers appeared oblivious to the carnage taking place a few paces away. Surely, he thought, the terrorists would not be content with a single massacre. The iconic Ivy would be their next stop.

Isherwood considered his options. Again he had two. He could make his escape or he could try to save as many lives as possible. The decision was the easiest of his life. As he staggered across the street, he heard an explosion from the direction of Charing Cross Road. Then another. Then a third. He was not a hero, he thought as he careened through the door of the Ivy, waving his arms like a madman, but he could act like one, if only for a moment or two. Perhaps Gabriel had been right. Perhaps it was not too late for him after all.

3

VAUXHALL CROSS, LONDON

They were twelve in number, Arabs and Africans by eth-nicity, Europeans by passport. All had spent time in the caliphate of ISIS—including a training camp, now destroyed, near the ancient Syrian city of Palmyra—and all had returned to Western Europe undetected. Later, it would be established they had received their orders via Telegram, the free cloud-based instant-messaging service utilizing end-to-end encryp-tion. They were given only an address and the date and time they were to appear. They did not know that others had re-ceived similar instructions; they did not know they were part of a larger plot. Indeed, they did not know they were part of a plot at all.

They trickled into the United Kingdom one by one, by train and by ferry. Two or three had to undergo a bit of questioning at the border; the rest were welcomed with open arms. Four made their way to the town of Luton, four to Harlow, and four to Gravesend. At each address a British-based operative of the network was waiting. So, too, were their weapons—explosive vests, combat assault rifles. The vests each contained a kilogram of TATP, a highly volatile crystalline explosive manufactured from nail polish remover and hydrogen peroxide. The assault rifles were AK-47s of Belarusan manufacture.

The British-based operatives quickly briefed the attack cells on their targets and the objectives of the mission. They were not suicide bombers but suicide warriors. They were to kill as many infidels as possible with their assault rifles, and only when cornered by police were they to detonate their explosive vests. The goal of the operation was not the destruction of buildings or landmarks, it was blood. No distinction was to be made between man or woman, adult or child. They were to show no mercy.

In late afternoon—in Luton, in Harlow, and in Gravesend—the members of the three cells shared a final meal. Afterward, they ritually prepared their bodies for death. Finally, at seven that evening, they climbed into three identical white Ford Transit vans. The British-based operatives handled the driving, the suicide warriors sat in back, with their vests and their guns. None of the cells knew of the existence of the others, but all were headed toward the West End of London and were scheduled to strike at the same time. The clock was Saladin's trademark. He believed that in terror, as in life, timing was everything.

The venerable Garrick Theatre had seen world wars, a cold war, a depression, and the abdication of a king. But never had it witnessed anything like what occurred at 8:20 that evening, when five ISIS terrorists burst into the theater and began firing into the crowd. More than a hundred would perish during the first thirty seconds of the assault, and another hundred would die in the terrible five minutes that followed, as the terrorists moved methodically through the theater, row by row, seat by seat. Some two hundred fortunate souls managed to escape through the side and rear exits, along with the entire cast of the production and the stagehands. Many would never work in the theater again.

The terrorists emerged from the Garrick seven minutes after entering it. Outside, they encountered two unarmed Metropolitan Police officers. After killing both, they headed to Irving Street and slaughtered their way from restaurant to restaurant, until finally, at the fringes of Leicester Square, they were confronted by a pair of Met special firearms officers. The officers were armed only with 9mm Glock 17 pistols. Even so, they managed to kill two of the terrorists before they were able to detonate their explosive vests. Two of the surviving terrorists set off their bombs in the lobby of the cavernous Odeon Cinema; the third, in a busy Italian restaurant. In all, nearly four hundred would perish in that portion of the attack alone, making it the deadliest in British history—worse, even, than the 1988 bombing of Pan Am Flight 103 over Lockerbie, Scotland.

But unfortunately the five-member cell was not acting alone. A second cell—the Luton cell, as it would become known— attacked the Prince Edward Theatre, also at twenty minutes past eight precisely, during a performance of *Miss Saigon*. The Prince Edward was far larger than the Garrick, 1,600 seats instead of 656, and so the death toll inside the theater was considerably higher. What's more, all five of the terrorists detonated their suicide vests in bars and restaurants along Old Compton Street. More than five hundred lives were lost in the span of just six minutes.

The third target was St. Martin's: five terrorists, twenty minutes past eight precisely. This time, however, a team of special firearms officers intervened. Later, it would be revealed that a passerby, a man identified only as a prominent London art dealer, had reported the attack to authorities seconds after the terrorists entered the theater. The same London art dealer had then helped to evacuate the dining room of the Ivy restaurant. As a result, only eighty-four would die in that portion of the attack. On any other night, in any other city, the number would have been unthinkable. Now it was a reason to give thanks. Saladin had struck terror into the heart of London. And London would never be the same.

By morning the scale of the calamity was plain to see. Most of the dead still lay where they had fallen—indeed, many still sat in their original theater seats. The commissioner of the Metropolitan Police declared the entire West End an active crime scene and urged both Londoners and tourists to avoid the area. The Underground canceled all service as a precautionary measure; businesses and public institutions remained closed throughout the day. The London Stock Exchange opened on time, but trading was suspended when share prices plummeted. The economic loss, like the loss of life, was catastrophic.

For reasons of security, Prime Minister Jonathan Lancaster waited until midday to tour the devastation. With his wife, Diana, at his side, he made his way on foot from the Garrick to the Prince Edward and finally to the St. Martin's. Afterward, outside the Met's makeshift command post in Leicester Square, he briefly addressed the media. Pale and visibly shaken, he vowed the perpetrators would be brought to justice. "The enemy is determined," he declared, "but so are we."

The enemy, however, remained curiously quiet. Yes, there

were several celebratory postings on the usual extremist Web sites, but nothing of authority from ISIS central command. Finally, at 5:00 p.m. London time, a formal claim of responsibility appeared on one of the group's many Twitter feeds, along with photographs of the fifteen operatives who had carried out the attack. A few terrorism analysts expressed surprise over the fact that the statement made no mention of anyone named Saladin. The savvier ones did not. Saladin, they said, was a master. And like many masters, he preferred to leave his work unsigned.

If the first day was characterized by solidarity and grief, the second was one of division and recriminations. In the House of Commons, several members of the opposition party lambasted the prime minister and his intelligence chiefs for failing to detect and disrupt the plot. Mainly, they asked how it was possible that the terrorists had managed to acquire combat assault rifles in a country with some of the most draconian gun control laws in the world. The head of the Met's Counter Terrorism Command issued a statement defending his actions, as did Amanda Wallace, the director general of MI5. But Graham Seymour, the chief of the Secret Intelligence Service, otherwise known as MI6, chose to remain silent. Until recently, the British government had not even acknowledged the existence of MI6, and no minister in his right mind would have ever dreamed of mentioning the name of its chief in public. Seymour preferred the old ways to the new. He was a spy by nature and upbringing. And a spy never spoke for attribution when a poisonous leak to a friendly reporter would suffice.

Responsibility for protecting the British homeland from terrorist attack fell primarily to MI5, the Metropolitan Police, and the Joint Terrorism Analysis Center. Still, the Secret Intelligence Service had an important role to play in detecting plots abroad before they reached Britain's vulnerable shores. Graham Seymour had warned the prime minister repeatedly that an ISIS attack on the United Kingdom was imminent, but his spies had failed to produce the hard, actionable intelligence necessary to prevent it. Consequently, he regarded the attack on London, with its horrendous loss of innocent life, as the greatest single failure of his long and distinguished career.

Seymour had been in his magnificent office atop Vauxhall Cross at the time of the attack—he had seen the flashes of the explosions from his window—and in the dark days that followed he rarely left it. His closest aides pleaded with him to get some sleep and, privately, fretted over his uncharacteristically worn appearance. Seymour curtly advised them their time would be better spent finding the vital intelligence that would prevent the next attack. What he wanted was a loose thread, a member of Saladin's network who could be manipulated into doing his bidding. Not a senior figure; they were far too loyal. The man Graham Seymour was looking for would be a small player, a runner of errands, a carrier of other people's bags. It was possible this man might not even know he was a member of a terror organization. It was even possible he had never heard the name Saladin.

Policemen, secret or otherwise, have certain advantages in times of crisis. They stage raids, they make arrests, they hold press conferences to reassure the public they are doing everything in their power to keep them safe. Spies, on the other hand, have no such recourse. By definition, they toil in secret, in back alleys and hotel rooms and safe houses and all the other godforsaken places where agents are persuaded or coerced into handing over vital information to a foreign power. Early in his career, Graham Seymour had carried out such work. Now he could only monitor the efforts of others from the gilded cage of his office. His worst fear was that another service would find the loose thread first, that he would once again be relegated to a supporting role. MI6 could not crack Saladin's network alone; it would need the help of its friends in Western Europe, the Middle East, and across the pond in America. But if MI6 were able to unearth the right piece of intelligence in a timely fashion, Graham Seymour would be first among equals. In the modern world, that was the best a spymaster could hope for.

And so he remained in his office, day after day, night after night, and watched with no small amount of envy as the Met and MI5 rolled up remnants of Saladin's network in Britain. MI6's efforts, however, produced nothing of consequence. Indeed, Seymour learned more from his friends in Langley and Tel Aviv than he did from his own staff. Finally, a week to the day after the attack, he decided a night at home would do him good. The computer logs would show his Jaguar limousine departed the parking garage, coincidentally, at 8:20 p.m. precisely. But as he was heading across the Thames toward his home in Belgravia, his secure phone purred softly. He recognized the number, along with the female voice that came on the line a moment later. "I hope I'm not catching you at a bad time," said Amanda Wallace, "but I have something that might be of interest. Why don't you stop by my place for a drink? My treat."

4

THAMES HOUSE, LONDON

Thames House, MI5's riverfront headquarters, was a building Graham Seymour knew well; he had worked there for more than thirty years before becoming the chief of MI6. As he made his way along the corridor of the executive suite, he paused in the doorway of the office that had been his when he was deputy director general. Miles Kent, the current deputy, was still at his desk. He was quite possibly the only man in London who looked worse than Seymour.

"Graham," said Kent, looking up from his computer. "What brings you to our little corner of the realm?"

"You tell me."

"If I did," said Kent quietly, "the queen bee would give me the sack."

"How's she holding up?"

"Haven't you heard?" Kent beckoned Seymour inside and closed the door. "Charles ran off with his secretary."

"When?"

"A couple of days after the attack. He was having dinner at the Ivy when the third cell entered the St. Martin's. Said it forced him to take a hard look in the mirror. Said he couldn't go on living the way he was."

"He had a mistress and a wife. What more did he want?"

"A divorce, apparently. Amanda's already moved out of the flat. She's been sleeping here at the office."

"There's a lot of that going around."

Seymour was surprised by the news. He had seen Amanda that very morning at 10 Downing Street and she'd made no mention of it. Truth be told, Seymour was relieved Charles's reckless love life was finally out in the open. The Russians had a way of finding out about such indiscretions and had never been squeamish about using them to their advantage.

"Who else knows?"

"I found out quite by accident. You know Amanda, she's very discreet."

"Too bad Charles wasn't." Seymour reached for the door but stopped. "Any idea why she wants to see me so urgently?"

"The pleasure of your company?"

"Come on, Miles."

"All I know," said Kent, "is that it has something to do with guns."

Seymour went into the corridor. The light over Amanda's door shone green. Even so, he knocked softly before entering. He found Amanda seated at her large desk, with her eyes cast downward toward an open file. Looking up, she treated Seymour to a cool smile. It looked, he thought, as if she had taught herself the gesture by practicing in front of a mirror.

"Graham," she said, rising. "So good of you to come."

She stepped slowly from behind the desk. She was dressed, as usual, in a tailored pantsuit that flattered her tall, awkward frame. Her approach was cautious. Graham Seymour and Amanda Wallace had entered MI5 in the same intake and had spent the better part of thirty years battling each other at every turn. Now they occupied two of the most powerful positions in Western intelligence, and yet their rivalry persisted. It was tempting to think the attack would alter the dynamics of their relationship, but Seymour believed otherwise. The inevitable parliamentary inquiry was coming. Undoubtedly, it would uncover serious lapses and missteps on the part of MI5. Amanda would fight tooth and nail. And she would do her utmost to make certain that Seymour and MI6 shouldered their fair share of the blame.

A drinks tray had been placed at the end of Amanda's gleaming conference table. She mixed a gin and tonic for Seymour and for herself a martini with olives and cocktail onions. Her toast was restrained, silent. Then she led Seymour to the seating area and gestured toward a modern leather armchair. The BBC flickered on the large flat-panel television. British and American warplanes were striking ISIS targets near the Syrian city of Raqqa. The Iraqi portion of the caliphate had been largely reclaimed by the central government in Baghdad. Only the Syrian sanctuary remained, and it was under siege. The loss of territory, however, had done nothing to diminish ISIS's ability to conduct terrorist operations abroad. The attack on London was proof of that.

"Where do you suppose he is?" asked Amanda after a moment.

"Saladin?"

"Who else?"

"We've been unable to definitively—"

"You're not speaking to the prime minister, Graham."

"If I had to guess, he's somewhere other than the rapidly shrinking caliphate of ISIS."

"Where?"

"Perhaps Libya or one of the Gulf emirates. Or he could be in Pakistan or across the border in Afghanistan controlled by ISIS. Or," said Seymour, "he might be closer at hand. He has friends and resources. And remember, he used to be one of us. Saladin worked for the Iraqi Mukhabarat before the invasion. His job was to provide material support to Saddam's favorite Palestinian terrorists. He knows what he's doing."

"That," said Amanda Wallace, "is an understatement. Saladin almost makes one nostalgic for the days of KGB spies and IRA bombs." She sat down opposite Seymour and placed her drink thoughtfully on the coffee table. "There's something I need to tell you, Graham. Something personal, something awful. Charles has left me for his secretary. She's half his age. Such a cliché."

"I'm sorry, Amanda."

"Did you know he was having an affair?"

"One heard rumors," said Seymour delicately.

"I didn't hear them, and I'm the director general of MI5. I suppose it's true what they say. The spouse is always the last to know."

"Is there no chance of reconciliation?"

"None."

"A divorce will be messy."

"And costly," added Amanda. "Especially for Charles."

"There'll be pressure for you to step aside."

"Which is why," said Amanda, "I'm going to require your

support." She was silent for a moment. "I know I'm largely to blame for our little cold war, Graham, but it's gone on long enough. If the Berlin Wall can come down, surely you and I can be something like friends."

"I couldn't agree more."

This time, Amanda's smile almost appeared genuine. "And now to the real reason I asked you to come." She pointed a remote toward the flat-panel television and a face appeared on the screen—a male of Egyptian descent, lightly bearded, approximately thirty years of age. It belonged to Omar Salah, the leader of the so-called Harlow cell who had been killed by a special firearms officer inside St. Martin's Theatre before he could detonate his explosive vest. Seymour was well acquainted with Salah's file. He was one of several thousand European Muslims who had traveled to Syria and Iraq after ISIS declared its caliphate in June 2014. For more than a year after Omar Salah's return to Britain, he had been the target of full-time MI5 surveillance, both physical and electronic. But six months prior to the attack, MI5 concluded that Salah was no longer an imminent threat. A4, the watchers, were stretched to the breaking point, and Salah appeared to have lost his taste for radical Islam and jihadism. The termination order bore Amanda's signature. What she and the rest of British intelligence didn't realize was that Salah was communicating with ISIS central command using encrypted methods that even the mighty American National Security Agency couldn't crack.

"It wasn't your fault," said Seymour quietly.

"Perhaps not," answered Amanda. "But someone will have to take the fall, and it's probably going to be me. Unless, of course, I can turn the unfortunate case of Omar Salah to my advantage." She paused, then added, "Or should I say *our* advantage."

"And how might we do that?"

"Omar Salah did more than lead a team of Islamic murderers into St. Martin's Theatre. He was the one who smuggled the guns into Britain."

"Where did he get them?"

"From an ISIS operative based in France."

"Says who?"

"Says Omar."

"Please, Amanda," said Seymour wearily, "it's late."

She glanced at the face on the screen. "He was good, our Omar, but he made one small mistake. He used his sister's laptop to conduct ISIS business. We seized it the day after the attack, and we've been scrubbing the hard drive ever since. This afternoon we found the digital remains of an encrypted message from ISIS central command, instructing Omar to travel to Calais to meet with a man who called himself the Scorpion."

"Catchy," said Seymour darkly. "Was there any mention of guns in the message?"

"The language was coded, but obvious. It's also consistent with a bulletin we received from the DGSI late last year. It seems the French have had the Scorpion on their radar for some time. Unfortunately, they don't know much about him, including his real name. The working theory is that he's part of a drug gang, probably Moroccan."

It made sense, thought Seymour. The nexus between ISIS and European criminal networks was undeniable.

"Have you told the French about any of this?" he asked.

"I won't leave the security of the British people in the hands of the DGSI. Besides, I'd like to find the Scorpion *before* the French. But I can't," she added quickly. "My mandate stops at the water's edge."

Seymour was silent.

"Far be it from me to tell you how to do your job, Graham. But if I were you, I'd send an officer to France first thing in the morning. Someone who speaks the language. Someone who knows his way around criminal networks. Someone who isn't afraid to get his hands dirty." She smiled. "You wouldn't happen to know anyone like that, would you, Graham?"

He had come to the port city in the south of England like many others before him, in the back of a government van with blacked-out windows. It had sped past the marinas and the old redbrick Victorian warehouses before finally turning onto a small track that carried it across the first fairway of a golf course, which on the morning of his arrival had been abandoned to the gulls. Just beyond the fairway was an empty moat, and beyond the moat was an ancient fort with walls of gray stone. Originally built by Henry VIII in 1545, it was now MI6's primary school for spies.

The van paused briefly at the gatehouse before entering the central courtyard, where the cars of the DS, the Directing Staff, stood in three neat rows. The driver of the van, who was called Reg, switched off the engine and with little more than a dip of his head signaled to the man in the backseat that he could see himself out. The Fort was not a hotel, he might have added, but didn't. The new recruit was a special case, or so the DS had been informed by Vauxhall Cross. Like all new recruits, he would be told at every opportunity that he was being admitted into an exclusive club. The members of this club lived by a different set of rules than their countrymen. They knew things, did things, that others did not. That said, the man in the backseat didn't strike Reg as the sort of fellow who would be moved by such flattery. In fact, he looked as though he had been living by a different set of rules for a very long time.

The Fort consisted of three wings—the east, the west, and the main, where most of the actual training took place. Directly above the gatehouse was a suite of rooms reserved for the chief, and beyond the walls was a tennis court, a squash facility, a croquet pitch, a helipad, and an outdoor shooting range. There was an indoor range as well, though Reg suspected his passenger would not require much in the way of weapons training, firearms or otherwise. He was a soldier of the elite variety. You could see it in the shape of the body, the set of the jaw, and in the way he shouldered the canvas duffel bag before striking out across the courtyard. Without a sound, noted Reg. He was definitely the silent type. He had been places he wished to forget and had carried out missions no one talked about outside safe-speech rooms and secure facilities. He was classified, this one. He was trouble.

Just inside the entrance to the west wing was the little nook where George Halliday, the porter, waited to receive him. "Marlowe," said the new recruit with little conviction. And then, almost as an afterthought, he added, "Peter Marlowe." And Halliday, who was the longest serving of the Directing Staff—a holdover from the days of King Henry, according to Fort legend—ran a pale, spidery forefinger down his list of names. "Ah, yes, Mr. Marlowe. We've been expecting you. Sorry about the weather, but I'd get used to it if I were you."

Halliday said this while stooping to remove a key from the row of hooks beneath his desk. "Second floor, last room on the left. You're lucky, it has a lovely view of the sea." He laid the key on the desktop. "I trust you can manage your bag."

"I trust I can," said the new recruit with something like a smile.

"Oh," said Halliday suddenly, "I nearly forgot." He turned and clawed a small envelope from one of the pigeonhole mail-boxes on the wall behind his desk. "This arrived for you last night. It's from 'C.'"

The new recruit scooped up the letter and shoved it into the pocket of his watch coat. Then he shouldered his canvas duffel—like a soldier, agreed Halliday—and carried it up the flight of ancient steps that led to the residential quarters. The door to the room opened with a groan. Entering, he allowed the duffel to slide from his sturdy shoulder to the floor. With the keen eye of a close-observation specialist, he surveyed his surroundings. A single bed, a nightstand and reading lamp, a small desk, a simple armoire for his things, a private toilet and bath. A recent gradu-ate of an elite university might have found the apartment more than adequate, but the new recruit was not impressed. A man of considerable wealth—illegitimate, but considerable nonethe-less—he was used to more comfortable lodgings.

He shed his coat and tossed it on the bed, dislodging the envelope from the pocket. Reluctantly, he tore open the flap and removed the small notecard. There was no letterhead, only three lines of neat script, rendered in distinctive green ink.

Britain is better off now that you are here to look after her . . .

An ordinary recruit might have retained possession of such a note as a memento of his first day as an officer in one of the world's oldest and proudest intelligence services. But the man known as Peter Marlowe was no ordinary recruit. What's more, he had worked in places where such a note could cost a man his life. And so after reading it—twice, as was his custom—he burned it in the bathroom sink and washed the ashes down the drain. Then he went to the room's small arrow-slit of a window and gazed across the sea toward the Isle of Wight. And he wondered, not for the first time, whether he had made the worst mistake of his life.

His real name, needless to say, was not Peter Marlowe. It was Christopher Keller, which was intriguing in its own right, for as far as Her Majesty's Government was concerned, Keller had been dead for some twenty-five years. Consequently, he was thought to be the first decedent to serve in any department of British intelligence since Glyndwr Michael, the homeless Welshman whose corpse had been used by the great wartime deceivers to feed false documents to Nazi Germany as part of Operation Mincemeat.

The Directing Staff of the Fort, however, did not know any of this about their new recruit. In fact, they knew almost nothing at all. They did not know, for example, that he was a veteran of the elite Special Air Service, that he still held the record for the regiment's forty-mile endurance trek across the rugged Brecon Beacons of South Wales, or that he had achieved the highest score ever in the Killing House, the SAS's infamous training facility where members honed their close-quarters combat skills. A further examination of his records—all of which had been sealed by order of the prime minister himself—would have revealed that in the late 1980s, during a particularly violent period of the war in Northern Ireland, he had been inserted into West Belfast, where he lived among the city's Roman Catholics and ran agents of penetration into the Irish Republican Army. Those same records would have mentioned, in rather vague terms, an incident at a farmhouse in South Armagh where Keller, his cover blown, had been taken for interrogation and execution. The exact circumstances surrounding his escape were murky, though it involved the death of four hardened IRA men, two of whom had been virtually cut to pieces.

After his hasty evacuation from Northern Ireland, Keller returned to SAS headquarters at Hereford for what he thought would be a long rest and a stint as an instructor. But after the Iraqi invasion of Kuwait in August 1990, he was assigned to a Sabre desert warfare squadron and dispatched to western Iraq, where he searched for Saddam Hussein's lethal arsenal of Scud missiles. On the night of January 28, 1991, Keller and his team located a launcher about one hundred miles northwest of Baghdad and radioed the coordinates to their commanders in Saudi Arabia. Ninety minutes later a formation of coalition fighter-bombers streaked low over the desert. But in a disastrous case of friendly fire, the aircraft attacked the SAS squadron instead of the Scud site. British officials concluded the entire unit was lost, including Keller.

In truth, he had survived the incident without a scratch, which was his knack. His first instinct was to radio his base and request extraction. Instead, enraged by the incompetence of his superiors, he started walking. Concealed beneath the robe and headdress of a desert Arab, and highly trained in the art of clandestine movement, he made his way through the coalition forces and slipped undetected into Syria. From there, he hiked westward across Turkey, Greece, and Italy until finally he washed ashore on the rugged island of Corsica, where he fell into the waiting arms of Don Anton Orsati, a crime figure whose ancient family of Corsican bandits specialized in murder for hire.

The don gave Keller a villa and a woman to heal his wounds. Then, when Keller was rested, he gave him work. With his northern European looks and SAS training, Keller was able to fulfill contracts that were beyond the capabilities of Orsati's Corsican-born assassins, the *taddunaghiu*. Posing as an executive for Orsati's small olive oil company, Keller roamed Western Europe for the better part of twenty-five years, killing at the don's behest. They accepted him as one of their own, the Corsicans, and he repaid their generosity by adopting their ways. He dressed as a Corsican, ate and drank as a Corsican, and viewed the rest of the world with a Corsican's fatalistic disdain. He even wore a Corsican talisman around his neck—a lump of red coral in the shape of a hand—to ward off the evil eye. Now, at long last, he had come home, to an ancient fortress of gray stone overlooking a cold granite sea. They were going to teach him to be a proper British spy. But first he would have to learn how to be an Englishman again.

The other members of Keller's intake were more in keeping with MI6's traditional tastes—white, male, and members of the middle or privileged classes. Moreover, all were recent graduates of either Oxford or Cambridge. All but Thomas Finch, who had attended the London School of Economics and worked as an investment banker in the City before finally submitting to MI6's repeated advances. Finch spoke Chinese fluently and thought himself especially clever. During their first session he had complained, only partially in jest, that he was taking a substantial cut in pay for the honor of serving his country. Keller could have made the same boast, but had the good sense not to. He told his fellow recruits he had worked in the retail food business and that in his spare time he enjoyed mountaineering, both of which happened to be true. As for his age—he was by far the oldest of the lot, perhaps the oldest recruit ever—he claimed to be something of a late bloomer, which was not at all the case.

The course was known formally as the IONEC, the Intelligence Officers New Entry Course. Its purpose was to prepare a recruit for an entry-level job at Vauxhall Cross, though additional training would be necessary before he would be ready to operate in the field, lest he do irreparable harm to his country's interests or his own career. There were two primary instructors—Andy Mayhew, big, ginger, garrulous, and Tony Quill, a whippet-thin former agent-runner who, it was said, could charm the habit off a nun and steal her rosary when she wasn't looking. Vauxhall Cross had scoured the records of both men to determine whether, in their previous lives, they might have encountered an SAS operative named Christopher Keller. They had not. Mayhew was largely a headquarters man. Quill was Iron Curtain and Middle East. Neither had ever set foot in Northern Ireland.

The first portion of the course dealt with MI6 itself—its history, its successes, its stunning failures, its structure. It was far smaller than its American and Russian counterparts but punched above its weight, as Quill was fond of saying, thanks to the native cunning and natural deceptiveness of those who ran it. Whereas the Americans depended on technology, MI6 specialized in human intelligence, and its officers were regarded as the finest recruiters and runners of agents in the business. The hard work of convincing men and women to betray their countries or organizations was carried out by the IB, the intelligence branch. Approximately three hundred and fifty officers were assigned to it; most worked in British embassies around the world, under the safety of diplomatic cover. Another eight hundred or so worked in the general services division. GS officers specialized in technical matters or held administrative positions in MI6's various geographic controllerates. Each controllerate was headed by a controller who reported to the chief. Though Mayhew and Quill did not know it, "C" had already determined that the recruit known as Peter Marlowe would not be working in any of the existing controllerates. He would be a controllerate unto himself. A controllerate of one.

Having poured the institutional concrete, Mayhew and Quill turned their attention to the tradecraft of human intelligence—the maintenance of proper cover, detecting and shaking surveillance, secret writing, dead drops, brush contacts, memory drills. For a spy's memory, said Quill, was his only friend in the world. And then, of course, there were the long and detailed lectures on how to spot and then successfully recruit human sources of intelligence. Keller had an unfair advantage over his classmates; he had recruited and run agents in a place where one small misstep would result in an atrocious death. In fact, he was quite certain he could have taught Mayhew and Quill a thing or two about conducting a clandestine meeting in such a way that both agent and officer survived the encounter. Instead, in the classrooms of the main wing, he adopted the demeanor of a quiet and attentive pupil, eager to learn but not to ingratiate or impress. He left that to Finch and to Baker, a literature student from Oxford who was already making notes for his first spy novel. Keller spoke only when spoken to and never once raised his hand or volunteered an answer. He was as invisible as a man could be in a cramped classroom of twelve students. But then that was his special talent—making himself invisible to those around him.

On the streets of nearby Portsmouth, where they performed the bulk of their field exercises, Keller's formidable skills were harder to conceal. He cleaned out his dead drop sites without raising so much as an eyebrow; his brush contacts were textbook. Six weeks into the course, MI5 sent down a team of A4 watchers to assist in a daylong countersurveillance drill. The point of the exercise was to demonstrate that proper physical surveillance—the real thing, not the banana-republic variety— was almost impossible to detect. The other recruits failed to spot a single one of their MI5 watchers, but Keller was able to correctly identify four members of a crack team who tailed him during an excursion to the Cascades shopping center. Incredulous, MI5 demanded a second chance, but the results were the same. The next day's session was dedicated not to identifying surveillance but shaking it. Keller dumped his team in five minutes flat and vanished without a trace. They found him later that night, singing French-accented karaoke at the Druid's Arms in Binsteed Road. He left the pub with the name, phone number, and address of everyone in the room, along with a proposal of marriage. Next morning Quill called Personnel at Vauxhall

Cross and asked where they had found the man called Peter Marlowe.

"We didn't find him," said Personnel. "He's 'C's' private stock."

"Send me ten more just like him," said Quill, "and Britain will rule the world again."

The real work of the IONEC was done in the evenings, in the recruits' private bar and dining hall. They were encouraged to drink—alcohol, they were told, played an important part in the life of a spy—and several times each week a special guest joined them for dinner. Controllers, policy experts, legendary operatives. A few still worked for the service. Others were cobwebbed figures in crumpled suits who recalled their duels with the KGB in Berlin and Vienna and Moscow. Russia was once again MI6's primary target and adversary—the great game, said a dried-out cold warrior, had been renewed. Quill warned his students that, in time, the Russians would make a play for each and every one of them, with flattery, with offers of money, or with blackmail. How they responded when the bear came calling would determine whether they slept at night or rotted in a self-made hell. He then played a video of Kim Philby's famous 1955 press conference where he denied he was a KGB spy. Quill called it the finest piece of lying he had ever seen or ever would.

James Bond might have had a license to kill, but real-world MI6 officers did not. Assassination as a tool was strictly forbidden, and most British spies rarely carried a gun, let alone fired one in the line of duty. Still, they were not merely champagne spies, not all of them at least, and the world was an increasingly dangerous place. Which meant they had to possess a basic understanding of how to operate a weapon—where one inserted the magazine, how one chambered the round, how one held the contraption so as not to shoot oneself or a fellow agent, that sort of thing. Here again, Keller's proficiency was difficult to camouflage. On the first day of weapons training, the instructor handed him a pistol, a Browning 9mm, and told him to fire it toward the human silhouette target fifteen meters down the range. Keller raised the weapon swiftly and without seeming to take aim poured all thirteen rounds through the target's head. When asked to repeat the exercise, he placed an entire magazine's worth of rounds through the target's left eye. Henceforth, he was excused from further firearms training. Nor was he required to take part in the IONEC's rudimentary self-defense course. Not after nearly dislocating the shoulder of an instructor who had foolishly pointed an unloaded gun in his direction. After that, no one, not even Mayhew, who was built like a rugby player, would set foot on the mat with him.

They were kept largely isolated from the civilian population around them, but Mayhew and Quill made no effort to sequester them from the outside world—far from it, in fact. A stack of British and international newspapers waited at breakfast each morning, and in the lounge was a television that received all of the global and European news networks. They huddled round it the night of the attack on London, in despair, in anger, and in the knowledge that this was the war in which they would all soon be fighting. One sooner than the rest.

The following week the IONEC reached its conclusion. All twelve members of the intake passed easily, with Peter Marlowe receiving the highest score and Finch a respectable but distant second. That evening they dined together one last time in the company of Mayhew and Quill. And in the morning they placed their room keys on old George Halliday's desk and carried their bags outside into the courtyard, where Reg the driver waited behind the wheel of a coach to take them, newly minted spies, up to London. One, however, was missing. They searched for him high and low, in the rooms of the east wing, the west, and the main, at the shooting range, the tennis court, the croquet pitch, and the gymnasium, until finally, at nine that morning, Reg set out for London with eleven recruits instead of twelve. It was Quill who found the length of rope beneath his window, and the tiny swatch of fabric flying like a pennant from the wire atop the perimeter fence, and the fresh footprints along the beach, made by a man in a hurry who weighed approximately two hundred well-defined pounds. A pity, thought Quill. Ten more just like him, and Britain would have ruled the world again.

WORMWOOD COTTAGE, DARTMOOR

The precise route of his escape, like Saladin's flight from America, was never reliably established. There were clues, however, such as the Volkswagen Jetta, pale blue, reported stolen from the car park of Morrisons supermarket in Gosport at a quarter past ten that same morning. It was discovered later that afternoon, some one hundred miles to the west in Devon, parked outside a post office and general store in the tiny hamlet of Coldeast. The tank had been topped off with petrol and on the dash was a note, handwritten, apologizing for any inconvenience to the owner. The Hampshire Constabulary, which had jurisdiction in the matter, commenced an investigation. It ended quite abruptly after a phone call from Tony Quill to the chief constable, who duly surrendered the note, along with all surveillance video from the Morrisons car park—though later the chief was heard to remark that he'd grown weary of the antics by the lads from King Henry's old gray fortress. Playing spy games on the streets of Portsmouth was one thing. But stealing some poor sod's car, even for the purposes of a training exercise, was just bad manners.

The town of Coldeast was noteworthy only in that it lay at the edge of Dartmoor National Park. The skies were pouring with rain on the day in question and it was prematurely dark. As a result, no one noticed Christopher Keller as he set off along the Old Liverton Road, a rucksack over one shoulder. By the time he reached the Liverton Village Hall, the night was as black as India ink. It was no matter; he knew the way. He turned into a hedgerowed track and followed it due north, past the Old Leys Farm. Once, he had to step onto the verge to allow a rattletrap farm truck to pass, but otherwise it seemed as though he were the last man on the face of the earth.

Britain is better off now that you are here to look after her . . .

At Brimley he tacked to the west and followed a series of footpaths to Postbridge. Beyond the village was a road that appeared on no map, and at the end of the road was a gate that whispered quiet authority. Parish, the caretaker, had neglected to unlock it. Keller scaled it without a sound and hiked up the long gravel drive toward the limestone cottage that stood atop a swell in the bleak moorland. A yellow light burned like a candle over the unlocked front door. Entering, Keller wiped his feet carefully on the mat. The air smelled of meat and aromatics and potato. He peered into the kitchen and saw Miss Coventry, powdered and vaguely formidable, standing before an open oven, an apron tied around her ample waist.

"Mr. Marlowe," she said, turning. "We were expecting you earlier."

"I got a bit of a late start."

"No trouble, I hope."

"None at all."

"But look at you! Poor lamb. Did you walk all the way from London?"

"Not quite," said Keller with a smile.

"You're dripping water all over my clean floor."

"Can you ever forgive me?"

"Unlikely." She relieved him of his sodden coat. "I've made up your old room for you. There's clean clothing and some kit. You've time for a nice hot bath before 'C' arrives."

"What's for dinner?"

"Cottage pie."

"My favorite."

"That's why I made it. A nice cup of tea, Mr. Marlowe? Or would you like something stronger?"

"Perhaps a little whiskey to warm the bones."

"I'll see to it. Now go upstairs before you catch your death."

Keller left his shoes in the entrance hall and climbed the stairs to his room. A change of clothing was laid out neatly on the bed. Corduroy trousers, an olive-drab sweater, undergarments, a pair of suede brogues, all appropriately sized. There was also a pack of Marlboros and a gold lighter. Keller read the engraving. *To the future* . . . No salutation, no name. None was necessary.

Keller stripped off his wet clothing and stood for a long time beneath a scalding shower. When he returned to his room, a tumbler of whiskey stood on the nightstand, atop a white MI6 doily. Dressed, he carried the drink downstairs to the drawing room, where he found Graham Seymour sitting before the fire, elegantly draped in tweed and flannel. He was listening to the news on the ancient Bakelite radio.

"The stolen car," he said, rising, "was a nice touch."

"Better to make a bit of noise in a case like this, isn't that what you taught me back in the day?"

"Did I?" Seymour gave a mischievous smile. "I'm only glad it was accomplished without resort to violence."

"An MI6 officer," said Keller with mock severity, "never resorts to violence. And if he does feel the need to draw a weapon or throw a punch, it's only because he hasn't done his job properly."

"We might have to rethink that approach," said Seymour. "I'm only sorry to lose a man like Peter Marlowe. I hear his IONEC scores were rather impressive. Andy Mayhew was so distraught over your disappearance he offered his resignation."

"But not Quill?"

"No," answered Seymour. "Quill's made of sterner stuff."

"I hope you weren't too hard on poor Andy."

"I took the blame myself, though I did order a full review of the Fort's perimeter security."

"Who else knows about our little ruse?"

"The controller for Western Europe and two of his most senior desk officers."

"What about Whitehall?"

"The Joint Intelligence Committee," said Seymour, shaking his head, "is totally in the dark."

The JIC were the overseers and taskmasters of MI5 and MI6. They set priorities, assessed the product, advised the prime minister, and made certain the spies played by the rules. Graham Seymour had reached the conclusion that the Secret Intelligence Service needed room to maneuver, that in a dangerous world, with threats all around, it had to get a bit of chalk on its cleats from time to time. Thus his renewed relationship with Christopher Keller.

"You know," said Seymour, his eyes moving over Keller's sturdy frame, "you almost look like one of us again. It's too bad you have to leave."

They went into the kitchen and sat down at the table in the

snug little alcove, with its leaded windows overlooking the moorland. Miss Coventry served them the cottage pie with a claret from the well-stocked cellar, and a green salad for their digestion. Seymour spent much of the meal interrogating Keller about the IONEC. Of particular interest was the quality of the other members of the intake.

"Don't you see the assessments and scores?" asked Keller.

"Of course. But I value your opinion."

"Finch gives snakes a bad name," said Keller, "which means he has the makings of a fine spy."

"Baker's scores were quite good, too."

"So was the first chapter of the thriller he's working on."

"And the course itself?" asked Seymour. "Did they manage to teach you anything?"

"That depends."

"On what?"

"How you intend to use me."

With a spy's careful smile, Seymour declined Keller's invitation to brief him on his maiden voyage as a full-fledged MI6 agent. Instead, as rain pelted the windows of the alcove, he spoke of his father. Arthur Seymour had spied for England for more than thirty years. But at the end of his career, when he was blown to kingdom come by Philby and the other moles and traitors, the service sent him down to the gray pile of stone by the sea to light the secret fire within the next generation of British spies. "And he hated every minute of it," said Seymour. "He saw it for what it was, the end of the line. My father always thought of the Fort as a crypt into which the Service tossed his battered old corpse."

"If only your father could see you now."

"Yes," said Seymour distantly. "If only indeed."

"He was hard on you, the old man?"

"He was hard on everyone, especially my mother. Fortunately, I was little more than an afterthought. I was with him in Beirut in the sixties when Philby was there, too. Then he shipped me off to school. After that, he was someone I saw only a couple of times a year."

"He must have been disappointed when you joined MI5."

"He threatened to disown me. He thought MI5 were policemen and proletarian plods, as did everyone else at MI6."

"So why did you do it?"

"Because I preferred to be judged on my own accomplishments. Or maybe," said Seymour after a moment, "I didn't want to join a service that had been gutted by traitors. Maybe I wanted to *catch* spies instead of recruit them. Maybe I wanted to stop IRA bombs from exploding in our streets." He paused, then added, "Which is where you came in."

There was a silence.

"We did good work together in Belfast, you and I. We stopped many attacks, saved countless lives. And what did you do? You ran off and joined Don Orsati's little band of assassins."

"You left a few things out of your account."

"Only for the sake of time." Seymour shook his head slowly. "I grieved for you, you bastard. And so did your parents. At your memorial service, I tried to comfort your father, but he was inconsolable. That was a terrible thing you did to them."

Keller ignited a cigarette and then handed the new gold lighter to Seymour. "Do you remember what the inscription says?"

"Point taken. It's all in the past. You've been fully restored,

Christopher. You're as good as new. All you need now is a nice girl to share that beautiful home of yours in Kensington." Seymour reached for Keller's cigarettes but stopped himself. "Eight million pounds, quite a tidy sum. By my calculation that leaves you with a mere twenty-five million, all of it earned by working for Don Orsati. At least the money is in a fine British financial institution now instead of those Swiss and Bahamian banks you were using. It's been repatriated, just like you."

"We had a deal," said Keller quietly.

"And I intend to abide by it. Don't worry, you can keep your ill-gotten money."

Keller made no reply.

"And the girl?" asked Seymour, changing the subject. "Any prospects? We'll have to vet her thoroughly, you realize."

"I've been a bit busy, Graham. I haven't had a chance to meet many girls."

"What about the one who proposed to you at the Druid's Arms?"

"She was quite drunk at the time. She was also under the impression I was French."

Seymour smiled. "She won't be the first to make that mistake."

It had been fifteen years since Christopher Keller had willingly allowed his photograph to be taken. On that occasion he had been perched atop a wobbly wooden stool in a little shop high in the mountains of central Corsica. The walls of the shop had been hung with portraits—brides, widows, patriarchs— all unsmiling, for the inhabitants of the village were a serious lot who were suspicious of outsiders and modern gadgets like cameras, which were thought to be dispensers of the evil eye. The photographer was a distant relative of Don Anton Orsati, a cousin of some sort, by marriage rather than blood. Even so, he had been fearful in the presence of the hard, silent Englishman who, it was rumored, carried out assignments for the Orsati clan that ordinary *taddunaghiu* could not. The photographer had taken six pictures that day; in none did Keller look remotely the same. They appeared in the six false French passports Keller used throughout his career as a professional assassin. Two of the passports were still valid. One he kept in a bank vault in Zurich, the other in Marseilles, a fact he had neglected to tell his new employers at the Secret Intelligence Service. One never knew, he reasoned, when one might require an ace in the hole.

The technician who took Keller's photograph for MI6 had been unnerved by his subject too and consequently had worked with unusual haste. The session took place not at Vauxhall Cross—Keller's exposure to the building was to be strictly limited—but in a basement in Bloomsbury. The finished product showed an unsmiling man of perhaps fifty who looked as though he had recently returned from a long holiday in the sun. His name, according to the passport in which the photo was eventually placed, was Nicholas Evans, and he was not fifty years old but forty-eight. MI6 provided Keller with a British driver's permit in the same name, along with three credit cards and an attaché case stuffed with files related to his cover, which had something to do with sales and marketing. Keller also took possession of an MI6 mobile phone, which would allow him to communicate securely with Vauxhall Cross while in the field. He assumed, rightly, that Vauxhall Cross could in turn use the phone to monitor his movements and, if necessary, eavesdrop on his conversations. Therefore, he planned to part company with the device at the first opportunity.

He left London the following morning on the 5:40 Eurostar to Paris. It arrived at a quarter past nine, leaving Keller the better part of two hours to determine whether he was being watched. Using the techniques taught to him by Mayhew and Quill at the Fort—and a few others he had picked up on the streets of West Belfast—he established beyond a shadow of a doubt that he was not.

His next train, the TGV to Marseilles, departed the Gare de Lyon at half past eleven. He passed the journey working diligently on his laptop for the sake of his cover while beyond his window the Cézanne colors of the south—chrome yellow, burnt sienna, viridian, ultramarine—flashed through his peripheral vision like a pleasant memory from childhood. He arrived in Marseilles at two and spent the next hour wandering the grimy, familiar streets of the city center until certain his arrival had gone unnoticed. Finally, in the Place de la Joliette, he entered a Société Générale private bank, where Monsieur Laval, his account manager, granted him access to his safe-deposit box. From it he took his false French passport, along with five thousand euros in cash. In it he placed his MI6 phone, passport, driver's permit, credit cards, and laptop computer.

Outside, he walked a short distance along the Quai du Lazaret to the ferry terminal, where he purchased a ticket for the overnight crossing to Corsica, with first-class accommodations. The man at the counter thought nothing of the fact he paid in cash. This was Marseilles, after all, and the ferry was bound for Ajaccio. In a nearby café he ordered a bottle of Bandol rosé and drank it halfway down the label while reading *Le Figaro*, content for the first time in many months. An hour later, alert but pleasantly inebriated, he was standing at the prow of the ferry as it carved its way southward into the Mediterranean, the words of an ancient proverb running through his thoughts. He who has two women loses his soul. But he who has two homes loses his mind.

Shortly before dawn, Keller woke to the smell of rosemary and lavender drifting through the half-open window of his cabin. Rising, he dressed in his gray-and-white English clothing and, twenty minutes later, filed off the ferry in the company of a family of lumpy Corsicans, who were more ill tempered than usual due to the earliness of the hour. In a bar across the street from the terminal, he asked if he could use the telephone to place a local call. Under normal circumstances, the proprietor might have shrugged his shoulders in dismay at such a request from a foreigner. Or, if so moved, he might have explained that the telephone had been out of order since the last *sirocco*. But Keller delivered his request flawlessly in the dialect of the island. And the proprietor was so shocked he actually smiled while placing the phone atop the bar. Then, unsolicited, he prepared for Keller a cup of strong coffee and a small glass of cognac, for it was very cold that morning and a man couldn't face such weather without a little something to fortify the blood.

The number Keller dialed was unknown to all but a few residents of the island and, more important, to the French authorities. The man who answered seemed pleased by the sound of Keller's voice and, curiously, not at all surprised. He instructed Keller to remain at the café; he would dispatch a car to collect him. It arrived an hour later, driven by a young man named Giancomo. Keller had known him since he was a boy. It was Giancomo's wish to be a *taddunaghiu* like Keller, whom he idolized. For now, he was an errand boy for the don. On Corsica there were worse things for a young man of twenty-five to be.

"The don said you were never coming back."

"Even the don," said Keller philosophically, "is wrong on occasion."

Giancomo scowled, as though Keller had uttered a heresy. "The don is like the Holy Father. He is infallible."

"Now and forever," said Keller quietly.

They were driving along the island's western coast. At the

town of Porto, they headed inland along a road lined with olive groves and laricio pine, and began the long, winding climb into the mountains. Keller lowered his window. There it was again, rosemary and lavender, the smell of the *macchia*. It covered Corsica from west to east, stem to stern, a dense and tangled carpet of undergrowth that defined the very identity of the island. The Corsicans seasoned their foods with the *macchia*, heated their homes with it in winter, and took refuge in it in times of war and vendetta. According to Corsican legend, a hunted man could take to the *macchia* and, if he wished, remain there undetected forever. Keller knew this to be true.

Eventually, they came to the ancient village of the Orsatis, a cluster of sandstone-colored houses with red-tile roofs, huddled around the bell tower of a church. It had been there, or so it was said, since the time of the Vandals, when people from the coasts took to the hills for safety. Beyond it, in a small valley of olive groves that produced the island's finest oil, was Don Orsati's estate. Two armed guards stood watch at the entrance. They touched their distinctive Corsican caps respectfully as Giancomo turned through the gate and started up the long drive.

He parked in the deep shadow of the forecourt, and Keller, alone, entered the villa and climbed the cold stone steps to the don's office. He was seated at a large oaken table, peering into an open leather-bound ledger. He was a large man by Corsican standards, well over six feet and broad through the back and shoulders. He was wearing a pair of loose-fitting trousers, dusty leather sandals, and a crisp white shirt that his wife ironed for him each morning, and again in the afternoon when he rose from his nap. His hair was black, as were his eyes. At his elbow was a decorative bottle of Orsati olive oil—olive oil being the legitimate front through which the don laundered the profits of death.

"How's business?" asked Keller at last.

"Which part? Blood or oil?" In Don Orsati's world, blood and oil flowed together in a single seamless enterprise.

"Both."

"Oil, not so good. This no-growth economy is killing me. And the British with this Brexit nonsense!" He waved his hand as though dispersing a foul odor.

"And blood?" asked Keller.

"Did you happen to see the story about the German businessman who disappeared from the Carlton Hotel in Cannes last week?"

"Where is he?"

"Five miles due west of Ajaccio." The don smiled. "Or thereabouts."

"Alive one hour," said Keller, quoting a Corsican proverb, "dead the next."

"Remember, Christopher, life is just as long as the time it takes to pass by a window." The don closed the ledger with a coffin finality and regarded Keller thoughtfully. "I didn't expect to see you back on the island so soon. Are you having second thoughts about your new life?"

"Third and fourth," replied Keller.

This pleased the don. He was still appraising Keller with his black eyes. It was like being studied by a canine.

"I hope your friends in British intelligence don't know you're here."

"It's possible," said Keller candidly. "But don't worry, your secret is safe with them."

"I don't have the luxury of not worrying. As for the British," said the don, "they're not to be trusted. You're the only inhabitant of that dreadful island I've ever cared for. If only they'd stop coming here for their summer holidays, everything would be right with the world."

"It's good for the island's economy."

"They drink too much."

"A cultural affliction, I'm afraid."

"And now," said the don, "you're one of them again."

"Almost."

"They've given you a new name?"

"Peter Marlowe."

"I prefer your old name."

"It wasn't available. Poor chap's deceased, you see."

"And your new employers?" asked the don.

"Every bed has lice," said Keller.

"Only the spoon," replied the don, "knows the pot's sorrows."

With that, a companionable silence settled between them. There was only the wind in the laricio pine and the crackling of the *macchia*-wood fire, which perfumed the air of the don's large office. At length, he asked why Keller had returned to Corsica; and the Englishman, with an indifferent movement of his head, implied he had come for reasons having to do with his new line of work.

"You were sent here by the British secret service?"

"More or less."

"Don't speak to me in riddles, Christopher."

"I didn't have an appropriate proverb at my fingertips."

"Our proverbs," said the don, "are sacred and correct. Now tell me why you're here."

"I'm looking for a man. A Moroccan who calls himself the Scorpion."

"And if I agree to help you?" The don tapped the leather cover of his ledger.

Keller said nothing.

"Money doesn't come from singing, Christopher."

"I was hoping you might do it as a personal favor."

"You abandon me, and now you want to utilize my services free of charge?"

"Is that a proverb, too?"

The don frowned. "And if I can find this man? What then?"

"My friends in British intelligence think it might be a good idea for me to go into business with him."

"What line of work is he in?"

"Drugs, apparently. But in his spare time he supplies guns to ISIS."

"ISIS?" Don Orsati shook his head gravely. "I suppose this has something to do with the attacks in London."

"I suppose it does."

"In that case," said the don, "I'll do it for nothing."

The average life span of *Capra aegagrus hircus*, otherwise known as the domestic goat, is fifteen to eighteen years. Therefore, the old goat belonging to Don Casabianca, a notable who owned much of the valley adjacent to the Orsatis', had most definitely overstayed its earthly welcome. By Keller's calculation the beast had been consuming valuable oxygen for more than twenty-four years, much of it in the shade of the three ancient olive trees that stood just before the sharp left-hand turn in the dirt-and-gravel track that led to Keller's villa. A nameless creature with the markings of a palomino and a red beard, it blocked the path whenever it saw fit, denying access to those of whom it did not approve. For Keller, a mainlander with no Corsican blood in his veins, it harbored a particular resentment. Theirs was a long-simmering contest of wills, and more often than not it was the goat that had got the better of it. Keller, on many occasions, had contemplated ending the stand-off with a well-placed shot between the goat's malevolent eyes. But that would have been a grave mistake. The goat enjoyed the protection of Don Casabianca. And if Keller were to harm one hair on its wretched head, there would be a feud. One never knew where a feud might end. It might be settled amicably over a glass of wine, with an apology or restitution of some sort. Or it might go on for months or even years. Consequently, Keller had no choice but to wait patiently for the goat's passing. He felt like a shiftless son who counted his inheritance while his wealthy father, purely out of spite, clung stubbornly to life.

"I was hoping," said Keller morosely, "to avoid this scene."

"He had a scare in October." Giancomo tapped a finger impatiently on the steering wheel. "Or maybe it was November."

"Really?"

"Cancer. Or maybe it was an infection of the bowels. Don Casabianca brought in the priest to administer last rites."

"What happened?"

"A miracle," said Giancomo, shrugging.

"How unfortunate." Keller and the goat exchanged a long, tense look. "Try honking the horn."

"You can't be serious."

"It might work this time."

"Obviously," said Giancomo, "you've been away for a while."

With a heavy exhalation, Keller climbed out of the car. The goat raised its chin defiantly and stood its ground while Keller, fingertips squeezing the bridge of his nose, pondered his options. His usual tactic was a full-frontal assault of shouted invective and waved arms; and in most cases the old goat would cede its ground and flee into the *macchia*, the hiding place of scoundrels and bandits. But on that morning, Keller had no stomach for a confrontation. He was travel-weary and a touch seasick from the ferry. Besides, the goat, battered old bastard that he was, had had a rough time of it lately, what with the cancer and the problem with its bowels and the extreme unction performed by the village priest. And since when did the Church countenance the dispensation of holy sacraments to cloven-hoofed bovidae? Only on Corsica, thought Keller.

"Listen," he said at last, leaning against the hood of the car, "life is too short for this sort of nonsense." He might have added that life is just as long as it takes to pass by a window, but he didn't think the goat, who was just a goat after all, would understand the analogy. Instead, Keller spoke of the importance of friends and family. He confessed that he had made many mistakes in life and that now, after many years in the wilderness, he was home again and almost happy. He had but one unresolved relationship, this one, and it was his wish to set it right before it was too late. Time the conqueror could not be kept at bay forever.

At this, the goat tilted its head to one side in the manner of a man whom Keller, many years earlier, had been hired to kill. Then it took a few steps forward and licked the back of Keller's hand before retreating to the shade of the three ancient olive trees. The sun shone brightly upon Keller's villa as Giancomo turned into the drive. The air smelled of rosemary and lavender.

Inside, Keller found his possessions—his extensive library, his modest collection of French Impressionist paintings—precisely as he had left them, though coated with a fine powdery layer of dust. It was Saharan dust, he reckoned, carried across the Mediterranean by the last *sirocco*. Tunisian, Algerian, perhaps Moroccan, just like the man whom Don Orsati had undertaken to find on Keller's behalf.

Entering the kitchen, he discovered the pantry and refrigerator provisioned with supplies. Somehow, the don had advance warning of Keller's return. He poured a glass of pale Corsican rosé and carried it upstairs to his bedroom. A loaded Tanfoglio pistol lay on the bedside table, atop a volume of McEwan. Several business suits hung neatly in the closet, the attire of the former director of northern European sales for the Orsati Olive Oil Company, and behind a concealed door was a large selection of clothing for any occasion or assassination. The tattered denim and wool of the wandering bohemian, the silk and gold of a jet-setting one-percenter, the fleece and Gore-Tex of a mountain-climbing outdoorsman. There was even the clerical suit and Roman collar of a Catholic priest, along with a breviary and traveling mass kit. It occurred to Keller that the disguises, like his false French passports, might prove useful in his new line of work, too. He thought of his MI6 mobile phone and laptop computer expiring slowly in a bank vault in Marseilles. Surely Vauxhall Cross was now aware the devices had not moved in more than twelve hours. At some point, Keller would have to tell Graham Seymour he was alive and well. At some point, he thought again.

Keller changed into a pair of wrinkled chinos and a rough woolen sweater, and carried the wine and the volume of McEwan downstairs to the terrace. Stretched on the wrought-iron chaise, he resumed reading the novel where he had left off, in midsentence, as though his interruption had been a few minutes instead of many months. It was the story of a young woman, a student at Cambridge, drawn into British intelligence in the early 1970s. Keller found he had little in common with the character, but enjoyed the book nonetheless. A shadow soon encroached on the page. He dragged the chaise across the terrace and placed it against the balustrade and remained there until the darkness and cold drove him inside. That night an icy *tramontana* blew from the northeast, loosening several tiles from Keller's roof. He wasn't displeased. It would give him something to do while he waited for the don to find the man called the Scorpion.

He passed the next few days without plan or purpose. The repair of the roof consumed only a portion of one morning, including the two hours he spent at the hardware store in Porto discussing the recent spate of winds with several men from the surrounding villages. It seemed the *tramontana*, which came from the Po, had blown more often than usual, as had the *maestrale*, which is how the fiercely independent Corsicans referred to the wind that came down from the Rhône Valley. All agreed it had been a difficult winter, which, according to Corsican proverbs, promised a benign spring. Keller, whose future was uncertain, declined comment.

Afternoons he climbed the rugged peaks at the center of the island—Rotondo, d'Oro, Renoso—and hiked across sunlit valleys of *macchia*. Most evenings he took his dinner with Don Orsati at the estate. Afterward, over brandy in the don's office, he would gently probe for details concerning the search for the Scorpion. The don spoke only in proverbs, and Keller, who was under the discipline of an intelligence service, answered with proverbs of his own. Mainly, they listened to the *tramontana* and the *maestrale* prowling in the eaves, which is how Corsican men preferred to pass the evening.

On the sixth morning of Keller's stay there was an attack in Germany, a single suicide bomber in a Stuttgart train terminal, two killed, twenty wounded. The usual questions ensued. Was the attacker a lone wolf, or was he acting at the behest of ISIS central command in the caliphate? The one they called Saladin. Keller watched the television coverage until midafternoon, when he climbed into his battered Renault station wagon and drove into the village. The central square lay at the town's highest point. On three sides were shops and cafés, on the fourth was an old church. Keller took a table at one of the cafés and watched a game of *boules* until the church bell tolled five o'clock. Its door opened a moment later and several parishioners, mostly elderly, came tremulously down the steps. One, an old woman dressed entirely in black, paused for a moment and glanced in Keller's direction before entering the crooked little house adjoining the rectory. Keller finished the last of his wine as darkness settled over the village. Then he laid a few coins on the table and headed across the square.

She greeted him, as always, with a worried smile and a warm, weightless hand to his cheek. Her skin was the color of flour; a black scarf covered her tinder-dry white hair. It was strange, thought Keller, how the marks of ethnicity and national origin were erased by time. Were it not for her Corsican language and mystical Catholic ways, she might have been mistaken for his old Auntie Beatrice from Ipswich.

"You've been on the island a week," she said at last, "and only now do you come to see me." She gazed deeply into his eyes. "The evil has returned, my child."

"Where did I contract it?"

"In the castle by the sea, in the land of Druids and sorcerers.

There was a man there with the name of a bird. Beware of him in the future. He does not wish you well."

The old woman's hand was still pressed to Keller's cheek. In the language of the island, she was known as a *signadora*. Her task was to care for those afflicted with the evil eye, though she had the power to see the past and future as well. When Keller was still working for Don Orsati, he never left the island without paying a visit to the old woman. And when he returned, the crooked little house at the edge of the square was always among his first stops.

She removed her hand from Keller's cheek and fingered the heavy cross around her neck. "You're looking for someone, are you not?"

"Do you know where he is?"

"First things first, my dearest."

With a movement of her hand, she invited Keller to sit at the small wooden table in her parlor. Before him she placed a plate filled with water and a vessel of olive oil. Keller dipped his forefinger in the oil. Then he held it over the plate and allowed three drops to fall onto the water. The oil should have gathered into a single gobbet. Instead, it shattered into a thousand droplets, and soon there was no trace of it.

"As I suspected," said the old woman with a frown. "And worse than usual. The world beyond the island is a troubled place, filled with evil. You should have stayed here with us."

"It was time for me to leave."

"Why?"

Keller had no answer.

"It was all the Israelite's doing. The one with the name of an angel."

"It was my choice, not his."

"You still haven't learned, have you? It's no use lying to me." She stared into the plate of water and oil. "You should know," she said, "that your path will lead you back to him."

"The Israelite?"

"I'm afraid so."

Without another word, she took hold of Keller's hand and prayed. After a moment she began to weep, a sign the evil had passed from his body into hers. Then she closed her eyes and appeared to be sleeping. When she awoke she instructed Keller to repeat the trial of the oil and the water. This time the oil coalesced into a single drop.

"Don't wait so long the next time," she said. "It's best not to allow the evil to linger in the blood."

"I need someone in London."

"I know of a woman in a place called Soho. She's Greek, a heretic. Use her only in cases of emergency."

Keller pushed the plate toward the center of the table. "Tell me about the one they call the Scorpion."

"The don will find him in a city at the other end of one of our ferries. It is not in my power to tell you which one. He is not important, this man. But he can lead you to the one who is."

"Who?"

"It is not in my power," she said again.

"How long will I have to wait?"

"When you go home, pack your bag. You'll be leaving us soon."

"You're sure?"

"You doubt me?" Smiling, she searched his eyes. "Are you happy, Christopher?"

"As happy as a man like me can be."

"But you still mourn for the one you lost in Belfast?"

He said nothing.

"It is understandable, my child. The manner of her death was terrible. But you killed the man who took her from you, the one called Quinn. You received your vengeance."

"Does vengeance truly heal such wounds?"

"You're asking the wrong person. After all, I'm a Corsican. You used to be one, too." She glanced at the strand of leather around Keller's neck. "At least you still wear your talisman. You're going to need it. She will, too."

"Who?"

Her eyes began to close. "I'm tired now, Christopher. I need to rest."

Keller kissed her hand and slipped a roll of euros into her palm.

"It's too much," she said softly as he took his leave. "You always give me too much."

Later that evening, in the firelit warmth of Don Orsati's office, Christopher Keller learned the man who called himself the Scorpion would be waiting two days hence at Le Bar Saint Étienne, on the rue Dabray in Nice. Keller feigned surprise. And the don, who knew that Keller had been to see the *signadora*, made scant effort to conceal his irritation over the fact that the mystical old woman, whom he had known since he was a boy, had once again stolen his thunder.

There was much about the encounter that even the *signadora*, with her extraordinary powers of second sight, could not have surmised. She did not know, for example, that the Scorpion's real name was Nouredine Zakaria, that he held both French and Moroccan passports, that he had been a low-level street criminal most of his life and had served time in a French prison, and that he was rumored to have spent several months in the caliphate, probably in Raqqa. Which meant it was possible he was under DGSI surveillance, though the don's men had seen no evidence of it. He was scheduled to arrive at Le Bar Saint Étienne, alone, at a quarter past two in the afternoon. He would be expecting a Frenchman named Yannick Ménard, a career criminal who specialized in the sale of weaponry. Ménard, however, would be unable to attend. He was now lying five miles due west of Ajaccio, in the watery graveyard of the Orsatis. And the guns he planned to sell Nouredine Zakaria—ten Kalashnikov combat assault rifles and ten Heckler & Koch MP7 compact machine guns with suppressors and ECLAN reflex sights—were in an Orsati warehouse outside the Provençal town of Grasse.

"How much would this be worth to your friends in London?" asked the don.

"I thought we agreed your work would be pro bono."

"Humor me."

"Ménard's death might complicate things," said Keller thoughtfully.

"How so?"

"The British frown on blood."

"Is it not true you have a license to kill?"

No, explained Keller, it was not.

Le Bar Saint Étienne occupied the ground floor of a three-story pie-shaped building at the corner of the rue Vernier. Its awning was green, its tables and chairs were aluminum and stained with spilt ice cream. It was a neighborhood spot, a place to grab a quick café crème or a beer or perhaps a sandwich. Tourists rarely ventured there unless they were lost.

On the opposite side of the intersection was La Fantasia. Here the fare was pizza, though the accommodations were identical. Keller arrived at half past one and after ordering a coffee at the counter took a table on the street. He was dressed as a man of the south. Not a well-to-do sort who lived in a villa in the hills or an apartment by the sea, but the kind who lived by his wits on the street. A waiter one day, a laborer the next, a thief by night. He'd done a bit of time in prison, this version of Keller, and was good with his fists and a knife. He was an excellent friend to have in times of trouble, and a dangerous enemy.

He drew a cigarette from his packet of Marlboros and lit it with a disposable lighter. His phone was disposable, too. Through an exhalation of smoke, he scanned the quiet street and the shuttered windows of the surrounding apartment buildings. He could see no sign of the opposition. Mayhew and Quill, his instructors at the Fort, would have reminded him that surveillance by a professional service was almost impossible to detect. Keller, however, was confident of his instincts. He had worked as an assassin in France for more than twenty years, and yet to the French police he was nothing more than a rumor. It was not because he was lucky. It was because he was very good at his job.

A small Peugeot transit van, dented and dusty, passed in the street, a North African face behind the wheel, another in the front passenger seat. So much for coming alone. Keller wasn't alone, either. In violation of all known MI6 rules, written and unwritten, he was carrying an illegal Tanfoglio pistol at the small of his back. Were the weapon to discharge—and were the round to strike another human being—Keller's might be the shortest career in the history of Her Majesty's Secret Intelligence Service.

The Peugeot eased into an empty spot along the rue Dabray as a second car, a Citroën sedan, stopped outside Le Bar Saint Étienne. It, too, contained a pair of North African–looking men. The passenger climbed out and sat down at one of the outdoor tables while the driver found an empty space along the rue Vernier.

Keller crushed out his cigarette and considered his situation. No sign of the French security service, he thought, only four members of a Moroccan criminal gang quite possibly linked to ISIS. He recalled the many lectures he had attended during the IONEC regarding the rules for making or aborting a meeting. Given current circumstances, MI6 doctrine dictated a hasty retreat. At the very least, Keller was obliged to check in with his controller in London for guidance. Too bad his secure MI6 phone was locked in a bank vault in Marseilles.

With the disposable phone, Keller snapped a photograph of the man waiting for him at Le Bar Saint Étienne. Then, rising, he left a few coins on the table and started across the street. He is not important, the old woman had said. But he can lead you to the one who is.

He was a citizen of the forgotten France, the great belts of suburbs, banlieues, that ringed large metropolitan centers like Paris and Lyon and Toulouse. For the most part, their residents lived in shabby high-rise housing blocks that were factories of crime, drug abuse, resentment, and, increasingly, radical Islam. The overwhelming majority of France's growing Muslim population wanted nothing more than to live in peace and care for their families. But a small minority had fallen victim to the siren song of ISIS. And some, like Nouredine Zakaria, were prepared to slaughter in the name of the caliphate. Keller had encountered many like him—members of North African street gangs—while working for Don Orsati. He suspected that Zakaria knew little of Islam, the tenets of jihadism, or the ways of the *salaf al Salih*, the original followers of the Prophet Muhammad whom the murderers of ISIS sought to emulate. But the Moroccan possessed something more valuable to ISIS than knowledge of Islam. As a career criminal, he was a natural operator who knew how to acquire weapons and explosives, how to steal cars and cell phones, and where to find places for members of a terrorist cell to lie low before and after an attack. In short, he knew how to get things done without attracting the attention of the police. For a terrorist group—or an intelligence service, for that matter—it was an essential skill.

He was shorter than Keller by an inch or two, and powerfully built. His was not a body sculpted in a fitness club. It was a prisoner's physique, honed by relentless calisthenics in a confined space. He looked to be about thirty-five, but Keller couldn't be sure; he had never been good at guessing the ages of North African men. In appearance he was an archetype—a high forehead with arcs at the temples, broad cheekbones, a full mouth, dark lips. Yellow-tinted aviators shielded his eyes; Keller had the impression they were almost black. On his right wrist was a large Swiss watch, no doubt stolen. The right wrist meant he was probably left-handed. So it was the left hand, not the right, that would reach for the gun he carried just inside his partially zipped leather jacket. The bulge was quite obvious. And intentional, thought Keller.

Presently, a Police Nationale unit rolled slowly past the café, an environmentally friendly Peugeot 308, a go-kart with lights and a flashy paint job. The officer behind the wheel cast a long look toward the two men seated outside Le Bar Saint Étienne. Keller watched the car round the corner while lighting a cigarette. When at last he spoke, he did so in the Corsican way, so that Nouredine Zakaria would know he was not a man to be taken lightly.

"You were instructed," he said, "to come alone."

"Do you see anyone else sitting here, my friend?"

"I'm not your friend. Not even close." Keller glanced toward the Citroën parked across the street, and at the Peugeot van on the rue Dabray. "What about them?"

"Guys from the neighborhood," said Zakaria with a dismissive shrug.

"Tell them to take a drive."

"Can't."

Keller started to rise.

"Wait."

Keller froze and after a moment's hesitation lowered himself back into his chair. Mayhew and Quill would have been pleased by their star pupil's performance; he had just established dominance over the source. It was a technique as old as the bazaar, the willingness to walk away from a deal. But Nouredine Zakaria was a man of the bazaar, too. Moroccans were born negotiators.

He started to reach inside his leather jacket.

"Easy," said Keller.

Slowly, the hand retrieved a mobile phone from an interior pocket. Like Keller's, it was a throwaway. The Moroccan used it to dispatch a brief text message. *Ping*, thought Keller, as the message surged across the French cellular network. A few seconds later two engines turned over, and two examples of French automotive prowess, one a Peugeot, the other a Citroën, moved off.

"Happy?" asked Nouredine Zakaria.

"Rapturous."

The Moroccan lit a cigarette of his own, a Gauloise. "Where's Yannick?"

"Under the weather."

"So you're the boss?"

Keller allowed the question to pass unanswered. The fact that he was the boss, he thought, was manifest.

"I don't like changes," the Moroccan said. "They make me uneasy."

"Change is good, Nouredine. It keeps everyone on their toes."

An eyebrow rose above the yellow-tinted aviators. "How do you know my real name?"

Keller managed to appear offended by the question. "I wouldn't be here," he said evenly, "if I didn't."

"You speak like a Corsican," Zakaria said, "but you don't look like one."

"Appearances can be deceiving."

The Moroccan made no reply. The dance was almost complete, thought Keller, the dance that two seasoned criminals engaged in before getting down to business. He had no interest in seeing it come to an end, not yet. He was no longer a contract killer, he was a gatherer of information. And the only way to get information was to talk. He decided to drop another coin in the jukebox and stay on the floor a little longer.

"Yannick tells me you're interested in acquiring twenty pieces of merchandise."

"Is twenty a problem?"

"Not at all. In fact, my organization generally deals in much larger quantities."

"How large?"

Keller glanced at the clouds, as if to say the sky was the limit. "To tell you the truth, twenty is hardly worth our time or effort. Yannick should have checked with me before making any promises. He has a bright future but he's young. And sometimes," added Keller, "he doesn't ask enough questions."

"Such as?"

"My organization operates a bit like a government," Keller explained. "We want to know who our buyers are and how they intend to use our merchandise. When the Americans sell airplanes to their friends the Saudis, for example, the Saudis have to promise they won't use the planes against the Israelis."

"Zionist pigs," murmured the Moroccan.

"Nevertheless," said Keller with a frown, "I trust you see my point. We won't fill your order without certain restrictions."

"What sort?"

"We would need your assurance that nothing will be used here in France or against citizens of the Republic. We're criminals, but we're also patriots."

"So are we."

"Patriots?"

"Criminals."

"Are you really?" Keller smoked in silence for a moment. "Listen, Nouredine, what you do in your spare time is of no concern to me. If you want to make jihad, go ahead. I'd probably make jihad too if I were in your position. But if you use the weapons on French soil, there's a good chance they'll be traced back to my boss. And that would make him extremely unhappy."

"I thought *you* were the boss."

A cloud of smoke came billowing across the table. Keller's eyes watered involuntarily. He had never cared for the smell of Gauloises.

"Say it for me, Nouredine. Swear to me that you won't use my guns against my countrymen. Promise me you won't give me a reason to hunt you down and kill you."

"You're not threatening me, are you?"

"I wouldn't dream of it. I just wouldn't want you to do something you might regret later. Because if you behave yourself, my boss can get you anything you want. Do you understand?"

The Moroccan crushed out his cigarette, slowly. "Listen, *habibi*, I'm beginning to lose patience. Shall we make business, or should I find someone else to sell me the guns? Someone who doesn't ask so many fucking questions."

Keller said nothing.

"Where are they?"

Keller glanced toward the west.

"Spain?"

"Not quite that far. I'll take you there, just the two of us."

"No, you won't." Zakaria picked up his mobile and with a second text summoned the Citroën. "Change in plan."

"I don't like changes."

"Change is good, *habibi*. It keeps everyone on their toes."

Keller, as instructed, sat in the passenger seat, with Noure-dine Zakaria directly behind him. The Moroccan wondered aloud whether Keller might want to place his hands on the dashboard, a suggestion Keller rejected with a few choice Corsican obscenities and a murmured proverb. Zakaria didn't bother to ask whether Keller had a gun. Keller was posing as an arms dealer, after all. Zakaria probably assumed he had an RPG in his back pocket.

The Citroën stopped once on the outskirts of Nice, long enough for another North African to slide into the backseat. He was a smaller version of Zakaria, a year or two younger perhaps, with a deep scar along one cheek. In all likelihood, Keller was now surrounded by three career criminals with ties to ISIS. As a result, he spent the next several minutes choreographing the complex sequence of moves that would be required to extricate himself from the car if the deal went sideways.

There was disagreement over the path they should take from Nice to their destination. Zakaria wanted to use the A8 Autoroute, but Keller convinced him the two-lane D4 was a better option. They picked it up at its source, along the beach near the airport, and followed it into the foothills of the Maritime Alps, through Biot and Valbonne and, finally, to the outskirts of Grasse. Keller glanced into the side-view mirror. It appeared that no other members of the gang were following. He took no comfort in this realization. The final exchange of money for goods was the most dangerous part of any criminal deal. It was not unusual for one of the parties, buyer or seller, to end up with a bullet in his head.

The Orsati Olive Oil Company warehouse in Grasse served as its primary distribution center for all of Provence. Even so, like most Orsati facilities, it was easily missed. It stood on a dusty road called the Chemin de la Madeleine, in an industrial quarter northeast of the town's historic center. Keller punched the code into the keypad at the front gate and entered the property on foot, followed by the Citroën. Next he opened the warehouse door and led Zakaria and the one with the scar on his cheek inside. Zakaria was clutching a stainless steel attaché case. Presumably, it contained a sum of sixty thousand euros—three thousand euros for each black-market weapon. Keller thought it a rather fair price. He threw a switch and, overhead, a row of fluorescent lights flickered to life. They illuminated several hundred wooden crates. Three contained weapons, the rest Orsati olive oil.

"Well played," said the Moroccan.

"This is the part," replied Keller, "where you show me the money."

He had expected the usual wrangle over protocol. Instead, Zakaria placed the attaché case on the concrete floor, opened the combination latches, and lifted the lid. Tens, twenties, fifties, and hundreds, all bound by rubber bands. Keller lifted one of the bundles to his nose. It smelled faintly of hashish.

Keller closed the attaché case and nodded toward the far corner of the warehouse. Zakaria and the second Moroccan hesitated and then started walking, with Keller a few steps behind, the attaché case dangling from his left hand. Eventually, they came to a neat stack of rectangular crates. With a nod, Keller instructed Zakaria to remove the lid from the topmost. Inside were five AK-47s of Belarusan manufacture. The Moroccan removed one of the guns and inspected it carefully. It was obvious he knew his way around firearms.

"We're going to need ammunition. I'm interested in acquiring five thousand rounds. Is that sufficient for your organization?"

"I should think so."

"I was hoping that would be your answer."

The Moroccan returned the Kalashnikov to the crate. Then he handed Keller a slip of paper, folded in half.

"What's this?"

"Consider it a small demonstration of goodwill."

Keller unfolded the paper and saw a few lines of French script rendered in red ink. He looked up sharply.

"Why?" he asked.

"To prove to me that you are not a cop." The Moroccan paused, then added, "Or a spy."

"Do I look like a spy to you?"

"Appearances," said Zakaria, "can be deceiving." His gaze settled on the second Moroccan, the one with the scar on his face. "Prove it to me, monsieur. Prove that you are really an arms dealer and not a French spy."

"And if I refuse?"

"Then it is highly unlikely you will leave this place alive."

The second Moroccan was standing a few feet from Keller's right shoulder, Zakaria directly in front of him, next to the crates. Smiling, Keller allowed the slip of paper to fall from his fingertips. By the time it had fluttered to the floor, he had drawn the Tanfoglio from the small of his back. He aimed it at the face of Nouredine Zakaria.

"Very impressive," said the Moroccan. "And all the while holding the money. But perhaps you don't read so well."

"I read just fine. My hearing is quite good, too. And I'm certain you just threatened me. Big mistake, *habibi*." Keller paused, then said, "Fatal, actually."

Zakaria glanced nervously at the second Moroccan, who made a fumbling attempt to draw a weapon from inside his coat. Keller's arm swung forty-five degrees to the right, and without hesitation he pulled the trigger of the Tanfoglio twice. The *tap-tap* of a trained professional. Both shots struck the Moroccan in the center of the forehead. Then the arm swung back to its original position. Had Zakaria remained motionless, he might have presented Keller with a quandary over how to proceed. Instead, he attempted to draw a weapon as well, thus making Keller's decision instinctual. *Tap-tap* . . . Another dead Moroccan.

Keller returned the Tanfoglio to the waistband of his trousers. Then he retrieved the slip of paper from the warehouse floor and read again the words Nouredine Zakaria had written in red ink.

Kill my friend or I will kill you.

Change in plan, thought Keller. He placed the attaché case on the warehouse floor next to the bodies and went outside, where the third Moroccan sat behind the wheel of the Citroën. Keller rapped a knuckle against the driver's-side window, and the glass slid down.

"I thought I heard shots," said the Moroccan.

"Your friend Nouredine insisted on testing the merchandise." Keller opened the door. "Come inside, my friend. He has something he wants you to see."

Keller spent that night in a small hotel near the Old Port of Cannes and in the morning hired a car to take him to Marseilles. It was a few minutes after ten when he arrived; he entered the Société Générale in the Place de la Joliette and requested access to his safe-deposit box. The batteries of his computer and mobile phone were long dead. He recharged both on the TGV to Paris and discovered in his in-box several unread messages from Vauxhall Cross, the tone of which rose in an ascending scale of alarm. He waited until he was safely aboard his second train, a London-bound Eurostar, before informing his controller he was homeward bound. He doubted his reception would be pleasant.

There were no further messages from Vauxhall Cross until his train drew into St. Pancras International. It was then he received a bland six-word transmission stating that he would be met in the arrivals hall. His welcoming committee turned out to be Nigel Whitcombe, Graham Seymour's youthful-looking aide-de-camp, food taster, and general factotum. Whitcombe spoke not a word as he drove Keller from Euston Street to a terrace of sooty postwar houses near the Stockwell Tube station. As Keller headed up the garden walk, clutching a stainless steel attaché case that contained sixty thousand euros of ISIS money, he composed the verbal report he would soon deliver to his chief. He had managed to find the ISIS operative known as the Scorpion and, as instructed, had tried to go into business with him. Regrettably, the first transaction had not gone as planned, and three members of an ISIS cell were now dead. Other than that, his first assignment as an officer of Her Majesty's Secret Intelligence Service had been rather uneventful.

C ouldn't you have missed?"

"I tried," answered Keller. "But the damn fools jumped in front of my bullets."

"Why were you even carrying a gun?"

"I considered bringing a bunch of daffodils, but I thought a gun would be better for my cover. After all, they were under the impression I sold them for a living."

"Where is it now?"

"The gun? Back on Corsica, I suppose."

"And the bodies?"

"A few miles to the west."

Seymour gazed disconsolately around the little sitting room. It was furnished with all the charm of an airport departure lounge. The safe house was hardly one of MI6's crown jewels— there were much grander Service properties in tony Mayfair and Belgravia—but Seymour used this one frequently owing to its proximity to Vauxhall Cross. The automatic recording system had long ago been disabled. Even so, he checked the power module to make certain the system had not been switched on by mistake. It was located in a cabinet in the galley kitchen. The lights and signal meters were darkened and lifeless.

He closed the cabinet and looked at Keller. "Did they really have to die?"

"They weren't exactly pillars of the community, Graham. Besides, I didn't have much choice in the matter. It was them or me."

"I'd advise your friend the don to give that warehouse a thorough scrubbing. Blood lingers, you know."

"Have you been watching *CSI* again?"

Seymour made no reply.

"The French police would never dare look in that warehouse," said Keller, "because they're on the don's payroll. That's the way it works in the real world. That's why the bad guys never get caught. At least the smart ones."

"But occasionally," said Seymour, "even spies get caught. And when it involves murder, they sometimes go to jail."

"Define murder."

"The unlawful killing of another—"

"'If we'd wanted to be in the Boy Scouts, we would have joined the Boy Scouts.'"

Seymour raised an eyebrow. "T. S. Eliot?"

"Richard Helms."

"My father loathed him."

"If you'd wanted the job handled by the book," said Keller, "you would have given it to a career officer who had his eye on a controllerate. But you sent me instead."

"I asked you to infiltrate the cell by posing as a Corsican arms dealer. I'm quite certain I never mentioned anything about killing three ISIS terrorists on French soil."

"It wasn't my intention going in. But let's not pretend to be troubled by my methods, Graham. We're beyond all that. We go back too far."

"We do indeed," said Seymour quietly. "All the way to a farmhouse in South Armagh."

He opened another cabinet door and pulled down a bottle of Tanqueray and a second bottle of tonic. Next he opened the refrigerator and peered inside. It was empty except for two dried-out limes. Their skins were the color of a paper sack.

"Heresy."

"What's that?"

"A gin and tonic without lime." Seymour grabbed a handful of ice from the freezer and divided it between two smudged tumblers. "Your actions are not without consequences. Chief among them is the fact that the one and only link between the attack and Saladin's network is now lying on the bottom of the Mediterranean."

"Where he won't be able to kill anyone else."

"Sometimes a live terrorist is more useful than a dead one."

"Sometimes," agreed Keller grudgingly. "What's your point?"

"My point," said Seymour, handing Keller his drink, "is that we now have no choice but to share Nouredine Zakaria's name with our friends in French intelligence."

"And what do we tell the French about Nouredine's current whereabouts?"

"As little as possible."

"If you don't mind," said Keller, "I think I'll skip that meeting."

"Actually, I have no intention of talking to them, either."

"Who are you planning to send?"

When Graham Seymour spoke the name, Keller smiled.

"Does he know about any of this?"

"Not yet."

"You're a devious bastard."

"It's in our blood." Seymour sipped his drink and frowned. "Didn't they teach you anything down at the Fort?"

KING SAUL BOULEVARD, TEL AVIV

I f there was an official record of the affair, which there certainly was not, it would have revealed the fact that Gabriel
Allon spent much of that same evening in the Op Center of King
Saul Boulevard. Of Christopher Keller's sojourn to France—or
the meeting at the Stockwell safe house—he knew nothing. He
had eyes only for the video display monitors, where a convoy of
four cargo trucks was moving west from Damascus toward the
border with Lebanon. On one screen was an overhead shot from
an Israeli Ofek 10 spy satellite floating high above Syria. On another, the view was from an IDF surveillance camera high atop
Mount Hermon. Both were utilizing infrared technology. As a
result, the engines of the trucks glowed white and hot against
a black background. The Office had it on the highest authority
that the convoy contained chemical weapons bound for Hezbollah, payment in kind for the radical Shiite group's support of
the embattled Syrian regime. For obvious reasons, the weapons
could not be allowed to reach their intended destination, which
was a Hezbollah storage depot in the Beqaa Valley.

The Op Center was far smaller than its Anglo and Ameri-

can counterparts, more Spartan and utilitarian, a secret warrior's chamber. There was a chair reserved for the chief and
a second for his deputy. Both men, however, were on their
feet, Navot with his heavy arms folded across his chest, Gabriel
with a hand to his chin and his head tilted slightly to one side.
His green eyes were fixed on the shot from the Ofek. He had
no assets on the ground, no operatives in harm's way. Still, he
was tense and unsettled. This is what it means to be the chief,
he thought. The terrible burden of command. Nor did he care
for the aerial high-tech trappings of tonight's operation. He
much preferred to deal with his enemies at a meter rather than
a mile.

All at once a memory was upon him. It was October 1972,
the Piazza Annibaliano in Rome, his first mission. An angel of
vengeance waiting by the coin-operated elevator, a Palestinian
terrorist with the blood of eleven Israeli coaches and athletes on
his hands.

"Excuse me, but are you Wadal Zwaiter?"

"No! Please, no!"

The distinctive ring of the chief's phone hauled Gabriel back
to the present. Navot reached for it instinctively, but stopped.
Smiling, Gabriel lifted the receiver to his ear, listened in silence,
and rang off. Afterward, he and Navot stood side by side, Boaz
and Jachin, each contemplating a screen.

Finally, Gabriel said, "The IAF is going to hit them the minute they cross the border."

Navot nodded thoughtfully. Waiting until the convoy was
in Lebanon would eliminate the risk of hitting any Russian or
Syrian forces, thus reducing the likelihood of starting World
War III.

"What were you thinking about just now?" Navot asked after a moment.

"The operation," answered Gabriel, surprised.

"Bullshit."

"How could you tell?"

"You were pulling a trigger with your right forefinger."

"Was I?"

"Eleven times."

Gabriel was silent for a moment. "Rome," he said at last. "I was thinking about Rome."

"Why now?"

"Why ever?"

"I thought you shot him with your left hand."

Gabriel watched the four-truck convoy moving steadily westward. At ten minutes past nine o'clock Tel Aviv time, it crossed into Lebanon.

"Uh-oh," said Navot.

"Should have checked navigation," quipped Gabriel.

There was a crackle over the secure communications net, and a few seconds later a pair of missiles flashed across the screen, left to right. Viewed through the infrared cameras, the resulting explosions were so bright Gabriel had to turn away. When he looked up again, he saw a single burning man running from the shattered convoy. He only wished it was Saladin. No, he thought coldly as he slipped from the Op Center. Better a meter than a mile.

Gabriel stopped in his office to collect his coat and briefcase before heading down to the underground garage and sliding into the back of his armored SUV. As he was nearing the outskirts of West Jerusalem his secure phone rang. It was Kaplan Street; the prime minister wanted a word. For ninety minutes, over a dinner of kung pao chicken and egg rolls, he held Gabriel captive, interrogating him on current operations and estimates. Iran was his primary obsession, with the new administration in Washington a close second. His relationship with the last American president had been disastrous. The new president had promised closer ties between Washington and Israel and was even threatening to formally relocate the U.S. Embassy from Tel Aviv to Jerusalem, a move that would likely ignite a firestorm of protest in the Arab and Islamic worlds. There were elements in the prime minister's coalition who wanted to seize upon the favorable conditions by rapidly expanding Jewish settlement in the West Bank. Annexation was in the air. Gabriel was a voice of caution. As chief of the Office, he needed the help of Arab intelligence services in Amman and Cairo to protect Israel's periphery. What's more, he was making important inroads with the Saudis and the Sunni emirates of the Gulf, who feared the Persians more than Jews. The last thing he wanted now was a unilateral move on the Palestinian front.

"When are you planning to go to Washington?" asked the prime minister.

"I haven't been invited."

"Since when do you need an invitation?" The Israeli leader attempted to pick up an egg roll with a pair of chopsticks and, failing, impaled it. "You sure you won't have one?"

"Thank you, no."

"How about some of the chicken?"

Gabriel held up a hand defensively.

"But it's kung pao," said the prime minister, incredulous.

It was nearly midnight by the time Gabriel's SUV turned into Narkiss Street. Once among the city's most tranquil, it now resembled something of an armed camp. There were security checkpoints at each end, and outside the old limestone apartment house at Number 16 a guard stood watch always. Otherwise, little had changed. The garden gate still screeched when opened, an overgrown eucalyptus tree still obscured the three little terraces, the light in the stairwell was still seasick green. Arriving on the third-floor landing, Gabriel found the door slightly ajar. He entered silently and saw Chiara seated at one end of the couch, an open book in her lap. He gently removed it from her grasp and looked at the cover. It was an Italian-language edition of an American spy thriller.

"Don't you get enough of this in real life?"

"It seems so much more glamorous when he writes about it."

"What's his hero like?"

"A killer with a conscience, a bit like you."

"Is he an art restorer, too?"

She made a face. "Who could invent such a thing?"

Gabriel removed his overcoat and suit jacket and tossed both provocatively across the back of an armchair. Chiara shook her head slowly in disapproval and, licking the tip of her forefinger, turned the page of her book. She was wearing a pair of ordinary gray sweatpants and a fleece pullover against the winter chill. Even so, with her long riotous hair drawn over one shoulder, she looked astonishingly beautiful. Chiara was nearing forty now, but neither time nor the intense stress of Gabriel's work had left a mark on her face. In it Gabriel saw traces of Arabia and North Africa and Spain and all the other places her ancestors had wandered before finding themselves in the ancient Jewish ghetto of Venice. But it was her eyes that had always enthralled him most. They were the color of caramel and flecked with gold, a combination he had been unable to reproduce on canvas. When they were happy, they filled him with a contentment he had never known. And when they were disappointed or angry, he felt like the lowliest creature to walk the earth.

"How are the children?" he asked.

"If you wake them . . ." She licked her forefinger and turned another page.

Gabriel removed his shoes and in stocking feet entered the nursery without a sound. Two cribs stood end to end against a wall that Gabriel had painted with clouds. Two infants, a boy and a girl, aged fourteen months, slept head to head, as they had in their mother's womb. Gabriel reached down toward his daughter, who was called Irene after her grandmother, but stopped. She was a creature of the night, easily woken, a spy by nature. Raphael, however, could sleep through anything, even the midnight touch of his father's hand.

Suddenly, Gabriel realized that three days had passed since he had last seen the children when they were awake. He had been chief for little more than a month and already he had missed important milestones—Raphael's first word, Irene's first halting steps. He had promised himself it would not be so, that he would not allow his work to intrude on his personal life. It was a fantasy, of course; the chief of the Office had no personal life. No family, no wife other than the country he was sworn to protect. It was not a life sentence, he assured himself. Just six years. The children would be seven at the end of his term. There would be plenty of time to make amends. Unless, of course, the prime minister imposed upon him to stay on. He calculated how old he would be at the end of two terms. The number depressed him. It was Abrahamic. *Noah* . . .

He slipped out and went into the kitchen, where the small café-style table had been laid with his supper. Tagliatelle with fava beans and cheese, an assortment of bruschetta, an omelet with tomato and herbs, all arranged as though for a photograph in a cookbook. Gabriel sat down and placed his mobile phone at the center of the table, gingerly, as if it were a live grenade. After accepting the job as chief, he had briefly considered moving his family to one of the secular suburbs of Tel Aviv to be closer to King Saul Boulevard. He realized now that it was better to remain in Jerusalem to be close to the prime minister's office. Three times he had been summoned to Kaplan Street in the middle of the night, once because the prime minister was restless and in need of company. They had discussed the state of the world while watching an American action film on television. Gabriel had nodded off during the climax and at dawn had been driven, bleary-eyed, to his desk.

"Wine?" asked Chiara, holding aloft a bottle of Galilean red.

Gabriel declined. "It's late," he said.

Chiara placed the wine on the counter. "How was the prime minister?"

"Unusually interested in Asian affairs."

"Chinese food again?"

"Kung pao and egg rolls."

"He's very consistent."

Chiara sat down opposite Gabriel and watched with appreciation as he filled his plate.

"Aren't you going to have something?" he asked.

"I ate five hours ago."

"Have a little something so I don't feel like a complete cad."

She picked up a slice of bruschetta smeared with chopped olives and Italian parsley and nibbled at the edge. "How was work?"

He gave a noncommittal shrug and twirled his fork in the tagliatelle.

"Don't even," she warned. "You're my only contact with the real world."

"The Office isn't exactly the real world."

"The Office," she countered, "is as real as it gets. Everything else is make-believe."

He gave her a declassified, white-paper version of that evening's strike on the convoy, but Chiara's beautiful eyes soon became bored. She much preferred Office gossip to the details of Office operations. The politics, the internecine battles, the romantic affairs. It had been many years since she had left active service, and yet, if given the chance, she would have returned to the field in a heartbeat. Gabriel had far too many enemies for that, enemies who had targeted his family before. And so Chiara had to be content playing the role of first lady. Unlike the previous chief's wife, the conniving Bella Navot, she was much beloved by the troops.

"Is this the way it's going to be for the next six years?" she asked.

"What's that?"

"Midnight dinners. You eating, me watching."

"We knew it was going to be difficult."

"Yes," she said vaguely.

"It's too late for second thoughts, Chiara."

"No second thoughts. I just miss my husband."

"I miss you, too. But there's nothing—"

"The Shamrons have invited us to dinner tomorrow night," she said suddenly.

"Tomorrow night is bad." He didn't explain why.

"Maybe we can drive up to Tiberias on Saturday."

"Maybe," he said without conviction.

A heavy silence fell between them.

"You know, Gabriel, God was not always kind to you."

"No, he wasn't."

"But he gave you a second chance to be a father. Don't let it go to waste. Don't be a man who comes and goes in darkness. That's all they'll remember. And don't try to justify it by telling yourself you're keeping them safe from harm. It's not enough."

Just then, his mobile phone flared. Hesitantly, he punched in his password and read the text message.

"The prime minister?" asked Chiara.

"Graham Seymour."

"What does he want?"

"A word in private."

"Here or there?"

"There," said Gabriel.

Without another word, he rang King Saul Boulevard and ordered Travel to make the necessary arrangements for what would be his first foreign trip as chief of the Office. There was a flight leaving Ben Gurion at seven, arriving in London at half past ten. Space would be made in first class for Gabriel and his detail. The British would handle security at their end.

With his itinerary complete, he killed the connection and, looking up, saw that Chiara had gone. Alone, he placed a second call to Uzi Navot and told him of his travel plans. Then he switched on the television and finished his dinner. With a bit of luck, he thought, he might get an hour or two of sleep. He would leave his children in darkness, he thought, and in darkness he would return. He would keep them safe from harm. And for his reward they might someday remember the midnight touch of his hand.

And so it was that Gabriel Allon, having slept fitfully if at all, slipped from his bed and into the womb of his armored SUV. He arrived at Ben Gurion Airport a few minutes before his flight's departure and, accompanied by two bodyguards, boarded planeside on the tarmac. He had no ticket, his name appeared on no manifest. As a rule, the *ramsad*, the chief of the Office, never traveled internationally under his real name, even to a reasonably friendly destination like the United Kingdom. Hostile actors such as the Iranians and the Russians had access to airline records, too. So did the Americans.

He passed the five-hour flight reading the newspapers, a rather pointless exercise for a man who knew too much, and upon arrival at Heathrow placed himself in the care of an MI6 reception team. Riding into central London in the back of a Jaguar limousine, he briefly regretted he had not tossed a necktie into his attaché case. Mainly, he stared out the window and recalled the many times he had crept into this city under different names, flying different flags, fighting different wars. The geography of London was for Gabriel a battlefield. *Hyde Park,*

Westminster Abbey, Covent Garden, the Brompton Road . . . He had
bled in London, grieved in London, and in an Office safe flat on
the Bayswater Road he had once recited secret marriage vows
to Chiara because he feared he would not survive the day to
come. His debt to the British secret services was profound. Britain had granted him sanctuary at the darkest times of his life,
and protected him when another country might have thrown
him to the wolves. In return, he had dealt with his fair share of
problems on behalf of Her Majesty's Government. By Gabriel's
calculation, the balance sheet was now roughly even.

At last, the car turned onto Vauxhall Bridge and sped across
the Thames, toward the temple of espionage on the opposite
embankment. On the uppermost floor Gabriel crossed an English garden of an atrium and entered the finest office in all of
spydom, where Graham Seymour, surrounded by several members of his executive staff, waited to receive him. A round of
introductions followed, brief, perfunctory. Then the senior staff
filed slowly out, and Seymour and Gabriel were alone. For a
long moment they appraised one another in silence. They were
as different as two men could be—in size and shape, in upbringing, in religious faith—but their bond was unbreakable. It had
been forged during numerous joint operations, waged against a
diverse cast of enemies and targets. Jihadist terrorists, the Iranian nuclear program, a Russian arms dealer named Ivan Kharkov. They distrusted one another only a little. In the espionage
trade, that made them the best of friends.

"So," said Seymour finally, "how does it feel to be a member
of the club?"

"Our chapter of the club isn't as grand as yours," said Gabriel,
glancing around the magnificent office. "Nor as old."

"Wasn't it Moses who dispatched a team of agents to spy out the land of Canaan?"

"History's first intelligence failure," said Gabriel. "Imagine how things might have turned out for the Jewish people if Moses had chosen another plot of land."

"And now that plot of land is yours to protect."

"Which explains why my hair is growing grayer by the day. When I was a boy growing up in the Valley of Jezreel, I used to have nightmares about the country being overrun by our enemies. Now I have those dreams every night. And in my dreams," said Gabriel, "it's always my fault."

"I've been having those dreams lately myself." Seymour gazed across the river toward the West End. "And to think it would have been worse if a prominent London art dealer hadn't spotted the terrorists entering the theater."

"Anyone I know?"

"Actually," said Seymour, "you might. Owns an Old Master gallery in St. James's. He's seventy-five in the shade but still runs around with younger women. In fact, he was supposed to have dinner with a girl half his age at the Ivy the night of the attack, but the girl stood him up. Best thing that ever happened to him." Seymour looked at Gabriel. "He hasn't mentioned any of this to you?"

"We try to keep our contact to a minimum."

"You must have rubbed off on him. He acted like a real hero."

"Are you sure we're talking about the same Julian Isherwood?"

Seymour smiled in spite of himself. "I have to hand it to your friend Saladin," he said after a moment. "He ran a very tight operation. Thus far, we've been able to identify only one other individual directly linked to the plot, an operative in France who supplied the automatic rifles. I dispatched one of our officers to locate this operative, but unfortunately there was a small mishap."

"What kind of mishap?"

"A fatality. Three, actually."

"I see," said Gabriel. "And the name of the operative?"

"Peter Marlowe. Did time in Northern Ireland. Used to work in the olive oil business on Corsica."

"In that case," said Gabriel, "consider yourself lucky that only three people died."

"I doubt the French will see it that way." Seymour paused, then added, "Which is why I need you to have a word with them on my behalf."

"Why me?"

"Despite your rather abysmal track record on French soil, you've managed to make some important friends inside the French security service."

"They won't be my friends for long if I get mixed up in your bungled operation."

Seymour said nothing.

"And if I agree to help you?" asked Gabriel. "What's in it for me?"

"The everlasting gratitude of Her Majesty's Secret Intelligence Service."

"Come now, Graham, you can do better than that."

Seymour smiled. "I can, indeed."

It was approaching dusk by the time Gabriel finally departed Vauxhall Cross. He did so not in the back of the Jaguar limousine but in the passenger seat of a small Ford hatchback piloted by Nigel Whitcombe. The young Englishman drove very fast and with the languid ease of someone who raced rally cars at the weekend. Gabriel balanced his secure attaché case on his knees and clung tightly to the armrest.

"Where's he living now?"

"I'm afraid that's classified," answered Whitcombe without a trace of irony.

"Maybe I should wear a blindfold then."

"I beg your pardon."

"Never mind, Nigel. But would you slow down a bit? I'd rather not be the first chief of the Office to die in the line of duty."

"I thought you *were* dead," said Whitcombe. "Died on the Brompton Road outside Harrods. That's what they wrote in the *Telegraph*."

Whitcombe eased off the throttle, but only slightly. He followed Grosvenor Road along the Thames and then headed north through Chelsea and Kensington to Queen's Gate Terrace, where finally he drew to a stop outside a large Georgian house the color of clotted cream.

"Is *all* that his?" asked Gabriel.

"Only the bottom two floors. It was a steal at eight million."

Gabriel checked the window on the first floor. The curtains were drawn and there appeared to be no light burning within. "Where do you suppose he is?"

"I'd rather not hazard a guess."

"Try his mobile."

"He's still figuring out how to use it."

"What does that mean?"

"I'll let him explain."

Whitcombe dialed the number. It rang several times without answer. He dialed it a second time with the same result.

"Think there's a key under the doormat?"

"I doubt it."

"Then I suppose we'll have to use mine instead."

Gabriel climbed out of the car and descended the short flight of steps that led to the basement entrance of the maisonette. He tried the latch; it was locked. Whitcombe frowned.

"I thought you had a key."

"I do." Gabriel drew a thin metal tool from the breast pocket of his overcoat.

"You can't be serious."

"Old habits die hard."

"You might find this difficult to believe," said Whitcombe, "but 'C' never carries a lock pick."

"Perhaps he should."

Gabriel slid the tool into the lock and worked it gently back and forth until the mechanism gave way.

"What if there's an alarm?" asked Whitcombe.

"I'm sure you'll think of something."

Gabriel turned the latch and opened the door a few inches. There was only silence.

"Tell Graham I'll find my own way home tonight. Tell him I'll call him from Paris as soon as I've cleaned up the mess with the French."

"What about your security detail?"

"I'm carrying more than a lock pick," said Gabriel, and went inside.

———

The doorway gave onto a kitchen that was the stuff of Chiara's dreams. An acre and a half of tastefully lit counter space, an island with a chef's sink, a pair of convection ovens, a Vulcan gas stove with a professional-grade hood. The refrigerator was a stainless steel Sub-Zero. Inside were several bottles of Corsican rosé and a lump of cheese flavored with rosemary and lavender and thyme. It seemed the owner's transition was still a work in progress.

Gabriel took down a wineglass from the cabinet and filled it with some of the rosé. Then he switched off the kitchen lights and carried the wine upstairs to the drawing room. It was furnished with only a single chair and ottoman and a billboard-size television. Gabriel moved to the window and, parting the curtains, peered into the street, where an expensively overcoated man was at that moment stepping from the back of a taxi. The man started up the front steps of the house but froze suddenly and shot a glance toward the window where Gabriel stood. Then he turned abruptly and descended the flight of steps toward the basement entrance.

A few seconds later Gabriel heard the sound of a door opening and closing, the flip of a switch, and a curse whispered in the dialect of those native to the island of Corsica. It was the foil wrapper from the bottle of rosé. Gabriel had left it in plain view on the counter. An amateur's mistake, he thought.

A bit of light was leaking up the stairwell from the kitchen, enough to silhouette the man who appeared in the entrance of the drawing room a moment later, a gun in his outstretched hands. At the end of the room where Gabriel stood, however, the darkness was absolute. He watched as the man pivoted left and then right with the compact movements of one who knew how to clear a room of well-armed adversaries. Then the man crept forward and with a flip of a switch flooded the room with light. He pivoted one final time, aiming the gun in Gabriel's direction, before quickly lowering the barrel toward the floor.

"You damn fool," said Christopher Keller. "You're lucky I didn't kill you."

"Yes," said Gabriel, smiling. "Not for the first time."

KENSINGTON, LONDON

A Walther PPK," said Gabriel, admiring Keller's gun. "How Bond-like of you."

"It's easy to conceal and packs quite a punch." Keller smiled. "A brick through a plate-glass window."

"I didn't realize MI6 officers were allowed to carry firearms."

"We're not." Keller filled a wineglass with the rosé and then offered the bottle to Gabriel. "You?"

"I'm driving."

Keller frowned and filled Gabriel's glass to within a centimeter of the rim. "How did you get in here?"

"You left the door unlocked."

"Bullshit."

Gabriel answered truthfully.

"Someday," said Keller, "you're going to have to teach me how to do that."

He removed his Crombie overcoat and tossed it carelessly onto the countertop. His suit was charcoal, his necktie was the color of tarnished silver. He almost looked respectable.

"Where were you?" asked Gabriel. "A funeral?"

"A meeting with my investment adviser. He took me to lunch at the Royal Exchange and informed me that the value of my portfolio had fallen by more than a million pounds. Thanks to Brexit, I've been taking quite a beating lately."

"The world is a dangerous and unpredictable place."

"Tell me about it," said Keller. "Your neck of the woods is starting to look like an island of peace and tranquillity, especially now that you're the one running the place. Sorry I couldn't make it to your little swearing-in party. I was tied up at the time and couldn't get away."

"The IONEC?"

Keller nodded. "Three months of unremitting boredom by the sea."

"But successful," said Gabriel. "Ran the watchers of A4 ragged. Record scores on the final exam. Too bad about France, though. That was no way to start a career."

"You're one to talk. Your career has been a series of disasters interspersed with the occasional calamity. And look what it got you. You're the chief now."

"Shamron always said that a career without controversy is not a proper career at all."

"How is the old man?"

"He endures," said Gabriel.

"He's rather like Israel, isn't he?"

"Shamron? He *is* Israel."

Keller lit a cigarette and blew a stream of smoke toward the ceiling.

"A new lighter?" asked Gabriel.

"You don't miss much."

Gabriel took the lighter from Keller's hand and read the inscription. "He must have worked very hard on that one."

"It's the thought that counts," said Keller. Then he asked, "How much did he tell you?"

"He told me that he sent you to France to track down the Moroccan who supplied the Kalashnikovs for the London attack. He said you managed to find this Moroccan in a matter of days despite the fact the DGSI never was able to learn his name. He suggested your former employer, the inimitable Don Anton Orsati, might have provided valuable assistance. He didn't go into detail."

"With good reason."

"It seems you met with this Moroccan, whose name was Nouredine Zakaria, at a café in Nice and led him to believe you were a Corsican arms dealer. To prove your bona fides, you agreed to sell him ten Kalashnikovs and ten Heckler & Koch MP7s for the very reasonable price of sixty thousand euros. Unfortunately, the deal didn't go down as planned, and you found it necessary to kill Zakaria and two of his associates, thus eliminating the only known link between Saladin's network and the attack on London. All things considered," said Gabriel, "I'd say you overstepped your brief."

"Shit happens."

"Quite. And now it's up to me to clean up the mess."

"For the record," said Keller, "it wasn't my idea to send you cap in hand to the French."

"You have me confused with someone else."

"Who's that?"

"Someone who removes his hat when he enters a room."

"So how do you intend to play it?"

"First, I'm going to ask the French for everything they have on Nouredine Zakaria. And then," said Gabriel, "I'm going to invite them to join my operation to find Saladin."

"*Your* operation? The French will never go for it. And neither will Graham."

"Graham signed off on it this afternoon. He also agreed to let me borrow you. You're working for me now."

"Bastard," said Keller, crushing out his cigarette. "I should have killed you when I had the chance."

They dined that evening in a small Italian restaurant near Sloane Square where neither of them was known. Afterward, Gabriel rode in a taxi alone to the Israeli Embassy, which was located in a quiet corner of Kensington just off the High Street. The ambassador and the station chief were inordinately pleased to see him, as were his bodyguards. Downstairs in the secure communications room—in the lexicon of the Office it was known as the Holy of Holies—he rang the private number of the man he needed to see in Paris. The call found him in his bed, in his sad little bachelor's apartment on the rue Saint-Jacques. He was not at all displeased to hear the sound of Gabriel's voice.

"I was wondering whether you might be able to spare a minute or two sometime tomorrow."

"I'm meeting with my minister all morning."

"My condolences. What about the afternoon?"

"I'm free after two."

"Where?"

"The rue de Grenelle."

Next Gabriel rang King Saul Boulevard and informed the Operations Desk that he would be extending his stay abroad by at least a day. Travel saw to his arrangements. He was tempted to spend the night in the old safe flat on Bayswater Road, but his bodyguards prevailed upon him to remain inside the station instead. Like most Office outposts, it contained a small bedroom for times of crisis. Gabriel stretched out on the hateful cot but sleep eluded him. It was the pull of an operation, the small thrill of being back in the field, even if "the field" was at that moment an embassy in one of the world's most exclusive neighborhoods.

Finally, in the hours before dawn, sleep claimed him. He rose at eight, took his breakfast with the officers of London Station, and at nine climbed into the back of an MI6 Jaguar bound for Heathrow Airport. His flight was British Airways 334. He boarded at the last minute, accompanied by his bodyguards, and took his seat next to the window in first class. As the aircraft rose over southeast England, he peered down at the gray-green fields sinking away beneath him. Inwardly, however, he was watching a large, powerfully built man, Arab in appearance, limping across a hotel lobby in Washington. Hair could be cut or dyed, a face could be altered with plastic surgery. But a limp like that, thought Gabriel, was forever.

I t was said of Paul Rousseau that he had plotted more bombings than Osama bin Laden. He did not dispute the claim,
though he was quick to point out that none of his bombs actually exploded. Paul Rousseau was a skilled practitioner in the
art of deception who had been granted authority to take "active
measures" to remove potential terrorists from circulation before
the terrorists could take active measures against the Republic
or its citizenry. The eighty-four officers of the Alpha Group,
Rousseau's elite unit of the DGSI, did not waste precious resources tailing suspected terrorists, listening to their phone
calls, or monitoring their maniacal musings on the Internet.
Instead, they shook the tree and waited for the poisonous fruit
to fall into their hands. In another country, in another time, a
civil libertarian might have condemned their methods as bor-
dering on entrapment. Paul Rousseau would not have disputed
that claim, either.

For the first six years of its existence, the Alpha Group was
one of official France's most closely held secrets, and its agents
operated with impunity. That changed in the aftermath of ISIS's

attack on Washington, when press reports in America revealed that Rousseau had been wounded in the truck bombing of the National Counterterrorism Center in suburban Northern Virginia. Subsequent reports, mainly in the French media, went on to detail some of the Alpha Group's more unsavory methods. Operations were compromised, assets identified. The interior minister and the chief of the DGSI responded by categorically denying that there was any such unit called the Alpha Group. But it was too late; the damage was done. Quietly, they urged Rousseau to forsake his anonymous headquarters on the rue de Grenelle and move his operation behind the walls of the DGSI's headquarters in Levallois-Perret. Rousseau, however, refused to budge. He had never been fond of the Paris suburbs. Nor could his agent-runners carry out their duties properly if they were seen entering and leaving a walled compound bearing a sign that read MINISTÈRE DE L'INTÉRIEUR.

And so, despite the elevated threat, Paul Rousseau and the Alpha Group continued to wage their quiet war on the forces of radical Islam from an elegant nineteenth-century building in the exclusive seventh arrondissement. A discreet brass plaque proclaimed that the building housed something called the International Society for French Literature, a particularly Rousseauian touch. Inside, however, all subterfuge ended. The technical support staff occupied the basement; the watchers, the ground floor. On the second floor was the Alpha Group's overflowing Registry—Rousseau preferred old-fashioned paper dossiers to digital files—and the third and fourth floors were the preserve of the agent-runners. Most came and went through the heavy black gate on the rue de Grenelle, either on foot or by car. Others entered through a secret passageway linking the building and the dowdy little antique shop next door, which was owned by an elderly Frenchman who had served in a secret capacity during the war in Algeria. Rousseau was the only member of the Alpha Group who had been allowed to read the shopkeeper's appalling file.

The fifth floor was somber and shadowed and quiet, save for the Chopin that occasionally drifted through Rousseau's open door. Madame Treville, his long-suffering secretary, occupied an orderly desk in the anteroom, and at the opposite end of a narrow hall was the office of Rousseau's ambitious young deputy, Christian Bouchard. It was an article of faith within the French security establishment that Bouchard would assume control of the Alpha Group if and when Rousseau ever decided to retire. He had tried that once before, after the death of his beloved Colette. The book he hoped to write, a multivolume biography of Proust, was but a pile of handwritten notes. He was now resigned to the fact that the fight against radical Islamic terrorism would be his life's work. It was not a fight France could lose. Rousseau believed the very survival of the Republic was at stake.

In Gabriel Allon, he had found a willing if unlikely partner. Their alliance had been formed in the wake of Saladin's Paris debut, the deadly bombing of the Isaac Weinberg Center for the Study of Anti-Semitism in France. Saladin had not chosen the target lightly; he had known of Gabriel's secret ties to the woman who ran it. So, too, had Paul Rousseau, and together he and Gabriel had placed an agent of penetration in Saladin's court. The operation had failed to prevent the attack on Washington, but it had all but ended decades of animosity and mistrust between the Office and the intelligence services of France.

A welcome consequence of the new relationship was that Gabriel was now free to travel in France without fear of arrest and prosecution. His litany of sins on French soil, the killings, the collateral damage, had been officially forgiven. He was as legitimate as a career spy could possibly be.

The Alpha Group's stringent new security measures required Gabriel to shed his motorcade and protection detail near the Eiffel Tower and to walk the remainder of the way alone. Usually, he entered the building through the gate on the rue de Grenelle, but at Rousseau's request he came through the passage in the antique shop instead. Rousseau was waiting for him upstairs on the fifth floor, in the glass-walled, soundproof conference room. He wore a crumpled tweed jacket that Gabriel had seen many times before and, as usual, was smoking a pipe in violation of French laws banning the use of tobacco in the workplace. Gabriel was a devout nonsmoker. Still, there was something about Rousseau's private rebellion he found reassuring.

He produced a photograph from his attaché case and slid it across the tabletop. Rousseau glanced at the face of the subject and then looked up sharply.

"Nouredine Zakaria?"

"You know him?"

"By reputation only." Rousseau held up the photograph. "Where did you get this?"

"It's not important."

"Oh, but it is."

"It comes from the British," conceded Gabriel.

"Which branch?"

"MI6."

"And why is MI6 suddenly interested in Nouredine Zakaria?"

"Because Nouredine is the one who supplied the Kalashnikovs for the attack in London. Nouredine is the one they call the Scorpion."

There is no worse feeling for a professional spy than to be told something by an officer from another service that he should have already known himself. Paul Rousseau endured this indignity while slowly reloading his pipe.

"How much do you know about him?" asked Gabriel.

"He works for the largest drug-trafficking network in Europe."

"Doing what?"

"The polite way of saying it is that he handles security."

"And the impolite way?"

"He's an enforcer and assassin. The Police Nationale believes he's personally killed at least twelve people. Not that they can prove it," added Rousseau. "Nouredine is as careful as they come. So is his boss."

"Who's that?"

"First things first." Rousseau held up the photo again. "Where did you get this?"

"I told you, from the British."

"Yes, I heard you the first time. But where did the British get it?"

"It's not important."

"Oh," said Rousseau, "but it is."

E xactly how many guns are we talking about?"

"I believe it was twenty."

"And where did this operative of British intelligence lay his hands on twenty Kalashnikovs and HKs?"

Gabriel's expression managed to convey both ignorance and indifference or something in between.

"And he posed as a Corsican?" asked Rousseau. "You're sure of it?"

"Is that noteworthy?"

"It might be. You see, only someone who's lived on the island for many years can imitate their speech."

Gabriel said nothing.

"He is a friend of yours, this British agent?"

"We're acquainted."

"He must be very well connected to have pulled off something like this. And quite talented."

"He has much to learn."

"What is your interest in this shabby affair?" asked Rousseau.

"My interest," said Gabriel, "is Saladin."

"Mine, too. Which is why I'm going to count to ten and restrain my anger. Because it's quite possible this British friend of yours has managed to prove something I've suspected for a long time."

"What's that?"

But Rousseau did not answer, at least not directly. Instead, adopting the demeanor of a professor, he took a detour backward in time, to the hopeful winter of 2011. In Tunisia and Egypt, a pair of oppressive regimes had been swept away by a sudden wave of popular anger and resentment. Libya was next. In January there were a smattering of protests over housing shortages and political corruption, protests that soon spiraled into a nationwide uprising. It quickly became apparent that Muammar Gaddafi, Libya's tyrannical ruler, would not follow the example of his counterparts in Tunis and Cairo and go quietly into the Arab night. He had ruled Libya with an iron fist for more than four decades, stealing its oil riches and murdering his opponents, sometimes only for the sake of his own entertainment. A man of the desert, he knew the fate that awaited him if he fell. And so he plunged his backward nation into a full-fledged civil war. Fearing a bloodbath, the West intervened militarily, with France taking a leading role. By October, Gaddafi was dead, and Libya was free.

"And what did we do? Did we flood Libya with money and other forms of assistance? Did we hold its hand while it tried to make the transition from a tribal society to a Western-style democracy? No," said Rousseau, "we did none of those things. In fact, we did almost nothing at all. And what happened as a result of our inaction? Libya became yet another failed state, and ISIS moved into the void."

The danger of an ISIS safe haven in North Africa, Rousseau continued, was obvious. It would allow the terrorists to infiltrate fighters and weaponry into Western Europe and attack virtually at will. But within months of ISIS's arrival in Libya, police forces from Greece to Spain noticed another disturbing trend. The flow of narcotics from North Africa, especially hashish from Morocco, rose to unprecedented levels. What's more, there was a change in the traditional smuggling routes. Where once the drug gangs were content to move their product across the Strait of Gibraltar one small boat or Jet Ski at a time—or overland to Egypt and then the Balkans—it was now coming across the water in massive cargo ships.

"Take, for example, the case of the *Apollo*, a Greek-registered rust bucket seized by the Italian navy off Sicily not long after ISIS set up shop in nearby Libya. The Italians had received a tip from a North African–based informant that the vessel contained an unusually large shipment of hashish. Even so, they were shocked by what they found. Seventeen metric tons, a record seizure."

But the *Apollo*, explained Rousseau, was only the beginning. Over the next three years, European authorities made several more stunning seizures. All the vessels had one thing in common; they had called on Libyan ports. And all the raids were based on tips from well-placed North African informants. All totaled, more than three hundred metric tons of narcotics, with an estimated street value of three billion dollars, were taken off the market. Then the informants suddenly stopped talking, and the seizures slowed to a trickle.

"But why? Why the sudden change in the smuggling route? Why were the producers suddenly forcing massive quantities of merchandise onto the market? And why," asked Rousseau, "did the informants go silent? Here in France we concluded there was a powerful new player on the scene. Someone with the muscle to seize control of the smuggling routes. Someone whose methods frightened the informants into silence. Someone who was willing to risk the loss of tons of precious cargo because they were more interested in making a great deal of money as quickly as possible. We determined there was only one group that fit that profile."

"ISIS."

Rousseau nodded slowly. "The marriage between hashish and terrorism," he said, "is as old as time itself. As you know, the word *assassin* is derived from the Arabic *hashashin*, the Shia killers who acted under the influence of hashish. Hezbollah, their descendants in Lebanon, finance their operations in part through the sale of hashish, much of it to customers in your country. And almost since its inception, ISIS has been an active player in the drug world, mainly by imposing taxes on product that moves through territory it controls. We now believe the Islamic State has taken over much of the European trade in illicit narcotics. And most of those drugs flow through the organization of one man. The man your friend works for," he added, tapping the photograph of Nouredine Zakaria.

Rousseau's pipe had gone dead. Much to Gabriel's disappointment, the Frenchman reached for his pouch.

"My greatest fear," Rousseau continued, "was that the relationship was more than financial, that ISIS would use the infrastructure of this man's distribution network to carry out attacks in Europe. If your British friend is correct, if Nouredine Zakaria supplied the weapons used in London, then it appears my fears have been realized. The question is, was Nouredine operating on his own? Or did he do it with his boss's blessing?"

"Maybe we should ask him."

"Nouredine's boss? Easier said than done. You see," explained Rousseau, "he's a very popular man here in France, especially among the rich and well connected. They dine in his restaurants and drink and dance in his nightclubs. They sleep in his hotels, shop in his boutiques, and adorn their fingers and necks with items from his exclusive line of jewelry. And, yes, on occasion, they smoke or snort or inject his drugs. The current president of the Republic is a personal friend. So are the interior minister and a good many others inside French law enforcement. They make certain that uncomfortable questions are never asked and that investigations never stray too close to his business empire."

"Does he have a name?"

"Jean-Luc Martel."

"JLM?"

Rousseau appeared genuinely surprised. "You know the name?"

"I've spent a lot time in your country over the years. Jean-Luc Martel is rather hard to miss."

"He's quite the celebrity, I'll grant you that. One of our most successful entrepreneurs. At least that's what they write about him. But it's all a sham. Martel's real business is drugs." Rousseau was silent for a moment. "And if I were to speak these words in my minister's office, he would laugh me out of the room. And then he would hurry off to dinner at Martel's new restaurant on the boulevard Saint-Germain. It's all the rage."

"So I've heard."

Rousseau smiled in spite of himself.

"Perhaps Martel can be reasoned with," said Gabriel. "An appeal to his patriotism."

"Jean-Luc Martel? Not possible."

"Then I suppose we'll have to turn him the old-fashioned way."

"How?"

"Leave that to me."

There was a silence.

"And if we can?" asked Rousseau.

"It might very well lead us to the one we're both looking for."

"Yes," said Rousseau. "It might indeed. But my minister will never approve."

"What your minister doesn't know won't hurt him."

The Frenchman gave a mischievous smile. "And the ground rules?"

"The same as last time. An equal partnership. I have autonomy abroad, you have veto power over anything that happens on French soil."

"What about the British?"

"I'll require the services of the one who speaks French like a Corsican."

"How much do I know about what really happened with Nouredine Zakaria and those guns?"

"About fifty percent."

"Do I want to know the rest?"

"Not a chance."

"In that case," said Rousseau, "I believe we have a deal."

———

Rousseau rang the Interior Ministry and ordered copies of two files, one bearing the name Nouredine Zakaria, the other the name of the man he worked for. The chief of the Registry, a fonctionnaire in the finest French tradition, immediately took issue with the request. Why was Rousseau, whose brief was restricted to jihadist terrorism, suddenly interested in a low-level Moroccan criminal and one of France's most celebrated businessmen? It was, the registrar pointed out, a rather odd pairing, like red wine and oysters. To his credit, Rousseau did not tell his nemesis that he found the analogy infantile at best. Instead, he pointed out that, as chief of a DGSI division, even a division that did not officially exist, he was entitled to see virtually every file in the French system. The registrar quickly capitulated, though he hinted at a delay of several hours, as the files were quite voluminous. Wasting the valuable time of others, thought Rousseau, was a bureaucrat's ultimate revenge.

As it turned out, it took slightly less than an hour to locate and copy the files in question. An Alpha Group motorcycle courier collected the documents at 4:52 and by a small miracle delivered them to the rue de Grenelle at eleven minutes past five. There was no disputing the time; the security guard, a recent addition, made a note of it in his logbook, as mandated by the Alpha Group's new protocols. The guard gave the documents a quick inspection—five hundred pages bound by a pair of metallic clips—before waving the courier into the building. For the sake of his fitness he took the stairs instead of the fickle lift, and at thirteen minutes past he placed the documents on the desk of Madame Treville. Here again, there was absolute certainty regarding the time. Madame Treville made a note of it in her desk diary, which was later recovered.

It was at this point that Christian Bouchard, ever alert to danger or opportunity, poked his well-groomed head from the door of his lair and, seeing the stack of recently delivered files on Madame Treville's desk, wandered over to have a look.

"JLM? Who ordered these?"

"Monsieur Rousseau."

"Why?"

"You'd have to ask him."

"Where is he?"

"The secure conference room." She lowered her voice and added, "With the Israeli."

"Allon?"

Madame Treville nodded gravely.

"Why wasn't I included?"

"You were at lunch when he arrived." She made this sound like an accusation. "Monsieur Rousseau asked me to deliver the files the moment they arrived. Perhaps you would like to do it for me."

Bouchard seized the stack of paper and carried it along the corridor to the secure conference room, where he found Gabriel and Rousseau behind a wall of soundproof glass, deep in conversation. He punched the code into the cipher lock, entered, and dropped the heavy files onto the table as though they were proof of a conspiracy.

It was then, the instant the five hundred pages landed with a leaden thud, that the bomb detonated. In fact, the timing was such that Gabriel initially thought the documents themselves had somehow exploded. Mercifully, he would have only a vague memory of what came next. He was aware that he was falling through a blizzard of glass and masonry and human blood, and that Paul Rousseau and Christian Bouchard were falling with him. When finally he came to rest, he felt as though he were in the confines of his own coffin. His last conscious thoughts were of his funeral, a knot of mourners surrounding an open grave on the Mount of Olives, two young children, a daughter who was called Irene after her grandmother, a boy who bore the name of a great painter. They would have no memory of him, his children. To them he was a man who had come and gone in darkness. And it was to the darkness he returned.

Part Two

A GIRL LIKE THAT

I t was the paper—the dossiers, the watch reports, the intercepted text messages and e-mails, the case histories—that
would expose the true nature of the secretive enterprise housed
inside the graceful old building on the rue de Grenelle. For
several hours after the attack it swirled through the streets of
the seventh arrondissement, from the Eiffel Tower to Les Inva-
lides to the gardens of the Musée Rodin, adrift on an uncertain
wind. There were numerous reports of uniformed police officers and agents in plain clothes frantically collecting the documents, even as rescue workers and paramedics were pulling
stunned survivors from the rubble. By early evening, however,
photographs of recovered documents, each bearing the logo of
the DGSI, began appearing on Twitter and other social media.
Le Monde broke the story first, followed soon after by the rest
of the mainstream French media. Finally, having no other recourse but the truth, the interior minister confirmed the obvious. The target of the second major bombing in Paris in less than
a year was not an obscure society dedicated to the promotion of
French literature; it was an elite unit of the DGSI whose very
existence the minister had recently denied. He then asked the

citizens of the Republic to surrender all recovered documents to the authorities and to cease posting images of them on the Internet. Compliance with the request was despairingly low.

Regrettably, the ensuing political scandal, and the many questions surrounding the Alpha Group's tactics, would overshadow the coldly calculated precision and brutality of the bombing itself. There was symbolism not only in the target but in the mode of delivery for the bomb—a white Renault Trafic transit van, the same model used in the attack on the Isaac Weinberg Center for the Study of Anti-Semitism in France ten months earlier. At just two hundred kilograms, however, it was far smaller than the Weinberg Center device. Even so, it was comparable in explosive power, which suggested to the experts that Saladin's bomb maker, whomever he was, had perfected his craft. The force of the blast left the Alpha Group headquarters in ruins and damaged buildings for several hundred meters up and down the length of the rue de Grenelle. Four pedestrians who happened to be walking past the van when it exploded were killed instantly, as were a mother and her six-year-old daughter who were entering the pharmacy across the street. Otherwise, the only fatalities were officers of the Alpha Group.

Of the van itself, almost nothing remained. A door came to rest near a *boucherie* in the rue Cler; a portion of the roof, in a playground in the Champ de Mars. Later, it would be established that the vehicle had been reported stolen three weeks earlier in a suburb of Brussels and that it had entered Paris from the northwest on the A13. Where the bomb had been assembled would never be reliably determined. Nor would the French authorities ever identify the man who parked the van directly beneath the window of Paul Rousseau's fifth-floor office. He was last seen climbing onto a motorcycle left for him in the Square de la Tour-Maubourg. The motorcycle, like the man, would never be found.

Fortunately, half of the Alpha Group's staff were off duty or in the field when the bomb exploded. Hardest hit were the technical staff and the watchers, whose workspaces occupied the basement and ground floor. Two young women from Registry were lost, as were nine of the Alpha Group's most experienced agent-runners. Paul Rousseau and Christian Bouchard suffered only moderate injuries, due in part to the fact they were in the secure conference room when the bomb exploded. Sadly, Madame Treville had chosen that very moment to tidy up Rousseau's cluttered office and was exposed to the full force of the detonation. She was pulled from the rubble alive, but died later that night as the rest of France wallowed in political intrigue.

But there was more intrigue to come. Indeed, on the day after the bombing, questions arose over whether the casualties inside the building were restricted solely to officers of the Alpha Group. The source of the controversy was a report that witnesses had seen two men—young, sturdy, and armed with pistols—frantically scouring the rubble in the immediate aftermath while repeatedly shouting a name. The name was Gavriel, which happened to be the Hebrew version of the name of the current chief of the Israeli secret intelligence service. This gave rise to speculation that the man in question, whose history in France was long and sordid, had been inside the building when the bomb detonated. The interior minister and the chief of the DGSI denied he had been present, or that he had even been in France. Given their recent track record, the statements were met with the skepticism they deserved.

In point of fact the man in question had indeed been inside the Alpha Group headquarters at the time of the attack and had spent forty-five long minutes buried in the rubble, bent and twisted like a contortionist, before finally being pried loose by his bodyguards and a French rescue team. Bloodied and coated in dust, he was taken to the nearby Val-de-Grâce military hospital, where he was sewn and patched and treated for several badly broken ribs, two fractured vertebrae in his lower back, and a severe concussion. Doctors would recall that he spoke fluent if slightly accented French, had been unfailingly polite if somewhat dazed, and had refused all pain medication despite the intense discomfort of his injuries. Later, however, after a visit from French intelligence officials, the doctors and attending nurses would deny all knowledge of him.

In truth, he remained at the hospital for three days, in a room next to the one occupied by Paul Rousseau and Christian Bouchard, cared for by a joint French-Israeli team of doctors and watched over by an identically composed team of bodyguards. Finally, after a round of X-rays and MRIs confirmed it was safe to move him, he was dressed in a clean suit and shirt and driven by ambulance to Charles de Gaulle Airport. There, after refusing all offers of assistance, he climbed a steep flight of stairs, stopping several times to rest and regain his balance, and entered the first-class cabin of an El Al jetliner. It was empty except for a beautiful woman with riotous dark hair. He lowered himself into the seat next to hers, rested his head on her shoulder, and closed his eyes. The woman's hair smelled of vanilla. Only then was he certain he was still alive.

———

Upon his return to Israel, Gabriel went directly to Narkiss Street and remained there, hidden from view, for the better part of the next week. At first, he kept mainly to his bed, rising only to catch the few minutes of late-winter sun that fell each afternoon on the little terrace. The pain of his injuries, while manageable, was immense. Each breath was an ordeal and even the smallest movement seemed to drive a hot iron spike into the base of his spine. And then there were the lingering effects of the concussion—the chronic headache, the sensitivity to light and sound, the inability to concentrate for more than a minute or two. He was most comfortable in a darkened room, behind a closed door. Alone, with only his muddled thoughts for company, he fretted that his condition was permanent, that he had suffered one wound too many, that he had exhausted his allotted ability to heal. No amount of retouching could restore him. He was a canvas beyond repair.

The rest of Israel, however, was blissfully unaware of the fact that its legendary intelligence chief was lying incapacitated in his bed, with four broken ribs, two cracked vertebrae, and a catastrophic headache without end. True, there were rumors, fed mainly by the press in France, but they were put to rest by fourteen seconds of video released by the prime minister's office and broadcast on Israeli television. It purported to show a meeting at Kaplan Street. In it, the prime minister wore a satisfied smile and a blue necktie; Gabriel wore gray and looked none the worse for wear. The video had been shot not long after he became chief and put in cold storage for an occasion such as this. There were other videos as well, different clothing, altered lighting conditions, lest Gabriel ever find it necessary to spend a significant period out of the public eye. He reckoned that time had come, though it had arrived far earlier in his tenure than he ever imagined. The chief of the Office had nearly died in a coldly calculated attack on the headquarters of a trusted friend and ally in the war on terror. Therefore, the chief had no recourse but to respond in kind. Such were the rules of the neighborhood. Gabriel would not delegate the task of vengeance to others. Nor would he lash out against meaningless targets in the deserts of Iraq and Syria. His target was a man. A man who had built a network of death that had laid siege to the great cities of the civilized world. A man who was financing his operations through the sale of narcotics in Western Europe. He was going to find this man and wipe him from the face of the earth. He would be painstaking in his approach, meticulous. For there was nothing more dangerous, he thought, than a patient man.

But he could not wage war against his enemy without a body and a brain. The pain gradually receded, like the waters of a severe flood, but his thoughts remained a jumble. The operation was somewhere out there, he knew it, but its plotlines and central characters were lost in the fog of the concussion. He determined that vigorous exercise was in order, not physical but mental, so he played Shamron's old memory games and, in his head, reread dense monographs on Titian, Bellini, Tintoretto, and Veronese. The effort fatigued him—it was exercise, after all—but slowly the operation came into sharper relief. Only the denouement eluded him. He saw a wealthy man, broken, exposed, and willing to do his bidding. But how would he maneuver the man to this place? Slowly, he reminded himself. Beware the fury of a patient man.

Pain disturbed his sleep, as did nightmares of tumbling downward through a maelstrom of masonry and glass and blood.

Nevertheless, he woke early on the fourth morning to find his headache gone and his thoughts clear. Rising before Chiara and the children, he went into the kitchen and made coffee, which he drank while watching the news on television. Afterward, he crept into the bathroom and confronted his reflection in the mirror. The image in the glass was by any objective measure disturbing. The left side of the face was reasonably intact, but the right—the side that had been turned toward the full force of the blast—was another story entirely. The eye was blackened and swollen, and there were numerous small cuts and abrasions left by flying glass and debris. It was not the face of a chief, he thought; it was the face of an avenger. He filled the basin with scalding water and slowly, painfully, scraped a week's growth from his chin and cheeks. Each stroke of the razor sent a charge of pain into the base of his spine, and a sneeze, wholly unexpected, left him doubled over for several seconds in agony.

Showered, he returned to the bedroom to find that Chiara had risen. He pulled on a pair of gabardine trousers and a dress shirt with only minimal pain, but the effort of tying his Oxford shoes nearly drove him to the sanctuary of his bed. Smiling tightly to conceal his discomfort, he went into the kitchen where Chiara was preparing a fresh pot of coffee.

"All better?" She handed him a cup of coffee and looked him up and down. "Please tell me you're not thinking about going to King Saul Boulevard."

In truth, he was. But the tone of Chiara's voice led him to reconsider. "Actually," he said, "I was hoping to spend some time with the children, and I wanted to look like a person again rather than a patient."

"Good recovery," said Chiara skeptically. Just then, there

came a chirp of laughter from the nursery. She smiled and whispered, "And so it begins."

He made a brave show of it. He helped Chiara dress the children, an activity that inflicted on him no small amount of pain, and supervised the chaotic food fight otherwise known as breakfast. He spent the remainder of the morning playing games, reading stories, watching developmental videos, and changing an endless parade of soiled diapers. Mainly, he wondered how Chiara managed to care for the children alone, day after day, without collapsing with exhaustion or losing her mind. Running one of the world's most formidable intelligence services suddenly seemed a rather trivial pursuit by comparison.

Nap time was an oasis. Gabriel slept, too, and when he woke he went onto the terrace to warm his weary body in the Jerusalem sun. This time, however, he brought a stack of reading material—the five hundred pages of Jean-Luc Martel's file, a copy of which he had carried out of France. Martel had been the target of on-and-off French interest for more than a decade. And yet, with the exception of two minor scrapes having to do with unpaid taxes, both of which were settled far from public view, his reputation remained beyond reproach. The most recent probe of his business empire had taken place two years earlier. It had been launched after a midlevel drug dealer offered to testify against Martel in exchange for a reduced prison sentence. In the end the case was closed for lack of evidence, though the chief investigating officer, a man with an unassailable character, retired early in protest. Perhaps not coincidentally, the drug dealer whose accusation started the probe was later found dead in his prison cell, his throat slashed.

The investigation produced reams of communications

intercepts—some salacious, many prosaic, all insignificant—and several hundred surveillance photos. Rousseau sent along a sampling of the best. There was Jean-Luc Martel at the Cannes Film Festival, Jean-Luc Martel at the Biennale in Venice, Jean-Luc Martel in the front row at Fashion Week in New York, Jean-Luc Martel on his 142-foot motor yacht in the Mediterranean, Jean-Luc Martel on the rue de Rhône in Geneva, and Jean-Luc Martel at the gala grand opening of his new restaurant in Paris, which was a smash because, according to one estimate, he dropped a cool five million euros to make certain every French celebrity of note was in attendance, along with an American reality television star who was famous for being famous, and a pair of American hip-hop artists who had unkind things to say about France's treatment of racial minorities.

In none of the photos was Martel alone; the woman was always with him. The unusually tall and long-limbed woman, with wide blue eyes and Nordic-blond hair that fell straight about her square shoulders. She was not French, but English—curious, for Martel was a public champion of all things Gallic. Her name meant nothing to Gabriel, but her flawless face was vaguely familiar. An ordinary Internet search produced more than four thousand highly professional images. Advertisements for clothing. For jewelry. For an exclusive line of wristwatches. For fragrance. For swimwear. For an Italian sports car of dubious reliability. But all that was in her past. She was now the nominal owner of a well-regarded art gallery in the Place de l'Ormeau in Saint-Tropez, against which the French authorities had found no fault. A further search of publicly available documents and news items revealed that she was an atrocious driver, had been arrested twice on minor drug charges, and had been involved in a string of questionable romantic entanglements—footballers, actors, a member of Parliament, an aging glam-rock star who had bedded every other fashion model in Britain. She had never been married, and had no children, parents, or siblings. She was, thought Gabriel, alone in the world.

In most of the French surveillance photographs, her gaze was averted, her face downcast. But in one, taken on the Île Saint-Louis in Paris, she was caught staring directly into the lens of the camera. It was this photograph that Gabriel showed to Uzi Navot late that evening, at the small table in Gabriel's kitchen. It was approaching midnight; Navot, who had spent the better part of the last decade on one fad diet or another, was slowly devouring the remnants of Chiara's dinner. He studied the photo carefully between bites. A former recruiter and runner of agents, he had a keen eye for talent.

"She's trouble," he said. "Avoid."

"Think she knows where her famous boyfriend really gets his money?"

"A girl like that . . ." Navot shrugged his heavy shoulders. "She knows. They always know."

"The gallery is in her name."

"You're thinking about getting rough with her?"

"It's not my first choice, but one should never limit one's options."

"How *do* you intend to play it?"

Gabriel explained while Navot finished the last of the food.

"You'll need a Russian arms dealer," Navot said.

"I have one."

"Is he married, or does he play the field?"

"Married," said Gabriel. "Very married."

"Which flavor?"

"A nice French girl."

"Anyone I know?"

Gabriel gave no answer. Navot stared at the photograph of the beautiful, long-limbed woman. "A girl like that won't come cheap," he said. "You're going to need money."

"I know where we can get money, Uzi." Gabriel smiled. "Lots of money."

KING SAUL BOULEVARD, TEL AVIV

It would be another seventy-two hours before Jean-Luc Martel, hotelier, restaurateur, clothier, jeweler, and international dealer of illicit narcotics, became the target of full-time Office surveillance, along with Olivia Watson, his not-quite wife. The delay had to do with their location, and the season of the year. Their location was the enchanted West Indian island of Saint Barthélemy, and the season was late winter, which meant there was not a rental villa or hotel room to be had in the entire resort. Under Gabriel's unrelenting pressure, Travel finally managed to lay its hands on a mosquito-infested hut overlooking the salt marshes of Saline. Mordecai and Oded, a pair of all-purpose Office field hands, settled there soon after, accompanied by two female escort officers, both of whom spoke American English. The French contributed no personnel, despite the fact that, technically speaking, it was their soil. Paul Rousseau's Alpha Group was in no condition to operate against anyone; it was still mourning its dead and searching for a new clandestine headquarters in Paris. And as far as the rest of official France was concerned—the various ministers, the heads of the intelligence and security services, the police and prosecutors—there *was* no operation.

The target of this nonexistent operation, however, had no difficulty in finding accommodation in Saint Barthélemy. He owned a large villa in the hills above the village of Saint-Jean, from which he could behold his luxury hotel, his boutique specializing in beachwear for women, and his restaurant, which he called Chez Olivia. The first batch of surveillance photos showed her stretched nude beside the pool at Martel's villa. The next depicted her in various stages of undress. Gabriel advised the team to devote its energies to more than photography. He already knew how Olivia Watson looked; what he wanted was hard intelligence. He was rewarded with another photo, this one showing Martel in flagrante delicto with one of the salesgirls from his boutique. Gabriel tucked the picture away for safekeeping, though he was dubious of its potential impact. When a woman entered into a relationship with a Frenchman, especially one as good-looking as Jean-Luc Martel, infidelity was part of the bargain. He only wondered whether Olivia Watson played by the same set of rules.

They would remain on Saint Barthélemy for the next ten days, unaware of the fact that several thousand miles away, in an anonymous office block in Tel Aviv, their lives were under a sustained if quiet assault. Eli Lavon, a skilled financial investigator, burrowed into JLM Enterprises, which, for all its Frenchness, was headquartered just across the border in secretive Geneva. With the help of Unit 8200, Israel's ultra-secret signals intelligence service, Lavon pondered JLM's balance sheets and tax records at his leisure. They revealed that the company was highly profitable indeed. Abnormally so, in the opinion of Lavon, who had a well-trained eye for dirty money. He then analyzed the company unit by unit. The restaurants, the hotels, the night-clubs, the boutiques and jewelry shops. All were in the black, a rather remarkable run of good fortune during a period of slug-gish overall economic growth. The same could be said for Gal-erie Olivia Watson in Saint-Tropez. Indeed, while the rest of the art world was struggling in the post–Great Recession market, Galerie Olivia Watson had sold more than two hundred million dollars' worth of art during the past eighteen months alone.

"Calder, Pollock, Rothko, Basquiat, three works by Roy Lichtenstein, three more by de Kooning, a couple of Rauschen-bergs, and more Warhols than I could count."

"Very impressive," said Gabriel.

"Especially when you consider the prices she's getting. I compared them to sales at auction houses in New York and London."

"And?"

"Not even close."

"Maybe she's a good negotiator," said Gabriel.

"I can tell you one thing. She's discreet. Nearly all the sales are totally private."

"Were you able to find any shipping waybills?"

"As a matter of fact, I was."

"And?"

"During the past six months, she's shipped four paintings to the same address in the Geneva Freeport."

Initially, Lavon conducted his probe from his office on the top floor. But once the hook had been set, he gathered up his files and migrated downward through the building, to the cramped subterranean chamber known as Room 456C. The rest of the old Barak team soon joined him. There was tall, balding Yossi Gavish, with his British-accented Hebrew and donnish air, and Rimona Stern, she of the sandstone-colored hair, childbearing hips, and acid tongue. Yaakov Rossman, the pockmarked former agent-runner who was now the chief of Special Ops, reclaimed his old spot at the communal table, next to the last chalkboard in all of King Saul Boulevard. Dina Sarid, the Office's walking database of Palestinian and Islamic terrorism, seized her usual place in the far corner. On the blank wall above her desk she hung an enlargement of the last known photograph of Saladin, the surveillance shot taken in the Tri-Border Area of South America. The message to the others was unmistakable. Jean-Luc Martel and Olivia Watson were mere stepping-stones. The ultimate prize was Saladin.

Gabriel, with his aching back and ribs, required no such reminder. Occasionally, he poked his head in the door to check on the team's progress, but for the most part he kept to the top floor and walked an administrative tightrope, a chief one minute, a field man and planner the next. Not since the days of Ari Shamron had a director general held the tiller of an operation so tightly. Even so, the rest of the Office's daily business—the myriad of smaller ops, the recruitments in progress, the analysis and assessment of current threats—proceeded as normal, thanks to the presence of Uzi Navot just across the hall. This was the maiden voyage of their new partnership, and it went off without a hitch. Navot even accompanied Gabriel to a meeting with the prime minister, though unlike Gabriel he proved powerless to resist the kung pao chicken. "It's the salt," he confessed as they filed out of Kaplan Street. "I'd eat my shoe if it was fried in oil and coated with soy sauce."

As Eli Lavon tunneled into the dubious hospitality conglomerate known as JLM Enterprises, Yossi Gavish and Rimona Stern focused their efforts on Jean-Luc Martel the man. The story of his humble beginnings had been told often. He did not hide from them; they were, like his mane of almost-black hair, part of his allure. As a child he had lived in a nothing village in the hills of Provence. It was the kind of place, he often recounted, through which the rich and beautiful passed on their way down to the sea. His father had laid tile, his mother had swept and mopped it. She was part Algerian, at least that was the rumor in the village. Jean-Luc's father beat her often. He beat Jean-Luc, too. The father disappeared when Jean-Luc was seventeen. Some months later his body was discovered at the bottom of an isolated ravine, a few miles from the village. The skull was in ruins, blunt force trauma, probably a hammer. Inside French law enforcement, it was widely regarded as Jean-Luc Martel's first murder.

In press interviews, Martel spoke often of the fact that he was a poor and disruptive student. University was not an option, so at eighteen he made his way to Marseilles, where he went to work waiting tables in a restaurant near the Old Port. He studied the business carefully—or so the story went—and scraped together enough money to open a restaurant of his own. In time, he opened a second, then a third. And thus an empire was born.

The five hundred pages of the French file, however, told a rather different version of Jean-Luc Martel's time in Marseilles. It was true he worked for a brief time as a waiter, but the restaurant was no ordinary restaurant. It was a money-laundering operation run by Philippe Renard, a high-ranking figure in the French *milieu* who specialized in the importation and distribution of illegal narcotics. Renard took an instant liking to the handsome young man from the hills, especially after learning that Jean-Luc had killed his own father. Renard taught his young apprentice everything there was to know about the business. He introduced him to suppliers in North Africa and Turkey. He counseled him on how to manage rivalries with other gangs so as to avoid needless bloodshed and publicity. And he instructed him on how to use seemingly legitimate businesses to launder and conceal profits. Martel rewarded Renard's trust by killing him the same way he killed his father, with a hammer, and seizing control of his business.

Overnight, Jean-Luc Martel became one of the most important drug figures in France. But he was not content to remain just one among many; total domination of the trade was his goal. And so he built an army of streetwise killers, mainly Moroccans and Algerians, and unleashed them on his rivals. When the blood finally stopped flowing, Martel was the only one standing. His expansion in the drug trade coincided with his rise in the legitimate world. Each side of the business fueled the other. JLM Enterprises was a criminal undertaking from top to bottom, a giant front-loading washing machine that produced hundreds of millions of clean euros each year.

He was married once, briefly, to a beautiful actress who played small parts in forgettable films. During the divorce proceedings, she threatened to tell the police everything she knew about the true source of her husband's income. An overdose of sleeping pills and alcohol was her fate. Afterward, he abstained from public romance for many months, which the press found endearing. The police weren't as impressed. Quietly, they tried to link Martel to his wife's death. The investigation turned up nothing.

When finally he emerged from his Blue Period, it was with Olivia Watson on his arm. She was thirty-three at the time, a member of that lost tribe of English expatriates who stumble into Provence and never seem to find their way home again. Too old for modeling, she was managing a small art gallery that sold minor works—"And *that*," explained Rimona Stern, "is being charitable"—to the tourists who besieged the village each summer. With Martel's financial help, she opened a gallery of her own. She also designed a line of beachwear and a collection of Provençal-style furnishings. Like the gallery, both bore her name.

"Apparently," added Rimona, "a fragrance is in development."

"What does it smell like?" asked Gabriel.

"Hashish," she quipped.

But was there another side to JLM Enterprises? A side other than hospitality and drugs? The case of Nouredine Zakaria suggested it was so. The Moroccan had managed to insert at least fifteen Kalashnikov assault rifles into the United Kingdom, an impressive feat of smuggling and logistics. Undoubtedly, he had used a portion of the network that moved Martel's drugs to Britain and the rest of Europe. But was Nouredine the exception, or were there others? Fortunately, the Office had in its possession several thousand French intelligence documents that Paul Rousseau had handed over after the attack on the Weinberg Center in Paris. With the help of an Alpha Group analyst in Paris, Dina Sarid compared the names in the database with known or reputed members of Jean-Luc Martel's army of dealers and enforcers, most of whom were of North African descent. Six names appeared on both lists: three Moroccans, two Algerians, and a Tunisian. Four of the men had served time in French prisons for drug offenses; two were thought to have spent time in Syria fighting for ISIS. But when Dina broadened the parameters to include second- and third-degree levels of association, the results were even more alarming. "JLM Enterprises," she concluded, "is an ISIS battalion in waiting."

Gabriel forwarded Dina's analysis to Paul Rousseau in Paris, and Rousseau put the worst of the worst under Alpha Group watch. That same evening the last member of the Barak team arrived in Tel Aviv aboard a flight from Zurich, where he had spent the past several days on a wholly unrelated matter. Entering Room 456C, he paused briefly before the enlarged photograph of Saladin, bade him an unpleasant evening, and sat down at his old desk, where Gabriel had personally placed two towering stacks of files. He opened the first and frowned. "Ivan Kharkov," he murmured. "Long time no see, you miserable son of a bitch."

It was Ari Shamron who once described Mikhail Abramov as "Gabriel without a conscience." It was not an altogether fair characterization, but nor was it far from the truth. Born in Moscow to a pair of dissident Soviet academics, Mikhail had served in the elite Sayeret Matkal, Israel's version of the British SAS, before joining the Office. His enormous talents, however, were not limited to the gun, thus the two stacks of files Gabriel had placed on his desk.

In appearance, he was Gabriel's opposite. Tall and lanky,

with a bloodless pallor and colorless gray eyes, he was the prince of ice to Gabriel's prince of fire. During those intense days of preparation, he all but ignored Jean-Luc Martel and Olivia Watson. They were lights on a distant shore—or, as Gabriel liked to say, on the other side of a horseshoe bay. Mikhail had only one assignment, to prepare himself for the role he would soon be playing. Not by coincidence, the character whose life he would inhabit had much in common with his quarry. Like Jean-Luc Martel, he was a man of two faces, one he showed to the rest of the world, the other he kept carefully hidden from view.

Much of Mikhail's course of study was self-directed, as it involved Russian armaments, a subject he knew well. But Gabriel, in yet another departure from Office tradition, personally oversaw the rest. On the evening Martel and Olivia Watson departed Saint Barthélemy, he summoned Mikhail to his suite for a final examination. Gabriel stood before a video monitor, a clicker in his hand, while Mikhail sat on the executive leather couch, his long legs propped on the coffee table, his eyes half closed with affected boredom, his default expression.

"Tintoretto," he said.

Gabriel pressed the clicker, and another image appeared on the screen.

"Titian," said Mikhail, suppressing an elaborate yawn.

The image changed.

"Rembrandt, for heaven's sake. Next."

When the image appeared, he placed a hand to his forehead in a show of deep thought. "Is that a Parmigianino or a Perugino?"

"Which is it?" asked Gabriel.

"Parmigianino."

"Right again."

"Why don't you give me something a bit more challenging?"

"How about this?"

Another image appeared on the screen. This time it was not a painting, but the face of a woman.

"Natalie Mizrahi," said Mikhail.

"That's not what I'm asking."

"Is she ready? Is that what you want to know?"

"Yes."

"Do you want me to talk to her?"

Gabriel switched off the video monitor and shook his head slowly. It wasn't the sort of job for a lover, he thought. Only a chief could ask such a thing.

Early the following afternoon, having cleared his in-box and returned the necessary phone calls, Gabriel eased into the back of his armored SUV and set out for the valley of his youth. The landscape beyond his window was yellowed like an old photograph. Overnight, a Palestinian arsonist had set fire to the Carmel Ridge. Whipped by high winds, the flames had consumed three thousand acres of highly combustible Aleppo pine and were now advancing toward the outskirts of Haifa. Israel's firefighters had proven themselves incapable of containing the blaze, leaving the prime minister no choice but to request international assistance. Economically crippled Greece had dispatched two hundred men; Russia had agreed to send a tanker aircraft. Even the ruler of Syria, who was battling for his very survival, had mockingly offered to come to Israel's aid. Gabriel found his country's impotence deeply unsettling. The Jewish people had drained the malarial swamps, watered the deserts, and prevailed in three existential conflicts against an enemy far greater in number. And yet a Palestinian with a pack of matches could bring the northwest corner of the country to a standstill and threaten its third-largest city.

Highway 6, Israel's main north-south motorway, was blocked at the Iron Interchange. Gabriel's motorcade turned onto Highway 65 and followed it eastward to Megiddo, the hillock where, according to the Book of Revelation, Christ and Satan would wage a climactic duel that would bring about the end of days. The ancient mound appeared peaceful, though it was shrouded in a sepia-toned veil of smoke from the distant fires on the ridge. They headed northward into the Valley of Jezreel, keeping to the side roads to avoid the diverted traffic, until finally a security gate, metal and spiked, blocked their path. Beyond it was Nahalal, a cooperative agricultural settlement, or moshav, founded by Jews from Eastern Europe in 1921, when Palestine was still in the hands of the British Empire. It was not the first Nahalal but the second. The first Jewish settlement on this plot of land had been established not long after the conquest of Canaan. As recorded in the nineteenth chapter of Joshua, it belonged to the tribe of Zebulun, one of the twelve tribes of ancient Israel.

Gabriel leaned out his window and jabbed the code into the keypad, and the security gate rolled open. Oleander and eucalyptus lined the gently curved lane that stretched before them. Modern Nahalal was circular in layout. Bungalows fronted the road, and behind the houses, like the folds of a hand fan, lay pastures and cultivated cropland. The children filing out of the cooperative's only school paid scant attention to Gabriel's large black SUV. Several of Nahalal's residents served in the security services or the IDF. Moshe Dayan, perhaps Israel's most famous general, was buried in Nahalal's cemetery.

At the southern end of the moshav, the SUV turned into the drive of a contemporary-looking house. A security guard in a khaki vest appeared instantly on the shaded veranda and, seeing Gabriel emerge slowly from the vehicle, raised a hand in greeting. In the other he gripped the stock of an automatic weapon.

"You just missed her."

"Where is she?"

The bodyguard inclined his head toward the farmland.

"How long ago did she leave?"

"Twenty minutes. Maybe a half hour."

"Please tell me she's not alone."

"She tried, but I sent a couple of the boys with her. They took one of the ATVs. None of us can keep up with her."

Smiling, Gabriel entered the bungalow. Its furnishings were spare and functional, more office than home. Once, the walls had been hung with outsize black-and-white photographs of Palestinian suffering—the long dusty walk into exile, the wretched camps, the weathered faces of the old ones dreaming of paradise lost. Now there were paintings. Some were Gabriel's, youthful works, derivative. The rest were his mother's. They were Cubist and Abstract Expressionist, full of fire and pain, produced by an artist at the height of her power. One depicted a woman in semi-profile, gaunt, lifeless, draped in rags. He recalled the week she had painted it; it was the week of Eichmann's execution. The effort had left her exhausted and bedridden. Many years later, Gabriel would discover the testimony his mother had recorded and then locked away in the archives of Yad Vashem. Only then would he understand that the Cubist depiction of an emaciated woman in rags was a self-portrait.

He went into the garden. Smoke rose above the Carmel Ridge like the plume of an erupting volcano, but the skies above the valley were clear and perfumed with the smell of earth and bovine excrement. Gabriel glanced over his shoulder and saw he was alone; his security detail seemed to have forgotten about him. He followed a dusty track past the animal enclosure, watched by blank-eyed dairy cows. The farm's pie slice of cropland stretched before him. The portion nearest the bungalow was under cultivation of some sort—Gabriel affected a resentful ignorance of all matters farming—but the distant section of the parcel lay tilled and fallow and awaiting the seed. Beyond the outer boundary was Ramat David, the kibbutz where Gabriel had been born and raised. It was established a few years after Nahalal, in 1926, and derived its name not from the ancient Jewish king but from David Lloyd George, the British prime minister whose government had looked favorably upon the idea of establishing a Jewish national home in the land of Palestine.

The residents of Ramat David were not from the East; they were largely German Jews. Gabriel's mother arrived there in the autumn of 1948. Her name was Irene Frankel then, and she soon met a man from Munich, a writer, an intellectual, who had taken the Hebrew name Allon. She had hoped to have six children, one child for each million lost to the Holocaust, but one was all her womb would bear, a boy she named Gabriel, the messenger of God, the defender of Israel, the interpreter of Daniel's visions. Their home, like most in Ramat David, was a place of sadness—of candles burning for parents and siblings who had not survived, of terrified screams in the night—and so Gabriel passed his days wandering the ancient valley of the tribe of Zebulun. As a child he had thought of it as *his* valley. And now it was his to watch over and protect.

The sun had slipped behind the burning ridge; daylight was in retreat. Just then, Gabriel heard what sounded like a distant cry for help. It was only the first notes of the call to prayer drifting down from the Arab village perched on the slopes of the hills to the east. As a child, Gabriel had known a boy from the village named Yusuf. Yusuf had referred to him as Jibril, the Arabic version of his name, and had told him stories of what it was like in the valley before the return of the Jews. Their friendship was a closely guarded secret. Gabriel never went to Yusuf's village, Yusuf never came to his. The divide had been unbridgeable. It was still.

The call to prayer slowly faded, along with the last of the light. Gabriel gazed across the darkening fields toward the bungalow. Where the hell were his bodyguards? He was grateful for the reprieve; he could not remember the last time he had been completely alone. All at once he heard the voice of a woman calling his name. For an instant he imagined it was his mother. Then, turning, he glimpsed a slender figure bounding toward him along the track, pursued by two men in an ATV. Suddenly, he felt a stab of pain at the small of his back. Or was it guilt? It's what we do, he reassured himself as he rubbed away the pain. It is our punishment for having survived in this land.

Like Gabriel, Dr. Natalie Mizrahi had had the distinct displeasure of seeing Saladin in the flesh. Gabriel's encounter with the monster had been fleeting, but Natalie had been obliged to spend several days with him in a great house of many rooms and courts near the northern Iraqi city of Mosul. There she had treated Saladin for two serious wounds suffered in an American air strike, one to his chest, the other to his right leg. Unfortunately, Natalie and Saladin had met again, in a tiny A-frame cabin in rural Northern Virginia. A Caravaggesque painting depicting the instant before her rescue hung in Gabriel's appalling gallery of memory. Try as he might, he had been unable to remove it. This, too, was something he and Natalie had in common.

The story of her journey into the dark heart of the caliphate of ISIS was one of the most remarkable in the annals of the Office. Indeed, even Saladin, who knew only part of it, predicted that one day someone would write a book about it. Born and educated in France, fluent in the Algerian dialect of Arabic, she immigrated to Israel with her parents to escape the rising tide of anti-Semitism in her homeland and took a position in the emergency room at the Hadassah Medical Center in West Jerusalem. Her arrival in Israel did not escape the notice of the talent spotters of the Office. And when Gabriel was searching for an agent to feed into Saladin's network, it was to Natalie he turned. At the little farmhouse in Nahalal, he peeled away the many layers of her identity and transformed her into Leila Hadawi, an Arab woman of Palestinian lineage, a black widow bent on vengeance. Then, with the help of Paul Rousseau and the Alpha Group, he fed her into the pipeline of French and other European Muslims heading to Syria to fight for ISIS.

She spent nearly a month in the caliphate, in an apartment house near al-Rasheed Park in downtown Raqqa, in a training camp in the ancient city of Palmyra, and, finally, at the house near Mosul where, threatened with death, she had saved the life of the greatest terror mastermind since Osama bin Laden. During the period of his recovery, he had shown her great kindness. He had referred to her only as Maimonides, the philosopher and Talmudic scholar who served as one of the real Saladin's court physicians in Cairo, and allowed her to be in his presence without veiling her face. Never once did she leave his side. She had monitored his vital signs, changed his bloody dressings, and muted his pain with injections of morphine. Many times she considered shoving him through death's door with an overdose. Instead, bound by her oath as a doctor and her belief that it was essential she report what she had witnessed, she had nursed Saladin back to health, an act of mercy he repaid by dispatching her to Washington on a suicide mission.

It had been three months since that night, and yet even now Gabriel noticed remnants of Leila Hadawi in Natalie's bearing and in her dark eyes. She had shed Leila's veil and Leila's rage, but not her quiet piety or her dignity. Otherwise, there was no visible trace of the ordeal she had suffered in the Islamic caliphate or in the cabin in Virginia, where Saladin had personally subjected her to a brutal interrogation. It had been his intention to execute Natalie in ISIS's preferred manner, by taking her head, and her imminent death had the effect of loosening his tongue. He admitted he had served in the Iraqi Mukhabarat under Saddam Hussein, that he had supplied material and logistical support to rejectionist Palestinian terrorists such as Abu Nidal, and that he had joined the Iraq insurgency after the American invasion of 2003. Those three elements of his curriculum vitae represented the sum total of what the intelligence services of the West knew of him. Even his real name remained a mystery. Natalie, however, had been granted access to Saladin's inner court, at a time when he was physically enfeebled. She knew every inch of his tall, powerful body, every mole and birthmark, every scar. It was only one of the reasons why Gabriel had come to the farm in Nahalal, in the valley of his birth.

The evening turned cold quickly, as it always did in the Galilee. Nevertheless, they sat outside in the garden, at the same table where ten months earlier Gabriel had conducted Natalie's initial recruitment. Now, as then, she sat very straight, with her hands folded neatly in her lap. She wore a snug-fitting blue tracksuit and neon-green trainers, soiled by the dust of the farm roads. Her dark hair was drawn away from her face and constrained at the base of her neck by an elastic band. Her wide, sensuous mouth was set in a half-smile. She looked happy for the first time in many months. Suddenly, Gabriel felt another stab of pain. This time it was real.

"You know," said Natalie, her expression serious, "you'll heal faster if you take something."

"Is it that obvious?"

"You're leaning to one side to keep pressure off the fractures."

Grimacing, Gabriel tried to imitate Natalie's erect posture.

"And your respiration," she said, "is very shallow."

"That's because it hurts to breathe. And every time I cough or sneeze I see stars."

"Are you getting any sleep?"

"Enough." Then he asked quietly, "You?"

Natalie drew the cork from a bottle of Galilean white and poured two glasses. She drank only a small amount from hers and then returned the glass to the tabletop. During the many months she had lived as a radicalized Muslim, she had largely abstained from alcohol. Her daily consumption of white wine— the Office talent spotters had regarded it as her one and only vice—had fallen sharply since her return to Israel.

"*Are* you?" asked Gabriel a second time.

"Sleeping? I was never really good at it, even before the operation. Besides," she added with a glance toward the exterior of the bungalow, "it's not exactly a house of secrets, is it? Every room is wired, and every move I make is recorded and analyzed by your psychiatrists."

Gabriel didn't bother with a denial. The bungalow was indeed wired for both audio and video, and a team of Office physicians had charted every facet of Natalie's recovery. Their assessments painted a portrait of an officer who was still struggling with the effects of post-traumatic stress disorder. The officer suffered from prolonged periods of insomnia, night terrors, and bouts of severe depression. Her daily training runs in the valley had improved her overall health and tempered her mood swings. So, too, had her romantic relationship with Mikhail, who was a regular visitor to Nahalal. All in all, it was the opinion of Natalie's doctors—and Mikhail—that she was ready to return to limited duty. Limited duty, however, was not what Gabriel had in mind. He had Saladin in his sights.

He shifted uncomfortably in his chair. Natalie frowned.

"At least drink some of the wine. It might take the edge off the pain."

He did. It didn't.

"He was the same way," said Natalie.

"Who?"

"Saladin. He didn't want pain medication. I practically had to torture him to convince him he needed it. And every time I fed morphine into his drip he fought to remain conscious. If only I'd—"

"You did the right thing."

"I'm not sure the victims in London would agree. Or Paris," she added. "You're lucky to be alive. And none of it would have happened if I'd killed him when I had the chance."

"We're not like them, Natalie. We don't do suicide missions. Besides," Gabriel went on, "someone else would have taken his place."

"There *is* no one else like Saladin. He's special. Trust me, I know."

She warmed her hand over the candle that burned between them. The direction of the wind shifted subtly, bringing with it the acrid scent of the fires. Gabriel preferred it to the smell of the valley. Even as a child he had hated it.

Natalie removed her hand from the flame. "I was beginning to think you'd forgotten about me."

"Not for a minute. And I haven't forgotten what you went through, either."

"That makes two of us."

She reached for her wine but stopped. Leila's temperance, it seemed, had reclaimed her.

"Mikhail assures me that one day I won't remember any of it, that it will be like an unpleasant memory from childhood, like the time I almost sliced my finger off playing with one of my mother's kitchen knives." She raised a hand in the darkness. "I still have the scar."

The wind died, the flame of the candle burned straight.

"Do you approve of him?" she asked.

"Mikhail?"

"Yes."

"It doesn't matter what I think."

"Of course it does. You're the chief."

He smiled. "Yes, Natalie, I approve. Wholeheartedly, in fact."

"And did you approve of that American girl he was involved with? The one who worked for the CIA? Her name," added Natalie coolly, "escapes me."

"Her name was Sarah."

"Sarah Bancroft," she added, stressing the first syllable of the rather patrician-sounding family name.

"Yes," said Gabriel. "Sarah Bancroft."

"It doesn't sound Jewish, Bancroft."

"With good reason. And no," said Gabriel, "I did not approve of the relationship. At least not in the beginning."

"Because she wasn't Jewish?"

"Because relationships between intelligence officers are inherently complicated. And relationships between officers who work for services from different countries are unheard of."

"But she was close to the Office."

"Very."

"And you were fond of her."

"I was."

"Who ended it?"

"I wasn't privy to all the details."

"Please," she said dismissively.

"I believe," he said guardedly, "it was Mikhail."

Natalie appeared to consider his last statement carefully. Gabriel hoped he hadn't spoken out of turn. One never really knew what passed between lovers, especially where old relationships were concerned. It was possible Mikhail had portrayed himself as the aggrieved party. No, he thought, that wasn't Mikhail's style. He had many fine qualities, but his heart was fashioned of cast iron.

"I suppose he'll be leaving soon," she said.

"I have a few more pieces to put into place."

"Operational spadework?"

He smiled.

"And how long do you suppose he'll be away?"

"Hard to say."

"I hear you're turning him into an arms dealer."

"A very rich one."

"He'll need a girl. Otherwise, Jean-Luc Martel won't believe he's real."

"Know much about him?"

"JLM?" She shrugged. "Only what I used to read in the newspapers."

"Think he's involved in drugs?"

"That was the rumor. I grew up in Marseilles, you know."

"Yes," said Gabriel flatly. "I think I might have read something about that once in your file."

"And I treated my fair share of heroin overdoses when I was working there," Natalie went on. "The word on the street was that it was Martel's heroin. But I suppose you can't believe everything."

"Sometimes you can."

A silence fell between them.

"So who's the lucky girl?" asked Natalie at last.

"Mikhail's girl? I have someone in mind for the part," said Gabriel, "but I'm not sure she wants it."

"Have you asked her?"

"Not yet."

"What are you waiting for?"

"Forgiveness."

"For what?"

Just then, a gust of wind rose suddenly and extinguished the flame. They sat alone in the darkness, saying nothing at all, and watched the mountains burn.

It took Natalie only a few minutes to toss her belongings into a bag. Then, still dressed in her tracksuit, she settled into the back of Gabriel's SUV and rode with him back to Tel Aviv. Doctrine dictated that she take up residence at a "jump site," a safe flat where Office agents assumed the identities they would carry with them into the field. Instead, Gabriel dropped her at Mikhail's flat off HaYarkon Street. He reckoned it wasn't a complete breach of protocol; after all, Mikhail and Natalie would be posing as husband and wife. With a bit of luck, they might even learn to dislike each other a little bit. Then no one would doubt the authenticity of their cover.

It was approaching nine o'clock by the time Gabriel's SUV started the long climb up the Bab al-Wad toward Jerusalem. Provided there were no accidents or security alerts—or calls from the prime minister—he would be at Narkiss Street by half past at the latest. The children would likely be asleep, but at least he could share a quiet meal with Chiara. But as they were approaching the western edge of the city, his mobile phone flared with an incoming message. He stared at it for a long moment, wondering whether he could pretend it had somehow been lost in transmission. Regrettably, he could not. He was about to make his second trip abroad as chief. But this time he was going to America.

22

LINCOLN MEMORIAL, WASHINGTON

Langley sent a plane for him, never a good sign. It was a Gulfstream G650 with a leather-and-teak interior, a large selection of in-flight movies, and baskets filled with unwholesome snack food. In the aft of the aircraft was a private stateroom. Gabriel stretched out on the narrow bed but could find no arrangement of his torso and limbs that did not cause him pain. The sky beyond his window never grew light; he was chasing the night westward. Sleepless, he had little else to do but wonder about the reason for his unexpected summons to Washington. He doubted it was social in nature. The new crowd in the White House wasn't in the business of playing nice.

The plane touched down at Dulles Airport at half past three and taxied to a private hangar where a convoy of three armorplated Suburbans waited, tailpipes gently smoking in the cold, damp air. The early hour meant that for once the traffic was light. As they crossed the Capital Beltway, Gabriel glanced toward the Liberty Crossing Intelligence Campus, the former headquarters of the Office of the Director of National Intelligence and the National Counterterrorism Center. A thicket of trees blocked the view of the devastation. As yet, Congress had not allocated the billions of dollars necessary to rebuild Liberty Crossing, once a shining symbol of the chaotic post–9/11 expansion of the American national security state. Like the members of Paul Rousseau's Alpha Group, the staffs of the ODNI and NCTC had been forced to seek accommodations elsewhere. Saladin, if nothing else, had made a lot of spies and analysts homeless.

The caravan of SUVs turned onto Route 123 and headed into McLean. Gabriel feared he was being taken to CIA Headquarters—he avoided it when he could—but they sped past the entrance without so much as slowing and made their way to the George Washington Memorial Parkway. It carried them along the Virginia side of the Potomac, to the glass-and-steel towers of Rosslyn. On the other side of the river rose the graceful spires of Georgetown University, but Gabriel's eye was drawn to the ugly rectangular slab of the Key Bridge Marriott, where Natalie had spent many hours trapped in a room with a French-Algerian terrorist named Safia Bourihane. Through a concealed video camera, Gabriel had watched Natalie record a martyrdom video and then wrap her body in a suicide vest. Only later, at the cabin in Virginia, would she learn the vest was inoperative. Saladin had deceived her. And Gabriel, too.

They continued southward along the river, past the fringes of Arlington National Cemetery, and turned onto Memorial Bridge. On the opposite bank, aglow as though lit from within, was the Lincoln Memorial. Normally, traffic flowing from Virginia to Washington was routed onto Twenty-Third Street. But the three SUVs of Gabriel's motorcade eased slowly over a concrete median and then parked in the esplanade on the memorial's southern flank. A few uniformed U.S. Park Police officers stood in the darkness, but otherwise the space was deserted. Just then, Gabriel's phone pulsed with an incoming text. He exited the SUV, made his way to the base of the memorial's steps, and with one hand pressed to the small of his back began to climb.

A heavy tarpaulin, moving in the faint wind, stretched across the entrance. Gabriel shouldered his way through the breach and stepped hesitantly into the central chamber. Lincoln peered down contemplatively from his marble throne, as though aggrieved by the damage around him. The base of the statue was pockmarked with tiny craters. So were the murals by Jules Guérin and the Ionic columns separating the central chamber from the side chambers, north and south. One of the columns had suffered significant structural damage at its base. It was there that a member of Saladin's network had placed a backpack filled with explosives and ball bearings. The blast had been powerful enough to send a shiver through the White House. Twenty-one people had died inside the memorial, another seven on the steps, where the terrorist opened fire with a handgun. And it was only the beginning.

Gabriel passed between a pair of scarred columns and entered the north chamber, where Adrian Carter, his face tilted upward, was reading the words of Lincoln's second inaugural address. He lowered his gaze toward Gabriel's face and frowned.

"It seems the rumors were true after all," he said.

"What rumors are those?"

"About you being inside the headquarters of the Alpha Group when that bomb went off."

"Bad timing on my part."

"Your specialty."

Carter resumed his study of the towering panel. He wore a toggle coat, wrinkled chinos, and shoes that looked as though they had been designed for walking in the woods of New England. The attire, combined with his tousled thinning hair and unfashionable mustache, gave him the air of a professor from a minor university, the sort who championed noble causes and was a constant thorn in the side of his dean. In truth, Carter was the chief of the CIA's Directorate of Operations, the longest serving in Agency history. His summons of Gabriel was a violation of protocol; generally speaking, the *ramsad* did not meet with deputies. Adrian Carter, however, was a special case. He was a spy's spy, a legend who in the dark days after 9/11 had drawn up the Agency's plan to destroy al-Qaeda and roll up its global networks. The black sites, the renditions, the enhanced interrogation methods—they all bore his fingerprints. For a decade and a half he had been able to tell himself, and his critics, that for all his many sins he had managed to protect the American homeland from a second terror spectacular. And in the blink of an eye, Saladin had made a liar of him.

"My father brought me here to see Dr. King in sixty-three," Carter said. "He was involved in the civil rights movement, my father. He was an Episcopal minister." He glanced at Gabriel. "Did I ever mention that?"

"Once or twice."

"I remember being very proud of my country that day," Carter went on. "I felt anything was possible. And I was proud when we elected our first African American president, despite all the nasty things he said about the Agency during the campaign. He and I had our disagreements over the years, but I never forgot what he represented. His election was a miracle. And it never would have happened were it not for the words Martin Luther King spoke here that day. This is our sacred space, our hallowed ground. Which is why I'll never forgive Saladin for what he did."

Carter turned away from the panel and moved slowly into the central chamber, where he paused at the feet of Lincoln.

"You're the expert. Can it be restored?"

"Marble isn't my medium," replied Gabriel. "But, yes, almost anything can be restored."

"And what about my country?" asked Carter suddenly. "Can it be fixed?"

"Your divisions are hairline cracks compared to ours. America will find its way."

"Will it? I'm not so sure." Carter took Gabriel by the arm. "Come with me. There's something I want to show you."

23

GEORGETOWN, WASHINGTON

I t is not easy for the chief of the Office and the deputy director of the Central Intelligence Agency to stroll unnoticed in
Washington, even in the hour before dawn, but they did their
best. Only a single bodyguard trailed them along the footpath
at the edge of the Potomac; the rest were confined to the con-
stellation of black Suburbans that moved in their orbit. Carter's
pace was deliberate, thoughtful. For that much at least, Gabriel
was grateful. His back was ablaze with pain, a fact he could not
hide from his old friend.

"How bad is it?" asked Carter.

"Unfortunately, they say I'm going to live."

"I hope the flight wasn't too hard on you."

"The Gulfstream made it tolerable."

"It belongs to a friend of mine named Bill Blackburn. Bill
used to work in the Special Activities Division. He was a real
knuckle-dragger back in the day. Central America, mainly. Did
a final lap in Afghanistan after nine-eleven. He owns a private
intelligence shop now. Calls it Black Ops."

"Clever."

"He is, actually. Bill does quite well for himself. I use him for jobs that require a bit of extra discretion."

"I thought you used me for those kinds of jobs."

"Bill and his men are down and dirty," explained Carter. "I save you for the ones that demand a little finesse."

"It's nice to have one's work appreciated."

They walked in silence for a moment. All around them the city groaned and stirred.

"Bill's been pestering me for years to come in with him," said Carter at last. "Says he'd pay me seven figures the first year. Apparently, I wouldn't have to do much. Bill wants to use me as a rainmaker to guarantee that the lucrative contracts keep flowing his way. The global war on terror has been very profitable for a lot of people in this town. I'm the only idiot who hasn't cashed in."

"You've earned it, Adrian."

"Would you take a job like that?"

"Not in a million years."

"Neither would I. Besides, I have more important things to do before they show me the door at Langley."

"Like what?"

"Like getting the man who did *that*."

Carter raised his eyes toward the Kennedy Center. A few minutes after the attack on the Lincoln Memorial, a suicide bomber had detonated his device in the Hall of States. Then three more terrorists had moved methodically through the rest of the complex—the Eisenhower Theater, the Opera House, the Concert Hall—slaughtering all those they encountered.

"I knew two of the victims," said Carter. "A young couple who lived around the corner from me out in Herndon. He did something in tech, she was a financial planner. They had life by the tail. Good careers, a mortgage, two beautiful kids. The house is for sale now and the kids live with their aunt in Baltimore. That's what happens when people like us make mistakes. People die. Lots of people."

"We did everything we could to stop the attacks, Adrian."

"My new director doesn't see it that way. He's a real hard-ass, a true believer. Personally, I've always thought it was dangerous to mix ideology and intelligence," said Carter. "It clouds one's thinking and makes one see exactly what one wants to see. My new director begs to differ. So do the earnest young men he's brought with him to the Agency. They think of me as a loser, which in their world is the worst thing a man can be. When I urge operational caution, they accuse me of weakness. And when I offer an assessment that's at variance with their worldview, they accuse me of disloyalty."

"Elections have consequences," said Gabriel.

"So do successful terrorist attacks on American soil. Apparently, it's all my fault despite the fact that I told anyone who would listen that ISIS was plotting to hit us with something big. According to the rumor mill, I'm yesterday's man."

"How long have you got?"

"A few weeks, maybe less. Unless," added Carter quietly, "I can do something to dramatically change the landscape."

At once, Gabriel understood why Adrian Carter had brought him to Washington aboard a private Gulfstream owned by an intelligence contractor named Bill Blackburn.

"Does your director know I'm in town?"

"I might have forgotten to mention it," said Carter.

They had reached the Thompson Boat Center. They crossed

a footbridge spanning Rock Creek and made their way past the Swedish Embassy to Harbor Place. Perhaps not coincidentally, it was the same route three ISIS gunmen had taken that night after leaving the Kennedy Center. Here their deadly handiwork was still in evidence. Nick's Riverside Grill, a popular tourist spot, was boarded up and closed for business until further notice. So were the more upscale Sequoia and Fiola Mare.

"How's your back holding up?" asked Carter as they walked along K Street beneath the Whitehurst Freeway.

"That depends on how much farther you intend to make me walk."

"Not far. There's just one more thing I'd like you to see."

They turned onto Wisconsin Avenue and climbed the slope of the hill to M Street. A block to the north was Prospect Street. They rounded the corner and after a few paces paused outside the entrance of Café Milano. Like the restaurants of Harbor Place, it was closed until further notice. Forty-nine people had died there. Still, the toll would have been far higher were it not for Mikhail Abramov, who had single-handedly killed four ISIS terrorists. The restaurant was noteworthy for another reason. It was the only target where Saladin had made a personal appearance.

"A rather tragic symbol of our enduring partnership," said Carter. "Mikhail saved a great many lives that night. But it might never have happened if I'd heeded your warning about the man you bumped into in the lobby of the Four Seasons."

"You know what they say about hindsight, Adrian."

"I do. And I've always found it to be an excuse for failure."

Carter turned without another word and led Gabriel into the heart of residential Georgetown. The neighborhood was beginning to awaken. Lights burned in kitchen windows; dogs led sleepy masters along redbrick sidewalks. At last, they arrived at the curved front steps of a large Federal-style townhouse on N Street, the Agency's most exclusive safe property. Inside, the stately old house was like a walk-in refrigerator, more evidence that Gabriel's visit to Washington was private in nature.

"Did someone forget to pay the power bill?" he asked.

"New regulations. The Agency is going green. I'd offer you some coffee but—"

"That's all right, Adrian. I really have to be going."

"Pressing matters at home?"

"A chief's work is never done."

"I wouldn't know." Carter wandered over to the thermostat and squinted at the dial, mystified.

"Please tell me you didn't drag me all the way to Washington to take a stroll down nightmare lane, Adrian. I was here, remember? I had an agent inside Saladin's operation."

"A damn fine piece of work on your part," said Carter. "But it was all for naught. Saladin beat you in the end. And I know how much you hate to lose, especially to a creature like him."

"What's your point?"

"Word on the street is you've got something cooking with the French other than a nice pot of coq au vin. Something involving Saladin. I want to remind you that it was my country he attacked last November, not yours. And if anyone's going to get him, it's me."

"Any ops in the works?"

"Several."

"Any of them about to bear fruit?"

"Not a one. Yours?"

Gabriel was silent.

"I've never been shy about crashing operational parties," said Carter. "All it would take is a single phone call to the chief of the DGSI, and it would be mine."

"He doesn't know about it."

"Must be a good one then."

"Must be," agreed Gabriel.

"Perhaps I can contribute."

"And thus preserve your hold on the Directorate of Operations."

"Absolutely."

"I appreciate your honesty, Adrian. It's refreshing in our line of work."

"Desperate times," said Carter.

"How much do you need to remain viable?"

"At this point, nothing short of Saladin can save me."

"In that case," said Gabriel, "I might be able to help."

They spoke in the drawing room, bundled in their overcoats, without the distraction of refreshment. Gabriel's version of the operation thus far was abridged but honest enough so that nothing was lost in translation. Carter did not flinch at the mention of Jean-Luc Martel's name; Carter was a man of the real world. He offered support where he could, mainly in the form of electronic and digital surveillance, America's strong suit. In return, Gabriel allowed Carter to take the operation to the seventh floor of Langley and present it as a joint undertaking between the Agency and its friends in Tel Aviv. From Gabriel's point of view, it was a high price to pay, and not without risk. But if it kept Carter in his job, it would be worth its weight in gold.

They left the safe house together shortly before eight o'clock and rode to Dulles Airport, where Bill Blackburn's Gulfstream sat fueled and ready for departure. The crew had already filed a flight plan to Ben Gurion, but upon entering the aircraft Gabriel asked to be taken to London instead. Stretched out on the bed in the private stateroom, he fell into a dreamless sleep. His mind was at peace for the first time in many days. He was about to make an old friend quite wealthy. It was, he thought, the least he could do.

Julian Isherwood was a man of many faults, but parsimony was not among them. Indeed, in his business dealings, as in his private life, he had always been rather too free with his wallet. He had acquired a good many paintings when he should have passed—his personal and professional collection was said to rival that of the Queen herself—and invariably it was his credit card that ended up on the collection plate each evening in the bar at Wilton's. Not surprisingly, his finances were in a state of perpetual disrepair. Of late, the situation had grown dire. His cheerless accountant, the appropriately named Blunt, had suggested a fire sale of available assets, coupled with a sharp reduction in outlays. Isherwood had balked. Most of his professional inventory was of little or no value. It was dead as a doornail, as they said in the trade. Burned to a crisp. Toast. And as for the idea of trimming his expenditures, well, that was simply out of the question. One had to live one's life, especially at his age. Besides, his actions on the night of the attack had imbued him with a sense of personal optimism. If Juicy Julian Isherwood could risk his life to save others, anything was possible.

It was this belief that brighter days were just over the horizon that compelled Isherwood to admit Brady Boswell, the director of a small but respected museum in the American Midwest, into his gallery in Mason's Yard late that afternoon. Boswell had a well-deserved reputation as a looker, not a buyer. He spent the better part of two hours pawing Isherwood's inventory before finally confessing that his acquisition budget was in worse condition than Isherwood's bank account, and that he was in no position to buy new carpeting for his museum, let alone a new painting to hang on its walls. Isherwood was tempted to tell Boswell that the next time he wanted to see Old Masters in London, he should try the National Gallery. Instead, he accepted the American's invitation to dinner, if only because he couldn't bear the thought of spending yet another evening listening to tubby Oliver Dimbleby describing his latest sexual conquest.

Boswell suggested Alain Ducasse at the Dorchester, and Isherwood, having no alternative at the tip of his tongue, agreed. They dined on Dorset crab and Dover sole and between them drank two bottles of Domaine Billaud-Simon Les Clos grand cru Chablis. Boswell spent much of the evening lamenting his country's dreadful politics. Isherwood listened attentively. Inwardly, however, he wondered why it was that enlightened Americans always found it necessary to bash their country whenever they set foot in the mother ship.

"I'm thinking about leaving." Boswell was sputtering with indignation. "Everyone is."

"Everyone?"

"Well, not everyone. Only people like me."

Only the crashing bores. America, thought Isherwood, would soon be a much more interesting place.

"Where would you go?"

"I'm eligible for Irish citizenship."

"Ireland? Good grief."

"Or I might get a little place here in England until things blow over."

"We have problems of our own. You're better off staying put."

The notion that modern England might not be a cultural paradise appeared to come as a shock to Brady Boswell. He was one of those Americans who formed their impressions of life in the United Kingdom by watching reruns of *Masterpiece Theater*.

"A shame about the terrorist attacks," said Boswell.

"Yes," said Isherwood vaguely.

"I was hoping to see something in the West End while I was here, but I'm not sure it's safe."

"Nonsense."

"Cognac?"

"Why not?"

Boswell ordered the most expensive on the list, and when the check arrived he adopted Oliver Dimbleby's favorite pose, that of a bewildered survivor of a natural disaster.

"Whom are you seeing tomorrow?" asked Isherwood as he discreetly slipped his credit card into the little leather coffin, the card he hoped wouldn't automatically self-destruct when inserted into the reader.

"I have Jeremy Crabbe in the morning and Roddy Hutchinson in the afternoon. I trust you won't tell them about my little funding issues. I wouldn't want them to think I'm not playing it straight."

"Your secret is safe with me."

It wasn't, actually. In fact, Isherwood planned to call Roddy first thing in the morning and advise him to come down with a sudden case of malaria. Otherwise, Roddy would be the one footing the bill for Brady Boswell's next meal.

Outside, Isherwood thanked Boswell for what had been the least enjoyable night out since his heroics at the Ivy. Then he placed the American in a cab—he was staying at some fleabag in Russell Square—and sent him on his way. Another taxi was waiting. Isherwood gave the driver the address for his house in Kensington and ducked into the back. But as the cab turned into Park Lane he felt the pulse of his mobile phone against his heart. He assumed it was the obligatory thank-you from Boswell and for an instant considered ignoring it. Instead, he withdrew the phone and squinted at the screen. The message was terse, a command rather than a request, and appeared to have no point of origin. Therefore, it could have come from only one person. Isherwood smiled. His evening, he thought, was about to get much more interesting.

"Change in plan," he informed the driver. "Take me to Mason's Yard."

Isherwood's gallery occupied three floors of a sagging Victorian warehouse once owned by Fortnum & Mason. On one side were the offices of a minor Greek shipping company, on the other a pub that catered to pretty office girls who rode motor scooters. The door was fashioned of shatterproof glass and protected by three state-of-the-art locks. It yielded to Isherwood's gentle touch.

"Bloody hell," he whispered.

The limited space of the gallery had compelled Isherwood to arrange his empire vertically—storerooms on the ground floor, business offices on the second, and on the third a glorious formal exhibition room modeled on Paul Rosenberg's famous gallery in Paris, where Isherwood had spent many happy hours as a child. Entering, he reached for the light switch.

"Don't," said a voice from the opposite end of the room. "Leave them off."

Isherwood crept forward, sidestepping a museum-style ottoman, and joined the man who appeared to be contemplating a large landscape by Claude. The man, like the painting, was shrouded in darkness. But his green eyes, when fixed on Isherwood, seemed to glow as if from an inner source of heat.

"I was beginning to wonder," said Gabriel, "if your dinner would ever end."

"So was I," answered Isherwood glumly. "Mind telling me how you got in here?"

"You'll recall that we were the ones who installed your security system."

Isherwood did indeed. He also recalled that the system received a serious upgrade after an operation involving a Russian arms dealer named Ivan Kharkov.

"Congratulations, Julian. My friends in British intelligence tell me you were quite the hero the other night."

"Oh, that." Isherwood gave a dismissive wave of his hand.

"Don't be so modest. Bravery is in rather short supply these days. And to think it wouldn't have happened if that pretty young girlfriend of yours hadn't stood you up."

"Fiona? How on earth do you know about her?"

"The British gave me a copy of the text message she sent while you were sitting at the restaurant."

"Is nothing sacred?"

"They also showed me a few minutes of CCTV video," said Gabriel. "I'm proud of you, Julian. You saved a good many lives that night."

"I can only imagine how I must have looked. An aging Don Quixote tilting at windmills."

Overhead, night rain pattered on the skylight.

"So what brings you to town?" asked Isherwood. "Business or pleasure?"

"I don't do pleasure, Julian. Not anymore at least."

"That makes two of us."

"That bad?"

"I'm in a bit of a dry patch, to say the least."

"How dry?"

"Saharan," said Isherwood.

"Perhaps I can provide a bit of rain."

"Nothing too dangerous, I hope. I'm not sure I can take any more excitement."

"No, Julian, it's not like that at all. I just need you to advise a friend of mine who's interested in building a collection."

"Israeli, this chap?"

"Russian, actually."

"Oh, dear. How does he make his money?"

"In ways he doesn't like to talk about."

"I see," said Isherwood. "I don't suppose this has anything to do with all the bombs that have been exploding lately."

"It might."

"And if I agree to serve as this chap's adviser?"

"The standard rules for such relationships will apply."

"By that, you mean I'll be able to charge him a commission for each painting I help him acquire."

"Actually," said Gabriel, "you can gouge the hell out of him. He won't be paying much attention."

"He likes Old Masters, your man?"

"Adores them. But he appreciates contemporary works, too."

"I won't hold that against him. How much is he willing to spend?"

"Two hundred," said Gabriel. "Maybe three."

Isherwood frowned. "He won't get far with that."

"*Million*, Julian. Two hundred million."

"You can't be serious."

Gabriel's expression said that he was. "He'll be arriving in London in a few days. Run him round to the auction houses and the galleries. Buy carefully but in a hurry. And make a bit of noise, Julian. I want people to notice."

"I can't do it on charm and good looks," said Isherwood. "I'll need actual money."

"Don't worry, Julian. The check is in the mail."

"Two hundred million?" asked Isherwood.

"Maybe three."

"Three is definitely better than two."

Gabriel shrugged. "So we'll do three."

Saladin struck again at half past eight the following morning. The target was Antwerp's Centraal train station, two suicide bombers, two gunmen, sixty-nine dead. Gabriel was in London's St. Pancras at the time, waiting to board a Eurostar to Paris. His train departed forty minutes late, though no reason was given for the delay. It seemed Saladin had succeeded in creating a new normal in Western Europe.

"If he keeps this up," said Christian Bouchard, "he's going to run out of targets."

Bouchard had been waiting for Gabriel in the arrivals hall of the Gare du Nord. Now he was behind the wheel of an Alpha Group Citroën, racing eastward on the boulevard de la Chapelle. He bore no visible traces of the injuries he had suffered in the attack on the rue de Grenelle. If anything, the handsome Frenchman looked better than ever.

"By the way," he said, "I owe you an apology for the way I acted before the bombing. I'm only glad it wasn't your last impression of me."

"To be honest, Christian, I don't remember even seeing you that day."

Bouchard smiled in spite of himself.

"Where are you taking me?"

"A safe house out in the twentieth."

"Any luck finding a new headquarters?"

"Not yet. We're a bit like the ancient Israelites," said Bouchard. "Scattered to the four winds."

The safe flat was located in a modern apartment block not far from a kosher supermarket. Paul Rousseau, seated at a cheap linoleum table in the kitchen, smoked his pipe incessantly throughout Gabriel's briefing. Rousseau had reason to be uneasy. He had let loose a foreign intelligence service on a prominent French businessman and was now feasting on the fruit of a poisonous tree. In short, he was on very thin ice indeed.

"I'm not happy about the Americans. These days their priority seems to be mergers and acquisitions."

"I did it for one reason and one reason only."

"Still . . ." Rousseau nibbled thoughtfully on the end of his pipe. "How sure are you about the gallery?"

"I should know more by the end of the day."

"Because if you can prove the gallery is dirty . . ."

"That's the idea, Paul."

"How soon do you intend to go operational?"

"As soon as I've acquired the necessary funding," said Gabriel.

"Is there anything else you require of us?"

"A property near Saint-Tropez."

"There's plenty to rent, especially at this time of year."

"Actually, I'm not in the market for a rental."

"You wish to buy?"

Gabriel nodded. "In fact," he said, "I already have a property in mind."

"Which one?"

Gabriel answered. Rousseau appeared incredulous.

"The one that was owned by—"

"Yes, that's the one."

"It's frozen."

"So unfreeze it. Trust me, I'll make it well worth your while. The taxpayers of France will be grateful."

"How much are you prepared to offer?"

Gabriel lifted his eyes toward the ceiling. "Twelve million feels about right."

"Apparently, it's fallen into quite a state of disrepair."

"We intend to renovate."

"In Provence?" Rousseau shook his head. "I wish you the best of luck."

Five minutes later, having checked a few more mundane operational boxes, Gabriel was once more in the passenger seat of Bouchard's Citroën. This time they drove from the twentieth arrondissement to the twelfth and stopped on the boulevard Diderot outside the Gare de Lyon. It looked as though it were under military occupation. It was the same at every train station in France.

"Sure you want to go in there?" asked Bouchard. "I can arrange a car if you prefer."

"I'll manage."

Long lines stretched from the station's entrance, where heavily armed police were searching handbags and suitcases and questioning anyone, especially young men, remotely Arab in appearance. The new normal, thought Gabriel as he was admitted into the soaring departure hall. The famous clock read five minutes past three, his train was boarding on Track D. Track Dalet, he thought. Why did it have to be that one? Couldn't they have chosen another?

He made his way along the platform, entered one of the first-class carriages, and settled into his assigned seat. Only when the memories had subsided did he draw his mobile. The number he dialed was in Bern. A man answered in Swiss German. Gabriel addressed him in the Berlin-accented German of his mother.

"I'm on my way to your beautiful country, and I was wondering whether you might show me a good time."

There was a silence, followed by a lengthy exhalation of breath.

"When are you getting in?"

"Six fifteen."

"How?"

"The TGV from Paris."

"What is it this time?"

"Same as the last. A quick peek, that's all."

"Nothing is going to explode, is it?"

Gabriel killed the connection and watched the platform sliding slowly past his window. Once again the memories arose. He saw a woman, scarred and prematurely gray, sitting in a wheelchair, and a man running wildly toward her, a gun in his hand. He closed his eyes and gripped the armrest to stop his hand from shaking. I'll manage, he thought.

The NDB, like Switzerland itself, was small but efficient. Headquartered in a drab office block in Bern, the service was responsible for keeping the many problems of a disorderly world from crossing the borders of the Swiss Confederation. It spied on the spies who plied their trade on Swiss soil, watched over the foreigners who hid their money in Swiss banks, and monitored the activities of the growing number of Muslims who made Switzerland their home. Thus far, the country had been spared a major terrorist attack by the likes of al-Qaeda or ISIS. It was no accident. Christoph Bittel, the chief of the NDB's counter-terrorism division, was very good at his job.

He was also punctual as a Swiss watch. Tall and thin, he was leaning against the hood of a German sedan when Gabriel emerged from the Gare de Cornavin in Geneva at half past six. The Swiss secret policeman frowned. In Switzerland, six fifteen meant six fifteen.

"Do you know the address for the vault?"

"Building Three, Corridor Eight, Vault Nineteen."

"Who's renting it?"

"Something called TXM Capital. But I suspect the real owner is JLM."

"Jean-Luc Martel?"

"One and the same."

Bittel swore softly. "I don't want any trouble with the French. I need the DGSI to protect my western flank."

"Don't worry about the French. As for your western flank, I'd be very afraid."

"Is it true what they say about Martel? That his real business is drugs?"

"We'll know in a few minutes."

They crossed the Rhône and then, a moment later, the mucus-green waters of the Arne. To the south lay a *quartier* of Geneva where tourists and diplomats rarely ventured. It was a land of tidy warehouses and low-slung office blocks. It was also the home of the secretive Geneva Freeport, a secure tax-free repository where the global superrich stashed away treasures of every kind: gold bars, jewelry, vintage wine, automobiles, and, of course, art. It was not art to be viewed and cherished. It was art as a commodity, art as a hedge against uncertain times.

"The place has changed since we were here," Bittel said. "The last straw was that scandal involving the Modigliani, the one that had been stolen by the Nazis. A lot of the collectors pulled out after that and moved their holdings to places like Delaware and London. The cantonal authorities have brought in a new man to run the place. He's a former Swiss finance minister, a real stickler for the letter of the law."

"Perhaps there's hope for your country after all."

"Let's skip this part," said Bittel. "I like it better when we're on the same side."

A row of featureless white structures appeared on their right, surrounded by an opaque green fence topped with concertina wire and security cameras. It might have been mistaken for a prison were it not for the red-and-white sign that read PORTS FRANCS. Bittel turned into the entrance and waited for the security gate to open. Then he pulled forward a few feet and slipped the car into park.

"Building Three, Corridor Eight, Vault Nineteen."

"Very good," said Gabriel.

"We're not going to find drugs in there, are we?"

"No."

"How can you be sure?"

"Because drug dealers don't lock away their product in secure tax-free storage facilities. They sell it to idiots who smoke it, snort it, and inject it into their veins. That's how they make their money."

Bittel entered the security office. Through the half-open blinds of the window, Gabriel could see him in close conversation with an attractive brunette. It was obvious they were speaking in French rather than Swiss German. Finally, there were a few nods and assurances, and then a key changed hands. Bittel carried it back to the car and slid behind the wheel again.

"You're sure there's nothing between you two?" asked Gabriel.

"Don't start with that again."

"Maybe you can introduce me. It would save you the trouble of having to make the drive down from Bern every time I need to look inside some criminal's vault."

"I prefer our current system."

Bittel parked outside Building 3 and led Gabriel inside. From the entrance stretched a seemingly endless hall of doors. They climbed a flight of stairs to the second level and made their way to Corridor 8. The door to Vault 19 was gray metal. Bittel inserted the key into the lock and, entering, switched on the light. The vault contained two chambers. Both were filled with flat rectangular wooden crates of the sort used to transport valuable art. All were identical in size, about six feet by four.

"Not again," said Bittel.

"No," said Gabriel. "Not again."

He examined one of the crates. Attached to it was a shipping waybill bearing the name Galerie Olivia Watson of Saint-Tropez. He pulled at the lid, but it wouldn't budge. It was nailed tightly into place.

"You wouldn't happen to have a claw hammer in your back pocket, would you?"

"Sorry."

"How about a tire tool?"

"I might have one in the trunk."

Gabriel scrutinized the remaining crates while Bittel went

downstairs. There were forty-eight. All had come from Galerie Olivia Watson. TXM Capital was the recipient of record for twenty-seven of the crates. The rest bore equally vague names—the kind of names, thought Gabriel, invented by clever lawyers and private bankers.

Bittel returned with the tire tool. Gabriel used it to pry open the first crate. He worked slowly, gently, so as to leave as few marks in the wood as possible. Inside he found a canvas wrapped in glassine paper, resting in a protective frame of polyurethane. It was all very professional looking, with the exception of the canvas itself.

"How contemporary," said Bittel.

"There's no accounting for taste," replied Gabriel.

He opened another crate. The contents were identical to the first. The same was true of the third crate. And the fourth. A canvas wrapped in glassine paper, a protective frame of polyurethane. All very professional, except for the canvases themselves.

They were blank.

"Mind telling me what this means?" asked Bittel.

"It means that Jean-Luc Martel's real business is drugs, and he's using his girlfriend's art gallery to launder some of the profits."

"Just what the Freeport needs. Another scandal."

"Don't worry, Christoph. It will be our little secret."

Which left only the money. The money necessary to take Gabriel's operation from development to the stage. The two or three hundred million to acquire a flashy art collection. The twelve million for a lavish villa on France's Côte d'Azur, and the five million, give or take, to make it presentable. And then there was the money for all of life's little extras. The cars, the clothes, the jewelry, the restaurants, the trips by private plane, the lavish parties. Gabriel had a figure in mind, to which he added another twenty million, just in case. Operations, like life itself, were uncertain.

"That's a lot of cash," said the prime minister.

"A half billion doesn't go as far as it used to."

"Where's the bank?"

"We have several to choose from, but the National Bank of Panama is our best option. One-stop shopping," explained Gabriel, "and little threat of retaliation, not after the Panama Papers scandal. Even so, we'll plant a few false flags to cover our tracks."

"Who are you going to hang it on?"

"The North Koreans."

"Why not the Iranians?"

"Next time," promised Gabriel.

The targeted funds were spread over eight separate accounts, all bearing the name of the same shell investment corporation. They were part of a vast fortune of looted money controlled by the ruler of Syria and his closest friends and relatives. Shortly before becoming chief, Gabriel had tracked down and then seized the lion's share of the fortune in a bid to moderate the ruler's murderous conduct in the Syrian civil war. But he had been compelled to return the money, more than eight billion dollars, in exchange for a single human life. He had paid the ransom without regret—it was, he always said, the best deal he had ever made. Even so, he had been looking for an excuse, any excuse, to have the final say. Finding Saladin was as good a reason as any.

Gabriel had not returned the eight billion directly to the Syrian ruler. He had deposited it, as instructed, in Gazprombank in Moscow, thus effectively placing it in the hands of the tsar, the Syrian ruler's closest friend and benefactor. The tsar had taken half of the money for himself—service charges, carrying costs, shipping and handling. The remaining funds, slightly more than four billion dollars, had been deposited in a string of secret accounts in Switzerland, Luxembourg, Liechtenstein, Dubai, Hong Kong, and, of course, the National Bank of Panama.

Gabriel knew this because, with the help of a highly secretive unit of Office computer hackers, he had been watching the money's every move. The unit had no official name because, officially, it did not exist. Those who had been briefed on its work referred to it only as the Minyan, for the unit was ten in number and exclusively male in gender. With but a few keystrokes, they could darken a city, blind an air traffic control network, or make the centrifuges of an Iranian nuclear-enrichment plant spin wildly out of control. In short, they had the ability to turn machines against their masters. Privately, Uzi Navot referred to the Minyan as ten good reasons why no one in his right mind would ever use a computer or a mobile phone.

The Minyan worked in a room just down the hall from the one where Gabriel's team was putting the final touches on the preoperational planning. Its nominal leader was a kid named Ilan. He was the cyber equivalent of Mozart. First computer code at five, first hack at eight, first covert op against the Iranians at twenty-one. He was thin as a pauper and had the pasty white pallor of someone who didn't get outside much.

"All I have to do is push a button," he said with an impish smile, "and *poof*—the money is gone."

"And no fingerprints?"

"Only North Korean."

"And there's no way they'll be able to trace the money from the Bank of Panama to HSBC in Paris?"

"Not a chance."

"Remind me," said Gabriel, "to keep my money under the mattress."

"Keep your money under the mattress."

"It was a rhetorical point, Ilan. I didn't want you to actually remind me."

"Oh."

"You have to get out into the real world once in a while."

"This *is* the real world."

Gabriel stared at the computer screen. Ilan stared at it, too.

"Well?" asked Gabriel.

"Well what?"

"What are you waiting for?"

"Authorization to steal a half billion dollars."

"It's not stealing."

"I doubt the Syrians will see it that way. Or the Panamanians."

"Push the button, Ilan."

"I'd feel better if you did it."

"Which one?"

Ilan indicated the enter key. Gabriel tapped it once. Then he walked down the hall and informed his team of the news. The necessary funding had come through. They were open for business.

He was spotted for the first time the following week, on the Wednesday, coming out of Bonhams on New Bond Street with Julian Isherwood at his heels. As luck would have it—or perhaps, with the benefit of hindsight, it wasn't luck at all—Amelia March of *ARTnews* happened to be standing on the pavement at the time, killing a few minutes before her two o'clock with the chairman of Bonhams' postwar and contemporary department. She was an art journalist, not a real one, but she had a nose for a story and an eye for detail. "Tall, trim, quite blond, rather pale, no color in the eyes at all. His suit and overcoat were perfect, his cologne smelled of money." She thought it odd he was in the company of a fossil like Julian. He looked as though his tastes ran to Modern rather than angels and saints and martyrs. Isherwood gave a hurried introduction before ducking with his accomplice into the back of a waiting Jaguar limo. Dmitri Something-or-Other. But of course.

Inside Bonhams, Amelia was able to determine that Isherwood and his tall, pale friend had spent several hours with Jeremy Crabbe, the auction house's maestro of Old Masters. She tracked down Jeremy at Wilton's later that evening. They spoke like a couple of spies in a Vienna coffeehouse after the war.

"Name's Antonov. Dmitri Antonov. Russian, I suppose, but it didn't come up in casual conversation. He's absolutely *made* of money. Does something with natural resources. Don't they *all*," drawled Jeremy. "Julian's attached himself like a barnacle to the hull of a ship. Apparently, he's acting as both dealer and adviser. Quite a cozy relationship, financially speaking. It seems Dmitri has taken several paintings off Julian's hands, and now they're hunting big game. But don't quote me on that. In fact, don't quote me on anything. This is all off the record. Strictly entre nous, darling."

Amelia agreed to keep the information confidential, but Jeremy wasn't so discreet. In fact, he told everyone in the bar, including Oliver Dimbleby. By evening's end it was all anyone was talking about.

In mid-March they were spotted at both Christie's and Sotheby's. They also paid a visit to Oliver's gallery in Bury Street, where after an hour of benign negotiation they committed to acquire a hilly dunescape by the Dutch painter Jacob van Ruisdael, two Venetian canal scenes by Francesco Guardi, and an entombment by Zelotti. Roddy Hutchinson sold him five paintings in all, including a still life with fruit and a lizard by Ambrosius Bosschaert II. The next day Amelia March published a small piece about a young Russian who was making waves in the London art market. Julian Isherwood, acting as the young Russian's spokesman, declined comment. "Any purchases made by my client were private," he said, "and they will remain so."

Early April saw Isherwood and his Russian friend across the Atlantic in New York, where their arrival was eagerly anticipated. They toured the auction houses and the galleries, dined in all the right restaurants, and even took in a Broadway musical. A gossip columnist from the *Post* reported they acquired several Old Master paintings from Otto Naumann Ltd. on East Eightieth Street, but once again Isherwood mumbled something about his client's desire for privacy. By all accounts, it went only so far. Those who met him were left with the impression he was a man who liked to be seen. The same was true of the beautiful young woman—apparently she was the wife, but this was never proven irrefutably—who accompanied him to America. She was trim, dark, French, and deeply unfriendly. "Never missed an opportunity to have a look at herself," said the manager of an exclusive Fifth Avenue jeweler. "A real piece of work."

But who was this man named Dmitri Antonov? And perhaps more important, where did he get his money? He was soon the focus of many Gatsbyesque rumors, some malicious, others well placed. It was said that he had killed a man, that he had killed many men, and that he had come by his fortune illicitly, all of which happened to be true. Not that it made him any less palatable to those who sold art for a living. They didn't much care how he made his money, so long as the check arrived on time and there were no problems at the other end. There weren't. He banked reputably at HSBC in Paris, but, curiously, all his purchases were forwarded to a vault in the Geneva Freeport. "He's one of those," said a woman who worked in the business office at Sotheby's. A superior quietly reminded her that "those" were the ones who kept places like Sotheby's in business.

The vault in the Freeport was the closest thing he had to a permanent address. In London he lived at the Dorchester, in Paris at the Hôtel de Crillon. And when business took him to Zurich, only the Terrazza Suite at the Dolder Grand would do. Even Julian Isherwood, who was tethered to him by cell phone and text, claimed not to know where he was from one day to the next. But there were rumors—here again they were only rumors—he had acquired a castle for himself somewhere in France. "He's using the Freeport as a temporary storage facility," Isherwood whispered into Oliver Dimbleby's ear. "Something big is in the works." Isherwood then swore Oliver to absolute secrecy, thus ensuring the news would go global by morning.

But where in France? Once again the rumor mill began to turn. For on the day the man called Dmitri Antonov left New York, there appeared a small item in *Nice-Matin* regarding a certain notorious piece of real estate near Saint-Tropez. Known as Villa Soleil, the sprawling seaside compound on the Baie de Cavalaire was once owned by Ivan Kharkov, the Russian oligarch and arms dealer who was shot to death outside an exclusive Saint-Tropez restaurant. For nearly a decade the property had been in the hands of the French government. Now, for reasons never made clear, the government was suddenly anxious to remove Villa Soleil from its books. Apparently, a buyer had been found. *Nice-Matin*, despite strenuous efforts, had not yet been able to identify him.

Renovation of the property commenced immediately. Indeed, on the day after the article appeared, an army of painters, plumbers, electricians, stonemasons, landscapers descended on Villa Soleil and remained there without interruption until the great palace by the sea was once again fit for human habitation. The enterprising nature of the workforce provoked no small amount of resentment among the neighbors, all of whom were battle-scarred veterans of Provençal construction projects. Even Jean-Luc Martel, who lived in a grand villa on the opposite side of the bay, was impressed by the speed with which the project was completed. Gabriel and the team knew this because, with the help of the mighty American NSA, they were now privy to all of Martel's private communications, including the molten e-mail he sent to his builder wondering why a renovation to his pool house was two months behind schedule. "Finish it by the end of April," he wrote, "or I'll fire you and hire the company that did Ivan's old place."

The interior decoration of Villa Soleil was conducted at the same un-Provençal pace, overseen by one of the Côte d'Azur's most prominent firms. There was only one delay, a pair of matching couches ordered from Olivia Watson's design shop in Saint-Tropez. Owing to a minor clerical error—in truth, it was quite intentional—the name of the villa's owner appeared on the order form. Olivia Watson shared the name with Martel, who in turn gave it to a columnist at *Nice-Matin* who had written favorably of him in the past. Gabriel and his team knew this because the mighty American NSA said it was so.

Which left only the paintings, the paintings acquired under the flawless eye of Julian Isherwood and stored in a vault in the Geneva Freeport. In mid-May they were transported to Provence in a convoy of panel vans, watched over by agents of a private security firm and several officers of a secret unit of the

DGSI known as the Alpha Group. Isherwood supervised the hanging with the assistance of the owner's French wife. Then they flew to Paris, where the owner himself was staying in his usual suite at the Crillon. That evening they dined at Martel's thriving new restaurant on the boulevard Saint-Germain, accompanied by a durable-looking man who spoke French with a pronounced Corsican accent. Martel was there, too, along with his glamorous English girlfriend. Gabriel and his team were not surprised by the presence of their quarry; they had known of Martel's plans several days in advance, and had reserved a table for four under the name Dmitri Antonov. Within minutes of the party's arrival, a bottle of champagne appeared, along with a handwritten note. The champagne was a 1998 Dom Pérignon, the note was from Jean-Luc Martel. *Welcome to the neighborhood. See you in Saint-Tropez* . . . It was, all in all, a promising beginning.

I think I'll go into the village a little later."

"Whatever for?"

"It's market day. You know how much I love the market."

"Ah, yes, wonderful."

"Can you come?"

"Can't, unfortunately. I have a few calls to make."

"Fine."

Ten days had elapsed since Mikhail and Natalie—otherwise known as Dmitri and Sophie Antonov—had settled into their new home on the Baie de Cavalaire, and already it seemed they were bored. It was not operational boredom, it was marital in nature. Gabriel had declared that the Antonovs' would not be an entirely blissful union. Few marriages were perfect, he argued, and the marriage between a Russian criminal and a Frenchwoman of dubious personal provenance would not be without its rough patches. He had also decreed that they were to maintain their cover identities at all times, even when they were safely behind the twelve-foot walls of Villa Soleil. Thus the frigid exchange over breakfast. It was conducted in English, as Dmitri Antonov's French was atrocious and his wife's Russian was nonexistent. The household staff, all officers of Paul Rousseau's Alpha Group, addressed only Madame Sophie. Monsieur Antonov they generally avoided. They thought him rude and coarse, and he regarded them, with some justification, as the worst domestic servants in all of Provence. Gabriel shared his opinion. Privately, he had urged Rousseau to knock them quickly into shape. Otherwise, they risked sinking the entire operation.

Mikhail and Natalie were seated like characters in a film, at a table on the broad colonnaded terrace overlooking the pool. It was the spot where they had taken their breakfast each of the nine preceding mornings, for Monsieur Antonov preferred it above all others. He had started his day with a vigorous thirty-minute swim in the pool. Now he wore a snowy white toweling robe against his pale skin. Natalie's eye was drawn to the rivulet of water running through the chiseled creek bed of his abdominal muscles toward the waistband of his bathing suit. Quickly, she looked away. Madame Sophie, she reminded herself, was annoyed with Monsieur Antonov. He could not worm his way back into her good graces with a petty display of physical beauty.

She poured a cup of strong black coffee from the silver pot and added a generous measure of steamed milk. In doing so she looked undeniably French. Next she plucked a Gitane from its packet and lit it. The cigarettes, like her churlish demeanor, were purely for the sake of her cover. A physician who had seen firsthand the terrible effects of tobacco on the human body, she was a devout nonsmoker. The first inhalation clawed at the back of her throat, but with a sip of the coffee she managed to suppress the urge to cough. It was very nearly perfect, the coffee;

only in the south of France, she thought, did it taste like this. The morning was clear and fine, with a soft wind that moved in the line of cypress pines marking the boundary between Villa Soleil and its neighbor. Wavelets flecked the Baie de Cavalaire, across which Natalie could make out the faint lines of the villa owned by Jean-Luc Martel, hotelier, restaurateur, clothier, jeweler, and international dealer of illicit narcotics.

"Croissant?" she asked.

"Pardon?" Mikhail was reading something on a tablet computer with great intensity and could not be bothered to lift his gaze to meet hers.

"I asked whether you wanted another croissant."

"No."

"How about lunch?"

"Now?"

"In Saint-Tropez. You can meet me there."

"I'll try. What time?"

"*Lunch*time, darling. The time people usually eat lunch."

He swiped a forefinger across the surface of the tablet but said nothing. Natalie stabbed out her cigarette and in the manner of Sophie Antonov stood abruptly. Then she leaned down and put her mouth close to Mikhail's ear.

"You seem to be enjoying this too much," she whispered in Hebrew. "I wouldn't get used to it if I were you."

She entered the villa and padded barefoot through its many cavernous rooms until she came to the base of the grand main staircase. Her accommodations, she thought, were far better than the ones she had endured in her first operation—the drab flat in the Paris banlieue of Aubervilliers, her squalid little room in an ISIS dormitory in Raqqa, the desert training camp outside Palmyra, the chamber in the house in Mosul where she had nursed Saladin back to health.

You are my Maimonides . . .

In the bedroom, the satin sheets were still in disarray. Evidently, the Alpha Group maids had not found time in their busy schedule to put the room in order. Natalie smiled guiltily. This was the one room in the house where she and Mikhail made no attempt to conceal their true feelings for one another. Strictly speaking, their actions the previous evening had been a violation of Office regulations, which forbade intimate relations between operatives in the field. It was famously one of the least enforced rules in the entire service. Indeed, the current chief and his wife were known to have disregarded the rule on numerous occasions. Besides, thought Natalie as she straightened the sheets, their lovemaking was for the sake of their cover. Even quarreling spouses were not immune to the dark pull of desire.

The walk-in closet was overflowing with designer clothing, shoes, and accessories, all paid for by the murderous ruler of Syria. Only the best for Madame Sophie. From a drawer she removed a pair of Lycra leggings and a sports bra. Her Nike trainers were on the shoe rack, next to a pair of Bruno Magli pumps. Dressed, she walked down a cool marble hall to the fitness room and stepped onto the treadmill. She hated running indoors but had no other option. Madame Sophie was not permitted to run outside. Madame Sophie had security issues. So, too, did Natalie Mizrahi.

She slipped on a pair of headphones and set out at an easy jog, but with each kilometer she increased the speed of the belt until she was clipping along at a brisk pace. Her breathing remained controlled and steady; the many weeks she had spent at the farm in Nahalal had left her in peak fitness. She finished with a final sprint and spent thirty minutes lifting weights before returning to the bedroom to shower and dress. White capri pants, a snug-fitting stretch pullover that flattered her breasts and slender waist, gold flat-soled sandals. Standing before the mirror, she thought again of the last operation, the hijab and pious clothing of Dr. Leila Hadawi. Leila, she thought, would not have approved of Sophie Antonov. In that, she and Natalie were in complete agreement.

She stepped onto the balcony and peered down toward the terrace where Mikhail was stretched on a chaise longue, exposing his colorless skin to the morning rays of the sun. In ten days his pallor had not changed. He seemed to be incapable of tanning.

"Sure you won't join me?" she called down.

"I'm busy."

Natalie dropped her Office mobile into her handbag and headed downstairs to the forecourt, where the Antonovs' black Maybach limousine waited next to the splashing fountain, an Alpha Group driver behind the wheel. In the backseat was a second officer of the Alpha Group. His name was Roland Girard. During the first operation he had served as the director of the small clinic in Aubervilliers where Dr. Leila Hadawi had practiced medicine. Now he was Madame Sophie's favorite bodyguard. There were rumors they were having a torrid affair, rumors that had reached the ears of Monsieur Antonov. Several times he had tried to fire the bodyguard, but Madame Sophie would not hear of it. As the Maybach eased through the imposing security gate, she lit another Gitane and stared moodily out her window. This time she could not suppress the urge to cough.

"You know," said Girard, "you don't have to smoke those wretched things when it's just the two of us."

"It's the only way I'll ever get used to them."

"What are your plans?" he asked.

"The market."

"And then?"

"I was hoping to have lunch with my husband, but it seems he can't be bothered."

Girard smiled but said nothing. Just then, Natalie's mobile pinged with an incoming message. After reading it she returned the device to her handbag and, coughing, smoked the last of the Gitane. It was nearly time for Madame Sophie to meet Madame Olivia. She needed the practice.

28

SAINT-TROPEZ, FRANCE

As they passed the turnoff for the Plage de Pampelonne, Natalie was overcome by memories. This time they were not Leila's memories, they were her own. It is a perfect morning in late August. Natalie and her parents have made the difficult drive from Marseilles to Saint-Tropez because no other beach in France—or the world, for that matter—will do. The year is 2011. Natalie has completed her medical training and has embarked on what promises to be a successful career in France's state-run health care system. She is a model French citizen; she cannot imagine living anywhere else. But France is changing rapidly beneath her feet. It is no longer a place where it is safe to be a Jew. Each day, it seems, brings news of another horror. Another child beaten or spat upon, another shop window broken, another synagogue sprayed with graffiti, another gravestone toppled. And so on that day in late August, on the beach at Pampelonne, Natalie and her parents do their best to conceal their Jewishness. They cannot, and the day does not pass without scornful looks and a murmured insult by the waiter who grudgingly serves their lunch. During the drive back to

Marseilles, Natalie's parents make a fateful decision. They will leave France and settle in Israel. They ask Natalie, their only child, to join them. She agrees without hesitation. And now, she thought, gazing out the tinted window of the Maybach limousine, she was back again.

Beyond the beaches were newly planted vineyards and tiny villas shaded by cypress and umbrella pine. Once they reached the outer edges of Saint-Tropez, however, the villas were concealed by high walls covered in flowering vines. These were the homes of the *merely* rich, not the superrich like Dmitri Antonov or Ivan Kharkov before him. As a child Natalie had dreamed of living in a grand house surrounded by walls. Gabriel had granted her wish. Not Gabriel, she thought suddenly. It was Saladin.

The driver eased the Maybach onto the avenue Foch and followed it into the *centre ville*. It was only June, not yet high summer, and so the crowds were manageable, even in the Place des Lices, site of Saint-Tropez's bustling open-air market. As Natalie made her way slowly through the stalls, she felt an overwhelming sense of loss. This was *her* country, she thought, and yet her family had been forced to leave it because of the most ancient hatred. The presence of Roland Girard focused her attention on the task at hand. He walked not at her side, but at her back. There was no mistaking him for a husband. He was there for one reason and one reason only, to protect Madame Sophie Antonov, the new resident of the scandalous palace on the Baie de Cavalaire.

All at once she heard someone calling her name from a café along the boulevard Vasserot. "Madame Sophie, Madame Sophie! It's me, Nicolas. Over here, Madame Sophie." She looked up and saw Christopher Keller waving to her from a table at Le Clemenceau. Smiling, she crossed the street, with Roland Girard a step behind. Keller rose and offered her a chair. When Natalie sat down, Roland Girard returned to the Place des Lices and stood in the dappled shade of a plane tree.

"What a pleasant surprise," said Keller when they were alone.

"Yes, it is." Natalie's tone was cool. It was the voice Madame Sophie used when addressing men who worked for her husband. "What brings you into the village?"

"An errand. You?"

"A bit of shopping." She glanced around the market. "Anyone watching?"

"Of course, Madame Sophie. You caused quite a stir."

"That was the point, wasn't it?"

Keller was drinking Campari. "Have you had a chance to visit any of the art galleries?" he asked.

"Not yet."

"There's a rather good one near the Old Port. I'd be happy to show it to you. It's a five-minute walk at most."

"Will the owner be there?"

"I'd say so, yes."

"How does our friend want me to play it?"

"He seems to think a good snub is in order."

Natalie smiled. "I think Madame Sophie can manage that quite nicely."

They walked toward the Old Port past the parade of shops lining the rue Gambetta. Keller wore white pants, black moccasins, and a formfitting black pullover. With his dark tan and gelled hair, he looked thoroughly disreputable. Natalie, playing the role of Madame Sophie, affected a deep and profound boredom. She loitered in several of the shop windows, including a boutique that bore the name Olivia Watson. Roland Girard, her ersatz bodyguard, stood vigilantly at her shoulder.

"What do you think of that one?" she asked, pointing toward a sheer dress that hung from a headless mannequin like a negligee. "Do you think Dmitri would notice me if I wore that? Or how about *that* one? That might get his attention."

Greeted by a professional silence, she walked on, swinging her handbag like a spoiled schoolgirl. Yossi Gavish and Rimona Stern were walking toward them along the narrow street, hands clasped, laughing at a private joke. Dina Sarid was evaluating a pair of sandals in the window of Minelli, and a little farther along the street Natalie spotted Eli Lavon rushing into a pharmacy with the urgency of a man whose bowels were in a state of rebellion.

At last, they arrived in the Place de l'Ormeau. It was not a proper square like the Place des Lices, but a tiny triangle at the intersection of three streets. In the center was an old wellhead, shaded by a single tree. On one side was a dress shop, on the other a café. And next to the café was the handsome four-story building—large by Saint-Tropez standards, pale gray instead of tan—occupied by Galerie Olivia Watson.

The heavy wooden door was closed and locked. Next to it was a brass placard, which stated in both French and English that viewing of the gallery's inventory was by appointment only. In the display window were three paintings—a Lichtenstein, a Basquiat, and a work by the French painter and sculptor Jean Dubuffet. Natalie wandered over to have a closer look at the Basquiat while Keller checked his mobile. After a moment she became aware of a presence at her back. The intoxicating scent of lilac made it clear it was not Roland Girard.

"Beautiful, isn't it?" asked a female voice in French.

"The Basquiat?"

"Yes."

"Actually," said Natalie to the glass, "I prefer the Dubuffet."

"You have good taste."

Natalie turned slowly and appraised the fourth work of art standing a few inches away, in the Place de l'Ormeau. She was shockingly tall, so tall in fact that Natalie had to lift her gaze to meet hers. She was not beautiful, she was professionally beautiful. Until that moment, Natalie had not realized there was a difference.

"Would you like to have a closer look?" the woman asked.

"I'm sorry?"

"At the Dubuffet. I have a few minutes before my next appointment." She smiled and extended a hand. "Forgive me, I should have introduced myself. I'm Olivia. Olivia Watson," she added. "This is my gallery."

Natalie accepted the proffered hand. It was unusually long, as was the bare arm, smooth and golden, to which it was attached. Luminous blue eyes stared out from a face so flawless it scarcely seemed real. It was set in an expression of mild curiosity.

"You're Sophie Antonov, are you not?"

"Have we met?"

"No. But Saint-Tropez is a small town."

"Very small," said Natalie coolly.

"We live across the bay from you and your husband," Olivia Watson explained. "In fact, we can see your villa from ours. Perhaps you'd like to come over some time."

"I'm afraid my husband is extremely busy."

"He sounds like Jean-Luc."

"Jean-Luc is your husband?"

"Partner," said Olivia Watson. "His name is Jean-Luc Martel. Perhaps you've heard of him. You and your husband had dinner at his new brasserie in Paris a couple of weeks ago. He sent you a bottle of champagne." She glanced at Keller, who appeared to be engrossed by something he was reading on his mobile. "He was there, too."

"He works for my husband."

"And that one?" Olivia Watson nodded toward Roland Girard.

"He works for me."

The luminous blue eyes settled on Natalie once more. She had studied hundreds of photographs of Olivia Watson in preparation for their first encounter, and yet the impact of her beauty was still a shock to the system. She was smiling slightly now. It was a sly smile, seductive, superior. She was well aware of the effect her appearance had on other women.

"Your husband is an art collector," she said.

"My husband is a businessman who appreciates art," said Natalie carefully.

"Perhaps he'd like to visit the gallery."

"My husband prefers Old Master paintings to contemporary works."

"Yes, I know. He made quite a splash in London and New York this spring." She delved into her handbag and produced a business card, which she offered to Natalie. "My private number is on the back. I have some special pieces I think might be of interest to your husband. And please come to our villa for lunch this weekend. Jean-Luc is eager to meet you both."

"My husband and I have other plans this weekend," said

Natalie briskly. "Good day, Madame Wilson. It was a pleasure to meet you."

"Watson," she called out as Natalie walked away. "My name is Olivia Watson."

She was still holding the business card between her thumb and forefinger. Keller walked over and plucked it from her grasp. "Madame Sophie can be a bit on the moody side. Don't worry, I'll have a word with the boss on your behalf." He offered his hand. "I'm Nicolas, by the way. Nicolas Carnot."

Keller walked with Natalie and Roland Girard back to the Place des Lices and saw them into the waiting Maybach. It departed the *centre ville* a few seconds later in a black blur, observed enviously by tourists and natives alike. Alone, Keller cut through the stalls of the market to the opposite side of the square and mounted the Peugeot Satelis motorbike he had left there. He headed west along the edge of the Golfe de Saint-Tropez, then south into the hills of the Var, until he came to the village of Ramatuelle. It was not unlike the village of the Orsatis in central Corsica, a cluster of small dun-colored houses with red-tile roofs, perched defensively atop a hill. There were larger villas hidden away in the wooded lowlands. One was called La Pastorale. Keller made certain he was not being followed before presenting himself at the iron security gate. It was painted green and quite formidable. He thumbed the intercom button and then turned to watch a delivery truck pass in the road.

"Oui?" came a thin metallic voice a moment later.

"C'est moi," said Keller. "Open the fucking gate."

The drive was long and winding and shaded by pine and

poplar. It terminated in the gravel forecourt of a large stone villa with yellow shutters. Keller made his way to the sitting room, which had been converted into a makeshift op center. Gabriel and Paul Rousseau were hunched over a laptop computer. Rousseau acknowledged Keller's arrival with a guarded nod—he was still deeply suspicious of this talented MI6 officer who spoke French like a Corsican and was comfortable in the presence of criminals—but Gabriel was smiling broadly.

"Well played, Monsieur Carnot. Taking the business card was a nice touch."

"First impressions matter."

"They do, indeed. Listen to this."

Gabriel tapped the keyboard of the laptop and a few seconds later came the voice of a woman shouting in anger in French. It was fluent and profane but marked by an unmistakable English accent.

"Who's she talking to?"

"Jean-Luc Martel, of course."

"How did he take it?"

"You'll hear in a minute."

Keller winced as Martel's voice boomed from the speakers.

"Clearly," said Gabriel, "he's not used to people telling him no."

"What's your next move?"

"Another snub. Several, in fact."

The speakers fell silent after Olivia Watson, with one final fusillade of shouted obscenities, terminated the call. Keller walked over to an array of video monitors and watched a Maybach limousine turning in to a palatial villa by the sea. A woman exited and made her way through cavernous rooms hung with Old Master paintings to a terrace overlooking a lagoon-size swimming pool. A man dozed there, his pale skin reddening beneath the unrelenting onslaught of the sun. The woman spoke something directly into his ear that the microphones could not capture and led him upstairs to a room where there were no cameras. Keller smiled as the door closed. Perhaps there was hope for Madame Sophie and Monsieur Antonov after all.

29

CÔTE D'AZUR, FRANCE

It was not true that Madame Sophie and Monsieur Antonov had plans that weekend. But somehow, with the help of a hidden hand, or perhaps by magic, plans materialized. Indeed, no sooner had the sun set on a perfect Friday afternoon than an unclasped diamond necklace of car headlights lay along the shore of the Baie de Cavalaire, flowing toward the gates of Villa Soleil, which blazed and sparkled and pulsed to the beat of music so loud it could be heard across the water, which was the point. The guests traveled from far and wide. There were actors and writers and faded aristocrats and thieves. There was the son of an Italian automaker who arrived amid a school of seminude women, and a pop star who had not had a hit record since music went digital. Half the London art world was there, along with a contingent from New York, which, it was rumored, had flown privately across the Atlantic at the host's expense. And there were many others who would later admit to having received no invitation at all. These lesser souls had heard about the affair through the usual channels—the Rivieran gossip mill, social media—and had beaten a path to Monsieur Antonov's gold-plated door.

If he was actually present that night, there was no sign of him. In fact, not a single guest would be able to offer reliable firsthand evidence of having seen him. Even Julian Isherwood, his art adviser, was at a loss to explain his whereabouts. Isherwood conducted a private tour of the villa's impressive collection of Old Master paintings for the handful of guests who displayed any interest in seeing it. Then, like everyone else, he became roaring drunk. By midnight the buffet had been devoured and women were swimming naked in the pool and the fountains. There was a fistfight, and the very public commission of a sexual act, and the threat of a lawsuit. Old rivalries flared, marriages collapsed, and many fine automobiles suffered damage. Everyone agreed a good time was had by all.

But the party did not end that night, it merely went into brief remission. By late morning, cars once again choked the roads, and a flotilla of white motor yachts lay anchored in the waters off Villa Soleil's dock, tended by Monsieur Antonov's shore craft. The second night's festivities were worse than the first, owing to the fact that most of the guests arrived drunk or were still drunk from the night before. Monsieur Antonov's large staff of security guards kept careful watch over the paintings, and several of the unruliest guests were ejected from the premises with quiet efficiency. Still, there was not one who actually shook hands with the host or even laid eyes on him. Oh, there was the middle-aged American divorcée the color of saddle leather who claimed to have spotted him observing the party, Gatsbylike, from a private terrace in the upper reaches of his palace, but she was quite inebriated at the time and her account was roundly dismissed. Mortified, she made a clumsy pass at a handsome young Formula One driver and had to console herself with the company of Oliver Dimbleby. They were last seen teetering into the night, with Oliver's hand on her backside.

There was a champagne brunch on Sunday, after which the last of the guests dispersed. The walking wounded saw themselves to the door, the comatose and nonresponsive departed by other means. Then an army of workmen arrived and erased all evidence of the weekend's destruction. And on Monday morning Monsieur Antonov and Madame Sophie were in their usual place on the terrace overlooking the pool, Monsieur Antonov lost in his tablet computer, Madame Sophie in her thoughts. At midday she went into the village, accompanied by Roland Girard, and had lunch with Monsieur Carnot at a restaurant in the Old Port owned by Jean-Luc Martel. Olivia Watson dined with a friend, a woman of nearly equal beauty, a few tables away. Leaving, she passed Madame Sophie's table without a word or glance, though Monsieur Carnot was quite certain he overheard an anatomical vulgarity that even he, a man of disrepute, never dared to utter.

There was another party the following weekend, smaller but no less felonious, and a blowout the next week that set a Côte d'Azur record for complaints to the gendarmes. At which point the Antonovs declared a cease-fire and life on the Baie de Cavalaire returned to something like normal. For the most part they remained prisoners of Villa Soleil, though several times each week Madame Sophie, after her morning run on the treadmill, traveled to Saint-Tropez in her Maybach limousine to shop or have lunch. Usually, she dined with Roland Girard or Monsieur Carnot, though on two occasions she was seen with a tall sunburned Englishman who had taken a villa for the summer near the hill town of Ramatuelle. He had a curvy, sarcastic wife whom Madame Sophie adored.

The couple were not the only ones staying at the villa. There was a small woman with dark hair who moved with a slight limp and carried herself with an air of early widowhood. And an elusive man of late middle age who never seemed to wear the same clothing twice. And a hard-looking man with a pock-marked face who seemed always to be contemplating an act of violence. And a Frenchman of professorial bearing who fouled the rooms of the villa with his ever-present pipe. And a man with gray temples and green eyes who was forever pleading with the Frenchman to find another habit, one that didn't endanger the health of those around him.

The occupants of the villa made no show of recreation or leisure; they had come to Provence on deadly serious business. The professorial Frenchman and the green-eyed man were ostensibly equal partners, but in practice the Frenchman deferred to his associate in nearly all matters. Both men spent significant time outside the villa. The Frenchman, for example, shuttled back and forth between Provence and Paris while the green-eyed man made several clandestine trips to Tel Aviv. He also traveled to London, where he negotiated the terms of the next phase of his endeavor, and to Washington, where he was berated for its slow pace. He was forgiving of his American partner's foul mood. The Americans had grown used to solving problems with the push of a button. Patience was not an American virtue.

But the green-eyed man was patience incarnate, especially when he was at the villa in Ramatuelle. The antics of Monsieur Antonov and Madame Sophie were of little concern to him. It was the beautiful Englishwoman who owned the art gallery in the Place de l'Ormeau who was his obsession. With the help of the other occupants of the villa, he watched her day and night. And with the help of his friend in America, he listened to her every phone call and read her every text message and e-mail.

She loathed the noisy new couple who lived on the opposite side of the Baie de Cavalaire—that much was evident—but she was intrigued by them nevertheless. Mainly, she wondered why it was that every D-list celebrity in the south of France had been invited to the Antonovs' villa, but she had been excluded. Her not-quite husband was of a similar mind. He was a celebrity himself, after all. A real celebrity, not one of those poseurs who had wormed their way into the Antonovs' dubious orbit. Soon he was making inquiries of his own about his new neighbor and the source of his considerable income. The more he heard, the more he became convinced that Monsieur Dmitri Antonov was a kindred spirit. He instructed his not-quite wife to extend another invitation. She replied that she would sooner slash her wrists than spend another minute in the company of that spoiled creature from the other side of the bay, or words to that effect.

And so the green-eyed man bided his time. He watched her every move and listened to her every word and read her every electronic missive. And he wondered whether she was worthy of his obsession. Was she the girl of his dreams, or would she break his operational heart? Would she surrender to him willingly, or would force be necessary? If so, he had force in abundance. Namely, the forty-eight blank canvases he had found in the Geneva Freeport. He hoped it wouldn't come to that. He thought of her as a painting in desperate need of repair. He would offer his services. And if she was foolish enough to refuse him, it was possible things might get nasty.

By the second week of July he had seen and heard enough. Bastille Day was fast approaching, after which the final crush of the summer season would commence. But how to bridge the divide that he himself had created? Only a formal invitation, he decided, would do. He wrote it out himself, in a hand so precise it looked as though it had rolled off a laser printer, and gave it to Monsieur Carnot to deliver to the gallery in the Place de l'Ormeau. He did so at eleven fifteen on a perfect Provençal morning, and by noon the following day they had received the answer they were hoping for. Jean-Luc Martel, hotelier, restaurateur, clothier, jeweler, and international dealer of illicit narcotics, was coming to Villa Soleil for lunch. And Olivia Watson, the girl of Gabriel's dreams, was coming with him.

W hat do you think, darling? Gun or no gun?"
Mikhail was admiring himself in the full-length mirror in the dressing room. He wore a dark linen suit—too dark for the occasion and the weather, which was warm even by Côte d'Azur standards—and a crisp white dress shirt un-buttoned to the breastbone. Only his shoes, a pair of fifteen-hundred-euro drivers, which he wore with no socks, were entirely appropriate. Their gold clasps matched the gold wrist-watch that lay on his wrist like a misplaced weather barometer. It had been handmade for him by his man in Geneva, a bargain at a million and a half.

"No gun," said Natalie. "It might send the wrong message."

She was standing next to him, her image reflected in the same mirror. She wore a sleeveless white dress and more jewelry than was necessary for an afternoon garden luncheon. Her skin was very dark from too much time in the sun. She thought it did not quite match the color of her hair, which had been light-ened several shades before her departure from Tel Aviv.

"Do you think it would ever get boring?"

"What's that?"

"Living like this."

"I suppose that depends on the alternative."

Just then, Natalie's mobile vibrated.

"What is it?"

"Martel and Olivia have just departed their villa."

Mikhail frowned at his wristwatch. "They were supposed to be here twenty minutes ago."

"JLM time," said Natalie.

The mobile vibrated a second time.

"What is it now?"

"It says we make a handsome couple."

Natalie kissed Mikhail's cheek and went out. Downstairs on the shaded terrace a trio of Alpha Group household servants was setting a luncheon table with inordinate care. At the opposite end of the terrace Christopher Keller was drinking rosé. Natalie tugged a Marlboro from his packet and addressed him in French.

"Can't you even pretend to be a little nervous?"

"Actually, I'm looking forward to finally meeting him. Here he comes now."

Natalie looked toward the horizon and saw a pair of black Range Rovers skirting the edge of the bay, one for Martel and Olivia, the other for their security detail. "Bodyguards at lunch," she said with Madame Sophie's disdain. "How gauche." Then she lit the cigarette and smoked for a moment without coughing.

"You're getting rather good at that."

"It's a filthy habit."

"Better than some. In fact, I can think of several that are far worse." Keller watched the approaching Range Rovers. "You really have to relax, Madame Sophie. It's a party, after all."

"Jean-Luc Martel and I come from the same part of France. I'm afraid he's going to look at me and see a Jewish girl from Marseilles."

"He's going to see whatever you want him to see. Besides," said Keller, "if you can convince Saladin that you're a Palestinian, you can do anything."

Natalie suppressed a cough and watched the Alpha Group servants putting the finishing touches on the table.

"Why *candles*?" she murmured. "We're doomed."

During the final hours of preparation for the long-awaited meeting between Jean-Luc Martel and Monsieur Dmitri Antonov, there had been an unusually heated debate between Gabriel and Paul Rousseau over what seemed to be a trivial detail. Specifically, whether the imposing gate of Villa Soleil should be open to Martel's arrival or left closed, thus placing before him one final metaphorical hurdle to clear. Rousseau lobbied in favor of a welcoming approach—Martel, he argued, had suffered enough. But Gabriel was in a less forgiving mood, and after a quarrel of several minutes he prevailed upon Rousseau to leave the gate closed. "And make him ring the bell like everyone else," said Gabriel. "As far as Dmitri Antonov is concerned, Martel is kitchen help. It's important we treat him as such."

And so it was that, at twenty-nine minutes past one o'clock, Martel's driver had to press the intercom button not once but twice before Villa Soleil's gate finally opened with an inhospitable groan. Roland Girard, in a dark suit and tie, roasted slowly in the sun-drowned forecourt, a radio to his ear. Thus, it was the face of an Alpha Group operative, not his host's, that Martel saw when he emerged from the back of his vehicle, dressed in a wedding-cake-white poplin suit, his trademark mane of hair twisting in the eddies of hot wind that swirled and died around the dancing waters of the fountain. Six cameras recorded his arrival, and the transmitter worn by Roland Girard captured a tense exchange concerning the fate of his bodyguards. It seemed Martel wanted them to accompany him into the villa, a request Girard politely but firmly denied. Incensed, Martel turned away and struck out across the court with a predatory swiftness, his manner that of a gangster entrepreneur, a rock-star hoodlum. Olivia was at that point an afterthought. She followed a few paces behind as though already preparing her apologies for his conduct.

By then, the Antonovs were standing in the shade of the portico, posed as if for a photograph, which was indeed the case. The greetings were gender-based. Madame Sophie welcomed Olivia Watson as though the frigid encounter outside the gallery had never occurred, while Martel and Dmitri Antonov shook hands like opponents preparing to thrash one another on the field of play. Through a tight smile, Martel said he had heard much about Monsieur Antonov and was pleased to finally make his acquaintance. He did so in English, which suggested he was aware of the fact that Monsieur Antonov did not speak French.

"Your villa is quite magnificent. But I'm sure you know its history."

"I'm told it was once owned by a member of the British royal family."

"I was referring to Ivan Kharkov."

"Actually, it was one of the reasons why I agreed to take it off the hands of the French government."

"You knew Monsieur Kharkov?"

"I'm afraid Ivan and I moved in rather different circles."

"I knew him quite well," boasted Martel as he walked next to his host across the villa's main hall, trailed by Madame Sophie and Olivia and watched by the unblinking eyes of the surveillance cameras. "I entertained the Kharkovs many times in my restaurants in Saint-Tropez and Paris. It was terrible, the way he died."

"The Israelis were behind it. At least that was the rumor."

"It was more than just a rumor."

"You sound rather sure of yourself."

"There isn't much that happens on the Côte d'Azur that I don't know about."

They went onto the terrace, where the last member of the luncheon party waited among the colonnades.

"Jean-Luc Martel, I'd like you to meet Nicolas Carnot. Nicolas is my closest aide and adviser. He's from Corsica originally, but don't hold that against him."

In the villa outside Ramatuelle, Gabriel watched intently as Jean-Luc Martel accepted the outstretched hand. There followed a tense few seconds as the two men took stock of one another as only creatures of similar birth, upbringing, and career aspirations can do. Clearly, Martel saw something he recognized in the hard-looking man from the island of Corsica. He introduced Monsieur Carnot to Olivia, who explained that they had met on two previous occasions at the gallery. But Martel didn't seem to hear her; he was admiring the bottle of Bandol rosé sweating in the ice bucket. His approval of the wine was no accident. It was featured prominently at all his bars and restaurants. Gabriel had ordered enough of the stuff to float a cargo ship filled with hashish.

At Madame Sophie's suggestion, they sat down on the couches and chairs arrayed at the far end of the terrace. She was cool and distant, an observer, like Gabriel. He was standing before the video monitors with his head tilted slightly to one side and a hand resting on his chin. The other he pressed to the small of his back, which was giving him fits. Eli Lavon stood next to him, and next to Lavon was Paul Rousseau. They watched anxiously as an officer of the Alpha Group, clad in a spotless white tunic, removed an exhausted bottle of rosé from the ice bucket and successfully replaced it with a fresh one. Quietly, Madame Sophie instructed him to bring the savories. This, too, he accomplished without casualties or collateral damage. Relieved, Paul Rousseau loaded a pipe and blew a cloud of smoke at the video screens. Madame Sophie appeared relieved, too. She lit a Gitane and, with thumb and ring finger, discreetly picked a fleck of tobacco from the tip of her tongue.

The conversation was polite but guarded, which was how Gabriel had intended it to be. It was conducted in English for the benefit of Dmitri Antonov, though occasionally he was cast adrift by a burst of French. He took no offense. In fact, he seemed to relish the quiet, for it gave him a respite from Martel's dogged inquiries regarding his business. He explained he had made a great deal of money trading in Russian commodities and had managed to cash out his chips before the Great Recession and the plunge in oil prices. He had recently embarked on a number of ventures in the West and Asia. Several, he said, had proven quite lucrative.

"Obviously," said Martel with a glance at his surroundings.

Monsieur Antonov only smiled.

"What sort of things are you investing in?"

"The usual," he answered evasively. "Mainly, I've been indulging my passion for art."

"Olivia and I would love to see your collection."

"Perhaps after lunch."

"You should really have a look at her inventory. She has many extraordinary pieces."

"I'd like that very much."

"When?" asked Martel.

"Tomorrow," said Gabriel to the video screens, and a few seconds later Dmitri Antonov said, "I'll drop by tomorrow, if that's convenient."

With that, they adjourned to the table for lunch. Here again, Gabriel had spared no expense and left nothing to chance. Indeed, he had hired the executive chef from a prominent Paris restaurant and flown him privately to Provence for the occasion. Madame Sophie had chosen the menu. Warm glazed potatoes with caviar, tapioca, and herbs; yellowfin tuna ribbons with avocado, spicy radish, and ginger marinade; diver scallops with caramelized cauliflower and a caper-raisin emulsion; black sea bass crusted with nuts and seeds, with a sweet-and-sour jus. Impressed, Martel asked to meet the chef. Madame Sophie, lighting another Gitane, demurred. The chef and his staff, she explained, were never permitted to leave the kitchen.

Over dessert the talk turned to politics. The election in America, the war in Syria, the ISIS terrorist attacks in Europe.

At the mention of Islam, Martel suddenly became animated. France as they once knew it was gone, he snarled. Soon it would be just another outpost in the Islamic Maghreb. Gabriel found it to be a rather convincing performance, though Olivia appeared to think otherwise. Bored, she asked Madame Sophie whether she might have one of her Gitanes.

"Jean-Luc has very strong opinions when it comes to the question of minorities in France," she confided. "I like to remind him that were it not for Arabs and Africans, he would have no one to wash the dishes in his restaurants or change the beds in his hotels."

Madame Sophie, with her expression, made it clear she found the topic distasteful. She asked the Alpha Group servants to bring the coffee. By then, it was approaching five o'clock. Everyone agreed a tour of the paintings would have to wait for another occasion, though they saw several as they made their way slowly through the vast sitting rooms and rose-colored halls, observed by the surveillance cameras.

"Are you really interested in coming to the gallery tomorrow?" asked Olivia as she paused to admire the pair of Venetian canal scenes by Guardi.

"Absolutely," answered Dmitri Antonov.

"I'm free at eleven."

"Afternoon is better," said Gabriel to the video screens, and Dmitri Antonov then explained that he had several important phone calls to make in the morning and would prefer to visit the gallery after lunch. "If that would be convenient."

"It would."

"Monsieur Carnot will make the necessary arrangements. I believe he has your number."

The Antonovs bid farewell to their guests on the portico, which by then was no longer in shadow but ablaze with a fine orange light. A moment later they were standing once more on the terrace, watching the black Range Rovers racing toward the villa on the other side of the Baie de Cavalaire. Presently, Madame Sophie's mobile purred.

"What does it say?" asked her husband.

"It says we were perfect."

"Did they enjoy themselves?"

"Martel is convinced you're an arms dealer masquerading as a legitimate businessman."

"And Olivia?"

"She's looking forward to tomorrow."

Smiling, Dmitri Antonov stripped off his suit and went down to the pool for a swim. Madame Sophie and Monsieur Carnot watched him from the terrace while they finished the last of the rosé. Madame Sophie's phone shivered with another incoming message.

"What now?" asked Monsieur Carnot.

"Apparently, Martel thinks I look like a Jew." She lit another Gitane and smiled. "Saladin said the same thing."

SAINT-TROPEZ, FRANCE

At ten the following morning the Place de l'Ormeau was deserted, save for a man of late middle age washing his hands in a thread of water from the wellhead. Olivia thought she had seen him in the village once or twice before but on closer inspection decided she was mistaken. The paving stones warmed her sandaled feet as she crossed the square to the gallery. Fishing her keys from her handbag, she unlocked the outer wooden door and stepped into the stifling vestibule. Next she opened the high-security glass door and, entering, disabled the alarm. She closed the door behind her. It locked automatically.

The interior of the gallery was dim and cool, a respite from the out-of-doors. In her private office Olivia threw a switch that opened the blinds and security grills. Then, as was her habit, she went upstairs to the exhibition rooms to make certain nothing was missing. The Lichtenstein, Basquiat, and Dubuffet displayed in her window were but the tip of the gallery's inventory. Olivia's substantial professional collection included works by Warhol, Twombly, de Kooning, Gerhard Richter, and

Pollock, along with numerous French and Spanish contemporary artists. She had acquired wisely and developed a reliable clientele among the megarich of the Côte d'Azur—men like Dmitri Antonov, she thought. It was an extraordinary achievement for a woman with no university degree and no formal artistic training. And to think that a few short years earlier she had been managing a little gallery that dispensed the scribblings of local artists to the sweaty tourists who staggered off the cruise ships and motor coaches. Sometimes she allowed herself to think she had arrived at this place as a result of her determination and business acumen, but in truth she knew better than that. It was all Jean-Luc's doing. Olivia was the public face of the gallery and it bore her name, but it was bought and paid for by Jean-Luc Martel. So, for that matter, was she.

After determining that her collection had survived the night intact, she went downstairs and found Monique, her receptionist, preparing a café crème at the automatic maker. She was a skinny, small-breasted girl of twenty-four, a Degas dancer come to life. Evenings, she worked as a hostess in one of Jean-Luc's restaurants. She looked as though she'd had a late night. Where Monique was concerned, that was more often than not the case.

"You?" she asked as the last of the steaming milk gurgled and spat into her cup.

"Please."

Monique handed Olivia the coffee and prepared another for herself. "Any appointments this morning?"

"Aren't you supposed to tell me that?"

Monique made a face.

"Who was it this time?"

"An American. *So* adorable. He's from somewhere called

Virginia." Spoken by Monique, it sounded like the most exotic and sensual place in the world. "He raises horses."

"I thought you hated Americans."

"Of course. But this one is very rich."

"Will you ever see him again?"

"Maybe tonight."

Or maybe not, thought Olivia. She had once been a girl like Monique. Perhaps she still was.

"If you consult your calendar," she said, "I'm sure you'll discover that Herr Müller is coming at eleven."

Monique frowned. "Herr Müller likes to look at my tits."

"Mine, too."

In fact, Herr Müller liked looking at Olivia more than at her paintings. He was not alone. Her looks were a professional asset, but on occasion they were a distraction and a waste of time. Rich men—and some not so rich—made appointments at the gallery just to spend a few minutes in her presence. Some screwed up the nerve to proposition her. Others fled without ever making their true intentions known. She had learned long ago how to project an air of unavailability. While technically single, she was JLM's girl. Everyone in France knew it. It might as well have been stamped on her forehead.

Monique sat down at the glass receptionist's desk. It had only a phone and the appointment calendar. Olivia didn't trust her with much else. All of the gallery's business and administrative affairs she saw to herself, with help from Jean-Luc. Monique was but another work of art, one that if so moved was capable of answering the phone. It was Jean-Luc, not Olivia, who had given her the job at the gallery. Olivia was all but certain they were lovers. She did not resent Monique. In fact, she pitied her a little. It would not end well. It never did.

Herr Müller was ten minutes late in arriving, which was not like him. He was fat and florid and smelled of last night's wine. A recent confrontation with a plastic surgeon in Zurich had left him with an expression of perpetual astonishment. He was interested in a painting by the American artist Philip Guston. A similar work had recently fetched twenty-five million in America. Herr Müller was hoping to acquire Olivia's for fifteen. Olivia turned him down.

"But I must have it!" he exclaimed while staring unabashedly at the front of Olivia's blouse.

"Then you'll have to find another five million."

"Let me sleep on it. In the meantime, don't let anyone else see it."

"Actually, I'm planning to show it this afternoon."

"Demon! Who?"

"Come now, Herr Müller, that would be indiscreet."

"Is it that Antonov character?"

She was silent.

"I went to a party at his villa recently. I barely survived. Others were not so fortunate." He chewed at the inside of his lip. "Sixteen. But that's my final offer."

"I'll take my chances with Monsieur Antonov."

"I knew it!"

At half past twelve Olivia dispatched him into the midday heat. When she returned to her desk she saw that she had received a text message from Jean-Luc. He was boarding his helicopter for a flight to Nice, where he had meetings all afternoon. She tried to text him back but received no reply. She supposed he was already airborne.

She returned the phone to her desk. A few seconds later it rang with an incoming voice call. Olivia didn't recognize the number. Even so, she accepted the call and lifted the phone to her ear.

"Bonjour."

"Madame Watson?"

"Yes."

"This is Nicolas Carnot. We had lunch yesterday at—"

"Yes, of course. How are you?"

"I was wondering whether you still had time to show Monsieur Antonov your collection."

"I've cleared my calendar," she lied. "What time would he like to come?"

"Would two o'clock work?"

"Two would be perfect."

"I'll need to stop by first to have a look around."

"I'm sorry?"

"Monsieur Antonov is careful about his security."

"I assure you, my gallery is quite safe."

There was a silence.

"What time would you like to come?" asked Olivia, exasperated.

"I'm free now if you are."

"Now is fine."

"Perfect. Oh, and one more thing, Madame Watson."

"Yes?"

"Your receptionist."

"Monique? What about her?"

"Give her an errand to run, something that will keep her out of the gallery for a few minutes. Can you do that for me, Madame Watson?"

———

Five minutes elapsed before the receptionist finally emerged from the gallery. She paused in the furnace of the square, her eyes moved left and right. Then she drifted torpidly past Keller's table at the café next door, with her arms hanging like limp long-stemmed flowers at her side. He typed a brief message into his mobile and fired it to the safe house at Ramatuelle. The reply bounced back instantly. Martel's helicopter was east of Cannes. Proceed as planned.

Like a good field operative, Keller had paid his check in advance. Rising, he went to the gallery and placed his thumb heavily upon the bell. There was no answer. Turnabout, he thought, was fair play. He rang the bell a second time. The deadbolts opened with a snap and he went inside.

There was something different about him, Olivia was sure of it. Outwardly, he was the same slick, indifferent creature with whom she had dined at the Antonovs' villa—the man of few words and unspecified duties—but his demeanor had changed. Suddenly, he seemed very sure of himself and the virtue of his cause. Crossing the gallery, he removed his sunglasses and propped them on his head. His smile was cordial but his blue eyes were all business. He addressed her without first offering his hand in greeting.

"I'm afraid there's been a slight change in plan. Monsieur Antonov won't be able to come after all."

"Why not?"

"A small matter that required his immediate attention. Nothing urgent, mind you. No cause for alarm." He said all this in his Corsican-accented French, through the same unthreatening smile.

"So why did you call me? And why," asked Olivia, "are you here?"

"Because some friends of Monsieur Antonov have taken an interest in your gallery and would like to have a word in private."

"What sort of interest?"

"It concerns several of your recent transactions. They were quite lucrative but somewhat unorthodox."

"The transactions of this gallery," she said coolly, "are private."

"Not as private as you think."

Olivia felt her face begin to burn. She walked slowly over to Monique's desk and lifted the receiver from its cradle. Her hand trembled as she dialed.

"Don't bother calling your husband, Olivia. He's not going to answer."

She looked up sharply. He had spoken these words not in French but in British-accented English.

"He's not my husband," she heard herself say.

"Oh, yes, I forgot. He's still in the air," he went on. "Somewhere between Cannes and Nice. But we've taken the additional precaution of blocking all his incoming calls."

"We?"

"British intelligence," he answered calmly. "Not to worry, Olivia, you're in very good hands."

She pressed the phone to her ear and heard the recording of Jean-Luc's voice mail.

"Put the phone down, Olivia, and take a very deep breath. I'm not going to hurt you, I'm here to help. Think of me as your last chance. I'd take it if I were you."

She returned the phone to its cradle.

"There's a good girl," he said.

"Who are you?"

"My name is Nicolas Carnot, and I work for Monsieur Antonov. It's important that you remember that. Now get your handbag and your phone and the keys to that beautiful Range Rover of yours. And please hurry, Olivia. We haven't much time."

The Range Rover was in its usual place, parked illegally outside Jean-Luc's restaurant in the Old Port. Olivia slid behind the wheel and, as directed, drove westward along the Golfe de Saint-Tropez. Twice she asked him to explain why her gallery was of sufficient interest to British intelligence to warrant such an elaborate ruse. Twice he remarked about the scenery and the weather in the manner of Nicolas Carnot, friend of Monsieur Dmitri Antonov.

"How did you learn to speak like that?"

"Like what?"

"A Corsican."

"My Auntie Beatrice was from Corsica. You're about to miss your turn."

"Which way?"

He pointed toward the turnoff for Gassin and Ramatuelle. She lurched the wheel hard to the left and a moment later they were headed south, into the rugged countryside separating the gulf and the Baie de Cavalaire.

"Where are you taking me?"

"To see some friends of Monsieur Antonov, of course."

She surrendered and drove in silence. Neither of them spoke again until after they had passed Ramatuelle. He directed her onto a smaller side road and eventually to the entrance of a villa. The gate was open to receive them. She parked in the forecourt and switched off the engine.

"It's not as nice as Villa Soleil," he said, "but you'll find it quite comfortable."

Suddenly, a man was standing at Olivia's door. She recognized him; she had seen him that morning in the Place de l'Ormeau. He helped her from the Range Rover and with only a movement of his hand guided her toward the entrance of the villa. The man she knew only as Nicolas Carnot—the man who spoke French like a Corsican and English with a posh West End accent—walked beside her.

"Is he from British intelligence, too?"

"Who?"

"The one who opened my door."

"I didn't see anyone."

Olivia turned around, but the man was gone. Perhaps he had been a hallucination. It was the heat, she thought. She was positively faint with it.

As she approached the villa, the door drew back and Dmitri Antonov stepped into the breach. "Olivia!" he exclaimed as though she were his oldest friend in the world. "So sorry to inconvenience you, but I'm afraid it couldn't be helped. Come inside and make yourself at home. Everyone's here. They're quite anxious to finally meet you in the flesh."

He said all this in his Russian-accented English. Olivia wasn't sure if it was real or performance. Indeed, at that moment, she wasn't sure of the ground beneath her feet.

She followed him across the entrance hall and beneath an

archway that gave onto the sitting room. It was comfortably furnished and hung with many canvases.

All were blank.

Olivia's legs seemed to liquefy. Monsieur Antonov steadied her and nudged her forward.

There were three other men present. One was tall and handsome and distinguished and undeniably English. He was saying something quietly in French to a crumpled figure in a tweed coat who looked as though he had been plucked from an antiquarian bookshop. Their conversation fell silent as Olivia made her entry, and their faces turned to her like sunflowers to the dawn. The third man, however, seemed entirely oblivious to her arrival. He was staring at one of the blank canvases, a hand pressed to his chin, his head tilted slightly to one side. The canvas was identical in dimensions to all the others but was propped upon an easel. The man looked comfortable before it, observed Olivia. He was of medium height and build. His hair was cropped short and gray at the temples. His eyes, which were fixed resolutely on the canvas, were an unnatural shade of green.

"I think," he said at last, "this one is my favorite. The draftsmanship is quite extraordinary, and the use of color and light are second to none. I envy his palette."

He blurted all this without pause in French, in an accent that Olivia couldn't quite place. It was a peculiar mixture, a bit of German, a dash of Italian. He was still gazing at the painting. His pose was unchanged.

"The first time I saw it," he went on, "I thought it was truly one of a kind. But I was mistaken. Paintings like this seem to be the specialty of your gallery. In fact, as far as I can tell, you've cornered the market on blank canvases." The green eyes finally turned to her. "Congratulations, Olivia. That's quite an achievement."

"Who are you?"

"I'm a friend of Monsieur Antonov."

"Are you from British intelligence, too?"

"Heavens no! But he is," he said, pointing toward the distinguished-looking Englishman. "In fact, he's the chief of the Secret Intelligence Service, which is sometimes referred to as MI6. His name used to be a state secret, but times have changed. Occasionally, he grants an interview and allows his photograph to be taken. Once upon a time that would have been heresy, but no more."

"And him?" she asked, nodding toward the crumpled figure in tweed.

"French," explained the green-eyed man. "He's the chief of something called the Alpha Group. Perhaps you've heard the name. Its headquarters in Paris were bombed not long ago, and several of his officers lost their lives. As you might expect, he's interested in finding the man who did it. And he'd like you to help him."

"Me?" she asked, incredulous. "How?"

"We'll get to that in a moment. As for my affiliation," he said, "I'm the odd man out. I'm from the place we don't like to talk about."

It was then she was finally able to place his peculiar accent. "You're from Israel."

"I'm afraid so. But back to the matter at hand," he added quickly, "and that's you and your gallery. It's not a real gallery, is it, Olivia? Oh, you sell the occasional painting, like that Guston you were trying to foist on poor Herr Müller this morning for the obscene price of twenty million euros. But mainly it serves as a washing machine that launders the profits of Jean-Luc Martel's real business, which is drugs."

A heavy silence fell over the room.

"This is the point," said the green-eyed man, "where you tell me that your—" He stopped himself. "Excuse me, but I'm a stickler for details. How *do* you refer to Jean-Luc?"

"He's my partner."

"Partner? How unfortunate."

"Why?"

"Because the word *partner* implies a business relationship."

"I think I'd like to call my lawyer."

"If you do, you'll lose the one and only chance you have to save yourself." He paused as if to assess the impact of his words. "Your gallery is a small but important part of a far-flung criminal enterprise. Its business is drugs. Drugs that come mainly from North Africa. Drugs that flow through the hands of the terrorist group that calls itself the Islamic State. Jean-Luc Martel is the distributor of those drugs here in Western Europe. He's in business with ISIS. Wittingly or unwittingly, he's helping to finance their operations. Which means you are, too."

"Good luck proving that in a French courtroom."

He smiled for the first time. It was cold and quick. "A show of bravery," he said with mock admiration, "but still no denial about your husband's business."

"He's not my husband."

"Oh, yes," he said scornfully, "I forgot."

They were the same words the man called Nicolas Carnot had spoken at the art gallery.

"As for calling your lawyer," the Israeli continued, "that won't be necessary. At least not yet. You see, Olivia, there are no police officers in this room. We are intelligence officers. We have nothing against the police, mind you. They have their job to do and we have ours. They solve crimes and make arrests, but our trade is information. You have it, we need it. This is your opening, Olivia. This is your one and only chance. If I were your lawyer, I'd advise you to take it. It's the best deal you're ever going to get."

There was another silence, longer than the last.

"I'm sorry," she said finally, "but I can't help you."

"You can't help us, Olivia, or you won't?"

"I don't know anything about Jean-Luc's business."

"The forty-eight blank canvases I found in the Geneva Freeport say you do. They were shipped there by Galerie Olivia Watson. Which means you will be the one to face charges, not him. And what do you think your *partner* will do then? Will he ride to your rescue? Will he step in front of the bullet for you?" He shook his head slowly. "No, Olivia, he won't. From everything I've learned about Jean-Luc Martel, he isn't that sort of man."

She made no response.

"So what will it be, Olivia? Will you help us?"

She shook her head.

"Why not?"

"Because if I do," she said evenly, "Jean-Luc will kill me."

Again he smiled. This time it appeared genuine.

"Did I say something funny?" she asked.

"No, Olivia, you told me the truth." The green eyes left her face and settled once more on the blank canvas. "What do you see when you look at it?"

"I see something Jean-Luc made me do in order to keep my gallery."

"Interesting interpretation. Do you know what I see?"

"What?"

"I see you without Jean-Luc."

"How do I look?"

"Come here, Olivia." He stepped away from the canvas. "See for yourself."

The blank canvases were removed from the walls and the easel, and a dark-haired woman of perhaps thirty-five silently served cold drinks. Olivia was invited to sit. In turn, the dapper Englishman and his crumpled French associate were properly introduced. Their names were familiar enough. So was the sharply angled face of the green-eyed Israeli. Olivia was all but certain she had seen it somewhere before, but couldn't decide where it had been. He introduced himself only as Gideon and paced the perimeter of the room slowly while everyone else sat perspiring in the unremitting heat. A rotating fan beat monotonously and to no effect in the corner; enormous flies moved like buzzards in and out of the open French doors. Suddenly, the Israeli ceased pacing and with a lightning movement of his left hand snatched one from the air.

"Did you enjoy it?" he asked.

"What's that?"

"Seeing your face in magazines and on billboards."

"It's not as easy as it looks."

"It's not glamorous?"

"Not always."

"What about the parties and the fashion shows?"

"For me, the fashion shows were work. And the parties," she said, "got rather boring after a while."

He flung the corpse of the fly into the glare of the garden and, turning, appraised Olivia at length. "So why did you choose such a life?"

"I didn't. It chose me."

"You were discovered?"

"In a manner of speaking."

"It happened when you were sixteen, did it not?"

"You've obviously read my clippings."

"With great interest," he admitted. "You auditioned to be an extra in a period film that was being shot along the Norfolk Coast. You didn't get the part, but someone on the production staff suggested you should consider modeling. And so you decided to forsake your studies and go to New York to pursue a career. By the time you were eighteen, you were one of the hottest models in Europe." He paused, then asked, "Did I leave anything out?"

"A great deal, actually."

"Such as?"

"New York."

"So why don't you pick up the story there," he said. "In New York."

It was hell, she told him. After signing on with a well-known agency, she was put up in an apartment on the West Side of Manhattan with eight other girls who slept in rotating shifts on bunk beds. During the day she was sent out on "go-sees" with potential clients and young photographers who were trying to break into the business. If she was lucky, the photographer would agree to take a few test shots that she could place in her portfolio. If not, she would leave empty-handed and return to the cramped apartment to fend off the roaches and the ants. At night she and the other girls hired themselves out to nightclubs to earn a bit of spending money. Twice Olivia was sexually assaulted. The second attack left her with a black eye that prevented her from working for nearly a month.

"But you persevered," said the Israeli.

"I suppose I did."

"What happened after New York?"

"Freddie happened."

Freddie, she explained, was Freddie Mansur, the hottest agent in the business and one of its most notorious predators. Freddie brought Olivia to Paris and into his bed. He also gave her drugs—weed, cocaine, barbiturates to help her sleep. As her caloric intake fell to near-starvation levels, her weight plummeted. Soon she was skin and bones. When she was hungry, she smoked a cigarette or blew a line. Coke and tobacco: Freddie called it the model diet.

"And the funny thing is, it worked. The thinner I got, the better I looked. Inside I was slowly dying, but the camera loved me. And so did the advertisers."

"You were a supermodel?"

"Not even close, but I did quite well. And so did Freddie. He took one-third of my earnings. And one-third of the salaries of all the other girls he was handling at the time."

"And sleeping with?"

"Let's just say our relationship wasn't monogamous."

By the time she was twenty-six, the cadaverous drug-addled

look with which she was associated went out of fashion, and her star began to fade. Much of her work took place on the runway, where her tall frame and long limbs remained much in demand. But her thirtieth birthday was a watershed. There was before thirty and after thirty, she explained, and after thirty the work all but dried up. She hung on for three more years until even Freddie advised her it was time to leave the business. He did so gently at first, and when she resisted he severed business and romantic ties with her and threw her into the street. She was thirty-three years old, uneducated, jobless, and washed up.

"But you were rich," said the Israeli.

"Hardly."

"What about all the money you made?"

"Money comes and money goes."

"Drugs?"

"And other things."

"You liked the drugs?"

"I needed them, there's a difference. I'm afraid Freddie left me with a few expensive habits."

"So what did you do?"

"I did what any woman in my position would have done. I packed my bags and went to Saint-Tropez."

With what remained of her money she took a villa in the hills—"It was a shack, really, not far from here"—and purchased a motor scooter secondhand. She spent her days on the beach at Pampelonne and her nights in the clubs and discos of the village. Naturally, she encountered many men there—Arabs, Russians, silver-haired Eurotrash. She allowed a few to take her to bed in exchange for gifts and money, which made her feel very much like a prostitute. Mainly, she searched for a suitable mate, someone to keep her in the style to which she had become accustomed. Someone who wasn't too repulsive. In short order, she concluded that she had come to the wrong place, and with her money dwindling she took a job working in a small art gallery owned by an expatriate Brit. Then, quite by chance, she met the man who would change her life.

"Jean-Luc Martel?"

She smiled in spite of herself.

"Where did you meet him?"

"At a party—where else? Jean-Luc was always at a party. Jean-Luc *was* the party."

In point of fact, she explained, it was not the first time they had met. The first time had been at Fashion Week in Milan, but Jean-Luc had been with his wife then and had barely looked Olivia in the eye when shaking her hand. But by the time of their second meeting, he was a recovering widower and very much in play. And Olivia fell madly and instantly in love with him.

"I was Rosemary and he was Dick. I was absolutely helpless with love."

"Rosemary and Dick?"

"Rosemary Hoyt and Dick Diver. They're the characters in—"

"I know who they are, Olivia. And you flatter yourself with the comparison."

His words were like a slap to her face. Her cheeks flamed with color.

"Did he give you gifts and money like the others?"

"Jean-Luc didn't have to pay for his girls. He was incredibly good-looking and fabulously successful. He was . . . Jean-Luc."

"And what do you suppose he saw in you?"

"I used to ask him the same thing."

"What was his answer?"

"He thought we made a good team."

"So it was a partnership from the beginning?"

"More or less."

"Did you ever discuss marriage?"

"I did, but Jean-Luc wasn't interested. We used to have the most terrible arguments about it. I told him that I wasn't going to waste the best years of my life being his concubine, that I wanted to marry him and have children. In the end we reached a compromise."

"What sort of compromise?"

"He gave me something in lieu of marriage and children."

"What was that?"

"Galerie Olivia Watson."

Olivia was used to men staring at her. Breathless men. Panting men. Men with damp, desirous eyes. Men who would do anything, pay almost any price, to have her in their beds. The three men arrayed before her now—the British spymaster, the French secret policeman, and the Israeli with no stated affiliation but a vaguely familiar face—were staring at her, too, but for a decidedly different reason. They seemed impervious to the spell of her looks. For them, she was not an object to be admired; she was a means to an end. An end they had not yet seen fit to reveal. She was not at all sure they liked her. All the same, she was relieved that such men still existed. A career in the modeling industry, and ten years in the make-believe world of Saint-Tropez, had left her with a rather low opinion of the species.

Galerie Olivia Watson . . .

The name, she told them, was Jean-Luc's idea, not hers. She had wanted to hang the proven moniker of JLM over the gallery's door, but Jean-Luc had insisted it bear her name rather than his. He gave her the money to purchase the fine old building on the Place de l'Ormeau and then financed the acquisition of a world-class collection of contemporary art. Olivia had wanted to acquire her inventory slowly and modestly, with a special emphasis on Mediterranean artists. But Jean-Luc wouldn't hear of it. He didn't do slow and modest, she explained. Only big and flashy. The gallery opened with a degree of glitz and glamour only JLM could provide. After that, he stepped aside and gave Olivia complete artistic and financial control.

"But only to a point," she said.

"What does that mean?" asked the Israeli. "One has complete control, or one doesn't. There's no middle ground."

"There is where Jean-Luc is involved."

He invited her to elaborate.

"Jean-Luc handled the gallery's books."

"You didn't find that odd?"

"Actually, I was relieved. I was a former fashion model, and he was a wildly successful businessman."

"How long did it take you to discover that something wasn't right?"

"Two years. Maybe a little longer."

"What happened?"

"I started looking at the gallery's records without Jean-Luc standing over my shoulder."

"And what did you find?"

"That I was acquiring and selling more works than I ever imagined possible."

"Your gallery was doing a brisk business?"

"That's putting it mildly. In fact, in only its second year in operation, Galerie Olivia Watson earned more than three hundred million euros in profit. Most of the sales were totally private and involved paintings I'd never seen."

"What did you do?"

"I confronted him."

"And how did he respond?"

"He told me to mind my own business." She paused, then added, "No pun intended."

"Did you?"

She hesitated before nodding slowly.

"Why?"

When she offered no explanation, he provided one for her.

"Because your life was perfect and you didn't want to do anything to upset it."

"All of us make compromises in life."

"But not all of us find refuge in the arms of a drug trafficker." He paused for a moment to allow the words to wound her sufficiently. "You did know that Jean-Luc's real business was narcotics, didn't you?"

"I still don't."

The Israeli greeted her answer with justifiable contempt. "We haven't much time, Olivia. It would be better not to waste it with pointless denials."

There was a silence. Into it crept the Englishman who called himself Nicolas Carnot. He went to the bookshelf and, craning his neck sideways, removed a volume with a tattered cover. It was *The Sheltering Sky* by the American novelist Paul Bowles. He tucked the book beneath his arm and with a glance at Olivia slipped out of the room again. She looked at the Israeli, who returned her gaze without judgment.

"You were about to tell me," he said at last, "when you became aware of the fact that your domestic and business partner was a drug trafficker."

"I heard rumors, just like everyone else."

"But unlike everyone else, you were in a unique position to know whether they were true or not. After all, you were the nominal owner of an art gallery that served as one of his most effective money-laundering fronts."

She smiled. "How naive of you."

"Why?"

"Because Jean-Luc is very good at keeping secrets." Then she added, "Almost as good as you and your friends."

"We are professionals."

"So is Jean-Luc," she said darkly.

"Have you ever asked him?"

"Whether he's a drug dealer?"

"Yes."

"Just once. He laughed. And then he told me never to ask him about his business again."

"Did you?"

"Never."

"Why not?"

"Because I'd heard other rumors," she said. "Rumors about what happened to people who crossed him."

"And yet you stayed," he pointed out.

"I *stayed*," she retorted, "because I was afraid to leave."

"Afraid to leave, or afraid you would lose your gallery?"

"Both," she admitted.

A flicker of a smile appeared on his lips and then vanished. "I admire your honesty, Olivia."

"If nothing else?"

"Like Nicolas Carnot, I'm inclined to reserve all judgments. Especially when there's valuable intelligence at stake."

"What sort of intelligence?"

"The organization of Jean-Luc's business, for example. You must have managed to collect a fair amount of information about how the company is structured. It's rather opaque, to say the least. Looking at it from the outside, we've managed to identify some of the players. There's a chief for each division—the restaurants, the hotels, the retail end of things—but try as we might, we haven't been able to identify the chief of JLM's illicit narcotics unit."

"You're joking."

"Only a little. Is he one man or two? Is it Jean-Luc himself?"

She said nothing.

"Time, Olivia. We haven't much time. We need to know how Jean-Luc manages his drug business. How he gives his orders. How he insulates himself so the police can't touch him. It doesn't happen by osmosis or telekinesis. Somewhere there's a trusted figure who handles his interests. Someone who can move in and out of his orbit without attracting suspicion. Someone he communicates with only in person, in a quiet voice, in a room where no phones are present. Surely you know who this man is, Olivia. Perhaps you're acquainted. Perhaps you're a friend of his."

"Not a friend," she said after a moment. "But I do know who he is. And I know what would happen to me if I were to tell you his name. He would kill me. And not even Jean-Luc would be able to stop him."

"No one's going to harm you, Olivia."

She regarded him skeptically. He feigned moderate offense.

"Think about the extraordinary lengths we went to in order to bring you here today. Haven't we demonstrated our professionalism? Haven't we proven ourselves worthy of your trust?"

"And when you're gone? Who will protect me then?"

"You won't need protection," he responded, "because you'll be gone, too."

"Where will I be?"

"That's up to you and your countryman to decide," he said with an inclination of his head toward the chief of British intelligence. "Oh, I suppose I could offer you a nice flat overlooking the sea in Tel Aviv, but I suspect you'd be more comfortable in England."

"What will I do for money?"

"Run an art gallery, of course."

"Which one?"

"Galerie Olivia Watson." He smiled. "Despite the fact that your professional inventory was purchased with drug money, we're prepared to let you keep it. With two exceptions," he added.

"Which ones?"

"The Guston and the Basquiat. Monsieur Antonov would like to write you a check for fifty million for both, which should allay any concerns Jean-Luc might have about how you spent this afternoon. And don't worry," he added. "Unlike Monsieur Antonov, the money is quite real."

"How generous of you," she said. "But you still haven't told me what this is about."

"It's about Paris," he answered. "And London. And Antwerp. And Amsterdam. And Stuttgart. And Washington. And it's about a hundred other attacks you've never heard about."

"Jean-Luc is no angel, but he's not a terrorist, either."

"True. But we believe he's in business with one, which means he's helping to finance his attacks. But I'm afraid that's all I'm going to say on the matter. The less you know, the better. That's the way it works in our trade. And all you need to know is that you're being given the opportunity of a lifetime. It's a chance to start over. Think of it as a blank canvas upon which you can paint any picture you want. And all it will cost you is a name." He smiled and asked, "Do we have a deal, Ms. Wilson?"

"Watson. My name is Olivia Watson. And, yes," she said after a moment, "I believe we have a deal."

They talked late into the afternoon, as the heat relented and the shadows grew long and thin in the garden and in the grove of silvery olive trees that climbed the next hillside. The circumstances of her repatriation to the United Kingdom. The manner in which she should conduct herself in Jean-Luc's presence during the days to come. The procedures she should follow in the case of some unforeseen emergency. The green-eyed Israeli referred to this as the break-the-glass plan and warned Olivia that it was to be engaged only in the event of extreme danger, for it would necessarily wipe out a great deal of time and effort and waste untold millions in operational expenses.

Only then did he ask Olivia for the name. The name of the man whom Jean-Luc trusted to run his multibillion-euro narcotics empire. The dirty side of JLM Enterprises, as the Israeli called it. The side that made everything else—the restaurants, the hotels, the boutiques and shops, the art gallery in the Place de l'Ormeau—possible. The first time Olivia uttered it, she did so softly, as though a hand were squeezing her throat. The Israeli asked her to repeat the name and, hearing it clearly, exchanged a long, speculative glance with Paul Rousseau. At length, Rousseau nodded slowly and then resumed contemplating his dormant pipe while on the other side of the room Nicolas Carnot returned the volume of Bowles to its original place on the shelf.

After that, there was no more discussion of drugs or terror or the real reason why Olivia had been brought to the modest villa outside Ramatuelle. Monsieur Antonov materialized, all smiles and Russian-accented bonhomie, and together they arranged the transfer of fifty million euros from his accounts to the gallery's. A bottle of champagne was opened to celebrate the sale. Olivia did not drink from the glass that was placed in her hand. The Israeli did not touch his glass, either. He was, thought Olivia, a man of admirable discipline.

Shortly after six o'clock, Nicolas Carnot returned her mobile phone. Precisely when he had taken it Olivia did not know. She reckoned he had plucked it from her handbag during the drive from Saint-Tropez. Glancing at the screen, she saw several text messages that had come through during her interrogation. The last was from Jean-Luc. It had arrived only a moment earlier. It said he was about to board his helicopter and would be home within the hour.

Olivia looked up, alarmed. "What should I say to him?"

"What would you usually say?" asked the Israeli.

"I'd tell him to have a safe trip."

"Then please do so. And you might want to mention that you have a fifty-million-euro surprise for him. That should brighten his mood. But don't give away too much. We wouldn't want to spoil it."

Olivia thumbed a response into the text box and held it up for him to see.

"Nicely done."

She tapped it into the ether.

"Time for you to be leaving," said the Israeli. "We wouldn't want your carriage to turn into a pumpkin, would we?"

Outside, a few windblown clouds were moving swiftly across the evening sky. Nicolas Carnot spoke only French during the drive south to the Baie de Cavalaire, and only of Monsieur Antonov and the paintings. They were to be delivered to Villa Soleil immediately upon receipt of the money. Madame Sophie, he said, had already chosen the spot where they would hang.

"She loathes me," said Olivia.

"She's not so bad once you get to know her."

"Is she French?"

"What else would she be?"

The Antonovs lived on the western side of the bay, Jean-Luc and Olivia in the east. As they were nearing the little Spar market on the corner of the boulevard Saint-Michel, Monsieur Carnot instructed her to stop. He squeezed her hand tightly and in English assured her that she had nothing to fear, that she was doing the right thing. Then he bade her a pleasant evening and, smiling as though nothing unusual had occurred that afternoon, climbed out. When she saw him last it was in the rearview mirror, speeding in the opposite direction atop a small motorcycle. Fleeing the scene of a crime, she thought.

Olivia continued eastward along the rim of the bay and a few minutes later entered the luxurious villa she shared with the man whom she had just betrayed. In the kitchen she poured herself a large glass of rosé and carried it outside onto the terrace. Through the sharp glare of the setting sun she could make out the faint outlines of Monsieur Antonov's monstrous villa.

Presently, her mobile phone trembled. She stared at the screen. HOME IN FIVE . . . WHAT'S THE SURPRISE? "The surprise," she said aloud, "is that your Russian friend and his bitch of a wife just wrote me a check for fifty million euros." She said it again and again, until even she believed it was true.

At 11:45 the following morning, the sum of fifty million euros appeared in the account of Galerie Olivia Watson, 9 Place de l'Ormeau, Saint-Tropez, France. The money did not have to travel far, as both sender and recipient did their banking at HSBC on the boulevard Haussmann in Paris. By midafternoon it was resting comfortably in a renowned Swiss bank in Geneva, in an account controlled by JLM Enterprises. And at five o'clock, two paintings—one by Guston, the other by Basquiat—were delivered by unmarked van to Villa Soleil. Olivia Watson followed in her black Range Rover. In the entrance hall she passed Christopher Keller, who was on his way out. He kissed her lavishly on both cheeks, commented on her appearance, which was dazzling, and then climbed onto his Peugeot Satelis motorbike. A moment later he was racing westward along the shore of the Mediterranean.

It was nearly dusk by the time he reached the outskirts of Marseilles. The violent drug gangs thrived in the city's northern banlieues, especially in the housing projects of Bassens and Paternelle, but Keller approached through the more tranquil suburbs to the east. The Tunnel Prado-Carénage delivered him to the Old Port, and from there he made his way to the rue Grignan. Slender and straight as a ruler, it was lined with the likes of Boss, Vuitton, and Armani. There was even a JLM jewelry boutique. Keller swore he could detect the sour odor of hashish as he passed.

As he continued across the city center, into the *quartier* of Marseilles known as Le Camas, the streets turned dirty and mean, and the shops and cafés catered to a decidedly immigrant and working-class clientele. One such enterprise, located on the ground floor of a graffiti-splattered building overlooking the Place Jean Jaurès, peddled discount electronic goods and mobile phones to a largely Moroccan and Algerian customer base. Its proprietor, however, was a Frenchman named René Devereaux. Devereaux owned a number of other small businesses in Marseilles—all of which were cash-oriented, some in the category loosely defined as adult entertainment—but the electronics shop served as something like his operational headquarters. His office was on the second floor of the building. The room contained no telephone or electronic devices of any kind, a curious set of circumstances for a man who purportedly sold such modern conveniences for a living. René Devereaux didn't care much for the telephone, and it was said that he had never once personally sent an e-mail or text message. He communicated with his business associates and subordinates only in person, oftentimes in the gritty square or at a streetside table at Au Petit Nice, a reasonably pleasant café located a few paces from his shop.

Keller knew all this because René Devereaux was a prominent figure in the world he had once inhabited. Everyone in the French criminal underground knew that Devereaux's real business was drug trafficking. Not just street-level trafficking, but trafficking on a continent-wide scale. The French police were likely aware of it, too, but Devereaux, unlike many of his competitors, had never spent a single day behind bars. He was a made man, an untouchable. Until tonight, thought Keller. For it was René Devereaux's name that Olivia Watson had spoken in the safe house outside Ramatuelle. Devereaux was the one who made the trains run on time, the one who moved the hashish from the docks of southern Europe to the streets of Paris and Amsterdam and Brussels. The one, thought Keller, who knew all of Jean-Luc Martel's secrets. They would have only one chance to get him cleanly. Fortunately, they had at their disposal some of the best field operatives in the business.

Keller left the motorbike at the edge of the Place Jean Jaurès and walked to Devereaux's shop. Peering at the merchandise in the cluttered display window he saw two men, both French in appearance, observing him from their outpost behind the counter. On the second floor, light burned behind the shuttered French door that gave onto the crumbling balcony.

Keller turned away and continued along the street for about fifty meters before stopping next to a parked van. Giancomo, Don Orsati's errand boy, sat behind the wheel. Two other Orsati operatives were crouched in the rear cargo compartment, smoking nervously. Giancomo, however, appeared outwardly calm. Keller suspected it was for his benefit.

"When was the last time you saw him?"

"About twenty minutes ago. He stepped onto the balcony to have a cigarette."

"Are you sure he's still in there?"

"We have a man watching the back of the building."

"Where are the others?"

The young Corsican nodded toward the Place Jean Jaurès. The square was crowded with residents of the *quartier*, many in the traditional clothing of Africa or the Arab world. Even Keller couldn't spot the don's men.

He looked at Giancomo. "No mistakes, do you hear me? Otherwise, you're liable to start a war. And you know how the don feels about wars."

"Wars are good for the don's business."

"Not when he's a combatant."

"Don't worry, I'm not a little boy anymore. Besides, I have this." Giancomo tugged at the talisman around his neck. It was identical to Keller's. "She sends her best, by the way."

"Did she say anything else?"

"Something about a woman."

"What about her?"

Giancomo shrugged. "You know how the *signadora* is. She talks in riddles."

Keller smoked a cigarette while walking to Au Petit Nice. Inside it was bedlam—Marseilles was playing Lyon—but there were a few tables to be had outside in the street. At one sat a man of medium build with dense silvery hair and thick black spectacles. At an adjacent table two dark-eyed men in their twenties were watching the pedestrians moving along the pavements with unusual intensity. Keller walked over to the silver-haired man and, uninvited, sat down. There was a bottle of pastis and a single glass. Keller signaled the waiter and requested a second.

"You know," he said in French, "you really should drink some."

"It tastes like licorice-flavored gasoline," replied Gabriel. He watched two robed men walking arm-in-arm in the street. "I can't believe we're back here again."

"Au Petit Nice?"

"Marseilles," said Gabriel.

"It was inevitable. When one is attempting to penetrate a European drug network, all roads lead to Marseilles." Keller watched the pedestrians, too. "Do you suppose Rousseau was true to his word?"

"Why wouldn't he be?"

"Because he's a spy. Which means he lies as a matter of course."

"You're a spy, too."

"But not long ago, I was employed by Don Anton Orsati. The same Anton Orsati," added Keller, "who's about to help us with a little dirty work tonight. And if Rousseau and his friends from the Alpha Group happen to be watching, it will place the don, peace be upon him, in a rather ticklish position."

"Rousseau wants nothing to do with what's about to happen here. As for the don," Gabriel went on, "helping us with this little piece of dirty work, as you so callously refer to it, is the best decision he's made since hiring you."

"How so?"

"Because after tonight no one will be able to lay a finger on him. He'll be immune."

"You think like a criminal."

"One has to in our line of work."

The waiter delivered the second glass. Keller filled it with pastis while Gabriel consulted his mobile phone.

"Any problems?"

"Madame Sophie and Monsieur Antonov are quarreling over where to hang the new paintings."

"And they were doing so well."

"Yes," said Gabriel vaguely as he returned the phone to his jacket pocket.

"Think they're going to make it?"

"I have my doubts."

Keller drank some of the pastis. "So what do you intend to do with all those paintings when the operation is over?"

"I have a feeling Monsieur Antonov will discover his Jewish roots and make a rather high-profile donation to the Israel Museum."

"And the fifty million euros you gave to Olivia?"

"I didn't *give* her anything. I purchased two paintings from her gallery."

"That," said Keller, "is a distinction without a difference."

"It's a rather small price to pay if it leads us to Saladin."

"If," said Keller.

"Is it my imagination," said Gabriel, "or is there something between you and—"

"It's your imagination."

"She's a very pretty girl. And when this is all over, she's going to be quite well off."

"I try to stay away from girls who latch onto rich French drug dealers."

"Are you forgetting what you used to do for a living?"

Frowning, Keller drank more of the pastis. "So Monsieur Antonov is Jewish?"

"Apparently so."

"I would have never guessed."

Gabriel shrugged indifferently.

"I'm a little Jewish. Did I ever mention that?"

"You might have."

A silence fell between them. Gabriel stared morosely into the street.

"I can't believe we're back here again."

"It won't be much longer."

Keller watched two men climb from the back of the van and enter the electronics shop owned by René Devereaux. Then he glanced at his watch.

"About five minutes. Maybe less."

From their exterior table at Au Petit Nice, Keller and Gabriel had only an obstructed view of what came next. A few seconds after the two men entered the shop, several flashes of light spilled from the display window into the street. They were faint—in fact, they might have been mistaken for the flicker of a television—and there was no sound at all. At least none that reached the noisy café. After that, the shop went entirely dark, with the exception of a small neon sign in the door that read FERMÉ. Pedestrians flowed past along the pavement as though nothing were out of the ordinary.

Keller's eyes returned to the van, where Giancomo was removing a large rectangular cardboard box from the rear compartment. It was an oddly shaped box, manufactured to Don Orsati's exacting standards by a paper-products factory on Corsica. It was quite obviously empty, for Giancomo had no trouble conveying it across the street and through the front door of the shop. But a few minutes later, when the box reappeared, it was borne by the two men who had entered the shop first, with Giancomo holding one side like a pallbearer. The two men inserted the box into the back of the van and crawled in after it while Giancomo reclaimed his place behind the wheel. Then the van slid away from the curb, rounded the corner, and was gone. From inside Au Petit Nice there arose a loud cheer. Marseilles had scored a goal against Lyon.

"Not bad," said Gabriel.

Keller checked the time. "Four minutes, twelve seconds."

"Unacceptable by Office standards, but more than adequate for tonight."

"You sure you don't want to join in the fun?"

"I've had enough to last a lifetime. But do send the don my best," said Gabriel. "And tell him the check is in the mail."

With that, Keller departed. A moment later, straddling the Peugeot Satelis, he flashed past Au Petit Nice, where a man with dense silver hair and thick black spectacles sat alone, wondering how long it would be before Jean-Luc Martel discovered that the chief of his illicit narcotics division was missing.

C eline was a Baia Atlantica 78 with three cabins, an MTV diesel engine capable of producing speeds of fifty-four knots, and a long slender prow that could accommodate a small helicopter. Keller, however, reached the vessel by less conspic-uous means—namely, a Zodiac dinghy that had been left for him at an isolated marina in the Rhône estuary, near the town of Saintes-Maries-de-la-Mer. He tied the craft to the aft swim platform and climbed up to the main salon, where he found Don Orsati watching the Marseilles-Lyon match on the satellite television. Dressed as he was now, in his simple Corsican cloth-ing and dusty sandals, he looked distinctly out of place amid the luxurious leather-and-wood fittings. Giancomo was on the bridge with the pilot.

"Marseilles scored again," said the don, disconsolate. He pointed the remote at the screen, and it turned to black.

Keller looked around the interior of the salon. "I expected something a bit more modest."

"I'm too old to be moving around the Mediterranean in the belly of a fishing trawler. Besides, you'll be glad to have twenty-four meters of boat beneath you later tonight. It's supposed to blow."

"Who does it belong to?"

"A friend of a friend."

"And the pilot?"

"He's mine."

Keller looked down and for the first time noticed several drops of drying blood.

"He had a gun on the desk when they went in," explained the don. "He took one in the shoulder."

"Is he going to live?"

"I'm afraid so."

"Has he seen your face?"

"Not yet."

"Did you bring a hammer?"

"A nice one," said the don.

"Where's Devereaux?"

"In the single. I didn't want him to make a mess in one of the masters."

Keller looked at the floor again. "Someone really should clean this up."

"Not me," said the don. "I can't stand the sight of blood."

One of the don's men was standing watch outside the door of the single. There was no sound from within.

"Is he conscious?" asked Keller.

"See for yourself."

Keller went in and closed the door behind him. The room was in darkness; it smelled of sweat and fear and faintly of blood. He switched on the built-in reading lamp and aimed the cone of light toward the figure stretched motionless upon the twin bed. Silver duct tape obscured the eyes and mouth. The hands were bound and secured to the torso, the legs and ankles were trussed. Keller scrutinized the wound to the right shoulder. There had been a substantial amount of blood loss, but for now the flow had stopped. Even so, the bedding was drenched. The friend of a friend, thought Keller, would need a new mattress when this was over.

He tore the duct tape from the eyes. René Devereaux blinked rapidly several times. Then, when Keller leaned into the light, showing Devereaux his face, the drug trafficker recoiled in fear. It seemed their acquaintance was mutual.

"Bonsoir, René. Thanks for dropping by. How's the shoulder?"

The eyes narrowed, the fear evaporated. Devereaux was trying to send the Englishman from Corsica a message, that he was not a man to be shot, kidnapped, and bound like a game bird. Keller removed the duct tape from Devereaux's mouth, thus allowing him to give voice to such sentiments.

"You're a dead man. You and that fat Corsican you work for."

"Are you referring to Don Orsati?"

"Fuck Don Orsati."

"Those are three very unwise words. I wonder whether you would dare to say them to the don's face."

"I would shit on the don. And the rest of his family."

"Would you, indeed?"

Keller went out. To the Corsican standing outside the door he said, "Ask his holiness to come down for a minute."

"He's watching the match."

"I'm sure he'll be able to tear himself away," said Keller. "And bring me the hammer."

The Corsican went up the companionway, and a moment later, with some difficulty, Don Orsati came down. Keller ushered him into the cabin and displayed him for René Devereaux to see. The don smiled at Devereaux's obvious discomfort.

"Monsieur Devereaux has something he wishes to tell you," said Keller. "Go ahead, René. Please tell Don Orsati what you said to me a moment ago."

Greeted by silence, Keller showed the don out. Then he stood menacingly over the captive drug trafficker. "Suffice it to say, you have a narrow window of opportunity. You can tell me what I want to know, or I can explain to the don all the naughty things you said about him and his beloved family. And then . . ." Keller held up his hands to indicate the uncertainty of Devereaux's fate under such an emotionally charged scenario.

"Since when have you been in the information business?" asked Devereaux.

"Since I made a career change. I'm working for British intelligence now. Haven't you heard, René?"

"You? A British spy? I don't believe it."

"Sometimes I don't believe it, either. But it happens to be true. And you're going to help me. You're going to be a confidential source, and I'm going to be your control officer."

"You can't be serious."

"Consider your current circumstances. They are as serious as it gets. So is our mission. You're going to help me find the man who's been orchestrating all the terrorist attacks here in Europe and in America."

"How am I going to do that? I'm a drug dealer, for God's sake."

"I'm glad we cleared that up. But you're no ordinary drug dealer, are you? *Dealer* is too small a word for what you do. You run an entire global network from that dump on the Place Jean Jaurès. And you do it," said Keller, "for Jean-Luc Martel."

"Who?" asked Devereaux.

"Jean-Luc Martel. The one with all the restaurants and the hotels and the hair."

"And the pretty English girlfriend," said Devereaux.

"So you *do* know him."

"Sure. I used to go to his first restaurant in Marseilles. He was a nobody then. Now he's a big star."

"Because of drugs," said Keller. "Hashish, to be specific. Hashish that comes from Morocco. Hashish that you distribute throughout Europe. Martel's empire would collapse if it wasn't for the hashish. But you would never dream of cutting him out, because that would mean finding a new method of laundering five or ten billion a year in drug profits. Your so-called legitimate businesses might be enough to make you look reasonably respectable to the French tax authorities, but there's no way they could handle all the profits from a global narcotics network. For that, you need a real business conglomerate. A conglomerate that takes in hundreds of millions of dollars a year in cash receipts. A conglomerate that acquires and develops large tracts of real estate."

"And buys and sells paintings." After a silence, Devereaux added, "I knew she was trouble the first time I met her."

"Who?"

"That English bitch."

Keller balled his right hand into a fist and drove it with all his strength into Devereaux's blood-soaked shoulder.

"But back to the matter at hand," he said while the Frenchman writhed on the bed in agony. "You're going to tell me everything you know about Jean-Luc Martel. The names of your suppliers in Morocco. The routes by which you bring the drugs into Europe. The methods you use for inserting the money into the financial bloodstream of JLM Enterprises. All of it, René."

"And if I do?"

"We're going to make a video," said Keller.

"And if I don't?"

"You're going to get the JLM treatment. And I'm not talking about a nice dinner or a night in a luxury hotel suite."

Devereaux managed a smile. Then, from deep within his throat, he produced a rich, gelatinous ball of phlegm and spat it into Keller's face. With a corner of the bedding, Keller calmly wiped away the mess before going out to retrieve the hammer from the Corsican. He struck Devereaux with it several times, concentrating his efforts on the right shoulder and avoiding the head and face entirely. Then he went up the companionway to the main salon, where he found Don Orsati watching the football match.

"Was it something he said or didn't say?"

"It was something he did," answered Keller.

"Was there blood?"

"A little."

"I'm glad you waited until I left. I can't stand the sight of blood." A thunderous cheer spilled from the television.

"It's a rout," said the don gloomily.

"Yes," answered Keller. "Let us hope."

Christopher Keller made three more trips to the smallest of *Celine*'s cabins—one at eleven, a second shortly after midnight, and a lengthy visit beginning at half past one that left René Devereaux, a hardened Marseilles criminal with much blood on his hands, weeping uncontrollably and begging for mercy. Keller bestowed it, but only on one condition. Devereaux was going to tell him everything, on camera. Otherwise, Keller was going to break every bone in Devereaux's body, slowly, with care and forethought and pauses for refreshment and reflection.

He had made a great deal of progress toward that eventuality already. Devereaux's right shoulder, in which a bullet was lodged, had suffered numerous fractures. Additionally, the right elbow was fractured, as was the left. Both hands were in deplorable condition, and the injury to the right knee, were it allowed to heal properly, would likely have left Devereaux with a permanent limp to match Saladin's.

Moving him to the salon, where a camera had been mounted atop a tripod, proved to be a challenge. Giancomo pulled him up the companionway while Keller pushed from beneath, giving much-needed support to the ruined leg. Cognac was provided, along with a powerful over-the-counter French pain medication that could make one forget a missing limb. Keller helped Devereaux into a bright yellow watch jacket and with a comb tidied up his lank, thinning hair. Then he switched on the camera and, after scrutinizing the shot carefully, posed his first question.

"What is your name?"

"René Devereaux."

"What do you do for a living?"

"I own an electronics shop on the Place Jean Jaurès."

"What is the real nature of your work?"

"Drugs."

"Where did you first meet Jean-Luc Martel?"

"At a restaurant in Marseilles."

"Who owned the restaurant?"

"Philippe Renard."

"What was Renard's real business?"

"Drugs."

"Where is Philippe Renard now?"

"Dead."

"Who killed him?"

"Jean-Luc Martel."

"How did he kill him?"

"With a hammer."

"What does Jean-Luc Martel do now?"

"He owns several restaurants, hotels, and retail businesses."

"What is his real business?"

"Drugs," said René Devereaux.

———

They put in at Ajaccio at half past nine. From there it was only a pleasant walk around the curving shoreline of the gulf to the airport. The next flight for Marseilles departed at noon. Keller arrived at eleven fifteen, having stopped for a late breakfast and to purchase a change of clothing. He dressed in an airport washroom and then cleared security with no possessions other than his wallet, a British passport, and his MI6 mobile. On it was a compressed and heavily encrypted video of René Devereaux's interrogation. At that moment it was perhaps the most important single piece of intelligence in the global war on terrorism.

Keller switched off the phone before takeoff and did not turn it on again until he was walking through the terminal in Marseilles. Mikhail was waiting outside, in the back of Dmitri Antonov's Maybach. Yaakov Rossman was behind the wheel. They listened to the interrogation through the car's magnificent sound system while heading eastward on the Autoroute.

"You missed your true calling," said Mikhail. "You should have been a television interviewer. Or a grand inquisitor."

"Repent, my son."

"Think he will?"

"Martel? Not without a fight."

"There's no way he can hide from this video. He's ours now."

"We'll see," said Keller.

It was approaching four in the afternoon by the time the Maybach turned through the gate of the safe house in Ramatuelle. Entering, Keller transferred the video file into the main operational computer network. A moment later René Devereaux's face appeared on the monitors.

"Where is Philippe Renard now?"

"Dead."

"Who killed him?"

"Jean-Luc Martel."

"How did he kill him?"

"With a hammer."

And on it went for the better part of two hours. Names, dates, places, routes, methods, *money* . . . It all came down to money. Under Keller's relentless questioning—and the threat, unseen on the video, of the hammer—René Devereaux surrendered the network's most precious secrets. How the money was collected from the street-level dealers. How the money was loaded into the laundry that was JLM Enterprises. And how, once it was cleaned and pressed, it was dispersed. The detail was granular, high resolution. There was no hiding from it. Jean-Luc Martel was in their sights. But who would be the one to offer a lifeline? Paul Rousseau declared it would be him. Martel, he said, was a French problem. Only a French solution would do.

And so, with Gabriel's help, Rousseau prepared an edited clip of the interrogation, thirty-three seconds in length. It was a teaser, an appetizer. "A love tap," as Gabriel called it. Martel was holding court in the bar of his restaurant in the Old Port when it appeared on his phone via an anonymous text. The phone itself was thoroughly compromised, allowing Gabriel and Rousseau and the rest of the team to watch the many shades of Martel's rising alarm as he viewed it. A second video appeared a few seconds later, just for good measure. It depicted a brief sexual encounter between Martel and Monique, Olivia's receptionist at the gallery. It had been shot with the same phone Martel now held in his hand, which, from the team's unique perspective, appeared to be shaking uncontrollably.

It was at this point that Rousseau dialed Martel directly. Not surprisingly, he did not answer, leaving Rousseau no option but to offer his terms in a voice message. They were the equivalent of unconditional surrender. Jean-Luc Martel was to present himself forthwith at Villa Soleil, alone, with no bodyguards. Any attempt to escape, warned Rousseau, would be thwarted. His planes and helicopters would be grounded, his 142-foot motor yacht would be stranded in port. "Obviously," said Rousseau, "your movements and communications are being monitored. You have one opportunity to avoid arrest and ruin. I'd advise you to take it."

With that, Rousseau terminated the call. Five minutes elapsed before Martel listened to the message. At which point the wait began. Gabriel stood before the monitors, a hand to his chin, his head tilted slightly to one side, while in the garden Christopher Keller smashed his MI6 phone to bits with a hammer. Rousseau watched from the French doors. He would give Martel one chance to save himself. He only hoped he was wise enough to take it.

CÔTE D'AZUR, FRANCE

This time they left the gate open for him, though at Gabriel's suggestion they blocked the road beyond Villa Soleil, lest he have a change of heart and try to make a run for it westward along the Côte d'Azur. He arrived, alone, at nine fifteen that same night, after a series of tense phone calls with Paul Rousseau. His appearance at the villa, he claimed, was by no means an admission of anything. He did not know the man in the video, his claims were ludicrous. His business was hospitality and luxury retail, not drugs, and anyone who claimed otherwise would face serious legal consequences. In response, Rousseau made it clear that this was not a legal question but a matter involving French national security. Martel, during a final tense exchange, actually sounded intrigued. He demanded to bring a lawyer. "No lawyers," said Rousseau. "They only get in the way."

Once again it was Roland Girard of Alpha Group who awaited him in the forecourt. His greeting was decidedly less cordial.

"Are you carrying a weapon?"

"Don't be ridiculous."

"Raise your arms."

Reluctantly, Martel complied. Girard searched him thoroughly, beginning with the back of the neck and ending with the ankles. Rising, the Alpha Group operative found himself staring into a pair of furious dark eyes.

"Is there something you wish to say to me, Jean-Luc?"

Martel was silent, a first.

"This way," said Girard.

He took Martel by the elbow and led him into the villa. Christopher Keller waited in the entrance hall.

"Jean-Luc! So sorry about the circumstances of the invitation, but we needed to get your attention." They were the last French words Keller spoke. The rest flowed in British-accented English. "Lives are at stake, you see, and we haven't much time. This way, please."

Martel remained frozen in place.

"Something wrong, Jean-Luc?"

"You're—"

"Not French," interjected Keller. "And I'm not from the island of Corsica, either. All that was for your benefit. I'm afraid you've been the target of a rather elaborate deception."

Dazed, Martel followed Keller into the grandest of Villa Soleil's sitting rooms, where long white curtains billowed and snapped like mainsails in the night wind. Natalie sat at one end of a couch, dressed in a tracksuit and her neon-green trainers. Mikhail sat opposite in a pair of jeans and a V-neck cotton pullover. Paul Rousseau was scrutinizing one of the paintings. And in the far corner of the room, alone on his own private island, Gabriel was scrutinizing Jean-Luc Martel.

It was Rousseau, turning, who spoke next.

"I wish we could say it is a pleasure to meet you, but it is not.

When we look at you, we wonder why it is we do what we do. Why we make the sacrifices. Why we take the risks. Quite honestly, your life is not worth protecting. But that's neither here nor there. We need your help, and so we have no choice but to welcome you, however grudgingly, into our midst."

Martel's eyes moved from face to face—the man he knew as Monsieur Carnot, the Antonovs, the silent figure watching him from his lonely outpost in the corner of the room—before settling once more on Rousseau.

"Who are you?" he asked.

"My name," replied Rousseau, "is not important. Indeed, in our line of work, names don't really mean much, as I'm sure you realize by now."

"Who do you work for?"

"A department of the Interior Ministry."

"The DGSI?"

"It's not relevant. In fact," Rousseau added, "the only salient aspect of my employment is that I'm *not* a police officer."

"And the rest?" asked Martel, glancing around the room.

"They are associates of mine."

He looked at Gabriel. "What about him?"

"Think of him as an observer."

Martel frowned. "Why am I here? What is this about?"

"Drugs," answered Rousseau.

"I told you, I'm not involved in drugs."

Rousseau exhaled slowly. "Let's skip this part, shall we? You know what you do for a living, and so do we. In a perfect world, you would be in handcuffs right now. But needless to say, this world of ours is far from perfect. It's a chaotic, dangerous mess. But your *work*," said Rousseau disdainfully, "has left you uniquely positioned to do something about it. We're prepared to be generous if you help us. And equally unforgiving if you refuse."

Martel squared his shoulders and stood a little taller. "That video," he said, "proves nothing."

"You've only heard a small portion of it. The entire video is nearly two hours in length and quite extraordinary in detail. In short, it lays bare all your dirty secrets. Were such a document to fall into the hands of the police, you would certainly spend your remaining years behind bars. Which is where," Rousseau added pointedly, "you belong. And if the tape were given to an enterprising reporter who's never bought into the JLM fairy tale, the impact on your business empire would be catastrophic. All your powerful friends, the ones you bribe with food and drink and luxury accommodations, would abandon you like rats fleeing a sinking ship. No one would protect you."

Martel opened his mouth to answer, but Rousseau plowed on.

"And then there is the matter of Galerie Olivia Watson. We've had the opportunity to review several of its transactions. They're questionable, to say the least. Especially those forty-eight blank canvases that were shipped to the Geneva Freeport. You've placed Madame Watson in an untenable situation. Her art gallery, like the rest of your empire, is a criminal enterprise. Oh, I suppose it's possible you might wriggle out of the noose, but your wife—"

"She's not my wife."

"Oh, yes, forgive me," said Rousseau. "How should I refer to her?"

Martel ignored the question. "Have you involved her in this?"

"Madame Watson knows nothing, and we would prefer to

keep it that way. There's no need to drag her into this. At least not yet." Rousseau paused, then asked, "How did you explain the fact that you were coming here tonight?"

"I told her I had a business meeting."

"And she believed you?"

"Why wouldn't she?"

"Because you have a bit of a track record." Rousseau gave a confiding smile. "What you do in your spare time is none of my business. We're French, you and I. Men of the world. My point is, it would not be altogether troubling to us if Madame Watson were left with the impression you were with another woman tonight."

"Not troubling for you," said Martel, "but for me . . ."

"I'm sure you'll think of something to say to her. You always do. But back to the matter at hand," said Rousseau. "It should be obvious by this point that you have been the target of a carefully planned operation. Now it's time to move to the next phase."

"The next phase?"

"The prize," said Rousseau. "You're going to help us find him. And if you don't, I'm going to make it my life's work to destroy you. *And* Madame Watson." After a silence, Rousseau added, "Or perhaps the thought of Madame Watson suffering for your crimes doesn't bother you. Perhaps you find such sentiments old-fashioned. Perhaps you're not that sort of man."

Martel returned Rousseau's gaze calmly. But when his eyes settled once more on Gabriel, his confidence appeared to waver.

"In any case," Rousseau was saying, "now might be a good time to listen to the rest of René Devereaux's interrogation. Not the entire thing, that would take too long. Just the relevant portion."

He glanced at Mikhail, who tapped a key on a laptop computer. Instantly, the room swelled with the sound of two men speaking in French, one with a distinct Corsican accent, the other as though he were in physical pain.

"*Where do the drugs come from?*"

"*We get them from all over. Turkey, Lebanon, Afghanistan, everywhere.*"

"*And the hash?*"

"*The hash comes from Morocco.*"

"*Who's your supplier?*"

"*We used to have several. Now we work with one man. He's the largest producer in the country.*"

"*His name?*"

"*Mohammad.*"

"*Mohammad what?*"

"*Bakkar.*"

Mikhail paused the recording. Rousseau looked at Jean-Luc Martel and smiled.

"Why don't we start there," he said. "With Mohammad Bakkar."

There are many reasons why an individual might agree to work on behalf of an intelligence service, few of them admirable. Some do it out of avarice, some for love or political conviction. And some do it because they are bored or disgruntled or vengeful at having been passed over for promotion while colleagues, whom they invariably regard as inferior, are pushed up the ladder of success. With a bit of flattery and a pot of money, these contemptible souls can be convinced to betray the secrets that pass between their fingertips or through the computer networks they are hired to maintain. Professional intelligence officers are more than happy to take advantage of such men, but secretly they despise them. Almost as much as the man who betrays his country for reasons of conscience. These are the useful idiots of the trade. For the professional, there is no lower form of life.

Nor does the professional trust those who volunteer their services, for oftentimes it is difficult to assess their true motives. Instead, he prefers to identify a potential recruit and then make the first move. Usually, he comes bearing gifts, but occasionally he finds it necessary to employ less savory methods. Consequently, the professional is always on the lookout for failings and weakness—an extramarital affair, a predilection for pornography, a financial indiscretion. These are the master keys of the trade. They unlock any door. Moreover, coercion is a great clarifier of intentions. It illuminates the dark corners of the human heart. The man who spies because he has no other choice is less of a mystery than one who walks into an embassy with a briefcase full of stolen documents. Still, the coerced asset can never be fully trusted. Inevitably, he will attempt to find some way to repay the injustice visited upon him, and he can be controlled only so long as his original sin remains a threat to him. Therefore, asset and handler invariably find themselves entangled in a love affair of the damned.

It was into this category of asset that Jean-Luc Martel, hotelier, restaurateur, clothier, jeweler, and international dealer of illicit narcotics, fell. He had not volunteered his services. Nor had he been lured to the table through the power of persuasion. He had been identified, assessed, and targeted with an elaborate and costly operation. His relationship with Olivia Watson had been torn asunder, his business associate had been beaten mercilessly with a hammer, he had been threatened with prison and ruin. Nevertheless, a recruitment still had to be made. Coercion could open a door, but to close a deal required skill and seduction. An accommodation would have to be reached. It was unavoidable. They needed Jean-Luc Martel much more than he needed them. Drug dealers were a dime a dozen. But Saladin was one of a kind.

He did not go easily to his fate, but this was to be expected; a man who kills both his father and his mentor is not a man who frightens easily. He evaded, he counterattacked, he made threats of his own. Rousseau, however, did not rise to Martel's bait. He was the perfect foil—unthreatening in appearance, slow to anger, patient to a fault. Martel tested Rousseau's forbearance often, such as when he demanded written assurances, beneath an official Interior Ministry letterhead, granting him immunity from prosecution, now and forever, amen. Such clemency was not Rousseau's to bestow, for he was operating without ministry mandate or even the knowledge of his masters at the DGSI. And so he smiled in the face of Martel's intransigence and, with a nod in Mikhail's direction, played a moment or two of René Devereaux's seaborne interrogation.

"He's lying," snapped Martel when the audio went silent. "It's a complete fantasy."

It was at this point, Gabriel would later recall—and the hidden cameras confirmed it was so—that the wind went out of Martel's sails. He settled next to Mikhail, a curious choice, and stared at the face of Natalie, who stared at the floor. A long silence ensued, long enough so that Rousseau saw fit to replay the relevant portion of the recording, the portion regarding a certain Mohammad Bakkar, one of Morocco's largest producers of hashish, by some accounts the largest, a man who liked to call himself the king of the Rif Mountains, the region of the country where hashish is grown and processed for export to Europe and beyond. The man who, according to René Devereaux, was Martel's one and only supplier.

"I take it," said Rousseau quietly, "you've heard the name."

And Martel, with the smallest of nods, confirmed that he had. Then the eyes moved from Natalie to Keller, who was standing protectively behind her. Keller had deceived him, Keller had betrayed him. And yet at that moment, it seemed that Jean-Luc Martel regarded Keller as his one and only friend in the room.

"Why don't you give us a bit of background?" suggested Rousseau. "We're amateurs, after all. At least when it comes to the business of narcotics. Help us understand how it all works. Enlighten us as to the wicked ways of your world."

Rousseau's request was not as innocent as it sounded. René Devereaux had already given Keller chapter and verse on Mohammad Bakkar's links to the network. But Rousseau wanted to get Martel talking, which would allow them to test the veracity of his words. A certain amount of deception was to be expected. Rousseau would demand absolute truth only where it mattered.

"Tell us a little about this man Mohammad Bakkar," he was saying. "Is he short or tall? Is he thin or is he fat like me? Does he have any hair or is he bald? Does he have one wife or two? Does he smoke? Does he drink? Is he religious?"

"He's short," answered Martel after a moment. "And, no, he doesn't drink. Mohammad is religious. Very religious, in fact."

"Do you find that surprising?" asked Rousseau quickly, seizing on the fact that Martel had at last answered a question. "That a hashish producer is a religious man?"

"I didn't say Mohammad Bakkar is a hash producer. His business is oranges."

"Oranges?"

"Yes, oranges. So, no, I'm not surprised he's a religious man. Oranges are a way of life in the Rif. The king has been trying for years to encourage the growers to plant other crops, but oranges are more lucrative than soybeans and radishes. Much more," Martel added with a smile.

"Perhaps the king should try harder."

"If you ask me, the king prefers things the way they are."

"How so?"

"Because oranges bring several billion dollars a year into the country. They help to keep the peace." Lowering his voice, Martel added, "Mohammad Bakkar is not the only religious man in Morocco."

"There are many extremists in Morocco?"

"You would know better than me," said Martel.

"ISIS has many cells in Morocco?"

"So I'm told. But the king doesn't like to talk about that," he added. "ISIS is bad for tourism."

"You have a business in Morocco, do you not? A hotel in Marrakesh, if I'm not mistaken."

"Two," boasted Martel.

"How's business?"

"Down."

"I'm sorry to hear that."

"We'll get by."

"I'm sure you will. And to what do you attribute this drop in business?" asked Rousseau. "Is it ISIS?"

"The attacks on the hotels in Tunisia had a big impact on our bookings. People are afraid Morocco is next."

"Is it safe for tourists there?"

"It's safe," said Martel, "until it isn't."

Rousseau permitted himself a smile at the astuteness of the observation. Then he pointed out that Martel's business interests allowed him to enter and leave Morocco, a notorious drug-producing country, without raising suspicion. Martel, with a shrug, did not dispute Rousseau's conclusion.

"Do you entertain Mohammad Bakkar at your hotel in Marrakesh?"

"Never."

"Why not?"

"He dislikes Marrakesh. Or what's become of Marrakesh, I should say."

"Too many foreigners?"

"And gays," said Martel.

"He dislikes homosexuals because of his religious beliefs?"

"I suppose."

"Where do you generally meet with him?"

"In Casa," said Martel, using the local shorthand for Casablanca, "or in Fez. He has a *riad* in the heart of the medina. He also owns several villas in the Rif and the Middle Atlas."

"He moves around a lot?"

"Oranges are a dangerous business."

Again Rousseau smiled. Even he was not immune to Martel's immense charm.

"And when you meet with Monsieur Bakkar? What do you discuss?"

"Brexit. The new American president. The prospects for peace in the Middle East. The usual."

"Obviously," said Rousseau, "you're joking."

"Not at all. Mohammad is quite intelligent, and he's interested in the world beyond the Rif."

"How would you describe his politics?"

"He's not an admirer of the West. He harbors a particular resentment toward France and America. As a rule, I try not to utter the word *Israel* in his presence."

"It angers him?"

"That's one way of putting it."

"And yet you do business with such a man."

"His oranges," said Martel, "are very fine."

"And when you're done talking about the state of the world? What then?"

"Prices, production schedule, delivery dates—that sort of thing."

"Prices fluctuate?"

"Supply and demand," explained Martel.

"A few years ago," Rousseau went on, "we noticed a distinct change in the way oranges were moving out of North Africa. Instead of coming across the Mediterranean one or two at a time aboard small vessels, it was tons of oranges in large cargo ships, all of which departed from ports in Libya. Was there a sudden glut on the market? Or is there some other reason to explain the shift in strategy?"

"The latter," said Martel.

"And that was?"

"Mohammad decided to take on a partner."

"An individual?"

"Yes."

"I suppose he would have to be a man, because someone like Mohammad Bakkar would never deal with a woman."

Martel nodded.

"He wanted to take a more aggressive market posture?"

"Much more aggressive."

"Why?"

"Because he wanted to maximize profits quickly."

"You met him?"

"Twice."

"His name?"

"Khalil."

"Khalil what?"

"That's all, just Khalil."

"He was a Moroccan?"

"No, he was definitely *not* a Moroccan."

"Where was he from?"

"He never said."

"And if you were to hazard a guess?"

Jean-Luc Martel shrugged. "I'd say he was an Iraqi."

I t was clear to everyone in the room—and once again the hidden cameras confirmed it was so—that Jean-Luc Martel did not understand the significance of the words he had just spoken. *I'd say he was an Iraqi* . . . An Iraqi who called himself Khalil. No family name, no patronymic or name of an ancestral village, only Khalil. Khalil who had found a partner in Mohammad Bakkar, a hashish grower of deep Islamic faith who hated America and the West and would fly into a rage at the mere mention of Israel. Khalil who wanted to maximize profits by forcing more product onto the European market. Gabriel, the silent observer of the drama he had conceived and produced, cautioned himself not to leap to a premature conclusion. It was possible the man who called himself Khalil was not the man they were looking for, that he was merely an ordinary criminal with no interests other than making money, that he was a wild goose chase that would waste precious time and resources. Still, even Gabriel found it difficult to control the banging of his heart. He had tugged at the loose thread and connected the dots, and the trail had led him here, to the former home of a vanquished foe. The other members of his team, however, seemed entirely indifferent to Martel's revelation. Natalie, Mikhail, and Christopher Keller were each peering into some private space, and Paul Rousseau had taken that moment to load his first pipe. A moment later his lighter flared and a cloud of smoke rolled over the two Venetian canal scenes by Guardi. Gabriel, the restorer, winced involuntarily.

If Rousseau were even remotely intrigued by the Iraqi who called himself Khalil, he gave no outward sign of it. Khalil was an afterthought, Khalil was of no importance. Rousseau was more interested, or so it seemed, in the nuts and bolts of Martel's relationship with Mohammad Bakkar. Who ran the show? That was what he wanted to know. Who held the upper hand? Was it Martel the distributor, or Bakkar the Moroccan grower?

"You don't know much about business, do you?"

"I'm an academic," apologized Rousseau.

"It's a negotiation," explained Martel. "But ultimately the producer holds the upper hand."

"Because he can cut out the distributor at any time?"

"Correct."

"Couldn't you find another source of drugs?"

"Oranges," said Martel.

"Ah, yes, oranges," agreed Rousseau.

"It's not so easy."

"Because of the quality of Mohammad Bakkar's oranges?"

"Because Mohammad Bakkar is a man of considerable power and influence."

"He would discourage other producers from selling to you?"

"Strongly."

"And when Mohammad Bakkar told you he wanted to

sharply increase the amount of oranges he was sending to Europe?"

"I advised against it."

"Why?"

"Any number of reasons."

"Such as?"

"Large shipments are inherently dangerous."

"Because they're easier for the authorities to find?"

"Obviously."

"What else?"

"I was concerned we would saturate the market."

"And thus drive down the price of oranges in Western Europe."

"Supply and demand," said Martel again with a shrug.

"And when you raised these concerns?"

"He gave me a very simple choice."

"Take it or leave it?"

"In so many words."

"And you took it," said Rousseau.

Martel was silent. Rousseau tacked abruptly.

"Shipping," he said. "Who's responsible for the shipping?"

"Mohammad. He puts the package in the mail and we pick it up at the other end."

"I assume he tells you when to expect the package."

"Of course."

"What are his preferred methods?"

"In the old days he used small boats to bring the merchandise directly across the Mediterranean from Morocco to Spain. Then the Spaniards tightened things up on the coast, so he started moving it across North Africa to the Balkans. It was a long and costly journey. A lot of oranges went missing along the way. Especially when they reached Lebanon and the Balkans."

"They were stolen by local criminal gangs?"

"The Serbian and Bulgarian mafia are quite fond of citrus products," said Martel. "Mohammad spent years trying to devise a way to get his oranges to Europe without having to go through their territory. And then a solution fell into his lap."

"The solution," said Rousseau, "was Libya."

Martel nodded slowly. "It was a dream come true, made possible by the president of France and his friends in Washington and London who declared that Gaddafi had to go. Once the regime crumbled, Libya was open for business. It was the Wild West. No central government, no police, no authority of any kind except for the militias and the Islamic psychos. But there was a problem."

"What's that?"

"The militias and the Islamic psychos," said Martel.

"They disapproved of oranges?"

"No. They wanted a cut. Otherwise, they wouldn't let the oranges reach the Libyan ports. Mohammad needed a local partner, someone who could keep the militias and the holy warriors in line. Someone who could guarantee that the oranges would find their way into the bellies of the cargo ships."

"Someone like Khalil?" asked Rousseau.

Martel made no reply.

"Do you remember a ship called the *Apollo*?" asked Rousseau. "The Italians seized it off Sicily with seventeen metric tons of oranges in its holds."

"The name," said Martel archly, "rings a bell."

"I assume it was your cargo."

Martel, with his expressionless gaze, confirmed that it was.

"Were there other ships before the *Apollo* that weren't intercepted?"

"Several."

"And remind me," said Rousseau, feigning bewilderment, "who bears the expense of a seizure? The producer or the distributor?"

"I can't sell the oranges if I don't receive them."

"So you're saying—and please forgive me, Monsieur Martel, I don't mean to belabor the point—that Mohammad Bakkar personally lost millions of euros when the *Apollo* was seized?"

"That's correct."

"He must have been furious."

"Beyond," said Martel. "He summoned me to Morocco and accused me of leaking the information to the Italians."

"Why would you do such a thing?"

"Because I was opposed to the large shipments in the first place. And the best way to make them stop would be to lose a ship or two."

"Were you responsible for the tip that led the Italians to the *Apollo*?"

"Of course not. I told Mohammad in no uncertain terms that the problem was at his end."

"By that," said Rousseau, "you mean North Africa."

"Libya," said Martel.

"And when the seizures continued?"

"Khalil plugged the leaks. And the oranges started to arrive safely again."

And there it was again. The name of Mohammad Bakkar's aggressive new partner. The man whom Paul Rousseau had been avoiding. After a prolonged pause to load and light another pipe, he wondered when it was that Jean-Luc Martel had first met this Iraqi who called himself Khalil. No family name. No patronymic or ancestral village. Only Khalil. Martel said it had been in 2012. The spring, he reckoned. Late March, perhaps, but he couldn't say for certain. Rousseau, however, would have none of it. Martel was the lord of a vast criminal enterprise, the details of which he carried around with him in his head. Surely, insisted Rousseau, he could recall the date of such a memorable meeting.

"It was the twenty-ninth of March."

"And the circumstances? Were you summoned, or was it previously scheduled?"

Martel indicated that his presence had been requested.

"And how is that done generally? It's a small point, I know, but I'm curious."

"A message is left for me at my hotel in Marrakesh."

"A voice message?"

"Yes."

"And the first meeting where Khalil was present?"

"It was in Casa. I flew there on my plane and checked into a hotel. A few hours later they told me where to go."

"Mohammad called you personally?"

"One of his men. Mohammad doesn't like to use the phone for business."

"And the hotel? Which one was it, please?"

"The Sofitel."

"And did you go alone?"

"Olivia came with me."

Rousseau frowned thoughtfully. "Do you always bring her?"

"Whenever possible."

"Why?"

"Appearances matter."

"Did she come to the meeting?"

"No. She stayed at the hotel while I went over to Anfa."

"Anfa?"

It was a wealthy enclave on a hill west of downtown, explained Martel, a place of palm-lined avenues and walled villas where the price per square meter rivaled London and Paris. Mohammad Bakkar owned a property there. As usual, Martel had to submit to a search before being allowed to enter. It was, he recalled now, more invasive than normal. Inside, he had expected to find Bakkar alone, as was customary for their meetings. Instead, another man was present.

"Describe him, please."

"Tall, broad shoulders, big face and hands."

"His skin?"

"Dark, but not too."

"How was he dressed?"

"Western. Dark suit, white shirt, no tie."

"Scars or distinguishing features?"

"No."

"Tattoos?"

"I could only see his hands."

"And?"

Martel shook his head.

"Were you introduced?"

"Barely."

"Did he speak?"

"Not to me. Only to Mohammad."

"In Arabic, I presume."

"Yes."

"Mohammad Bakkar speaks Maghrebi Arabic."

"Darija," said Martel.

"And the other man? Was he a Darija speaker, too?"

Martel shook his head.

"You can tell the difference?"

"I learned to speak a bit of Arabic when I was a child. I got it from my mother," he added. "So, yes, I can tell the difference. He spoke like someone from Iraq."

"And you didn't wonder about this man's affiliation, given the fact that ISIS had taken over much of Iraq and Syria, and established a base of operations in Libya? Or perhaps you didn't want to know," added Rousseau contemptuously. "Perhaps it's better not to ask too many questions in a situation like that."

"As a general rule," said Martel, "they can be bad for business."

"Especially when the likes of ISIS are involved." Rousseau checked his anger. "And the second meeting? When was that?"

"Last December."

"*After* the attacks on Washington?"

"Definitely."

"The exact date, please."

"I believe it was the nineteenth."

"And the circumstances?"

"It was our annual winter meeting."

"Where did it take place?"

"Mohammad kept changing the location. We finally met in a little village up in the Rif."

"What was on the agenda?"

"Prices and approximate shipping dates for the new year. Mohammad and the Iraqi wanted to push even more product onto the market. Lots of product. And quickly."

"How was he dressed this time?"

"Like a Moroccan."

"Meaning?"

"He was wearing a djellaba."

"A traditional Moroccan robe with a hood."

Martel nodded. "And his face was thinner and sharper."

"He'd lost weight?"

"Plastic surgery."

"Was there anything else different about him?"

"Yes," said Martel. "He walked with a limp."

CÔTE D'AZUR, FRANCE

There was a part of Paul Rousseau that had no stomach for the deal that would have to be made. Jean-Luc Martel, he would say later, was proof positive France had erred in doing away with the guillotine. But Khalil the Iraqi—Khalil whose face had been altered, Khalil who walked with a limp—was well worth the price. Coercion alone would not be sufficient to drag Martel across the finish line. He would have to be transformed into a full-fledged asset of the Alpha Group—"an operative of French intelligence, so help me God," lamented Rousseau—and only a promise of full immunity from prosecution would be sufficient to secure his unwavering cooperation. Rousseau had no power to make such a promise; only his minister could. Which presented Rousseau with yet another dilemma, for his minister still knew nothing of the operation. He was a man who, famously, did not like surprises. Perhaps in this case he would find it in his heart to make an exception.

For now, Rousseau held his nose and put Martel through his paces. They went over it all again, slowly, meticulously, forward, backward, sideways, and every other way that Rousseau, who was looking for any inconsistency, any reason to question the authenticity of his source, could imagine. Particular attention was paid to the agenda of the winter meeting where Khalil the Iraqi had been present, especially the schedule for upcoming deliveries. Three large shipments were due in the next ten days. All would be concealed inside cargo ships bound from Libya. Two would be arriving at French ports—Marseilles and nearby Toulon—but the third would dock in the Italian port of Genoa.

"If those drugs go missing," said Martel, "there's going to be hell to pay."

"Oranges," said Rousseau. "Oranges."

It was at this point that Gabriel interjected himself into the proceedings for the first time. He did so with only the thinnest of introductions, and bearing several blank sheets of paper and a pencil and sharpener. For the better part of the next hour, he sat at the side of the man whose life he had turned inside out, and with his help produced composite sketches of the two versions of Khalil the Iraqi—the 2012 version who wore Western clothing, and the version who appeared in Morocco after the attacks on Washington wearing a traditional djellaba and walking with a noticeable limp. Martel had a famous eye for detail—he had said so himself many times in press interviews—and claimed to never forget a face. He was demanding, too, a trait he revealed fully when Gabriel could not produce a suitable chin for the surgically retooled version of Khalil. They went through three drafts before Martel, with unexpected enthusiasm, gave his approval.

"That's him. That's the man I saw last December."

"You're sure?" pressed Gabriel. "There's no rush. We can do another draft, if you like."

"It's not necessary. That's exactly how he looked."

"And the limp?" asked Gabriel. "You never said which leg was injured."

"It was the right."

"You're positive about that?"

"No question."

"Did he offer any explanation?"

"He said he'd been in a car accident. He didn't say where."

Gabriel studied the finished sketches for a long moment before holding them up for Natalie to see. Her eyes widened involuntarily. Then, regaining her composure, she looked away and nodded slowly. Gabriel set aside the first sketch and contemplated the second at length. It was the new face of terror. It was the face of Saladin.

They dragged him upstairs to Madame Sophie's bedroom, smeared the side of his neck with Madame Sophie's blood-red lipstick, and hosed him down with enough of Madame Sophie's perfume that he left a vapor trail as he drove through the early-morning light, beaten and burned, toward his villa on the other side of the Baie de Cavalaire. He did not go alone. Nicolas Carnot, otherwise known as Christopher Keller, sat in the passenger seat, Martel's mobile in one hand, a gun in the other. Behind them, in a second vehicle, were four officers of the Alpha Group. Previously, they had been employed by Dmitri Antonov at Villa Soleil. Now, like Nicolas Carnot, they were working for Martel. The exact circumstances surrounding their decision to forsake one master for another were cloudy, but such things were liable to happen in Saint-Tropez in the summertime.

It was twelve minutes past five exactly when the two vehicles turned into the drive of Martel's villa. Olivia Watson knew this because she had lain awake all night and had rushed to the bedroom window at the sound of car doors opening and closing in the forecourt. Now, she feigned sleep as the bed shifted beneath the weight of her errant lover. She rolled over, their eyes met in the half-light.

"Where have you been, Jean-Luc?"

"Business," he murmured. "Go back to sleep."

"Is there a problem?"

"Not anymore."

"I tried to call you but my phone isn't working. There's no Internet either, and our landline is dead."

"There must be an outage." His eyes closed.

"Why is Nicolas downstairs? And who are those other men?"

"I'll explain everything in the morning."

"It *is* the morning, Jean-Luc."

He was silent. Olivia moved closer.

"You smell like another woman."

"Olivia, please."

"Who was she, Jean-Luc? Where have you been?"

The reckoning Paul Rousseau had been dreading occurred early that afternoon at the Interior Ministry in Paris. Like Jean-Luc Martel, he did not meet his fate alone; Gabriel went with him. They crossed the courtyard shoulder to shoulder and marched up the grand staircase to the minister's imposing office, where Rousseau, never one for polite small talk, immediately confessed his operational sins. British intelligence, he said, had identified the source of the assault rifles used in the London attack as a French Moroccan named Nouredine Zakaria, a career criminal connected to one of France's largest drug-trafficking networks. Without the authorization of his chief or the Interior Ministry, Rousseau and the Alpha Group had worked with two allied services—the British and, quite obviously, the Israelis—to penetrate the aforementioned network and turn its leader into an asset. The operation, he went on, had proven successful. Based on intelligence provided by the source, the Alpha Group and its partners could say with moderate confidence that ISIS had seized control of a significant portion of the illicit trade in North African hashish and that Saladin, the mysterious

Iraqi mastermind of the group's external operations division, was likely hiding in Morocco, a former French protectorate.

The minister reacted about as well as could be expected, which was not well at all. A tirade ensued, much of it profane. Rousseau offered his resignation—he had written out a letter in longhand during the trip north from Provence—and for a long moment it seemed the minister was prepared to accept it. At length, he dropped the letter into his shredder. Ultimate responsibility for protecting the French homeland from terrorist attack, Islamic or otherwise, rested on the minister's narrow shoulders. He was not about to lose a man like Paul Rousseau.

"Where is Nouredine Zakaria now?"

"Missing," said Rousseau.

"Has he gone to the caliphate?"

Rousseau hesitated before answering. He was prepared to obfuscate, but in no way would he tell an outright lie. Nouredine Zakaria, he said quietly, was dead.

"Dead how?" asked the minister.

"I believe it occurred during a business transaction."

The minister looked at Gabriel. "I suppose you had something to do with this."

"Zakaria's demise predated our involvement in this affair," responded Gabriel with lawyerly precision.

The minister was not mollified. "And the leader of the network? Your new asset?"

"His name," said Rousseau, "is Jean-Luc Martel."

The minister looked down and rearranged the papers on his desk. "That would explain your interest in Martel's file on the day your headquarters was bombed."

"It would," said Rousseau, holding his ground.

"Jean-Luc has been the target of numerous inquiries. All have reached the same conclusion, that he is not involved in drugs."

"That conclusion," said Rousseau carefully, "is incorrect."

"You know better?"

"I have it on the highest authority."

"Who?"

"Jean-Luc Martel."

The minister scoffed. "Why would he tell you such a thing?"

"He didn't have much of a choice."

"Why?"

"René Devereaux."

"The name rings a bell."

"It should," said Rousseau.

"Where is Devereaux now?"

"The same place as Nouredine Zakaria."

"Merde," said the minister softly.

There was a silence. Dust floated in the sunlight streaming through the window like fish in an aquarium. Rousseau cleared his throat gently, a signal he was about to venture onto treacherous ground.

"I know that you and Martel are friends," he said at last.

"We are acquainted," countered the minister quickly, "but we are not friends."

"Martel would be surprised to hear that. In fact, he invoked your name several times before finally agreeing to cooperate."

The minister could not hide his anger at Rousseau for airing dirty French laundry in front of an outsider, and an Israeli at that. "What is your point?" he asked.

"My point," said Rousseau, "is that I'm going to need Martel's continued cooperation, which will require a grant of immunity. Such a grant might be sensitive given your relationship, but it's necessary for the operation to move forward."

"What is your goal?"

"Eliminating Saladin, of course."

"And you intend to use Martel in some sort of operational capacity?"

"It is our only option."

The minister made a show of thought. "You're right, a grant of immunity would be difficult. But if *you* were to request it—"

"You'll have the paperwork by the end of the day," interjected Rousseau. "Frankly, it's probably for the best. You're not the only one in the current government who's *acquainted* with Martel."

The minister was shuffling papers again. "We gave you wide latitude when we created the Alpha Group, but needless to say you've overstepped your authority."

Rousseau accepted the rebuke in penitential silence.

"I won't be kept in the dark any longer. Is that clear?"

"It is, Minister."

"How do you intend to proceed?"

"In the next ten days, Martel's Moroccan supplier, a man named Mohammad Bakkar, is going to send several large shipments of hashish from ports in Libya. It is vital that we intercept them."

"You know the names of the vessels?"

Rousseau nodded.

"Bakkar and Saladin will suspect there's an informant."

"That is correct."

"They'll be angry."

Rousseau smiled. "That is our hope, minister."

The first ship, a Maltese-registered floating coffin called the *Mediterranean Dream*, was not due to leave Libya for another four days. Her point of departure was Khoms, a small commercial seaport east of Tripoli; and after a brief stop in Tunis, where she was scheduled to take on a load of produce, she would make directly for Genoa. The other two vessels, one flying a Bahamian flag, the other Panamanian, were both scheduled to depart Sirte in one week's time, thus presenting Gabriel and Rousseau with a minor quandary. They agreed that seizing the *Mediterranean Dream* while the other two vessels were still in port in Libya would be a miscalculation, as it would provide Mohammad Bakkar and Saladin an opportunity to reroute the merchandise. Instead, they would wait until all three vessels were in international waters before making their first move.

The delay weighed heavily on them both, especially Gabriel, who had watched Saladin's retouched face emerge from the labors of his own hand. He carried the sketch with him always, even to his bed in Jerusalem, where he passed four restless nights at the side of his wife. At King Saul Boulevard he sat through endless briefings on matters he had left in the capable hands of Uzi Navot, but everyone could see his thoughts were elsewhere. During a meeting of the Cabinet his mind drifted as the ministers bickered endlessly. In his notebook he sketched a face. A face partially concealed by the hood of a djellaba.

Rousseau woke Gabriel early the next morning with news that the *Mediterranean Dream* had left Tunis overnight and was now in international waters. But did it contain a concealed shipment of hashish from Morocco? Only one source said it would, the man who lived across the Baie de Cavalaire from Dmitri and Sophie Antonov. The man whose many sins had been officially forgiven and who was now under the complete and total control of a consortium of three intelligence services.

To the uninitiated eye, however, there appeared to be no outward change in his conduct, save for the constant presence at his side of Christopher Keller. Indeed, everywhere Martel went, Keller was sure to follow. To Monaco and Madrid for a pair of previously scheduled business meetings. To Geneva for an eye-opening session with a Swiss banker of questionable ethics. And finally to Marseilles, from which the chief of Martel's illicit narcotics division had vanished without a trace, leaving behind two dead bodyguards in his electronics shop overlooking the Place Jean Jaurès. The Marseilles police were under the impression René Devereaux had been killed by an underworld rival. Devereaux's associates, including one Henri Villard, were of the same opinion. During a meeting with Martel and Keller in a safe flat near the Gare Saint-Charles, Villard was on edge about the upcoming shipments. He was afraid, rightly, that there had been a leak. Martel calmed his fears and instructed him to collect the cargo in the usual manner. Close scrutiny of the recording produced by the phone in Keller's pocket—and of Villard's movements and communications after the meeting—suggested Martel had not tried to send a clandestine warning to his old network. The hashish was on its way, the payment was loaded into the pipeline. For both the drug dealers and the spymasters, all systems appeared to be go.

The message that would set the next act in motion was delivered through the usual channel, interior minister to interior minister, with no undue sense of urgency. A paid informant inside one of France's most prominent drug gangs claimed that a large shipment of North African hashish would be arriving in Genoa the following day, aboard the Maltese-registered *Mediterranean Dream*. The Italians, if they didn't have anything better to do, might want to check it out. They did indeed. In fact, units of the Guardia di Finanza, the Italian law-enforcement agency responsible for combating drug trafficking, boarded the vessel within minutes of its arrival and began breaking open the containers. Their search would eventually yield four metric tons of Moroccan hashish, not a record by any means but a respectable haul. Afterward, the Italian minister rang his French counterpart and thanked him for the information. The French minister said he was pleased to have been of assistance.

While major news in Italy, the seizure attracted little notice in France, least of all in the former fishing village of Saint-Tropez. But when French customs police raided two ships the following day—the Toulon-bound *Africa Star* and the Marseilles-bound *Caribbean Endeavor*—even sleepy Saint-Tropez was impressed. The *Africa Star* would yield three metric tons of hashish, the *Caribbean Endeavor* only two. But it would also surrender something that Gabriel and Paul Rousseau had not anticipated: a lead cylinder, forty centimeters in height, twenty in diameter, concealed inside a spool of insulated wire manufactured by a plant in an industrial quarter of Tripoli.

The cylinder bore no markings of any kind. Still, the French customs police, who were trained in how to handle potentially hazardous material, knew better than to open it. Calls were made, alarm bells rung, and by early evening the container had been transported securely to a French government laboratory outside Paris, where technicians analyzed the talcum-like powder they found inside. In short order they determined it was the highly radioactive substance cesium-137, or cesium chloride. Paul Rousseau and the interior minister were told of the discovery at eight that evening, and at twenty minutes past, with Gabriel trailing a step behind, they were rushing through the doors of the Élysée Palace to break the news to the president of the Republic. Saladin was coming for them once again, this time with a dirty bomb.

Part Three

THE DARKEST CORNER

Precisely how the Americans learned of the concealed shipment of cesium would never be determined to anyone's
satisfaction, least of all the French. It was one of those mysteries
that would linger long after the operational dust had settled.
Nevertheless, they *did* hear about it—that very night, in fact—
and before the sun had risen they demanded that all the relevant parties traipse to Washington for an emergency summit.
Graham Seymour and Amanda Wallace, the cousins, politely
demurred. Faced with the prospect of a radiological dispersion
device in the hands of Saladin's network, they could not afford
to be seen running off to the former colonies for help. They
were all for transatlantic cooperation—in fact, they were dan-
gerously dependent on it—but for them it was a simple matter
of national pride. And when Gabriel and Paul Rousseau added
their objections, the Americans quickly capitulated. Gabriel had
been confident of such an outcome; he had a good idea of what
the Americans were ultimately after. They wanted Saladin's
head on a pike, and the only way they were going to get it was
by taking control of Gabriel's operation. It was better to deny

them a home-field advantage. The five-hour time difference alone would be enough to keep them off balance.

A small delegation was too much to hope for. They arrived on a Boeing jetliner emblazoned with the official seal of the United States and traveled to the site of the conference—a disused MI6 training facility located in a rambling Victorian manor house in Surrey—in a long noisy motorcade that slashed its way through the countryside as though it were dodging IEDs in the Sunni Triangle of occupied Iraq. From one of the vehicles emerged Morris Payne, the Agency's new director. Payne was West Point, Ivy League law, private enterprise, and a former deeply conservative member of Congress from one of the Dakotas. He was big and bluff, with a face like an Easter Island statue and a baritone voice that rattled the beams in the old house's vaulted entrance hall. He greeted Graham Seymour and Amanda Wallace first—they were the hosts after all, not to mention distant family—before turning the full force of his water-cannon personality on Gabriel.

"Gabriel Allon! So good to finally meet you. One of the greats. A legend, truly. We should have done this a long time ago. Adrian tells me you slipped into town without coming to see me. I won't hold that against you. I know you and Adrian go way back. You've done good work together. I hope to continue that tradition."

Gabriel reclaimed his hand and looked at the men surrounding the new director of the world's most powerful intelligence service. They were young and lean and hard, ex-military like their boss, all well schooled in the sharp elbows of Washington bureaucratic combat. The change from the previous administration was striking. If there was a silver lining it was that they were reasonably fond of Israel. Perhaps too fond, thought Gabriel. They were proof that one needed to be careful what one wished for.

Tellingly, Adrian Carter was not among those in the director's close orbit. He was at that moment crawling out of an SUV along with the rest of the senior operators. Most were unfamiliar to Gabriel. One, however, he recognized. He was Kyle Taylor, the chief of the Agency's Counterterrorism Center. Taylor's presence was a troubling gauge of Langley's intentions; it was said of Taylor that he would drone his mother if he thought it would earn him Carter's job and his seventh-floor office. He wore his relentless ambition like a carefully knotted necktie. Carter, however, looked as though he had just been awakened from a nap. He walked past Gabriel with only the smallest of nods.

"Don't get too close," Carter whispered. "I'm contagious."

"What do you have?"

"Leprosy."

Morris Payne was now pumping Paul Rousseau's hand as though trying to earn his vote. At Graham Seymour's prompting, he moved into the old house's formal dining room, which long ago had been converted into a safe-speech facility. There was a basket at the entrance for mobile phones and, on the Victorian sideboard, an array of refreshments that no one touched. Morris Payne sat down at the long rectangular table, flanked on one side by his hard young aides and on the other by Kyle Taylor, the drone master. Adrian Carter was relegated to the far end—the spot, thought Gabriel, where he could doodle to his heart's content and dream of a job in the private sector.

Gabriel lowered himself into his assigned seat and promptly

DANIEL SILVA

turned over the little name placard that some industrious MI6
functionary had placed there. To his left, and directly across
from Morris Payne, was Graham Seymour. And to Seymour's
left was Amanda Wallace, who looked as though she feared
being splattered by blood. Morris Payne's reputation preceded
him. During his brief tenure he had largely completed the task
of transforming the CIA from an intelligence service into a
paramilitary organization. The language of espionage bored
him. He was a man of action.

"I know you're all in crisis mode," Payne began, "so I won't
waste anyone's time. You're all to be commended. You prevented a calamity. Or at least delayed one," he added. "But the
White House is insisting—and, frankly, we agree—that Langley needs to take the lead on this and bring the operation home.
With all due respect, it makes the most sense. We have the reach
and the capability, and we have the technology."

"But we have the source," responded Gabriel. "And all the
reach and technology in the world won't replace him. We found
him, we burned him, and we recruited him. He's ours."

"And now," said Payne, "you're going to turn him over to us."

"Sorry, Morris, but I'm afraid that's not going to happen."

Gabriel glanced toward the end of the table and saw Adrian
Carter attempting to suppress a smile. It was hardly an auspi-
cious beginning. Unfortunately, it went rapidly downhill from
there.

Voices were raised, the table pounded, threats issued. Threats
of retaliation. Threats of cooperation suspended and critical aid
withheld. Not long ago, Gabriel would have had the luxury of

calling the director's bluff. Now he had to proceed with caution. The British were not the only ones who were dependent on Langley's technological might. Israel needed the Americans even more, and under no circumstances could Gabriel afford to alienate his most valuable strategic and operational partner. Besides, for all his bluster and bravado, Morris Payne was a friend who saw the world roughly as Gabriel did. His predecessor, a fluent speaker of Arabic, had made a point of referring to Jerusalem as al-Quds. Things could definitely be worse.

At Graham Seymour's suggestion, they broke for food and drink. Afterward, the mood lightened considerably. Morris Payne admitted that during the flight across the Atlantic he had taken the time to review Gabriel's Agency file.

"I have to say, it was impressive reading."

"I'm surprised you were able to squeeze it aboard your plane."

Payne's smile was genuine. "We both grew up on farms," he said. "Ours was in a remote corner of South Dakota, and yours was in the Valley of Jezreel."

"Next to an Arab village."

"We didn't have Arabs. Only bears and wolves."

This time it was Gabriel who smiled. Payne picked at the edge of a dried-out tea sandwich.

"You've operated in North Africa before. Personally, I mean. You were involved in the Abu Jihad operation in Tunis in eighty-eight. You and your team landed on the beach and blasted your way into his villa. You killed him in his study in front of one of his children. He was watching videos of the intifada at the time."

"That's not true," said Gabriel after a moment.

"Which part?"

"I didn't kill Abu Jihad in front of his family. His daughter walked into the study after he was already dead."

"What did you do?"

"I told her to go take care of her mother. And then I left."

A silence fell over the room. It was Morris Payne who broke it.

"Think you can do it again? In Morocco?"

"Are you asking whether we have the capability?"

"Humor me," said Payne.

Morocco, replied Gabriel, was well within the operational reach of the Office.

"You have decent relations with the king," Payne pointed out. "Relations that would be endangered if something went wrong."

"So do you," replied Gabriel.

"Do you intend to work with the Moroccan services?"

"Did you work with the Pakistanis when you went after Bin Laden?"

"I'll take that as a no."

"In all likelihood," said Gabriel, "Saladin is hiding in circumstances similar to the way Bin Laden was living in Abbottabad. What's more, he enjoys the protection of a drug lord, a man who undoubtedly has friends in high places. Telling the Moroccans about the operation would be like telling Saladin himself."

"How sure are you he's really there?"

Gabriel placed the two composite sketches on the table. He tapped the first one, Saladin as he had appeared in the spring of 2012, not long after ISIS had set up shop in Libya.

"He looks an awful lot like the man I saw in the lobby of the Four Seasons in Georgetown before the attack. Check the hotel security footage. I'm sure you'll come to the same conclusion." Gabriel tapped the second sketch. "And this is the way he looks now."

"According to a drug dealer named Jean-Luc Martel."

"We don't always get to choose our assets, Morris. Sometimes they choose us."

"Do you trust him?"

"Not at all."

"Are you prepared to ride into battle with him?"

"Do you have a better idea?"

It was obvious he didn't. "What if Saladin doesn't bite?"

"He just lost a hundred million euros worth of hashish. And the cesium."

The American looked at Paul Rousseau. "Have your people been able to identify the source?"

"The most likely explanation," said Rousseau, "is that it came from Russia or one of the other former Soviet republics or satellites. The Soviets were rather indiscriminate in their use of cesium, and they left canisters of the stuff scattered all over the countryside. It's also possible it came from Libya. The rebels and militias overran Libya's nuclear facilities when the regime collapsed. The IAEA was particularly concerned about the Tajoura research facility. Perhaps you've heard of it."

Payne indicated he had. "When is your government planning to make an announcement?"

"About what?"

"The cesium!" snapped Payne.

"We're not."

Payne appeared incredulous. It was Gabriel who explained.

"An announcement would needlessly alarm the public. More

important, it would alert Saladin and his network to the fact that their radiological material had been discovered."

"What if another shipment of cesium got through? What happens if a dirty bomb goes off in the middle of Paris? Or London? Or Manhattan, for that matter?"

"Going public won't make that any more or less likely. Keeping quiet, however, has its advantages." Gabriel placed a hand on Graham Seymour's shoulder. "Have you had a chance to read *his* file, Director Payne? Graham's father worked for British intelligence during the Second World War. The Double Cross Committee. They didn't tell the Germans when they arrested their spies in Britain. They kept those captured spies alive in the minds of their German controllers and used them to feed deceptive information to Hitler and his generals. And the Germans never tried to replace those captured spies because they believed they were still on the job."

"So if Saladin thinks the material got through, he won't try to send more—is that what you're saying?"

Gabriel was silent.

"Not bad," said the American, smiling.

"This isn't our first rodeo."

"Did you have rodeos in the Jezreel Valley?"

"No," said Gabriel. "We did not."

After that, there was just one final piece of business to attend to. It was not something that could be addressed in front of a roomful of spies. It was a bilateral issue, one that needed to be handled at the highest level, chief to chief. A quiet side room wouldn't do. Only the walled garden, with its crumbled fountains and weedy footpaths, provided the necessary level of privacy.

Despite the fact it was midsummer, the weather was cool and gray and the overgrown hedges dripped with the rain of a recent shower. Gabriel and Morris Payne walked side by side, slowly, thoughtfully, separated by an inch at most. Viewed from the leaded windows of the old manor house, they made an unlikely pairing—the big, beefy American from the Dakotas, the diminutive Israeli from the ancient Valley of Jezreel. Morris Payne, jacketless, gestured broadly as he made his points. Gabriel, listening, rubbed the small of his back and when appropriate nodded in agreement.

Five minutes into the conversation, they stopped and turned to face one another, as if in confrontation. Morris Payne jabbed a thick forefinger into Gabriel's chest, hardly an encouraging sign, but Gabriel only smiled and returned the favor. Then he raised his left hand above his head and moved it in a circular fashion while the right hovered palm-down at his hip. This time it was Morris Payne who nodded in assent. Those watching from inside understood the significance of the moment. An operational accord had been struck. The Americans would handle the skies and cyber, the Israelis would run the show on the ground and, if presented the opportunity, send Saladin quietly into the night.

With that, they turned and started back toward the house. It was clear to those watching from inside that Gabriel was saying something that displeased Morris Payne greatly. There was another pause and more fingers pointed toward chests. Then Payne turned his big Easter Island face toward the gray sky and gave a capitulatory exhalation of breath. Passing through the meeting room, he snared his jacket from the back of his chair and headed outside, followed by his unsmiling executive staff and, a few paces behind, by Adrian Carter and Kyle Taylor. Gabriel and Graham Seymour waved to them from the portico as though bidding farewell to unwanted company.

"Did you get everything you wanted?" asked Seymour through a frozen smile.

"We'll see in a minute."

The scrum of Americans was now beginning to divide into smaller cells, with each cell making for one of the waiting SUVs. Morris Payne stopped suddenly and called out for Carter to join him. Carter detached himself from the rest of the operators and, watched enviously by Kyle Taylor, climbed into the director's SUV.

"How did you manage that?" asked Seymour as the motorcade rumbled into life.

"I asked nicely."

"How long do you reckon he'll survive?"

"That," said Gabriel, "depends entirely on Saladin."

Next morning the whole of King Saul Boulevard charged into battle. Even Uzi Navot, who had been tending other operational fires during Gabriel's many prolonged absences, was drawn into the intense planning. It was, as the Americans liked to say, all hands on deck. The Office had fought for and won the right to retain control of the operation. But with that victory had come the enormous responsibility of getting it right. Not since the American raid on Osama bin Laden's compound in Abbottabad had there been a targeted killing operation of this magnitude. Saladin pulled the levers of a global terror network that had proven itself capable of striking virtually at will—a network that had managed to obtain the radiological material for a dirty bomb and smuggle it to the doorstep of Western Europe. The stakes, they reminded themselves at every turn, could not be any higher. The security of the civilized world quite literally hung in the balance. So, too, did Gabriel's career. Success would only burnish his reputation, but a failure would wipe away all that had come before and add his name to the list of disgraced chiefs who had overreached and then stumbled.

If Gabriel was concerned about potential damage to his personal legacy, he didn't show it. Not even to Uzi Navot, who wore a groove in the patch of carpet stretching from his door to the office that once had been his. There was a rumor he had actually tried to talk Gabriel out of it, that he had advised his old rival to make a gift of Jean-Luc Martel and Saladin to the Americans and turn his attention to matters closer to home, like the Iranians. The risks of the operation were far too great, worried Navot, and the rewards too small. At least that was the version of the conversation that flashed through the corridors and cipher-protected rooms of King Saul Boulevard. But Gabriel, according to this account, had held fast to his operation. "And why wouldn't he?" asked a sage from Travel. Saladin had bested Gabriel that terrible night in Washington. And then, of course, there was Hannah Weinberg, Gabriel's friend and sometime accomplice, whom Saladin had killed in Paris. No, said the sage, Gabriel was not going to leave Saladin to his friends in Washington. He was going to put him in the ground. In fact, if given the chance, he was likely to do the deed himself. It wasn't business for Gabriel any longer. It was strictly personal.

But a personal stake in an operation was oftentimes perilous. No one recognized this more than Gabriel; his career spoke for itself. Therefore, he leaned heavily on Uzi Navot and the other members of his staff to vet every detail. Organizationally, it was Yaakov Rossman, the chief of Special Ops, who bore responsibility for planning and executing the mission. And with Gabriel looking over his shoulder, he hastily put the pieces in place. Morocco was not Lebanon or Syria, but it was still hostile territory. More than twenty times the size of Israel, it was a vast country with a varied terrain of agricultural plains, rugged mountains, Saharan sand deserts, and several large cities, including Casablanca, Rabat, Tangier, Fez, and Marrakesh. Finding Saladin, even with the help of Jean-Luc Martel, was going to be a difficult undertaking. Killing him with no collateral casualties—and then getting out of the country safely—would be one of the sternest tests the Office had ever faced.

The coastline would be their collaborator, just as it had been in Tunis in April 1988. On that night, Gabriel and a team of twenty-six elite Sayeret Matkal commandos had come ashore in rubber rafts not far from Abu Jihad's villa, and after completing their mission they had departed in the same fashion. During the weeks prior to the raid, they had rehearsed the landing countless times on an Israeli beach. They had even built a mock-up of Abu Jihad's seaside villa in the middle of the Negev so that Gabriel could practice making his way from the front door to the upstairs study where the PLO's second-in-command habitually spent his evenings. Such meticulous preparation, however, would not be possible for the operation against Saladin, for they had no idea where in Morocco he was hiding. Truth be told, they could not say for certain he was actually there. What they knew was that a man matching his appearance had been in Morocco several months earlier, after the attack on Washington. In short, they had much less than the Americans had before the raid on Abbottabad. And much more to lose.

Which meant they had to be prepared for any eventuality, or at least as many as reasonably possible. A large team would be required, larger than operations past, and each member would need a passport. Identity, the division of the Office that maintained agent legends, quickly exhausted its existing stock, thus requiring Gabriel to ask his partners—the French, the British, and the

Americans—to make up the shortfall. All initially balked. But under Gabriel's unrelenting pressure, all eventually capitulated. The Americans even agreed to reactivate an old U.S. passport that bore the name Jonathan Albright and a photograph that looked vaguely like Gabriel's.

"You're not actually thinking of going?" asked Adrian Carter over a secure video link.

"In summer? Oh, no," said Gabriel. "I wouldn't dream of it. It's far too hot in Morocco at this time of year."

There were cars and motorcycles to rent, open-ended airline tickets to book, and lodgings to acquire. Most of the team would stay in hotels, where they would be under the nose of Morocco's internal security service: the Direction de la Surveillance du Territoire, or DST. But for the field command post, Gabriel required a proper safe house. It was Ari Shamron, from his fortress-like home in Tiberias, who offered a solution. He had a friend—a well-to-do Moroccan Jewish businessman who had fled the country in 1967 after the cataclysm of the Six-Day War—who still owned a large villa in the old colonial section of Casablanca. At present, the villa was unoccupied, save for a pair of guardians who lived in a guesthouse on the property. Shamron recommended an outright sale over a short-term rental, and Gabriel readily agreed. Fortunately, money was not an issue; Dmitri Antonov, despite his recent spending spree, was still dripping with it. He wrote a check for the entirety of the purchase price and dispatched a French lawyer—in point of fact, he was an officer of Alpha Group—to Casablanca to collect the deed. By day's end the Office had taken possession of a forward operating base in the heart of the city. All it needed now was Saladin.

His network was quiet during those long days of planning—there were no attacks, directed or lone wolf—but ISIS's many social media channels were ablaze with chatter that something big was coming. Something that would eclipse the attacks on Washington and London. It only added to the pressure inside King Saul Boulevard, and at Langley and Vauxhall Cross. Saladin needed to be removed from circulation, sooner rather than later.

But would his demise put a stop to the bloodshed? Would his network die with him? "Unlikely," said Dina Sarid. In fact, her greatest fear was that Saladin had built the equivalent of a dead man's switch into the network—a switch that would automatically set off a string of murderous strikes in the event of his passing. What's more, ISIS had already demonstrated a remarkable adaptability. If the physical caliphate in Iraq and Syria were lost, said Dina, a virtual caliphate would arise in its place. A "cybercaliphate," as she called it. Here the old rules would not apply. Martyrs-in-waiting would be radicalized in hidden corners of the dark Web and then guided toward their targets by masterminds they had never met. Such was the brave new world that the Internet, social media, and encrypted messaging had brought about.

Of more immediate concern, however, was the three hundred grams of cesium chloride resting in a French government laboratory outside Paris. The cesium chloride that, as far as Saladin was concerned, was still aboard an impounded cargo ship in the port of Toulon. But had he entrusted his entire stockpile to a single clandestine shipment? Was a portion of it already in the hands of an attack cell? Would the next bomb that exploded in a European city contain a radioactive core? As the days passed with no contact from Jean-Luc Martel's Moroccan supplier, Paul Rousseau and his minister wondered whether it was time to warn their European counterparts of the elevated threat. But Gabriel, with the help of Graham Seymour and the Americans, convinced them to remain quiet. A warning, even if it were couched in routine language, risked exposing the operation. Inevitably, there would be a leak. And if it leaked, Saladin would conclude there was a link between the seizure of his drugs and the seizure of the radioactive powder hidden inside a spool of insulated wire.

"Maybe he's already reached that conclusion," said Rousseau dejectedly. "Maybe he's beaten us yet again."

Secretly, Gabriel feared the same. So, too, did the Americans. And during a heated secure videoconference on the second Friday of August, they renewed their demand that Gabriel hand over Jean-Luc Martel, and thus his operation, to Langley's control. Gabriel objected, and when the Americans pressed their case he took the only course available to him. He wished the Americans a pleasant weekend. Then he rang Chiara and informed her they were going to Tiberias for Shabbat dinner.

Tiberias, one of Judaism's four holy cities, lies on the western shore of the body of water that most of the world refers to as the Sea of Galilee and Israelis call Lake Kinneret. Just beyond its outskirts there is the small moshav of Kfar Hittim, which stands on the spot where the real Saladin, on a blazing summer afternoon in 1187, defeated the thirst-crazed armies of the Crusaders in a climactic battle that would leave Jerusalem once again in Muslim hands. He had shown his vanquished enemies no mercy. In his tent he had personally sliced off the arm of Raynald of Châtillon after the Frenchman refused to convert to Islam. The rest of the surviving Crusaders he condemned to execution by decapitation, the prescribed punishment for unbelievers.

A kilometer or so to the north of Kfar Hittim was a rocky escarpment that overlooked both the lake and the scalding plain where the ancient battle had occurred. And it was there, of all places, that Ari Shamron had chosen to make his home. He claimed that when the wind was right he could hear the clashing of swords and the screams of the dying. They reminded him, or so he said, of the transient nature of political and military power in this turbulent corner of the eastern Mediterranean. Canaanites, Hittites, Amalekites, Moabites, Greeks, Romans, Persians, Arabs, Turks, British: all had come and gone. Against overwhelming odds, the Jews had managed to pull off one of history's greatest second acts. Two millennia after the fall of the Second Temple, they had come back for a return engagement. But if history were a guide, they were already on borrowed time.

There are few people who can claim to have helped to build a country, and fewer still an intelligence service. Ari Shamron, however, had managed to accomplish both. Born in eastern Poland, he immigrated to British-ruled Palestine in 1937 as disaster loomed over the Jews of Europe, and had fought in the war that followed the creation of the State of Israel in 1948. In the aftermath of the conflict, with the Arab world vowing to strangle the new Jewish state in its infancy, he joined a small organization that insiders referred to only as "the Office." Among his first assignments was to identify and assassinate several Nazi scientists who were helping Egypt's Gamal Abdel Nasser build an atomic bomb. But the crowning achievement of his career as a field operative would come not in the Middle East but on a street corner in the industrial Buenos Aires suburb of San Fernando. There, on a rainy night in May 1960, he dragged Adolf Eichmann, the stationmaster of the Final Solution, into the back of a waiting car, the first stop on a journey that for Eichmann would end in an Israeli noose.

For Shamron, however, it was only the beginning. Within a few short years, the intelligence service he joined at its creation would be his to run, and the country would be his to protect.

From his lair inside King Saul Boulevard, with its gunmetal-gray filing cabinets and permanent stench of Turkish tobacco, he penetrated the courts of kings, stole the secrets of tyrants, and killed countless enemies. His tenure as chief lasted longer than any of his predecessors'. And in the late 1990s, after a string of botched operations, he was dragged happily out of retirement to right the ship and restore the Office to its former glory. He found an accomplice in a grieving field operative who had locked himself away in a small cottage at the edge of the Helford Passage in Cornwall. Now, at long last, the field operative was the chief. And the burden of protecting Shamron's two creations, a country and an intelligence service, was his to bear.

Shamron had been chosen for the Eichmann mission because of his hands, which were unusually large and powerful for so small a man. They were bunched atop his olive wood cane when Gabriel entered the house with a child in each arm. He entrusted them to Shamron and returned to his armored SUV to collect three platters of food that Chiara had spent the afternoon preparing. Gilah, Shamron's long-suffering wife, lit the Shabbat candles at sundown while Shamron, in the Yiddish intonations of his Polish youth, recited the blessings of the bread and the wine. For a brief moment it seemed to Gabriel that there was no operation and no Saladin, only his family and his faith.

It did not last long. Indeed, throughout the meal, as the others gossiped about politics and lamented the *matsav*, the situation, Gabriel's attention wandered time and again to his mobile phone. Shamron, watching from his place at the head of the table, smiled. He offered no words of sympathy over Gabriel's obvious discomfort. For Shamron, operations were like oxygen. Even a bad operation was better than no operation at all.

When the meal was over, Gabriel followed Shamron downstairs to the room that doubled as his study and workshop. The innards of an antique radio lay scattered across his worktable like the debris of a bombing. Shamron sat down and with a snap of his old Zippo lighter ignited one of his wretched Turkish cigarettes. Gabriel batted away the smoke and pondered the memorabilia arranged neatly on the shelves. His eye fell instantly upon a framed photograph of Shamron and Golda Meir, taken on the day she ordered him to "send forth the boys" to avenge the eleven Israeli coaches and athletes murdered at the Munich Olympic Games. Next to the photograph was a glass case, about the size of a cigar box. Inside, mounted on a background of black cloth, were eleven .22-caliber shell casings.

"I've been saving those for you," said Shamron.

"I don't want them."

"Why not?"

"They're macabre."

"You were the one who figured out how to squeeze eleven rounds into a ten-shot magazine, not me."

"Maybe I'm afraid that one day someone will have a box like that on his shelf with my name on it."

"Someone already does, my son." Shamron switched on his magnifying work lamp.

"You're showing remarkable restraint."

"How so?"

"You haven't asked me once about the operation."

"Why would I do that?"

"Because you're pathologically incapable of minding your own business."

"Which is why I'm a spy." He adjusted the magnifying lamp and scrutinized a worn-out piece of circuitry.

"What kind of radio is it?"

"An RCA Art Deco model with a marbleized Catalin polymer covering. Standard and shortwave. It was manufactured in 1946. Imagine," said Shamron, pointing out the original paper sticker on the base, "somewhere in America in 1946, someone was putting together this radio while people like your mother and father were trying to put together their lives."

"It's a radio, Ari. It had nothing to do with the Shoah."

"I was just making an observation." Shamron smiled. "You seem tense. Is something bothering you?"

"No, not at all."

They lapsed into silence while Shamron tinkered. Repairing old radios was his only hobby, other than meddling in Gabriel's life.

"Uzi tells me you're thinking about going to Morocco," he said at last.

"Why would he do a thing like that?"

"Because he couldn't talk you out of it, and he thought I could."

"I haven't made a final decision."

"But you've asked the Americans to renew your passport."

"Reactivate," said Gabriel.

"Renew, reactivate—what difference does it make? You never should have accepted it in the first place. It belongs in a little glass coffin like those shell casings."

"It's proven useful on numerous occasions."

"Blue and white," said Shamron. "We do things for ourselves, and we don't help others with problems of their own making."

"Maybe once," answered Gabriel, "but we can't operate like that any longer. We need partners."

"Partners have a way of disappointing you. And that passport won't protect you if something goes wrong in Morocco."

Gabriel picked up the little display case with the spent .22 rounds. "If my memory is correct, and I'm sure it is, you were in the backseat of a car in the Piazza Annibaliano while I was inside that apartment house dealing with Zwaiter."

"I was the chief of Special Ops then. It was my place to be in the field. A more appropriate analogy," Shamron went on, "would be Abu Jihad. I was the chief then, and I stayed aboard that naval vessel while you and the rest of the team went ashore."

"With the defense minister, as I recall."

"It was an important operation. Almost as important," said Shamron quietly, "as the one you're about to carry out. It's time for Saladin to leave the stage, with no encores or curtain calls. Just make sure you don't give him what he really wants."

"What's that?"

"You."

Gabriel returned the case to its place on the shelf.

"Will you permit me a question or two?" asked Shamron.

"If it will make you happy."

"Bolt-holes?"

Gabriel explained that there would be two. One was an Israeli corvette. The other was the *Neptune*, a Liberian-registered cargo vessel that in reality was a floating radar and eavesdropping station operated by AMAN, Israel's military intelligence service. The *Neptune* would be stationed off Agadir, on Morocco's Atlantic coast.

"And the corvette?" asked Shamron.

"A little Mediterranean port called El Jebha."

"I assume that's where the Sayeret team will come ashore."

"If I require it. After all," said Gabriel, "I have a former Say-eret officer and a veteran of the British Special Air Service at my disposal."

"Both of whom will have their hands full maintaining control of this Jean-Luc Martel character." Shamron shook his head slowly. "Sometimes the worst thing about a successful recruitment is that you're stuck with the asset. Whatever you do, don't trust him."

"I wouldn't dream of it."

Shamron's cigarette had extinguished itself. He lit another and returned to work on the radio while Gabriel stared at the photograph on the shelf, trying to reconcile the black-and-white image of a spymaster in his prime with the elderly figure before him. It had happened so quickly. Soon, he thought, it would happen to him. Not even Raphael and Irene could stave off the inevitable.

"Aren't you going to get that?" Shamron asked suddenly.

"Get what?"

"Your phone. It's driving me to distraction."

Gabriel looked down. He had been so lost in thought he hadn't noticed the message from the Ramatuelle safe house.

"Well?" asked Shamron.

"It seems Mohammad Bakkar would like a word with Jean-Luc Martel about those missing drugs. He was wondering whether he could come to Morocco early next week."

"Will he be free?"

"Martel? I think we can fit it into his schedule."

Smiling, Shamron plugged the radio into the power strip on his worktable and switched it on. A moment later, after adjusting the tuning dial, he found a bit of music.

"I don't recognize it," said Gabriel.

"You wouldn't, you're too young. It's Artie Shaw. The first time I heard this . . ." He left the thought unfinished.

"What's it called?" asked Gabriel.

"'You're a Lucky Guy.'"

Just then, the radio died and the music fell silent.

Shamron frowned. "Or maybe not."

T he road linking Casablanca's Mohammed V International Airport with the center of Morocco's largest city and financial hub was four lanes of smooth coal-black asphalt, along which Dina Sarid, a reckless motorist by nature and nationality, drove with extraordinary care.

"What are you so worried about?" asked Gabriel.

"You," she replied.

"What have I done now?"

"Nothing. I've just never driven a chief before."

"Well," he said, staring out his window, "there's a first time for everything."

Gabriel's overnight bag lay on the backseat, his attaché case was balanced on his knees. In it was the American passport that had allowed him to sail unmolested through Moroccan border control and customs. Things might have changed in Washington, but in much of the world it was still good to be an American.

All at once the traffic slowed to a halt.

"A checkpoint," explained Dina. "They're everywhere."

"What do you suppose they're looking for?"

"Maybe the chief of Israeli intelligence."

A line of orange pylons guided the traffic onto the shoulder of the road, where a pair of gendarmes was inspecting the vehicles and their occupants, watched over by a DST tough in plainclothes and sunglasses. While lowering her window, Dina spoke a few words to Gabriel in fluent German—German being the language of her cover identity and false passport. The bored gendarmes waved her forward, as though they were chasing away the flies. The DST man's thoughts were clearly elsewhere.

Dina quickly raised her window against the heavy, merciless heat and turned the air conditioner on full. They passed a large military installation. Then it was farmland again, small plots of rich dark earth, tended mainly by inhabitants of the surrounding villages. The stands of eucalyptus reminded Gabriel of home.

At last, they reached the ragged edges of Casablanca, North Africa's second-largest city, eclipsed only by the megalopolis of Cairo. The farmland did not surrender entirely; there were patches of it between the smart new apartment blocks and the shantytowns of corrugated metal-and-cinderblock shacks that were home to hundreds of thousands of Casablanca's poorest residents.

"They call them Bidonvilles," said Dina, pointing out one of the shantytowns. "I suppose it sounds better than a slum. The people there have nothing. No running water, barely enough to eat. Every once in a while the government tries to clear away the Bidonvilles with bulldozers, but the people come back and rebuild. What choice do they have? They have nowhere else to go."

They passed a plot of thin brown grass where two barefoot boys were watching over a flock of skinny goats.

"The one thing they *do* have in the Bidonvilles," Dina was saying, "is Islam. And thanks to Wahhabi and Salafist preachers, it's getting more and more extreme. Do you remember the attack in 2003? All those boys who blew themselves up came from the Bidonvilles of Sidi Moumen."

Gabriel did remember the attacks, of course, but in much of the West they were largely forgotten: fourteen bombings against mainly Western and Jewish targets, forty-five dead, more than a hundred wounded. They were the work of an al-Qaeda affiliate known as Salafia Jihadia, which in turn had ties to the Moroccan Islamic Combatant Group. For all its natural beauty and Western tourism, Morocco remained a hotbed of radical Islam where ISIS had managed to establish deep roots and numerous cells. More than thirteen hundred Moroccans had traveled to the caliphate to fight for ISIS—along with several hundred more ethnic Moroccans from France, Belgium, and the Netherlands—and Moroccans had played an outsize role in ISIS's recent terror campaign in Western Europe. And then there was Mohammed Bouyeri, the Dutch Moroccan who shot and stabbed filmmaker and writer Theo van Gogh on a street in Amsterdam. The killing was not the spontaneous act of one troubled man; Bouyeri was a member of a cell of radical North African Muslims based in The Hague known as the Hofstad Network. For the most part, Morocco's security services had managed to deflect the country's extremism outward. Still, there were plenty of plots at home. Morocco's interior ministry had boasted recently that it had broken up more than three hundred terror plots, including one involving mustard gas. There were some things, thought Gabriel, that were better left unsaid.

They breasted a hill and the pale blue Atlantic opened before them. The Morocco Mall, with its futuristic IMAX movie theater and Western boutiques, occupied a newly developed stretch of land along the coast. Dina followed the Corniche toward downtown, past beach clubs and restaurants and sparkling white seafront villas. One was the size of a commercial building.

"It belongs to a Saudi prince. And over there," said Dina, "is the Four Seasons."

She slowed so Gabriel could have a look. At the gated entrance to the grounds, two security guards in dark suits were searching the undercarriage of an arriving car for explosives. Only if it passed inspection would it be allowed to proceed along the drive to the hotel's covered motor court.

"There's a magnetometer just inside the door," said Dina. "All bags and guests, no exceptions. We'll have to bring the guns in from the beach. It won't be a problem."

"Think the boys from Salafia Jihadia know that, too?"

"I hope not," said Dina with a rare smile.

They continued along the Corniche past the massive Hassan II Mosque, the outer walls of the ancient medina, and the sprawling port. Finally, they entered Casablanca's old French colonial center, with its wide curving boulevards and its unique blend of Moorish, Art Nouveau, and Art Deco architecture. It had once been a place where cosmopolitan Casablancans strolled elegant colonnades dressed in the latest fashions from Paris, and dined in some of the world's finest restaurants. Now it was a monument to decay and danger. Soot blackened the floral stucco facades; rust rotted the wrought-iron balustrades. The smart set kept to the trendy *quartiers* of Gauthier and Maarif, leaving old Casablanca to the robed, the veiled, and the street vendors who sold spoiled fruit and cheap cassettes of sermons and Koranic verses.

The one sign of progress was the shining new streetcar that snaked along the boulevard Mohammed V, past the boarded-up shops and the arcades where the homeless dozed on beds of cardboard. Dina followed a tram for several blocks and then turned into a narrow side street and parked. On one side was an eight-story apartment building that looked as though it were about to collapse beneath the weight of the satellite dishes sprouting like mushrooms from the balconies. On the other was a crumbling, vine-covered wall with a once-ornate cedar door. Guarding it was a panting feral dog.

"Why are we stopping?" asked Gabriel.

"We're here."

"Where?"

"The command post."

"You're joking."

"No."

Gabriel eyed the canine warily. "What about him?"

"He's harmless. It's the rats you have to worry about."

Just then, one scurried past along the pavement. It was the size of a raccoon. The dog recoiled in fear. So did Gabriel.

"Maybe we should go back to the Four Seasons."

"It's not safe."

"Neither is this place."

"It's not so bad once you get used to it."

"What's it like on the inside?"

Dina switched off the engine. "It's haunted. But otherwise it's quite nice."

———

They sidestepped the panting dog and passed through the cedar doorway, into a hidden paradise. There was an azure-blue swimming pool, a red clay tennis court, and a seemingly endless garden of bougainvillea, hibiscus, banana trees, and date palms. The immense house was built in the Moroccan tradition, with tiled interior courtyards where the incessant murmur of Casablanca faded to silence. The labyrinthine rooms seemed frozen in time. It might have been 1967, the year the owner tossed a few belongings into a bag and fled to Israel. Or perhaps, thought Gabriel, it was a more genteel age. An age when everyone in the neighborhood spoke French and worried about how long it would be before the Germans were parading down the Champs-Élysées.

The two caretakers were named Tarek and Hamid. They had purchased the job from the previous caretakers, who had grown too old to look after the place. They avoided the interior of the house, keeping to the gardens and the small guest cottage instead. Their wives, children, and grandchildren lived in a nearby Bidonville.

"We're the new owners," said Gabriel. "Why can't we just fire them?"

"Bad idea," said Yaakov Rossman. Before transferring to the Office, Yaakov had worked for Shabak, Israel's internal security service, running agents in the West Bank and Gaza Strip. He spoke fluent Arabic and was an expert on Arab and Islamic cultures. "If we try to let them go, it will cause an uproar. It would be bad for our cover."

"So we'll give them a generous severance package."

"That's an even worse idea. Every relative they have from every corner of the country will be pouring through our door looking for money." Yaakov shook his head reproachfully. "You really don't know much about these people, do you?"

"So we keep the caretakers," said Gabriel. "But what's this nonsense about the place being haunted?"

They were standing in the cool silence of the house's main internal courtyard. Yaakov glanced nervously at Dina, who in turn looked at Eli Lavon. It was Lavon, Gabriel's oldest friend in the world, who eventually answered.

"Her name is Aisha."

"Muhammad's wife?"

"Not that Aisha. Different Aisha."

"Different how?"

"Aisha is a jinn."

"A what?"

"A demon."

Gabriel looked to Yaakov for a fuller explanation.

"Muslims believe that Allah fashioned man out of clay. The jinns he made from fire."

"Is that bad?"

"Very. By day the jinns live among us in inanimate objects, leading lives quite like ours, but they come out after dark in any form they desire."

"They're shape-shifters," said Gabriel dubiously.

"And wicked," said Yaakov, nodding gravely. "Nothing gives them more pleasure than harming humans. Belief in the jinns is particularly strong here in Morocco. It's probably a holdover from the pre-Islamic beliefs of the traditional Berber religion."

"Just because Moroccans believe it doesn't mean it's true."

"It's in the Koran," said Yaakov defensively.

"That doesn't make it true, either."

There was another exchange of nervous glances between the three veteran Office agents.

Gabriel frowned. "You don't actually believe this drivel, do you?"

"We heard a lot of strange noises in the house last night," said Dina.

"It's probably infested with rats."

"Or jinns," said Yaakov. "The jinns sometimes come in the form of rats."

"I thought we only had one jinn."

"Aisha is their leader. Apparently, there are many others."

"Says who?"

"Hamid. He's an expert."

"Really? And what does Hamid suggest we do about it?"

"An exorcism. The ceremony takes a couple of days and involves the slaughter of a goat."

"It could interfere with the operation," said Gabriel after giving the idea due consideration.

"It could," agreed Yaakov.

"Aren't there countermeasures we can deploy short of a full-blown exorcism?"

"All we can do is try not to make her angry."

"Aisha?"

"Who else?"

"What makes her angry?"

"We can't open the windows, sing, or laugh. We're also not allowed to raise our voices."

"Is that all?"

"Hamid sprinkled salt, blood, and milk in the corners of all the rooms."

"That's a relief."

"He also told us not to shower at night or use the toilet."

"Why not?"

"The jinns live just beneath the surface of water. If we disturb them . . ."

"What?"

"Hamid says we will suffer a great tragedy."

"That doesn't sound good." Gabriel looked around the beautiful courtyard. "Does this place have a name?"

"Not that anyone can remember," said Dina.

"So what shall we call it?"

"The Dar al-Jinns," said Lavon gloomily.

"That might upset Aisha," said Gabriel. "Something else."

"How about the Dar al-Jawasis?" asked Yaakov.

Yes, that was better, thought Gabriel. The Dar al-Jawasis.

The House of Spies.

They arranged for the wives and eldest daughters of Tarek and Hamid to come to the house and prepare a traditional Moroccan meal. They arrived in short order, two plump veiled women and four beautiful young girls, laden with straw baskets overflowing with meat and vegetables from the markets of the old medina. They spent the entire afternoon cooking in the huge kitchen, chattering softly in Darija to avoid disturbing the jinns. Soon the entire house smelled of cumin and ginger and coriander and cayenne.

Gabriel poked his head through the kitchen door around seven o'clock and saw endless platters of Moroccan salads and appetizers, and huge clay pots of couscous and tagine. There was enough to feed a village, so at Gabriel's insistence the women invited the rest of their relatives from the Bidonville to partake of the feast. They ate together in the largest of the courtyards—the destitute Moroccans and the four strangers whom they assumed to be Europeans—beneath a canopy of diamond-white stars. To conceal their facility with Arabic, Gabriel and the others spoke only in French. They talked of the jinns, of the broken promises of the Arab Spring, and of the murderous band of killers who called themselves the Islamic State. Tarek said that several young men from his Bidonville, including the son of a distant cousin, had gone to the caliphate. The DST staged raids in the Bidonville from time to time and carted off the Salafis to the Temara interrogation center to be tortured.

"They have stopped many attacks," he said, "but one day soon there's going to be another big attack like the one in 2003. It's only a matter of time."

It was on that note that the meal concluded. The women and their relatives returned to the Bidonville, taking all the leftover food with them, while Tarek and Hamid went into the garden to keep watch for the jinns. Gabriel, Yaakov, Dina, and Eli Lavon bade one another good night and retired to their separate rooms. Gabriel's overlooked the sea. One of the guardians had etched a circle around the bed in coal to protect it from the demons, and in the four corners were salted droplets of blood and milk. Exhausted, Gabriel fell instantly into a deep sleep, but shortly before dawn he awoke with a desperate urge to relieve himself. He lay in bed for a long time debating what to do before finally checking the time on his mobile. It was a few minutes after five o'clock. Sunrise was at 6:49. He closed his eyes. Better not to tempt fate, he thought. Better to leave Aisha and her friends undisturbed.

Later that morning Jean-Luc Martel, hotelier, restaurateur, clothier, jeweler, international dealer of illicit narcotics, and asset of French and Israeli intelligence, boarded his private Gulfstream aircraft, JLM Deux, at Nice's Côte d'Azur Airport and flew to Casablanca. He was accompanied by his not-quite wife, his not-quite friends who lived in the monstrous villa on the other side of the bay, and a British spy who until recently had earned his living as a professional assassin. In the annals of the global war against Islamic terrorism, no operation had ever had such a beginning. It was a first, everyone agreed. Against all reason, and with no justification, they hoped it would be the last.

Martel had arranged for a pair of Mercedes limousines to ferry the party from the airport to the Four Seasons. They roared past the flashy new apartment blocks and the squalor of the Bidonvilles before turning onto the seafront Corniche and making their way at motorcade speed to the hotel's heavily defended entrance. JLM and party were expected. As a result, the cars received only a cursory inspection before being waved into the motor court, where a small battalion of bellmen waited to receive them. Doors were flung open, and a mountain of matching luggage was loaded onto the waiting trolleys. Then the baggage and its owners squeezed through the choke point of the magnetometer. All were admitted without delay, save for Christopher Keller, who twice set off the alarm. The hotel's chief of security, after finding no prohibited objects on Keller's person, joked that he must have been made out of metal. Keller's tight, unfriendly smile did nothing to allay his suspicions.

A chapel silence hung over the cool of the refrigerated lobby, it being high summer in Morocco and therefore the low season for beachfront hotels. Followed by their caravan of belongings, JLM and party flowed toward reception, Martel and Olivia Watson dazzling in white, Mikhail and Natalie feigning boredom, Keller still smarting over his treatment at the door. The hotel's general manager handed over the room keys—as usual, Monsieur Martel had been granted the luxury of an advance check-in—and offered a few syrupy words of welcome.

"And will you be dining in the hotel this evening?" he wondered.

"Yes," answered Keller quickly. "A table for five, please."

It was an upside-down hotel—lobby on the top floor, guest floors below. JLM and party were on the fourth. Martel and Olivia were in a room together, with Mikhail and Natalie on one side and Keller on the other. When the bags had been delivered, and the bellmen tipped and dismissed, Mikhail and Keller opened the interior communicating doors, turning the three rooms effectively into one.

"That's much better," said Keller. "Lunch, anyone?"

The message arrived at the House of Spies shortly after noon, as Hamid and Tarek were standing over the toilet in Gabriel's bathroom, reciting verses of the Koran to drive away the jinns. It stated that JLM and party had arrived safely at the Four Seasons, that there had been no communication from Mohammad Bakkar or his surrogates, and that JLM and party were now sharing a lunch at the hotel's terrace restaurant. Gabriel fired the message securely to the Op Center at King Saul Boulevard, which in turn forwarded it to Langley, Vauxhall Cross, and DGSI headquarters in Levallois-Perret, where it was greeted with a level of interest that far outweighed its operational significance.

The prayers over the toilet bowl ended a few minutes after one, lunch at half past. Dina and Yaakov Rossman departed the House of Spies a few minutes later in one of the rented cars. Dina was wearing a pair of loose cotton trousers and a white blouse, and was clutching a shoulder bag that bore the name of an exclusive French designer. Yaakov looked as though he were about to make a night raid into Gaza. By two o'clock they were reclining in a private cabana at the Tahiti Beach Club on the Corniche. Gabriel instructed them to remain there until further notice. Then he turned up the volume on the audio feed from the three connecting rooms at the Four Seasons.

"Someone needs to bring the bag into the hotel," said Eli Lavon.

"Thanks, Eli," replied Gabriel. "I would have never thought of that myself."

"I was just trying to be helpful."

"Forgive me, it was the jinns talking."

Lavon smiled. "Who did you have in mind?"

"Mikhail is the most obvious candidate."

"Even I would be suspicious of Mikhail."

"Then maybe it's a job for a woman."

"Or two," suggested Lavon. "Besides, it's time they declared a truce, don't you think?"

"They got off on the wrong foot, that's all."

Lavon shrugged. "Could've happened to anyone."

There was a security guard at the gate that led from the back of the hotel's secluded grounds to the Plage Lalla Meriem, Casablanca's main public beach. Dressed in a dark suit despite the midafternoon heat, he watched the women—the tall Englishwoman whom he had seen several times before, and a Frenchwoman of sour disposition—making their way across the flat dark sand toward the water's edge. The Englishwoman wore a shimmering floral wrap knotted at her narrow waist and a top of translucent material, but the Frenchwoman was more modestly attired in a cotton sundress. Instantly, the beach boys were upon them. They placed two chaises at the tideline and erected two umbrellas against the scalding sun. The Englishwoman asked for drinks and, when they arrived, tipped the boys far too much. Despite many visits to Morocco, she had no familiarity with Moroccan money. For that reason, and others, the boys fought over the privilege of waiting on her.

The security guard returned to the game he was playing on his mobile phone; the beach boys, to the shade of their hut. Natalie stepped out of her sundress and placed it in her Vuitton beach bag. Olivia unknotted her wrap and removed her top. Then she stretched out her long body on the chaise and turned her flawless face to the sun.

"You don't like me very much, do you?"

"I was only playing a role."

"You played it very well."

Natalie adopted Olivia's reclined pose and closed her eyes to the sun. "The truth is," she said after a moment, "you're not really worth disliking. You were simply a means to an end."

"Jean-Luc?"

"He's a means to an end, too. And in case you were wondering, I like him even less than I like you."

"So you *do* like me?" said Olivia playfully.

"A little," Natalie admitted.

Two muscled Moroccan men in their midtwenties walked past in the ankle-deep surf, chatting in Darija. Listening, Natalie smiled.

"They're talking about you," she said.

"How can you tell?"

Natalie opened her eyes and stared at Olivia blankly.

"You speak Moroccan?"

"Moroccan isn't a language, Olivia. In fact, they speak three different languages here. French, Berber, and—"

"Maybe this was a mistake," said Olivia, cutting her off.

Natalie smiled.

"How is it you speak Arabic?"

"My parents were from Algeria."

"So you're an Arab?"

"No," said Natalie. "I'm not."

"So Jean-Luc was right after all. When we left your villa that afternoon he said—"

"That I look like a Jew from Marseilles."

"How do you know?"

"How do you think?"

"You were listening?"

"We always are."

Olivia rubbed oil onto her shoulders. "What were those Moroccans saying about me?"

"It would be difficult to translate."

"I can only imagine."

"You must be used to it by now."

"You, too. You're very beautiful."

"For a Jewish girl from Marseilles."

"Are you?"

"I was once," said Natalie. "Not anymore."

"Was it that bad?"

"Being a Jew in France? Yes," said Natalie, "it was that bad."

"Is that why you became a spy?"

"I'm not a spy. I'm Sophie Antonov, your friend from across the bay. My husband is in business with your boyfriend. They're doing something together here in Casablanca that they don't like to talk about."

"*Partner*," said Olivia. "Jean-Luc doesn't like to be known as my boyfriend."

"Any problems?"

"Between Jean-Luc and me?"

Natalie nodded.

"I thought you said you were listening."

"We are. But you know him better than anyone."

"I'm not so sure about that. But, no," said Olivia, "he doesn't seem to suspect that I was the one who betrayed him."

"You didn't *betray* him."

"How would you describe it?"

"You did the right thing."

"For once," said Olivia.

The two muscled Moroccans had returned. One stared at Olivia without reserve.

"Are you planning to tell me why we're here?" she asked.

"The less you know," replied Natalie, "the better."

"That's the way it works in your trade?"

"Yes."

"Am I in danger?"

"That depends on whether you remove any more clothing."

"I have a right to know."

Natalie gave no answer.

"I suppose it has something to do with those shipments of hashish that were seized."

"What hashish?"

"Never mind."

"Exactly," said Natalie. "Anything I tell you will only make it harder for you to play your role."

"What's that?"

"The loving partner of Jean-Luc Martel who has no idea how he really makes his money."

"It comes from his hotels and restaurants."

"And his art gallery," said Natalie.

"The gallery is mine." Drowsily, Olivia said, "There's one of your friends."

Natalie looked up and saw Dina walking slowly toward them along the water's edge.

"She seems very sad," said Olivia.

"She has reason to."

"What happened to her leg?"

"It's not important."

"None of my business—is that what you're saying?"

"I was trying to be polite."

"How refreshing." Olivia raised a hand to her brow to shade her eyes from the glare. "It's funny, but it looks like she has the same bag as you."

"Does she really?" Natalie smiled. "Isn't that a coincidence."

It was the job of the security guard to monitor all passersby along the beach, lest there be a replay of the unfortunate 2015 incident in Tunis, where a Salafist terrorist had pulled an AK-47 assault rifle from his umbrella and massacred thirty-eight guests at a five-star hotel, the majority of them British subjects. Not that the security guard could do much if faced with a similar set of circumstances. He had no weapon himself, only a radio. In the event of a terrorist incident, he was to issue an alert and then take "any and all" available measures to neutralize the attacker or attackers. Which meant that in all likelihood the security guard would lose his life trying to protect a bunch of half-naked, well-to-do Westerners. It was not the way he wished to die. But jobs were scarce in Casablanca, especially for boys from the Bidonvilles. Better to stand watch on the Plage Lalla Meriem than to sell fruit from a pushcart in the old medina. He'd done that, too.

It had been a slow afternoon, even for August, and so the woman approaching from the west, from the direction of Tahiti and the other beach clubs, received the guard's full attention. She was small and dark-haired and, unlike most Western women who came to the beach, modestly dressed. There was a sadness about her, as though she had been recently widowed. From her right shoulder hung a beach bag. Louis Vuitton, a very popular model that summer. The guard wondered whether the woman realized that it cost more than many Moroccans would see in a lifetime.

Just then, one of the women reclining near the water's edge, the unfriendly Frenchwoman, raised an arm in greeting. The sad-looking girl walked over and sat down at the end of the Frenchwoman's chaise. The beach boys offered to bring a third, but the sad-looking woman declined; evidently, she would not be staying long. The tall, beautiful Englishwoman seemed annoyed by the intrusion. Bored, she stared listlessly out to sea while the Frenchwoman and the sad-looking girl talked intimately and shared cigarettes, which the Frenchwoman had produced from her own beach bag, also a Louis Vuitton, the same model in fact.

At length, the sad-looking girl rose and took her leave. The Frenchwoman, now wearing her sundress, walked with her for about a hundred meters along the tideline. Then the two embraced and went their separate ways, the sad-looking girl toward the beach clubs, the Frenchwoman to her chaise. A few words passed between her and the tall, beautiful Englishwoman. Then the Englishwoman rose and knotted her wrap around her waist. Much to the security guard's delight, she did not bother with the sheer top. And he in turn was so distracted by the sight of her picture-perfect body that he did not bother to take more than a cursory glance inside their beach bags a moment later when they passed through the gate and reentered the hotel's grounds.

Together the two women boarded an elevator and rode it to the fourth floor, where they were admitted into the row of three rooms that had been turned into one. The tall, beautiful Englishwoman entered the suite she shared with Monsieur Martel. At once, he drew her close and murmured something into her ear that the Frenchwoman couldn't quite hear. It was no matter; inside the House of Spies they were listening. They always were.

CASABLANCA, MOROCCO

There was no contact from Mohammad Bakkar or his surrogates that night, and none the following morning, either. From King Saul Boulevard to Langley, and points in between, the mood turned bleak. Even Paul Rousseau, from his lair deep inside DGSI headquarters in Levallois-Perret, began to have his doubts. He feared that somewhere, somehow, the operation had sprung a leak and was taking on water. The most likely culprit was his unlikely asset. The asset he had burned and recruited without the consent of his chief or his minister. The asset to whom he had given a grant of blanket immunity. The hard young men around CIA Director Morris Payne shared Rousseau's pessimism. Unlike the Frenchman, however, they were not prepared to wait indefinitely for the phone to ring. They were soldiers by trade rather than spies and believed in taking the fight directly to the enemy. Payne, it seemed, was similarly inclined. He summoned Adrian Carter to his office and made his views clear. Carter in turn passed them along to Gabriel via a secure videoconference. Carter was in the Agency's

Counterterrorism Center. Gabriel was in the makeshift op center at the House of Spies.

"No big hand motions," he said.

"Translation?"

"Mohammad Bakkar is the star of the show. And the star of the show gets to set the time and place of the meeting."

"Even a star needs good advice from time to time."

"It's not in keeping with the way the relationship has worked in the past. If I instruct Martel to initiate contact, Bakkar will smell a rat."

"Maybe he already does."

"Calling him won't change that."

"The seventh floor is of the opinion it might settle things one way or another."

"Is that so?"

"And the White House—"

"Since when has the White House been involved in this?"

"They have been from the beginning. The president is said to be monitoring the situation carefully."

"How comforting. Exactly how many people in Washington know about this, Adrian?"

"Hard to say." Carter frowned. "What's that noise?"

"It's nothing."

"It sounds as though someone is praying."

"They are."

"Who?"

"Tarek and Hamid. They're trying to drive away the jinns."

"The what?"

"Jinns," said Gabriel.

"I prefer mine with a splash of tonic and a lime."

Gabriel asked Carter about the status of the pair of drones that Morris Payne had committed to the operation. One was a Sentinel stealth surveillance drone. The other was a Predator. Carter explained that the Sentinel had been moved into the theater and could be airborne over Morocco as soon as Gabriel had a target. The Predator, with its two deadly Hellfire missiles, was on a hot standby. The CIA had no authority to launch a strike in Morocco; only the president could. And even then, said Carter, it would have to be a last resort.

"The Moroccans," he said, "will go ape shit."

"How long will it take to get the Predator into position to take a shot?"

"Depends on the location of the target. Two hours, bare minimum."

"Two hours is too long."

"They're not the swiftest cats in the jungle. But all this is moot," said Carter, "unless Mohammad Bakkar summons your boy to a meeting."

"He'll call," said Gabriel, and killed the connection.

Privately, however, he was not so sure. And when noontime came and went with no contact, he succumbed temporarily to the same despair that had taken hold among his partners in Paris and Washington. He distracted himself by tending to his characters—the Antonovs and their friends Jean-Luc Martel and Olivia Watson. He sent Martel and Mikhail into the wilds of Casablanca to view potential sites for a new hotel that JLM Enterprises had no intention of building. Natalie and Olivia he dispatched to the massive Morocco Mall, where, armed with Martel's credit cards, they pillaged several exclusive boutiques. Afterward, they shared a late lunch with Christopher Keller in the Quartier Gauthier. Keller detected no evidence of surveillance, Moroccan DST or otherwise. Eli Lavon, who tailed Martel and Mikhail during their ersatz search for property, returned with an identical report.

In midafternoon, with Gabriel's mood darkening, there was another crisis involving the jinns. Hamid had found an open window in one of the bedrooms—in point of fact, it was Dina's—and feared several new demons had entered the house as a result. With Yaakov, he raised again the idea of an exorcism. He knew a man from his Bidonville who would handle it for a reasonable price, sacrificial goat included. Gabriel overruled him; they would rely on salt, blood, and milk and hope for the best. Hamid was clearly dubious. "As you wish," he said gravely. "But I fear it will end badly. For all of us."

By five o'clock even Gabriel was convinced the House of Spies was haunted and that Aisha and her fiery friends were plotting against him. He sent Natalie and Olivia down to the beach to catch the afternoon's last sun and went for a walk alone—with no bodyguards or weapons—through the dirty arcades of old Casablanca. He wandered aimlessly for a time, across crowded squares, along boulevards thick with evening traffic, until he found a café where most of the patrons wore Western clothing. At a table in the darkest corner sat three Americans: two young men and a girl.

In French he ordered a café noir. Too late, he realized he had no Moroccan currency. It was no matter; the waiter was more than happy to accept euros. Outside, the din of the street was oppressive. It smothered the sound of the television over the bar, and the quiet conversation of the three Americans, and the vibration, at twelve minutes past six o'clock, of Gabriel's mobile phone. He read the message a moment later and smiled. It seemed Mohammad Bakkar wanted a word with Jean-Luc Martel in Fez the following evening.

Gabriel dispatched a brief message to Adrian Carter at Langley before slipping the phone into his pocket. Then he ordered another coffee and drank it in the manner of a man who had all the time in the world for everything.

A few minutes before noon the following day, Christopher Keller stood outside the entrance of the hotel, watching the porters loading the bags into the cars. Martel came along a moment later, followed by Mikhail, Natalie, and Olivia. He was holding a printout of the bill, which he handed to Keller.

"Give it to your people. Tell them I expect to be fully reimbursed."

"I'll get right on that."

Keller dropped the bill into a rubbish bin and slid into the back of the first Mercedes. Martel joined him while the others climbed into the second car. They followed the coastline to Rabat, then headed inland through groves of cork oak to the foothills of the Middle Atlas Mountains. In spring the hills would be green with rain and snowmelt, but now they were brown and dry. Olive trees thrived on the ridges, and in the lowlands were fields of irrigated row crops. Martel stared glumly out the window while Keller monitored the flow of e-mails, text messages, and incoming voice calls on the Frenchman's phone. With Martel's help, he dashed off responses to those items requiring immediate attention. The rest he ignored. Even Jean-Luc Martel, he reasoned, needed a holiday now and then.

On Gabriel's instructions, they stopped for lunch in Meknes, the smallest of Morocco's four ancient imperial cities. It was there that Eli Lavon determined conclusively that they were being watched by a man, Moroccan in appearance, perhaps late thirties, wearing sunglasses and an American baseball cap. After lunch, the same man followed them to the Roman ruins of Volubilis, which they toured in the afternoon's fiercest heat. Lavon snapped a photo of the man while he was pretending to admire the triumphal arch, and sent it to Gabriel at the Casablanca safe house. Gabriel then bounced it to Christopher Keller, who showed it to Martel when they were back in the car again.

"Recognize him?"

"Maybe."

"What does that mean?"

"It means I might have seen him before."

"Where?"

"At the meeting in the Rif last December. After the attack on Washington."

"Who was he with? Bakkar?"

"No," said Martel. "He was with Khalil."

It was approaching six when they reached the Ville Nouvelle of Fez, the modern section of the city where most residents preferred to live. Their next hotel, the Palais Faraj, was at the edge of the ancient medina. It was a labyrinth of colorful tile floors and cool dark passageways. The owner had automatically upgraded Martel and Olivia to the Royal Suite. Keller was staying in a smaller room next door, and Mikhail and Natalie were down the hall. They took Olivia for a walk through the souks of the medina while Martel and Keller sat on the Royal Suite's private terrace and waited for the phone to ring. The air was hot and still. It smelled of wood smoke and faintly of piss from the nearby tanneries.

"How long is he going to make us wait?" asked Keller.

"Depends."

"On what?"

"His mood, I suppose. Sometimes he calls right away. And sometimes . . ."

"What?"

"He changes his mind."

"Does he know we're here?"

"Mohammad Bakkar," said Martel, "knows everything."

When another twenty minutes passed with no call or text, Martel stood abruptly. "I need a drink."

"Order something from room service."

"There's a bar upstairs," said Martel, and before Keller could object, he was headed toward the door. Outside in the foyer he pressed the call button for the elevator, and when it didn't appear instantly he mounted the stairs instead. The bar was on the top floor, small and dark, with a view across the rooftops of the medina. Martel ordered the most expensive bottle of Chablis on the wine list. Keller asked for a café noir.

"You sure you won't have some?" asked Martel, holding a glass of the wine approvingly up to the light.

Keller indicated he was fine with just coffee.

"No drinking on duty?"

"Something like that."

"I don't know how you do it. You haven't slept for days. I

suppose you get used to it in your line of work," added Martel thoughtfully. "Spying, that is."

Keller glanced at the barman. The room was otherwise empty.

"Have you always been a spy?" asked Martel.

"Have you always been a drug dealer?"

"I was *never* a drug dealer."

"Ah, yes," said Keller. "Oranges."

Martel studied him carefully over the rim of his wineglass. "It looks to me as though you spent some time in the military."

"I'm not the soldiering type. Never been one to follow orders. Don't play nicely with others."

"So maybe you were a special kind of soldier. SAS, for example. Or should I call it the Regiment? Isn't that how you and your comrades refer to it?"

"I wouldn't know."

"Bullshit," said Martel evenly.

Smiling for the benefit of the Moroccan barman, Keller looked out the window. Darkness was settling on the ancient medina, but there was still a bit of pink sunlight on the highest peaks of the mountains.

"You should watch your language, Jean-Luc. The lad behind the bar might take offense."

"I know Moroccans better than you do. And I know a former SAS man when I see one. Every night in my hotels and restaurants, some rich Brit arrives with a private security detail. And they're always ex-SAS. I suppose it's better to be a spy than an errand boy for some British bond trader who wants to look important."

Just then, Yossi Gavish and Rimona Stern entered the bar and sat down at a table on the other side of the room.

"Your friends from Saint-Tropez," said Martel. "Shall we invite them to join us?"

"Let's take the bottle downstairs."

"Not yet," said Martel. "I've always liked the view from here at sunset. It's a World Heritage Site—did you know that? And yet most of the people who live down there would gladly unload their crumbling old *riad* or *dar* to some Westerner so they can get a nice clean apartment in the Ville Nouvelle. It's a shame, really. They don't know how good they've got it. Sometimes the old ways are better than the new."

"Spare me the café philosophizing," said Keller wearily.

Rimona was laughing at something Yossi had said. Keller checked Martel's incoming texts and e-mails while Martel contemplated the darkening medina.

"You speak French very well," he said after a moment.

"I can't tell you how much that means to me, Jean-Luc."

"Where did you learn it?"

"My mother was French. I spent a lot of time there when I was young."

"Where?"

"Normandy, mainly, but Paris and the south, too."

"Everywhere but Corsica."

There was a silence. It was Martel who broke it.

"Many years ago, while I was still in Marseilles, there was a rumor going around about an Englishman who was working as a contract killer for the Orsati clan. He was ex-SAS, or so they said. Apparently, he was a deserter." Martel paused, then added, "A coward."

"Sounds like the stuff of a spy novel."

"Truth is sometimes stranger than fiction." Martel held

Keller's steady gaze. "How did you know about René Devereaux?"

"Everyone knows about Devereaux."

"It was your voice on that tape."

"Was it?"

"I can only imagine the things you must have done to make him talk. But you must have had another source," Martel added. "Someone who knew about my ties to René. Someone close to me."

"We didn't need a source. We were listening to your phone calls and reading your e-mails."

"There were no phone calls or e-mails." Martel smiled coldly. "I suppose all it took was a bit of money. That's how I got her, too. Olivia loves money."

"She had nothing to do with it."

Martel was clearly dubious. "Does she get to keep it?"

"What's that?"

"The fifty million you gave her for those paintings. The fifty million you paid her to betray me."

"Drink your wine, Jean-Luc. Enjoy the view."

"Fifty million is a lot of money," said Martel. "He must be very important, this Iraqi who calls himself Khalil."

"He is."

"And if he shows his face? What happens then?"

"The same thing," said Keller quietly, "that will happen to you if you ever lay a hand on Olivia."

Martel was unmoved by the threat. "Maybe someone should get that," he said.

Keller looked down at the phone, which was shivering on the low table between them. He checked the number of the incoming call and then handed the device to Martel. The conversation was brief, a mixture of French and Moroccan Arabic. Then Martel rang off and surrendered the phone.

"Well?" asked Keller.

"Mohammad changed the plan."

"When are you meeting him?"

"Tomorrow night. And it's not just me," said Martel. "We're all invited."

Christopher Keller was not the only one monitoring Jean-Luc Martel's phone. At the Casablanca safe house, Gabriel was keeping watch over it, too. He had listened to the steady stream of voice calls throughout the long afternoon, and read the many text messages and e-mails. And at seven fifteen that evening he eavesdropped on the brief exchange between Martel and a man who didn't bother to introduce himself. He listened to the recording of the conversation three times from beginning to end. Then he adjusted the time code to 19:16:13 and clicked the play icon.

"Mohammad and his partner would like to meet your friends. One friend in particular."

"Which one?"

"The tall one. The one with the pretty French wife and lots of money. He's Russian, yes? An arms dealer?"

"Where did you hear a thing like that?"

"It's not important."

"Why do they want to meet him?"

"A business proposition. Do you think your friend would be interested? Tell him it will be well worth his while."

Gabriel clicked PAUSE and looked at Yaakov Rossman. "How do you suppose Mohammad Bakkar and his partner figured out how Dmitri Antonov really makes his money?"

"Maybe he heard the same rumors Jean-Luc Martel heard. The rumors we spread like chicken feed from London to New York to the south of France."

"And the business proposition?"

"I doubt it involves hashish."

"Or oranges," said Gabriel. Then he said, "It sounds to me as though the person who really wants to meet with Dmitri Antonov is Mohammad's partner. But why?"

"Can we stipulate that Mohammad's so-called partner is Saladin?"

"Let's."

"Maybe he wants to buy arms. Or maybe he's looking to lay his hands on some loose Russian radiological material to replace the supply he lost when that ship was seized."

"Or maybe he wants to kill him." Gabriel paused, then added, "And his pretty French wife."

Gabriel clicked PLAY.

"Where?"

"Drive south to Erfoud and—"

"Erfoud? That's—"

"Seven hours at this time of year, maybe less. Mohammad has made arrangements for a couple of four-wheel drives. Those Mercedes sedans of yours will be useless where you're going."

"Which is?"

"A camp in the Sahara. Quite luxurious. You'll arrive around sunset. The staff will prepare a meal for you. Very traditional Moroccan. Very nice. Mohammad will come after dark."

Gabriel paused the recording.

"A camp at the edge of the Sahara. Very traditional, very nice."

"And very isolated," said Yaakov.

"Maybe Saladin's thinking the same thing."

"You think we're blown?"

"I'm paid to worry, Yaakov."

"Any suspects?"

"Only one."

Gabriel opened a new audio file on his computer and after adjusting the time code clicked PLAY.

"You speak French very well."

"I can't tell you how much that means to me, Jean-Luc."

"Where did you learn it?"

"My mother was French. I spent a lot of time there when I was young."

"Where?"

"Normandy, mainly, but Paris and the south, too."

"Everywhere but Corsica."

Gabriel clicked PAUSE.

"He was bound to make the connection at some point," said Yaakov. "They come from the same world. They're two sides of the same coin."

"Keller was never involved in the drug trade."

"No," said Yaakov archly. "He just killed people for a living."

"I believe in redemption."

"I should hope so."

Gabriel frowned and clicked PLAY.

"But you must have had another source. Someone who knew about my ties to René. Someone close to me."

"We didn't need a source. We were listening to your phone calls and reading your e-mails."

"There were no phone calls or e-mails. I suppose all it took was a bit of money. That's how I got her, too. Olivia loves money."

Gabriel paused the recording.

"He was bound to make that connection, too," said Yaakov.

In the House of Spies there was silence, but in the Royal Suite of the Palais Faraj the inhabitants of Gabriel's operation were now quarreling about whether to dine in the hotel or at a restaurant in the medina. They did so in the manner of the bored and very rich. So convincing was their performance that even Gabriel, who had created them, could not tell whether the row was genuine or staged for the benefit of the Moroccan DST, which surely was listening, too.

"Maybe we've lost Martel," said Gabriel at last. "Who knows? Maybe we never had him in the first place."

"Is that the jinns talking again?"

Gabriel said nothing.

"He's been under our control from the moment we burned him. Blanket coverage. Physical, electronic, cyber. Keller's practically been sleeping in the same room with him. We own him body and soul."

"Maybe we missed something."

"Like what?"

"A missing telephone patter or some sort of impersonal communication."

"Newspaper, no newspaper? Umbrella, no umbrella?"

"Exactly."

"No one reads newspapers anymore, and it doesn't rain in Morocco this time of year. Besides," said Yaakov, "if Mohammad Bakkar thought Martel had switched sides, he would have never summoned him in the first place."

In Fez, the argument over dinner had grown genuinely

heated. Exasperated, Gabriel settled the matter for them, with a terse text to Mikhail. JLM and party would be dining at the hotel that evening.

"Wise move," said Yaakov. "Better to make an early night of it. Tomorrow's likely to be a long day."

Gabriel was silent.

"You're not thinking about aborting, are you?"

"Of course I am."

"You've come too far," objected Yaakov. "Send them to the camp, have the meeting. Identify Saladin and light him up. And when he leaves, let the Americans drop some ordnance on him and turn him into a puff of smoke."

"Sounds so easy."

"It is. The Americans do it every day."

Gabriel said nothing.

"What are you going to do?" asked Yaakov.

Gabriel reached down and clicked PLAY.

"You'll arrive around sunset. The staff will prepare a meal for you. Very traditional Moroccan. Very nice. Mohammad will come after dark . . ."

Natalie awoke in sheets drenched with sweat, blinded by sunlight. Squinting, she gazed out at the patch of sky framed by the window, momentarily confused as to her whereabouts. Was she in Fez or Casablanca or Saint-Tropez? Or was she back in the large house of many rooms and courts near Mosul? *You are my Maimonides* . . . She rolled over and stretched a hand toward the drawstring for the blinds, but it was just beyond her reach. Mikhail's half of the bed was still in shadow. Shirtless, he slept undisturbed.

She closed her eyes tightly against the sun and tried to gather up the fragments of the morning's last dream. She had been walking through a garden of ruins—Roman ruins, she was certain of it. They were not the ruins of Volubilis, which they had visited the previous day, but of Palmyra in Syria. Natalie was certain of this, too. She was one of the few Westerners to visit Palmyra after its capture by the Islamic State, and had seen with her own eyes the devastation the holy warriors of ISIS had inflicted there. She had toured the ruins by moonlight, accompanied by an Egyptian jihadist called Ismail who was training at the same camp. But in her dream another man had been at her side. He was tall and powerfully built, and walked with a slight limp. An object of some sort, dripping and mangled, hung from his right hand. Only now, in the heat haze of morning, did Natalie comprehend that the object was her head.

She sat up in bed, slowly, so as not to wake Mikhail, and placed her feet on the bare floor. The tiles felt as though they had just come out of a kiln. All at once she felt nauseated. She supposed it was the dream that had sickened her. Or perhaps it was something she had eaten at dinner, some Moroccan delicacy that had not agreed with her.

Whatever the case, she was soon rushing into the bathroom to be sick. Afterward, her head throbbed with the opening shots of an encroaching migraine. Today of all days, she thought. She swallowed two tablets of pain reliever with a handful of tap water and stood for several minutes beneath a cool shower. Then, wrapped in a thin toweling robe, she went into the small sitting room and prepared a cup of strong black coffee with the Nespresso automatic. Madame Sophie's cigarettes beckoned from the end table. She smoked one for the sake of her cover, or so she told herself. It did nothing for her head.

You are very brave, Maimonides. Too brave for your own good . . .

If only that were true, she thought. How many might still be alive if she had found the courage to let him die? Washington, London, Paris, Amsterdam, Antwerp, and all the others. Yes, the Americans wanted him. But Natalie wanted him, too.

She went into the walk-in closet. Her clothing for the day lay folded on a shelf. Otherwise, her bags were packed. So were Mikhail's. The labels spoke of exclusive manufacture, but the luggage, like Dmitri Antonov himself, was counterfeit. The smallest contained a false bottom. In the hidden compartment were a Beretta 92FS, two magazines loaded with 9mm rounds, and a sound suppressor.

After Natalie agreed to work for the Office, Mikhail had trained her to properly load and discharge a firearm. Now, crouched on the floor of the closet, she quickly threaded the aluminum suppressor into the end of the barrel, rammed one of the magazines into the grip, and chambered the first round. Then she raised the weapon, holding it with two hands, the way Mikhail had taught her, and took aim at the man holding her head in his hand.

Go ahead, Maimonides, make a liar of me . . .

"What are you doing?" came a voice from behind her.

Startled, Natalie pivoted and pointed the gun at Mikhail's chest. She was breathing heavily; the grip of the Beretta was wet in her trembling hands. Mikhail stepped forward and slowly, gently, lowered the barrel of the gun toward the floor. Natalie relaxed her grip and watched while he swiftly returned the Beretta to its original state and placed it in the hidden compartment of the counterfeit bag.

Rising, he placed a forefinger to Natalie's lips and pointed toward the ceiling to indicate the presence of Moroccan DST transmitters. Then he led her outside, onto the terrace, and held her close.

"Who are you?" he whispered into her ear, in Russian-accented English.

"I'm Sophie Antonov," she answered dully.

"What are you doing in Morocco?"

"My husband is putting together a deal with Jean-Luc Martel."

"What kind of business is your husband in?"

"He used to do minerals. Now he's an investor."

"And Jean-Luc Martel?"

She didn't answer. She felt suddenly cold.

"Would you like to explain to me what that was all about?"

"Nightmares."

"What kind of nightmares?"

She told him.

"It was just a dream."

"It almost happened once."

"It won't happen again."

"You don't know that," she said. "You don't know how good he is."

"We're better."

"Are we really?"

There was a silence.

"Send a message to the command post," Natalie whispered finally. "Tell them I can't do it. Tell them I can't be around him. I'm afraid I'll bring down the entire operation."

"No," said Mikhail. "I will send no such message."

"Why not?"

"Because you're the only one who can identify him."

"You saw him, too. In the restaurant in Georgetown."

"Actually," replied Mikhail, "I was trying very hard not to look at him. I barely remember his face."

"What about the security video from the Four Seasons?"

"It's not good enough."

"I can't be in his presence," she said after a moment. "He'll remember me. Why wouldn't he? I was the one who saved his miserable life."

"Yes," said Mikhail. "And now you're going to help us kill him."

He took her back to bed and did his best to make her forget the dream. Afterward, they showered together and dressed. Natalie spent a long time arranging and rearranging her hair in the mirror.

"How do I look?" she asked.

"Like a Jew from Marseilles," said Mikhail with a smile.

Upstairs, the hotel staff was clearing away the last of the breakfast buffet. Over coffee and bread, Mikhail read the morning papers on his tablet while Natalie, affecting tedium, contemplated the ancient chaos of the medina. Finally, shortly before eleven, they went downstairs to the lobby, where Martel and Christopher Keller were seeing to the bill. Outside, Olivia was watching the porters tossing luggage into the waiting cars.

"Sleep well?" she asked.

"Never better," said Natalie.

She ducked into the back of the second car and took her place next to the window. A face she did not recognize stared back at her in the glass.

Maimonides . . . So good to see you again . . .

The Counterterrorism Center had once been located in a single room on Corridor F on the sixth floor of CIA Headquarters. With its televisions and ringing telephones and stacks of files, it had looked like the newsroom of a failing metropolitan daily. Its officers worked in small teams dedicated to specific targets: the Red Army Faction, the Irish Republican Army, the Palestine Liberation Organization, Abu Nidal, Hezbollah. There was also a unit, formed in 1996, that focused on a little-known Saudi extremist named Osama bin Laden and his burgeoning network of Islamic terror.

Not surprisingly, the CTC had expanded in size since the attacks of 9/11. It now occupied a half acre of prime Agency real estate on the ground floor of the New Headquarters Building, and was accessed through its own lobby and security turnstiles. Owing to security concerns, the real name of the CTC's chief was no longer a matter of public record. He was known to the outside world, and to the rest of Langley, only as "Roger." Kyle Taylor liked the name. No one, he reckoned, was afraid of a man named Kyle. But a Roger was someone to be feared, especially if he commanded a fleet of armed drones and had the power to vaporize a man for being in the wrong place at the wrong time.

Uzi Navot had first encountered Kyle Taylor a decade earlier, when Taylor was working at the CIA's station in London. Their dislike of one another was mutual and instantaneous. Navot viewed Taylor—who was fluent in no language other than English, and therefore unsuited for work in the field—as little more than an indoor spy and a boardroom warrior. And Taylor, who harbored a traditional CIA resentment of the Office and Israel, and perhaps a little more, regarded Navot as conniving and not to be trusted. Otherwise, they got on famously.

"Your first time in the Center?" asked Taylor after easing Navot's path through security.

"No. But it's been a while."

"We've probably grown since the last time you were here. We had to. On any given day we're running ops in Afghanistan, Pakistan, Yemen, Syria, Somalia, and Libya."

He sounded like a corporate salesman talking about his firm's unprecedented third-quarter expansion. "And now Morocco," said Navot quietly, egging Taylor on.

"Actually, given the political sensitivity of the mission, very few people in the building know about it. Even here in the Center," Taylor added. "It's special access only. We're using one of our smaller op rooms. We'll be totally black."

Taylor led Navot along a corridor lined with numbered doors, behind which nameless, faceless analysts and operators tracked terrorists and plots around the globe. At the end of the hall was a short flight of metal stairs and another checkpoint, through which Taylor and Navot passed without scrutiny. Beyond it was an ill-lit foyer and a cipher-protected door. Taylor punched the code rapidly into the keypad and stared directly into the lens of the biometric reader. A few seconds later the door opened with a snap.

"Welcome to the Black Hole," he said, leading Navot inside. "The others are already here." Taylor introduced Navot to Graham Seymour, perhaps forgetting they were well acquainted, perhaps not, and then to Paul Rousseau. "And Adrian I assume you know."

"Very well," said Navot, accepting Carter's outstretched hand. "Adrian and I have been through the wars together, and we have the scars to prove it."

It took a moment for Navot's eyes to fully adjust to the gloom. Outside, it was early morning of what promised to be an oppressive summer's day, but in the restricted ops room deep inside Langley it was a permanent night. At desks around the perimeter sat several technicians, their youthful faces lit by the glow of computer screens. Two wore flight suits, the two who were piloting the pair of drones now loitering above eastern Morocco without the knowledge of the Moroccan government. Images from the aircraft's high-resolution cameras flickered on the screens at the front of the room. The Predator, with its two Hellfire missiles, was already above Erfoud. But the Sentinel stealth drone was southeast of Fez, thus granting its camera an unobstructed view of the Palais Faraj. Navot watched as Christopher Keller and Jean-Luc Martel stepped into the hotel's forecourt. A few seconds later, two Mercedes sedans slipped beneath an archway and turned south toward the mountains.

Navot sat down next to Graham Seymour. Kyle Taylor had pulled Adrian Carter into a corner of the room for a private consultation. The tension between them was obvious.

"Any idea who's running the show?" asked Navot.

"For the moment," replied Graham Seymour, "I'd say the ball is in Gabriel's court."

"For how long?"

"Until the minute Saladin shows his face. If that happens," said Seymour, "all bets are off."

The traffic in the Ville Nouvelle was a nightmare. Even in ancient Fez there seemed to be no escaping it. Eventually, the commercial buildings receded and small plots of cultivated farmland appeared, along with new apartment buildings. They were three-level blockhouses, old before their time, with garages on the ground level. Most of the garages had been converted into tiny restaurants and shops, or were being used as pens for animals. Sheep and goats grazed among newly planted olive trees. Families shared picnic lunches in whatever shade they could find.

Gradually, the land tilted toward the distant peaks of the Middle Atlas, and the olive trees gave way to dense groves of carob and argan and Aleppo pine. Eagles circled overhead, searching for jackals. And above the eagles, thought Christopher Keller, the drones were searching for Saladin.

The first town of any significance was Imouzzer. Built by the French, it was inhabited by some thirteen thousand members of the Aït Seghrouchen, a prominent Berber tribe that spoke a distinct dialect of the ancient Berber tongue. The air was several degrees cooler—they were now above four thousand feet in elevation—and the souks and male-only cafés along the main street were crowded. Keller scanned the faces of the young and old alike. They were noticeably different from the faces he had seen in Casablanca and Fez. European features, fairer hair and eyes. It was as if they had crossed an invisible border.

Just then, Keller's mobile phone pulsed with an incoming message. He read it and then looked at Martel.

"Our friends are under the impression we're being followed again. They think it might be the same man who was with us yesterday in Meknes and Volubilis. They'd like us to get a better photo of him."

"What do they have in mind?"

Keller instructed the driver to pull over at a kiosk at the far end of town. The car carrying Mikhail, Natalie, and Olivia stopped behind them, as did a dusty Renault. In the side-view mirror, Keller could see the passenger—cropped dark hair, wide cheekbones, sunglasses, American baseball cap—but the driver was obscured.

"Get us a couple bottles of water," he told Martel.

"It's not the friendliest of towns."

"I'm sure you can take care of yourself."

Martel climbed out and walked over to the kiosk. Keller peered into the side-view mirror and saw the passenger stepping from the Renault. Through the heavily tinted rear window of the Mercedes, Keller snapped a photo of the passing figure. The result was a useless blurred profile. But a moment later, when the man returned to the Renault, Keller captured a clear three-quarter image of the man's face. He showed it to Martel when the Frenchman slid into the backseat with two sweating bottles of Sidi Ali mineral water.

"That's definitely him," said Martel. "He's the one I saw in the Rif last winter with Khalil."

As the car eased away from the curb, Keller sent the photo to the Casablanca command post. Then he checked the side-view mirror. The second Mercedes was directly behind them. And behind the Mercedes was a dusty Renault with two men inside.

Many years of close and sometimes controversial cooperation between the CIA and the Moroccan DST had earned Langley access to Morocco's long list of known jihadists and fellow travelers. As a result, it took the analysts in the Counterterrorism Center a matter of minutes to identify the man in Keller's photograph. He was Nazir Bensaïd, a former member of the Moroccan Salafia Jihadia who was jailed after the Casablanca suicide bombings in 2003. Released in 2012, Bensaïd made his way to Turkey and eventually to the caliphate of ISIS. The government of Morocco was under the impression that he was still there. Obviously, that was not the case.

A photo of Bensaïd taken at the time of his imprisonment soon appeared on the display screens of the Black Hole in the CTC, along with another photo snapped in 2012 during the Moroccan's arrival at Istanbul's Ataturk Airport. Both photos were forwarded to Gabriel, who sent them on to Keller. Keller confirmed that Nazir Bensaïd was the man he had just seen.

But what was Nazir Bensaïd doing in a town of thirteen thousand Berbers in the Middle Atlas Mountains? And why was he now following Keller and the others toward Erfoud? It was possible that Bensaïd had slipped back into Morocco to work in the hashish business of Mohammad Bakkar. But the more likely explanation was that he was looking after the interests of Bakkar's partner, the tall Iraqi who called himself Khalil and walked with a limp.

Inside the Black Hole the technicians digitally marked the Renault sedan and its two occupants, while at Fort Meade in Maryland the NSA locked onto the signals being emitted by their mobile phones. Adrian Carter rang the seventh floor to break the news to CIA Director Morris Payne, who quickly relayed it to the White House. By seven thirty Washington time, the president and his senior national security team were gathered in the Situation Room complex, watching the video feeds from the two drones.

At the House of Spies in Casablanca, Gabriel and Yaakov Rossman watched the video, too, while down the hall two caretakers prayed for deliverance from demons fashioned of fire. Through the speakers of his laptop computer, Gabriel could hear the excited chatter at the CTC in Langley. He wished he could share their optimism, but he could not. The entire operation was now in the hands of a man whom he had deceived and blackmailed into doing his bidding. We don't always get to choose our assets, he reminded himself. Sometimes they choose us.

The four-wheel drives were waiting in a hot, dusty square outside the Café Dakar in Erfoud. They were Toyota Land Cruisers, newly washed, white as bone. The drivers wore cotton trousers and khaki vests, and conducted themselves with the smiling efficiency of professional tour guides. They were not. They were Mohammad Bakkar's boys.

South of Erfoud was the great Tafilalt Oasis, with its endless groves of date palms—eight hundred thousand in all, according to the French-language guidebook Natalie clutched tightly in her hand. Gazing out her window, she thought again of that night in Palmyra, and of her dream that morning. *Saladin walking beside her in the light of a violent moon, her head in his hand* . . . She looked away and saw Olivia watching her intently from the opposite side of the Toyota's backseat.

"Are you all right?" she asked.

Silent, Natalie stared straight ahead. Mikhail was in the passenger seat next to the driver. The second Toyota, the one carrying Keller and Jean-Luc Martel, was about a hundred meters ahead. Behind them the road was empty. Even the Renault, the one that had been following them since Fez, was nowhere to be seen.

The palm groves receded, the landscape turned harsh and rocky. At Rissani the paved road ended, and soon the great sand sea of Erg Chebbi appeared. The village of Khamlia, a cluster of low mud-colored houses, lay at the southern end of the dunes. There they left the main road and turned onto a pitted desert track. Natalie monitored their progress on her mobile; they were a blue dot moving eastward across an uninhabited land toward the Algerian border. Then suddenly the blue dot froze as they ventured beyond cellular service. Mikhail had brought a satellite phone for just such an eventuality. It was behind Natalie, in the same bag as the Beretta.

For half an hour they drove as all around them the great wind-sculpted dunes turned brick-red with the gathering dusk. They passed a small encampment of nomadic Berbers who were boiling water for tea at the entrance of a black camel-hair tent. Otherwise, there was not another living soul. Only the mountainous dunes and the vast sheltering sky. The emptiness was unbearable; Natalie, despite the close proximity of Olivia and Mikhail, felt painfully alone. She scrolled through the photos on her phone, but they were Madame Sophie's memories, not hers. She could scarcely recall the farm at Nahalal. Hadassah Medical Center, her former place of employment, was all but lost to her.

At last, the camp appeared, a cluster of colorful tents arranged in the cleft of a dune. Another white Land Cruiser had arrived before them; Natalie supposed it was for the staff. She allowed one of the robed porters to take her bags, but Mikhail, adopting the supercilious manner of Dmitri Antonov, succeeded in carrying his into the camp unassisted. There were three tents arranged around a central court, and a fourth a short distance away with showers and toilets. The court was carpeted and adorned with large pillows and a pair of couches along a low-slung table. The tents were carpeted, too, and furnished with proper beds and writing tables. There was no evidence of electricity, only candles and a large fire in the court that threw shadows on the face of the dune. Natalie counted six staff in all. Two were visibly armed with automatic rifles. She suspected the others were armed as well.

With sunset, the air turned cooler. In her tent Natalie slipped on a fleece pullover and then went to wash for dinner. Olivia joined her a moment later.

Quietly, she asked, "Why are we here?"

"We're going to have a lovely dinner in the desert," answered Natalie.

Olivia's eyes met Natalie's in the mirror. "Please tell me someone is watching us."

"Of course they are. And listening, too."

Natalie went out without another word and found the table laid with a lavish Moroccan feast. The staff kept their distance, appearing every so often to refill their glasses from on high with sickly-sweet mint tea. Nevertheless, Natalie, Mikhail, and Christopher Keller held fast to their cover. They were Sophie and Dmitri Antonov and their friend and associate, Nicolas Carnot. They had settled in Saint-Tropez earlier that summer and after a fitful courtship had made the acquaintance of Jean-Luc Martel and his glamorous not-quite wife, Olivia Watson. And now, thought Natalie, they were all five at the very end of the earth, waiting for a monster to rise from the night.

Maimonides . . . So good to see you again . . .

Shortly after nine o'clock the staff cleared away the platters of food. Natalie had scarcely eaten. Alone, she walked to the edge of the camp to smoke one of Madame Sophie's Gitanes. She stood where the firelight ended and the darkness began. She stood, she thought, at the earth's sharp edge. Forty or fifty yards into the desert, one of the armed staff members kept watch. He wore the white robes and headdress of a Berber tribesman from the south. Pretending not to see him, Natalie dropped her cigarette and started across the sand. The guard, startled, blocked her path and gestured for her to return to the camp.

"But I wish to see the dunes," she said in French.

"It is not allowed. You can see them in the morning."

"I prefer now," she answered. "At night."

"It is not safe."

"So you'll come with me. Then it will be safe."

With that, she set off across the desert again, followed by the Berber guard. His garments were luminous; his skin, black as pitch, was indistinguishable from the night. She asked his name. He told her he was called Azûlay. It meant "the man with nice eyes."

"It is true," she said.

Embarrassed, he looked away.

"Forgive me," said Natalie.

They walked on. Overhead, the Milky Way glowed like phosphorus powder, and a minaret moon shone hot and bright. Before them rose three dunes, ascending in scale from north to south. Natalie removed her shoes and, trailed by Azûlay the Berber, climbed the highest dune. It took her several minutes to reach the summit. Exhausted, she dropped to her knees in the warm, soft sand to catch her breath.

Her eyes searched the land. To the west a thin strand of lights stretched intermittently from Erfoud, through the palm groves of the Tafilalt Oasis, to Rissani and Khamlia. In the east and south there was only empty desert. But to the north Natalie glimpsed a pair of headlights bobbing toward her through the dunes. After a moment the lights vanished. Perhaps, she thought, it had been a mirage, another dream. Then the lights reappeared.

Natalie turned and scurried down the slope of the dune to the spot where she had left her shoes. *You're the only one who can identify him . . .* But he would remember her, too. And why ever not? After all, she thought, I was the one who saved his miserable life.

The drones spotted the vehicle long before Natalie did, at five minutes past nine Morocco time, as it emerged from the southeastern corner of the sand sea at Erg Chebbi. Toyota Land Cruiser, white, seven occupants. It stopped at the camp's edge and six men climbed out, leaving the driver behind. Viewed from above with thermal-imaging technology, it appeared that none of the men walked with a limp. Five, visibly armed, remained at the perimeter of the camp while the sixth strode into the central court between the tents. There he greeted Jean-Luc Martel, then, a few seconds later, Mikhail. As expected, there was no audio coverage; the cellular void of the desert had struck the phones mute. Kyle Taylor, from the back of the room, provided one possible soundtrack of the exchange.

"Mohammad Bakkar, I'd like you to meet a friend of mine, Dmitri Antonov. Dmitri, this is Mohammad Bakkar."

"Maybe," said Adrian Carter. "Or maybe Saladin had a little work done to that leg, along with his face."

"He couldn't hide the limp in Washington," said Uzi Navot. "And he couldn't hide it from Jean-Luc Martel earlier this year.

Besides, does Mikhail look as though he's talking to the worst terrorist since Bin Laden?"

"He's always struck me as a rather cool customer," said Carter.

"Not that cool."

They were watching the scene through the camera of the Sentinel. Mikhail, greenish and aglow with body heat, stood a few feet from the fire with his arms akimbo, addressing with evident calm the man who had just arrived. Keller and Olivia had already withdrawn from the central court and entered one of the tents. Natalie, after returning from her sojourn in the dunes, had joined them. The Predator was searching the surrounding desert. There were no other heat signatures.

Navot turned and looked at Kyle Taylor. "Has the NSA identified any new phones in the camp?"

"They're working on it."

"Odd, don't you think?"

"How so?"

"They're not that hard to find. We're quite good at it, but you're even better."

"Unless the phone is powered off and the SIM card is removed."

"What about satellite phones?"

"Easy."

"So why isn't Mohammad Bakkar carrying one? Rather dangerous to be riding around in the desert without a satphone, don't you think?"

"Saladin knows that phones are death sentences."

"True," agreed Navot. "But how is Bakkar planning to tell him to come to the camp? Carrier pigeon? Smoke signal?"

"What's your point, Uzi?"

"My point," said Navot, "is that Mohammad Bakkar isn't carrying a satphone because he doesn't need one to signal Saladin."

"Why not?"

"Because Saladin is already there." Navot pointed toward the screen. "He's the one behind the wheel of the Toyota."

Jean-Luc Martel's physical description of Mohammad Bakkar proved accurate on at least one point; the Moroccan from the Rif Mountains was short, perhaps five foot four inches in height, and stout of build. His religious zealotry was not outwardly evident. He wore no kufi or unkempt beard, and smoked a cigarette in violation of the Islamic State's ban on tobacco. His clothing was European and expensive. A zippered cashmere sweater, neatly pressed twill pants, a pair of suede moccasins wholly unsuited to the desert. His wristwatch was large, gold, and Swiss; its crystal shone with reflected firelight. His French was excellent, as was his English, which he used to address Mikhail.

"Monsieur Antonov. It is so nice to finally meet. I've heard so much about you."

"From Jean-Luc?"

"Jean-Luc is not my only friend in France," he said confidingly. "You caused quite a sensation in Provence this summer."

"It wasn't my intention."

"Wasn't it?" He smiled genially. "Those parties of yours were all the rage. The stories reached Marrakesh. Quite scandalous."

"One has to live one's life."

"Yes, of course. But there are limits, are there not?"

"I've never thought so."

At this, Mohammad Bakkar smiled. "I trust you enjoyed the food?"

"Magnificent."

"You like Moroccan cuisine?"

"Very much."

"You've been here before? To Morocco?"

"No, never."

"How is that? My country is very popular with sophisticated Europeans."

"Not with Russians."

"This is true. The Russians prefer Turkey for some reason. But you're not really a Russian, are you, Monsieur Antonov? Not anymore."

Mikhail's heart banged once against his rib cage. "I still carry a Russian passport," he said.

"But France is your home."

"For the time being."

Mohammad Bakkar seemed to give this point undue consideration. "And the camp?" he asked, looking around him. "Is it to your liking?"

"Very much so."

"I tried to make it as traditional as possible. I hope you don't mind the fact that there's no electricity. The tourists come out here to the Sahara and expect all the creature comforts of their lives in the West. Electricity, phones, the Internet . . ."

"No Internet here." Mikhail held up his phone. "Useless."

"Yes, I know. That is why I chose this place."

Mikhail rose and started to take his leave.

"Where are you going?" asked Mohammad Bakkar.

"You and Jean-Luc have business to discuss."

"But it concerns you. At least part of it." Bakkar gestured toward the couches. "Please, sit down, Monsieur Antonov." Again he smiled. "I insist."

At the Casablanca command post, Gabriel watched as Mikhail sat down on one of the couches. A member of the staff appeared, tea was poured. At the right side of the image three human heat signatures were visible inside one of the tents. Two of the signatures were quite obviously female. The other was Christopher Keller. A moment earlier Gabriel had dispatched an encrypted message to Keller's satellite phone regarding the possible identity of the man behind the wheel of the newly arrived Toyota Land Cruiser. Keller's hands were now noticeably active, with what Gabriel could not see. Cold metal was not visible via infrared.

Keller placed the object at the small of his back and moved swiftly to the entrance of the tent, where he stood for several seconds, presumably while he surveyed the operational landscape. Then he took up a satellite phone and worked the screen. A few seconds later a message arrived on Gabriel's computer.

READY WHEN YOU ARE . . .

With the aid of the drones, Gabriel surveyed the operational landscape, too. Four men stood watch around the camp in the desert—north, south, east, and west, like points on a compass. All were armed. The men who arrived with Mohammad Bakkar were armed, too. Perhaps Bakkar himself. Mikhail, fearing a search by Bakkar's men, was not. That meant it would be at least ten against one. The chances were better than even that Keller and the rest of the team would not survive a close-quarters firefight, even one conducted by the man who had achieved the highest score ever recorded in the SAS's infamous Killing House. Besides, it was possible that Uzi Navot and Langley were mistaken about the identity of the man in the Toyota. Better to let it play out. Better to let him show his face and then take the shot where there was no chance of collateral damage. For the moment, the isolated spot in the darkest corner of southeastern Morocco was their enemy. But not for long. Soon, he thought, the desert would be their ally.

Gabriel ordered Keller to stand down and asked Langley to focus one of the drone cameras on the Land Cruiser at the camp's edge. The image appeared on his screen a moment later, courtesy of the Predator. A man wearing a hooded djellaba, both hands resting on the wheel, no cigarette. Gabriel reckoned that eventually he would join the others. To do so, he would have to climb out of the vehicle and walk several paces. And then Gabriel would know whether it was him. A man's physical appearance could be changed in many ways, he thought. Hair could be cut or dyed, a face could be altered with plastic surgery. But a limp like Saladin's was forever.

At first, Mohammad Bakkar spoke only Darija, and only to Jean-Luc Martel. It was obvious from his demeanor and tone that he was angry. Mikhail, during his time with Sayeret Matkal, had learned a bit of Palestinian Arabic, enough to function during night raids in Gaza and the West Bank and southern Lebanon. He was by no means fluent or even conversant. Still, he managed to understand the gist of what the Moroccan from the Rif Mountains was saying. It seemed several large shipments of an unspoken product had recently gone missing under unexplained circumstances. The losses incurred by Bakkar's organization were substantial—hundreds of millions, in fact. Somewhere, he said, there had been a leak of information. It had not occurred at his end. Evidently, he ran a very tight ship. Therefore, the mistake was clearly Martel's. Bakkar implied it had been intentional. After all, Martel had never approved of the rapid expansion of their shared business to begin with. Amends would have to be made. Otherwise, Bakkar intended to find another distributor for his product and cut Martel out of the picture entirely.

A violent quarrel ensued. Martel, in rapid and fluent Moroccan Arabic, implied that Mohammad Bakkar, not he, was to blame for the recent seizures. He reminded Bakkar that he had opposed scaling up the amount of product flowing into Europe, and for this very reason. By his calculation, they were losing more than a quarter of their product to seizures instead of the usual ten percent, an unsustainable rate in the long term. Caution was the only solution. Smaller shipments, no more container vessels. It was, thought Mikhail, a rather impressive performance on Martel's part. A trained agent could not have done it any better. By the end of it even Mohammad Bakkar appeared convinced that he and his organization were somehow responsible for the leaks. He resolved to get to the bottom of it. In the meantime, he had twenty metric tons of product sitting in his clandestine production facilities in the Rif, awaiting shipment. He was eager to move forward. New funds were clearly needed.

"I don't want to bear the costs for the last disaster alone. It isn't just."

"Agreed," said Martel. "What did you have in mind?"

"A fifty percent price increase. One time only."

"Fifty percent!" Martel waved his hand dismissively. "Madness."

"It is my final offer. If you wish to remain my distributor, I suggest you take it."

It was not Mohammad Bakkar's final offer, not even close. Martel knew this, and so did Bakkar himself. This was Morocco, after all. Passing the bread at dinner was a negotiation.

And on it went for several more minutes, as fifty shrank to forty-five and then forty and finally, with an exasperated glance toward the heavens, thirty. And all the while Mikhail was watching the man who was watching him. The man sitting behind the wheel of the Toyota, with an unobstructed view into the center of the camp. He wore a djellaba with the pointed hood up, and his face was in deep shadow. Even so, Mikhail could feel the leaden weight of his gaze. He could feel, too, the absence of a gun at the small of his back.

"Khalas," said Bakkar at last, rubbing his hands together. "Twenty-five it is, payable on receipt of the merchandise. It is far too little, but what choice do I have? Would you like the shirt off my back, too, Jean-Luc? I can always find another."

Martel was smiling. Mohammad Bakkar signed the deal with a handshake and then turned to Mikhail.

"You will forgive me, but Jean-Luc and I had serious business to discuss."

"So it seemed."

"You don't speak Arabic, Monsieur Antonov?"

"No."

"Not even a little?"

"Even coffee is a challenge."

Mohammad Bakkar nodded sympathetically. "Different pronunciations for different countries. An Egyptian would say the word differently from a Moroccan or a Jordanian or, say, a Palestinian."

"Or a Russian," laughed Mikhail.

"Who lives in France."

"My French is almost as bad as my Arabic."

"So we'll speak English."

There was a silence.

"How much has Jean-Luc told you about our business together?" asked Bakkar finally.

"Very little."

"But surely you must have some idea."

"Oranges," said Mikhail. "You supply the oranges that Jean-Luc uses in his restaurants and hotels."

"And pomegranates," said Bakkar agreeably. "Morocco has very fine pomegranates. The best in the world, if you ask me. But the authorities in Europe don't want our oranges and pomegranates. We've lost several large shipments lately. Jean-Luc and I were discussing how it happened and what to do next."

Mikhail listened, expressionless.

"Unfortunately, we lost more than just fruit in the recent seizures. Something irreplaceable." Bakkar looked at Mikhail speculatively. "Or perhaps not."

Bakkar beckoned for more tea. Mikhail watched the man in the Toyota while the glasses were filled.

"What sort of business are you in, Monsieur Antonov?"

"I'm sorry?"

"Your business," repeated Bakkar. "What is it you do?"

"Oranges," said Mikhail. "And pomegranates."

Bakkar smiled. "It is my understanding," he said, "that your business is arms."

Mikhail said nothing.

"You're a careful man, Monsieur Antonov. I admire that."

"It pays to be careful. Fewer shipments go missing."

"So it's true!"

"I am an investor, Monsieur Bakkar. And I have been known on occasion to broker deals that involve the movement of goods from Eastern Europe and the former Soviet republics to troubled places around the world."

"What sort of goods?"

"Use your imagination."

"Guns?"

"Armaments," said Mikhail. "Firearms are only a small part of what we do."

"What sort of merchandise are we talking about?"

"Everything from Kalashnikovs to helicopters and fighter jets."

"Aircraft?" asked Bakkar, incredulous.

"Would you like one? Or how about a tank or a Scud? We're running a special this month. I'd place your order now, if I were you. They won't last long."

"None for me," said Bakkar, holding up his hands, "but an associate of mine might be interested."

"In Scuds?"

"His needs are very specific. I would prefer to let him explain."

"Not yet," said Mikhail. "First, you tell me a little bit about him. Then I'll decide whether I want to meet with him."

"He is a revolutionary," said Bakkar. "I assure you, his cause is just."

"They always are," said Mikhail skeptically. "Where's he from?"

"He has no country, not in the Western sense of the word. Borders are meaningless to him."

"Interesting. But where will I ship his arms?"

Bakkar's expression turned suddenly serious. "Surely you are aware that the recent political turmoil in our region has erased many of the old borders drawn by diplomats in Paris and London. My associate comes from such a place. A place of great upheaval."

"Upheaval is what keeps me in business."

"I should think so," said Bakkar.

"What is your associate's name?"

"You may call him Khalil."

"And before the upheaval?" asked Mikhail quickly, as though the name meant nothing to him. "Where was he from?"

"As a child he lived along the banks of one of the rivers that flowed from the Garden of Eden."

"There were four," said Mikhail.

"That's correct. The Pishon, the Gihon, the Euphrates, and the Tigris. My associate lived along the banks of the Tigris."

"So your associate is an Iraqi."

"He was once. He's not any longer. My associate is a subject of the Islamic caliphate."

"I trust he's not in the caliphate now."

"No. He's right over there." Bakkar inclined his head toward the Toyota. Then he looked at Mikhail and asked, "Are you carrying a weapon, Monsieur Antonov?"

"Of course not."

"Would you mind terribly if one of my men searched you?" Bakkar smiled amiably. "You are an arms dealer, after all."

There was a gathering at the driver's-side door of the Toyota— five men by Gabriel's count, all armed. Finally, the door swung open, and with some difficulty the man inside climbed out. He remained next to the vehicle, protected by a circle of guards, for another long moment while Mikhail was thoroughly searched. And only when the search was complete did he make his way toward the center court of the camp. The armed guards surrounded him in a tight scrum. Even so, Gabriel could see that he was favoring the right leg. Step one of the two-step authentication process was complete. Step two, however, could not be accomplished from on high, with the use of an American drone. Only a face-to-face encounter would suffice.

Gabriel dispatched a message to Christopher Keller, stating that the subject had just entered the camp and that he had walked with a noticeable limp. Then he watched as the subject extended a hand toward an officer of Israeli intelligence.

"Dmitri Antonov," said Gabriel softly, "I'd like you to meet my friend Saladin. Saladin, this is Dmitri Antonov."

There were two Israeli officers at the remote desert camp who could potentially provide the second stage of the authentication required to launch a targeted killing operation on the soil of a sometime ally in the war on terror. The first was seated before the subject himself, with no weapon or communications device. The second was a few feet away in a comfortably furnished tent. The officer outside had had only a fleeting encounter with the subject in a famous Georgetown restaurant. But not the officer in the tent. She had spent several days with the subject in a house of many rooms and courts near Mosul and had spoken to him at length. She had also, in a cabin at the edge of the Shenandoah in Virginia, heard the subject sentence her to death. It was not a sound she would ever forget. She did not need to see the subject's face to know it was him. His voice told her it was so.

There was a third officer who had seen the subject in person as well—the officer who was waiting anxiously in a haunted house, in the old colonial section of Casablanca. When the confirmation of the subject's identity landed on his computer, he forwarded it immediately to the Black Hole at Langley.

"Got him!" shouted Kyle Taylor.

"Not yet," cautioned Uzi Navot, gazing at the image on the screen. "Not by a mile. Not even close."

He was taller than Mikhail remembered, and broader through the chest and shoulders. Perhaps it was because he'd had sufficient time to recover from his injuries. Or perhaps, thought Mikhail, it was his clothing. He had been wearing a dark business suit that night and had been seated across from a beautiful young woman whose dark hair was dyed blond. Occasionally, he had stolen glances at the television above the bar to view the results of his handiwork. Bombs had exploded at the National Counterterrorism Center in Virginia and at the Lincoln Memorial. But there was more to come. Much more.

Mikhail's first impression of Saladin's new face was that it did not suit him. It was too thin through the nose and cheekbones, and the movie-idol chin was something a vain man might choose from a magazine in his plastic surgeon's office. Substantial work had been done to the eyes as well, but the irises themselves were as Mikhail remembered—wide and dark and bottomless and shimmering with profound intelligence. They were not the eyes of a madman, they were the eyes of a professional. One would never want to play a game of chance against such eyes, nor sit across from them in an interrogation chamber. Or a camp at the edge of the Sahara, thought Mikhail, surrounded by several hardened jihadis armed with automatic weapons. He resolved to conduct the meeting swiftly and then send Saladin on his way. But not too swiftly. Saladin was about to present Mikhail with his weapons wish list, which meant there was priceless intelligence to be gained. The opportunity was unprecedented. It could not be squandered.

The introductions had been brisk and businesslike. Mikhail had accepted the proffered hand without hesitation. The hand that had condemned so many to death. The hand of the murderer. It was thick and strong and very warm to the touch. And dry, observed Mikhail. No sign of nerves. Saladin was not anxious or uncomfortable, he was in his element. Like his namesake, he was a man of the desert. The Moroccan mint tea, however, was clearly not to his liking.

"Too sweet," he said, making a face. "It's a wonder Moroccans have any teeth."

"We don't," said Mohammad Bakkar.

There was restrained laughter. Saladin tilted his face to the sky and searched the stars.

"Do you hear that?" he asked after a moment.

"What?" asked Mikhail.

"Bees," said Saladin. "It sounds like bees."

"Not here. Flies, perhaps, but not bees."

"I'm sure you are right." His English was heavily accented but assured. He lowered his gaze and fixed it securely on Mikhail. "I take it we have cleared up any lingering confusion about your profession."

"We have."

"And you are in fact a Russian?"

"I'm afraid so."

"I won't hold that against you," said Saladin. "Your government has committed horrible atrocities in Syria while trying to prop up the regime."

"When it comes to Syria," responded Mikhail, "Russia has no monopoly on atrocities. The Islamic State has plenty of blood on its hands, too."

"When one is making an omelet," said Saladin, "it is necessary to break eggs."

"Or slaughter innocent civilians?"

"No one is innocent in this war. So long as the unbelievers kill our women and children, we will kill theirs." He shrugged his heavy shoulders. "It is as simple as that. Besides, a man in your line of work is in no position to lecture anyone about collateral casualties."

"There's a difference between collateral casualties and the deliberate targeting of civilians."

"A narrow one." He drank some of the tea. "Tell me, Monsieur Antonov, are you a spy?"

"I live in a mansion in the south of France that's filled with art. I'm no spy."

"In Russia," said Saladin knowingly, "spies come in all shapes and sizes."

"I am not, nor have I ever been, a Russian intelligence officer."

"But you are close to the Kremlin."

"Actually, I do my best to avoid them."

"Come now, Monsieur Antonov. Everyone knows that the Kremlin picks the winners and losers in Russia. No one is allowed to become rich without the tsar's approval."

"You know my country well."

"I had many dealings with Russia in my past life. I know how the system works. And I know that a man in your line of work cannot function without the protection of friends in the SVR and the Kremlin."

"All true," said Mikhail. "And I would quickly lose my friends if they ever learned I was thinking about doing business with the likes of you."

"That doesn't sound like a compliment."

"It wasn't meant as one."

"I admire your honesty."

"And I yours," said Mikhail.

"Are you opposed in principle to doing business with us?"

"I have few—principles, that is."

"I pity you."

"Don't."

Saladin smiled. "I'm looking to acquire some merchandise for future operations."

"Weapons?"

"Not weapons," said Saladin. "Material."

"What kind of material?"

"The kind," said Saladin, "that the government of the former Soviet Union produced in great quantity during the Cold War."

Mikhail allowed a moment to pass before answering. "That's a dirty business," he said quietly.

"Very dirty," agreed Saladin. "And lucrative."

"What exactly are you looking for?"

"Cesium chloride."

"I assume you intend to use it for medical purposes."

"Agricultural, actually."

"I was under the impression that your organization took possession of material like that in Syria and Libya."

"Where did you hear something like that?"

"The same place you heard I was an arms dealer."

"It is true, but a portion of our supply recently went missing." He was staring at Jean-Luc Martel.

"And the rest of it?" asked Mikhail.

"That is none of your affair."

"Forgive me, I meant no—"

Saladin held up a hand to indicate that no offense had been taken. "Is it possible," he asked, "for you to obtain such material?"

"It's possible," said Mikhail carefully, "but extremely risky."

"Nothing worth doing is without risk."

"I'm sorry," said Mikhail after a moment, "but I can't be a party to this."

"To what?"

Mikhail made no reply.

"Will you at least hear my offer?"

"Money isn't the issue."

"Money," said Saladin, "is always the issue. Name your price, and I will pay it."

Mikhail made a show of thought. "I can make inquiries," he said at last.

"How long?"

"As long as it takes. It's not something that can be done quickly."

"I understand."

"Do you require technical assistance, too?"

Saladin shook his head. "Only the material itself."

"And if I acquire it? How do I contact you?"

"You don't," said Saladin. "You contact your friend, Monsieur Martel. And Monsieur Martel will contact Mohammad."

He stood abruptly and held out his hand. "I look forward to hearing from you."

"You will." Mikhail once again accepted the hand and held it tightly.

Saladin released his grip and turned his face once more to the sky. "Do you hear that?"

"The bees are back?"

Saladin made no reply.

"You must have excellent hearing," said Mikhail, "because I can't hear a bloody thing."

Saladin was still searching the stars. At length, he looked at Mikhail. The dark eyes narrowed thoughtfully.

"Your face is familiar to me, Monsieur Antonov. Is it possible we've met before?"

"No," said Mikhail, "it is not possible."

"In Moscow perhaps? In another life?"

The eyes moved slowly from Mikhail to Jean-Luc Martel and then to Mohammad Bakkar. At last, he looked at Mikhail again.

"Your wife is not Russian," he said.

"No. She's French."

"But her skin is very dark. Almost like an Arab." Saladin smiled and then explained how he knew this. "Two of my men saw her sunbathing on the beach in Casablanca. They saw her again in the medina of Fez yesterday. She covered her hair. My men were impressed."

"She's very respectful of Islamic culture."

"But she's not a Muslim."

"No."

"Is she a Jew?"

"My wife," said Mikhail coldly, "is none of your concern."

"Perhaps she should be. Would it be possible to meet her, please?"

"I never mix business and family."

"Wise policy," said Saladin. "But I would still like to see her."

"She has no facial veil."

"Morocco is not the caliphate, Monsieur Antonov. Inshallah, it will be soon, but for now I see uncovered faces everywhere I look."

"And how would you respond if I insisted on seeing your wife without a veil?"

"I would very likely kill you."

He brushed past Mikhail without another word and walked over to the tent.

He swept aside the flap and entered. Candles burned on the desk where Keller sat reading a worn paperback novel and next to the bed where Natalie and Olivia lay stretched on opposite sides of a backgammon board. They conversed quietly, and in the manner of people who have all the time in the world for everything.

At length, Keller looked up. "Just the man I've been waiting for," he said jovially in French. "Would you mind bringing us some tea? And some sweets. The ones soaked in honey. There's a good man."

Keller turned the page of his book. The candles trembled as Saladin crossed the room in three swift strides and stood at the foot of the bed. Natalie tossed the dice onto the board and, pleased by the results, contemplated her next move. Olivia glared at Saladin in disapproval.

"What are you doing in here?"

Saladin, silent, studied Natalie carefully. Her gaze was downward toward the board; her face was in profile and partially obscured by a lock of blond hair. When Saladin moved the hair aside, she drew away sharply.

"How dare you touch me!" she snapped in French. "Get out of here, or I'll call my husband."

Saladin held his ground. Natalie stared at him, unblinking.

Maimonides . . . So good to see you again . . .

Calmly, she said, "Is there something you wish to ask me?"

Saladin's gaze moved briefly to Keller before settling once more on Natalie.

"Forgive me," he said after a moment. "I was mistaken."

He turned away and went into the night.

Natalie looked at Keller. "You should have killed him when you had the chance."

In the Black Hole at Langley there was an audible gasp of relief when Saladin finally emerged from the tent. The drones watched as he spoke a few words directly into the ear of Mohammad Bakkar. Then the two men moved to the camp's edge and, surrounded by bodyguards, conferred at length. Several times Saladin pointed to the sky. Once, he seemed to stare directly into the lens of the Predator's camera.

"Game over," said Kyle Taylor. "Thanks for playing."

"There's a reason why he's still alive after all these years," said Uzi Navot. "He's very good at the game."

Navot watched as Mikhail slipped into the tent and accepted an object from Christopher Keller. It was not visible via infrared. Even so, Navot assumed that the two men, both veterans of elite special forces units, were now armed. And heavily outnumbered.

"What's the distance between Saladin and that tent?"

"Forty feet," answered Taylor. "Maybe a bit less."

"What's the blast radius of a Hellfire?"

"Don't even think about it."

Mohammad Bakkar had returned to the center court of the camp and was speaking to Martel. Even from twenty thousand feet, it was obvious the exchange was heated. All around them the camp was in motion. Guards were climbing into Land Cruisers, engines were turning over, lights were flaring.

"What the fuck is going on?" asked Taylor.

"Looks to me," said Navot, "as though he's shuffling the deck."

"Bakkar?"

"No," said Navot. "Saladin."

He was staring at the sky again, staring into the unblinking eye of the drone. And smiling, observed Navot. He was definitely smiling. Suddenly, he raised an arm, and four identical SUVs were swirling around him in a counterclockwise direction, in a cloud of sand and dust.

"Four vehicles, two Hellfires," said Navot. "What are the chances of picking the right one?"

"Statistically," said Taylor, "it's fifty-fifty."

"Then maybe you should take the shot now."

"Your team won't survive it."

"You're sure?"

"I've done this a time or two, Uzi."

"Yes," said Navot, watching the screen. "But so has Saladin."

Gabriel and Yaakov Rossman were watching the same image in the Casablanca command post—four SUVs circling a man whose heat signature was gradually dying beneath a veil of sand and dust. Finally, the SUVs slowed briefly to a stop, long enough for the man to enter one—which one, it was impossible to tell. Then all four set off across the desert, separated by enough space so that a single fifty-pound warhead could not take out two for the price of one.

The Predator pursued the SUVs northward across the desert while the Sentinel remained behind to keep watch over the camp. The four perimeter guards had withdrawn to the center court, where Mohammad Bakkar was once again in an animated conversation with Jean-Luc Martel. An object passed between them, from Bakkar's hand to the hand of Gabriel's unlikely asset. An object that was invisible to the thermal imaging sensors of the drone. An object that Jean-Luc slipped into the right-hand pocket of his jacket.

"Shit," said Yaakov.

"I couldn't agree more."

"Think he's gone over to the other side?"

"We'll know in a minute."

"Why wait?"

"You have a better idea?"

"Send a message to Mikhail and Keller. Tell them to come out of that tent, guns blazing."

"And what if Bakkar's men return fire with those Kalashnikovs?"

"They'll never get them off their shoulders."

"And Martel?" asked Gabriel. "What if he's standing in the wrong place at the wrong time?"

"He's a drug dealer."

"We wouldn't be here without him, Yaakov."

"You think he wouldn't betray us to save his own neck? What do you think he's doing right now? Send the message," said Yaakov. "Put them all down and let's get our people out of there before the Americans light up the desert with those Hellfire missiles."

Gabriel quickly sent not one message but two—one to Dina Sarid and the other to the satellite phone in Keller's possession. Dina replied instantly. Keller didn't bother.

"I respectfully disagree," said Yaakov.

"Duly noted."

Gabriel looked at the shot from the Predator. Four identical Toyota SUVs racing northward across the desert.

"Which one do you suppose he's in?"

"The second," said Yaakov. "Definitely the second."

"I respectfully disagree."

"Which one then?"

Gabriel stared at the screen. "I haven't a clue."

The Hotel Kasbah stood at the western edge of the great sand sea at Erg Chebbi. Dina and Eli Lavon were drinking tea in the terrace bar when the message came through from Gabriel; Yossi and Rimona were poolside. Five minutes later, having sanitized their rooms, they were all four in the hotel's cramped lobby, asking the night manager for the name of a nearby club where they might find a bit of music and dancing. He gave them the name of an establishment in Erfoud, which was to the north. They headed south instead, Yossi and Rimona in a rented Jeep Cherokee, Dina and Eli Lavon in a Nissan Pathfinder. At Khamlia they turned off the main road, into the desert, and waited for the sky to burn.

But in which Toyota Land Cruiser was the prize riding? After months of plotting and scheming and recruiting and deal making, it all came down to that. Four vehicles, two missiles. The odds of success were one in two. The price of failure would be a broken relationship with an important Arab ally— and perhaps far worse. Saladin's dead body would atone for all manner of secret sins. But Saladin on the loose in Morocco after a botched drone strike would be a diplomatic and security catastrophe. Many careers hung in the balance. Many lives, too.

There was no shortage of opinions. Graham Seymour swore it was the third Toyota, Paul Rousseau the fourth. Adrian Carter leaned toward the first vehicle but was willing to entertain the notion it was the second. Inside the White House Situation Room, the president and his senior aides were equally divided. CIA Director Morris Payne was all but certain he had seen Saladin enter the third SUV. But the president, like Paul Rousseau, was adamant it was the fourth. At the Black Hole in Langley, that was reason enough to eliminate number four from further consideration.

Expert opinion was divided, too. The drone teams analyzed the recordings of Saladin's initial flight from the camp, along with the live video and sensory data. The data pointed to number three with high probability, though one junior analyst was convinced that Saladin was not in any of the SUVs, that he had fled the camp on foot and was now making his way across the desert alone.

"He walks with a limp," remarked Uzi Navot caustically. "He'll be out there longer than Moses and the Jews of Egypt."

In the end it was left to Kyle Taylor—a veteran operations officer who had overseen more than two hundred successful drone strikes in Pakistan, Afghanistan, Iraq, Syria, Libya, Yemen, and Somalia—to make the final call. He did so swiftly and decisively and without bothering to consult with Adrian Carter. At 5:47 p.m. Washington time, 10:47 p.m. in Morocco, the order passed to the drone teams to ready the ordnance. Seventy-four seconds later, two of the Toyota Land Cruisers, the first and the third, exploded in a blinding flash of white light. Uzi Navot was the only one in the Black Hole or the White House Situation Room who wasn't watching.

The sound of the explosions reached the camp a second or two after the burst of light on the horizon. Keller and Mikhail had already drawn their Berettas by the time Jean-Luc Martel entered the tent.

"What are you going to do? Shoot me?"

"I might," answered Keller.

"That would be a miscalculation on your part." Martel glanced to the north and asked, "What just happened out there?"

"Sounded like thunder to me."

"I don't think Mohammad is liable to believe that. Not after what his Iraqi friend told him before he left."

"And what was that?"

"That Dmitri and Sophie Antonov are Israeli agents who were sent here to kill him."

"I hope you disabused Mohammad of that notion."

"I tried," said Martel.

"Is that why he gave you that gun?"

"What gun?"

"The one in the right-hand pocket of your jacket." Keller managed a smile. "The drones never blink."

Martel extracted the weapon slowly.

"An FN Five-seven," said Keller.

"The standard-issue sidearm of the SAS."

"Actually, we call it the Regiment." Keller was holding the Beretta with both hands. He released his left and stretched it toward Martel. "I'll take that."

The Frenchman only smiled.

"You're not thinking about doing something foolish, are you, Jean-Luc?"

"I did that once already. Now I'm going to look after myself." He glanced at Olivia, who was sitting at the edge of the bed next to Natalie. "And her, of course."

Keller lowered the gun. "Tell Mohammad I'd like to have a word with him."

"Why would I do that?"

"So he can hear my offer."

"*Your* offer? And what would that be?"

"Our safe passage in exchange for the lives of Mohammad and his men."

Martel emitted a low, bitter laugh. "You seem to have misread your situation. You're the one who has several Kalashnikovs pointed at you, not me."

"But I have a drone," said Keller. "And if anything happens to us, the drone is going to turn Mohammad into a pile of ash. You, too."

"Predator drones carry two Hellfire missiles. And I'm quite certain I heard two explosions just now."

"There's another drone above us."

"Is there really?"

"How did I know there was a gun in your pocket?"

"Lucky guess."

"You'd better hope so."

Martel approached Keller slowly and stared directly into his eyes. "Let me explain what's about to happen," he said quietly. "I'm going to leave here with Olivia. And then Mohammad's men are going to cut you and your friends to pieces with AK-47 fire."

Keller said nothing.

"You're not so tough without the don's protection, are you?"

"You're a dead man."

"Whatever you say."

Martel turned away from Keller and reached a hand toward Olivia. She sat motionless next to Natalie.

Martel's eyes narrowed in rage. "How much did they pay you to betray me, my love? I know you didn't do it out of the goodness of your heart. You haven't got one."

He seized Olivia's arm, but she tore it from his grasp.

"How noble of you," Martel said acidly. Then he placed the barrel of the FN to the side of her head. "Get on your feet."

Keller raised his gun and leveled it at Martel's chest.

"What are you going to do? Shoot me? If you do that, we all die."

Keller was silent.

"You don't believe me? Pull the trigger," said Martel. "See what happens next."

In the Black Hole at Langley, only Uzi Navot was watching the Sentinel's shot of the scene unfolding at the camp. Everyone else in the room was staring, transfixed, at the adjoining screen, where the wreckage of two Land Cruisers was burning brightly on the floor of the Sahara. But they were not the only vehicles to suffer damage in the strike. The driver of the second SUV had lost control after the explosions and had collided at high speed with an outcropping of desert rock. Badly damaged, the vehicle now lay on its passenger side, its headlamps still aglow. There appeared to be two men inside. In the ninety seconds since the crash, neither had moved.

"Three for the price of two," said Kyle Taylor, but no one in the room responded. They were all too busy watching the only surviving SUV, which had doubled back and was approaching the vehicle now lying beached and broken on its side. A moment later two men were frantically dragging a third from the wreckage.

"What are the chances," asked Kyle Taylor, "that he's Saladin?"

Adrian Carter watched as the two men hastily loaded the third into the back of the intact SUV.

"I'd say it's about one hundred percent. The question is, is he still alive?"

The surviving SUV was soon racing north with its headlights off, followed by the now-defanged Predator. The drone's sensors estimated the vehicle's speed at ninety-two miles per hour.

"Off road," said Carter, "with no headlights."

"Looks like we missed," said Taylor.

"Yeah," agreed Carter. "And he's still alive."

In Casablanca, Gabriel had eyes only for the video feed from the Sentinel drone. Greenish, ghostly versions of Keller and Mikhail were aiming weapons at Jean-Luc Martel, and Martel was holding a gun to the head of one of the women—Natalie or Olivia, Gabriel could not tell. Mohammad Bakkar and four of his men were outside the tent, weapons leveled toward the entrance. Owing to the center court's confined dimensions, they were tightly grouped. Gabriel calculated the odds. They were better, he reckoned, than doing nothing at all. He started to type out a message, but stopped and dialed instead. A few seconds later he watched a greenish, ghostly version of Christopher Keller reaching into his coat pocket.

"Answer it," said Gabriel through gritted teeth. "Answer the phone."

The Beretta was in Keller's right hand, the vibrating satphone in his left. His thumb was hovering over the screen.

"Don't," whispered Martel hoarsely.

"What are you going to do, Jean-Luc?"

Martel grabbed a handful of Olivia's hair and ground the barrel of the FN into her temple. Keller tapped the touchscreen and raised the phone swiftly to his ear.

Gabriel addressed him calmly.

"They're standing directly outside the entrance of your tent, Bakkar and four others. They're tightly packed, their guns are locked and loaded."

"Any other good news?"

"Saladin is still alive."

Keller lowered the phone without severing the connection and looked at Mikhail. "They're outside the tent waiting to kill us. Five men, all armed. Directly outside the entrance," Keller added pointedly.

"All of them?" asked Mikhail.

Keller nodded, then looked at Martel. "Khalil the Iraqi is a piece of charred meat. Several pieces, actually. Tell Mohammad to let us go, or he'll be next."

Martel dragged Olivia toward the entrance of the tent, the gun still to her head. Keller allowed the satphone to fall from his left hand while swiftly raising his right. He fired two shots, the *tap-tap* of a trained professional. Both found Martel's face. Then he pivoted to his right and along with Mikhail unleashed a stream of fire toward the five men standing outside.

As return fire tore through the skin of the tent, Natalie pulled Olivia to the floor. Martel lay next to them, the FN still in his lifeless hand. Natalie ripped the gun from his grasp, aimed it through the entrance, and pulled the trigger. And all the while, at the House of Spies in Casablanca, Gabriel was watching and listening. Watching as the members of his team fought for their lives. Listening to the sound of gunfire and the screams of Olivia Watson.

60

THE SAHARA, MOROCCO

From Gabriel's perspective, it seemed to last an eternity; from Keller's, a second or two. When the return fire from outside the tent fell silent, he expelled the spent magazine from his Beretta and rammed the spare into place while next to him Mikhail did the same. Then he looked down at Natalie and was surprised to see Martel's weapon in her outstretched hands. Olivia was screaming hysterically.

"Is she all right?"

The side of Olivia's face was covered with blood and brain matter. Natalie quickly searched her for a gunshot wound, but found nothing. The blood and brain matter were Martel's.

"She's fine."

Maybe someday, thought Keller, but not anytime soon. He reached down and snatched up the phone. "What's going on out there?"

"Not much," answered Gabriel.

"Any sign of movement?"

"The one in the middle. From up here, the rest look dead."

"Pity," said Keller. "What now?"

———

Ten miles to the north, the last surviving Toyota Land Cruiser was racing across an uninhabited patch of desert, pursued by the Predator.

"What's the loiter time on that drone?" asked Navot.

"Eight hours and change," said Adrian Carter. "Unless the Moroccans figure out that we carried out a clandestine drone strike on their territory. Then it's a hell of a lot less."

"And that one?" asked Navot, nodding toward the shot of the camp from the Sentinel.

"Fourteen hours."

"How stealth is it?"

"Stealth enough so that the Moroccans will never be able to find it."

One of the phones in front of Carter flashed with an incoming call. He brought the receiver to this ear, listened, and then swore softly.

"What is it?" asked Navot.

"NSA is picking up a lot of traffic from Morocco."

"What kind of traffic?"

"Sounds like the shit is hitting the fan."

Another phone flashed. This time it was Morris Payne calling from the Situation Room.

"Understood," said Carter after a moment, and hung up. Then he looked at Navot. "The Moroccan ambassador just called the White House to ask if the United States had attacked his country."

"What are you going to do?"

"The loiter time on those drones just got a whole lot shorter."

"The stealth drone, too?"

"What stealth drone?"

Carter gave the order to the drone teams. Instantly, the Predator banked sharply to the east toward the Algerian border. Its thermal imaging camera stayed with the surviving SUV for another two minutes, until finally the heat signature evaporated from the screens of the Black Hole. The Sentinel was next. The last image Navot saw was of two men slipping out of a tent in the desert, weapons in their outstretched hands.

It was true that all five men in the camp's center court had been shot, but two were still alive. One was Mohammad Bakkar. The other was one of the guards. Mikhail ended the guard's life with a single gunshot to the head while Keller examined Bakkar by starlight. The Moroccan hashish producer had been hit twice in the chest. His pullover was drenched in blood, and there was blood in his mouth. It was obvious he did not have long to live.

Keller crouched next to him. "Where is he going, Mohammad?"

"Who?" asked Bakkar, choking on the blood.

"Saladin."

"I don't know anyone by that name."

"Perhaps this will refresh your memory."

Keller placed the barrel of the Beretta against Mohammad Bakkar's ankle and pulled the trigger. The Moroccan's screams filled the night.

"Where is he?"

"I don't know!"

"Of course you do, Mohammad. You gave him sanctuary

here in Morocco after the attack on Washington. You gave him the money he needed to attack my country."

"And what country is that? Are you French? Or are you a fucking Jew like him?"

Bakkar was looking at Mikhail, who was standing over Keller's shoulder. Keller placed the barrel of the Beretta against the Moroccan's lower leg and pulled the trigger.

"I'm British, actually."

"In that case," said Bakkar, moaning in agony, "fuck your country."

Keller fired a shot into the side of Bakkar's knee.

"Allahu Akbar!"

"Be that as it may," said Keller calmly, "where is he?"

"I told you—"

Another shot into what was left of the knee. Bakkar was starting to lose consciousness. Keller slapped him hard across the face.

"Did he order you to kill us?"

Bakkar nodded.

"And what were you supposed to do after that?"

The Moroccan's eyes were closing. Keller was losing him.

"Where, Mohammad? Where is he going?"

"One of my . . . houses."

"Where? The Rif? The Atlas?"

Bakkar was choking on the blood.

"Where, Mohammad?" asked Keller, shaking the Moroccan violently. "Tell me where he's going so I can help you."

"Fez," gasped Bakkar. "He's going to Fez."

The light was going out of the Moroccan's eyes. Despite the blood and the pain, he looked like a deeply contented man.

"You're lying to me, aren't you, Mohammad?"

"Yes."

"Where's he going?"

"Who?"

"Saladin."

"Paradise," said Bakkar. "I'm going to paradise."

"I rather doubt that, actually," said Keller.

Then he placed the gun to Bakkar's forehead and pulled the trigger one last time.

Of the five dead men in the center court of the camp, only Mohammad Bakkar was in possession of a mobile phone. A Samsung Galaxy, it was in the front pocket of his trousers, with the SIM card and battery removed. Keller reassembled the device and powered it on while Mikhail and Natalie tended to Olivia. There were no vehicles left in the camp—Saladin, in his desperate attempt to escape, had taken all four—which meant they had no choice but to walk out of the desert. They took only what they could carry easily. Warm clothing, phones, passports, wallets, and two Kalashnikovs with fully loaded magazines. They didn't bother trying to find a torch among the camp's supplies. There was moon enough to light their path.

They left the camp at five minutes past eleven o'clock local time and headed due west into a sea of sand. Keller walked at the front of the line, followed by the two women and lastly by Mikhail. In Keller's right hand was Mohammad Bakkar's mobile phone. He checked the status of the battery. Twelve percent.

"Shit," he said. "Anyone have a charger?"

Even Olivia managed to laugh.

In Casablanca, Gabriel and Yaakov Rossman took quiet stock of what remained of the operation. Its wreckage lay scattered across the desert of southern Morocco, from the Algerian border to the dunes of Erg Chebbi. Two Toyota Land Cruisers were smoldering ruins, a third lay damaged on its side. And a fourth—the one presumably carrying a wounded Saladin, a Saladin who looked as though he might require emergency medical treatment—had last been seen speeding northwest toward the Middle Atlas Mountains. Jean-Luc Martel, a prominent if deeply corrupt French businessman, lay dead at a remote camp, along with Mohammad Bakkar, Morocco's largest hashish producer, and four of his men. Bakkar's mobile phone was now in the possession of a British intelligence officer. The battery meter read ten percent and falling fast.

"Other than that," said Gabriel, "it all went exactly according to plan."

"Saladin would be dead if the Americans had picked the right car."

Gabriel said nothing.

"You're not thinking about—"

"Of course I am."

Gabriel looked down at the computer screen. On it was a map of southern Morocco. Two blue lights were moving eastward across the desert from Khamlia; a single red light was moving slowly westward. They were approximately two miles apart.

"In a few minutes," said Yaakov, "the southeastern corner of Morocco is going to be crawling with soldiers and gendarmes. It won't take them long to find a couple of burning Toyotas and a camp full of dead bodies. And then all hell is going to break loose."

"It already has."

"Which is why you need to order the team to dump those weapons and make for the bolt-hole at Agadir. With a bit of luck, they'll arrive before dawn and we'll pull them out right away. If not, they'll lie low in a beach hotel and leave after dark tomorrow night."

"That's the safe play."

"Actually, there's nothing safe about it."

"And us?" asked Gabriel.

"The gendarmes will be blocking roads all over the country soon. Better to stay here tonight and leave by plane in the morning. We'll fly to Paris or London and then catch a flight back to Ben Gurion."

"What about Saladin?"

"He can see to his own travel arrangements."

"That's what I'm afraid of."

On the computer screen the blue lights had reached the red light, and after a moment all three were moving westward across the desert toward the village of Khamlia.

"What are you going to tell them?" asked Yaakov.

Gabriel rapidly typed out the message and clicked SEND. It was four words in length.

PLUG IN THE PHONE . . .

61

THE SAHARA, MOROCCO

They had no means for a secure upload—not in the cellular dead zone of the southern desert—so they searched the Samsung the old-fashioned way, call by call, text by text, Internet history. Natalie, the team's most fluent speaker and reader of Arabic, handled the device itself while Keller relayed the data to the Casablanca command post over the satellite phone. They were sitting in the backseat of the Nissan Pathfinder, with Dina behind the wheel and Eli Lavon serving as her navigator and spotter. Mikhail was in the Jeep Cherokee with Olivia.

"How is she?" asked Gabriel.

"About as well as you would expect. We need to get her out of here. Tonight, if possible."

"I'm working on it. Now give me the next number."

It appeared Mohammad Bakkar had not had the Samsung long. The first incoming call listed in the directory was the previous evening at 7:19 p.m. The time corresponded to the call that Jean-Luc Martel had received while sitting with Keller in the bar of the Palais Faraj in Fez. So, too, did the number. It seemed that the man who had called Martel to arrange the meeting at the camp in the desert had immediately called Mohammad Bakkar to say the meeting was on. Bakkar had then placed a call of his own, at 7:21.

"Give me that number," said Gabriel.

Keller recited it.

"Read it again."

Keller did.

"That's Nazir Bensaïd."

Bensaïd was the Moroccan jihadist and ISIS member who had followed Martel and the team from Casablanca to Fez, and from Fez into the Middle Atlas Mountains.

"Bakkar called someone else a few minutes after that," said Keller.

"What's the number?"

Keller relayed it to him.

"Does it appear anywhere else?"

Keller put the question to Natalie, who quickly searched the directories. Bakkar had placed another call to the number at 5:17 that afternoon. He had received one at 5:23.

Keller relayed the information to Gabriel.

"Who do you suppose that is?"

"The guest of honor?"

Gabriel severed the connection and raised Adrian Carter at Langley over the secure link.

"Where's Nazir Bensaïd?" he asked.

"His phone is back in Fez. Whether Nazir is still attached to it is unclear."

Gabriel then gave Carter the number Mohammad Bakkar had called three times—once the previous day at 7:21 p.m., and twice that afternoon, before the meeting in the desert.

"Any idea who it belongs to?" asked Carter.

"If I had to guess," said Gabriel, "it's Saladin."

"Where did you find it?"

"Directory assistance."

"Why didn't we think of that? I'll give it to the NSA. In the meantime," said Carter, "tell your team not to lose that phone."

Twenty minutes after they passed the encampment of Berber nomads, Mohammad Bakkar's phone reconnected to Morocco's cellular network. It received no old texts or voice mails, and no new communication of any kind. Keller passed the news along to Gabriel and then asked for instructions. Gabriel ordered them to follow the N13 north to the village of Rissani, at the edge of the Tafilalt Oasis. Once there, they were to switch to the N12 and make their way westward to Agadir.

"I assume Saladin will be waiting for us when we arrive?"

"Doubtful," said Gabriel.

"So why are we going there?"

"Because Agadir is a lot nicer than the Temara interrogation center."

"What about the guns?"

"Dump them in the desert. In all likelihood, you're going to run into roadblocks."

"And if we do?"

"Improvise."

The connection went dead.

"What were his instructions?" asked Eli Lavon.

"He wants us to improvise."

"What about the weapons?"

435

"He thinks we should hang on to them," said Keller. "Just in case."

It was after midnight by the time they reached the village of Khamlia. As Dina turned north on the N13, a pair of helicopters thundered overhead on an easterly course.

"Could be a routine patrol," said Keller.

"Could be," said Eli Lavon skeptically.

The Kalashnikov that Keller had taken from the camp was hidden in a duffel bag in the rear storage compartment; the Berretta was at the small of his back. He glanced over his shoulder and saw the headlamps of the Jeep Cherokee, trailing about a hundred yards behind. He wondered how Olivia would fare during a prolonged interrogation by Moroccan gendarmes. Not well, he reckoned.

Turning around, he saw flashing emergency lights approaching them at speed. The vehicles sped past in a blur.

"That didn't look good," said Lavon. "Are you sure Gabriel doesn't want us to dump the guns?"

Keller didn't answer. He was staring at Mohammad Bakkar's phone, which was vibrating in his hand. It was an incoming text message, Arabic script, from the same number Bakkar had called that afternoon. Keller held up the device for Natalie to see. Her eyes widened as she read.

"What does it say?" asked Keller.

"He wants to know if we're dead."

"Really? I wonder who that could be from."

Keller picked up the satphone and started to dial, but stopped when he saw a gendarme standing in the middle of the highway, a traffic torch in his hand.

"What should I do?" asked Dina.

"By all means," said Keller, "you should stop."

Dina eased to the side of the road and braked to a halt. Behind her, Yossi Gavish did the same in the Jeep Cherokee.

"What should I tell them?" asked Dina.

"Improvise," suggested Keller.

"What happens if they don't believe me?"

Keller looked down at the message on Mohammad Bakkar's phone.

"If they don't believe you," he said, "they die."

Dina spoke to the gendarme in German, very quickly, and with fear in her voice. She said that she and her friends had been camping in the desert, that there had been explosions of some sort, and gunfire. Fearful for their lives, they had fled the camp with only the clothes on their backs.

"In French, Madame. Please, in French."

"I don't speak French," answered Dina in German.

"English?"

"Yes, I speak English."

But it was so heavily accented she might as well have still been speaking German. Frustrated, the gendarme checked her passport while his partner circled the vehicle slowly. The beam of his torch lingered for a moment on Keller's face, long enough for Keller to consider reaching for the Beretta. Finally, the gendarme moved to the back of the SUV and rapped a knuckle on the glass.

"Open it," he said in Arabic, but his partner overruled him. He returned Dina's passport and asked where they were planning to go next. And when Dina answered in German, he waved her forward with his red-tipped torch. The Jeep Cherokee, too.

Keller handed Bakkar's phone to Natalie. "Answer him."

"What should I say?"

"Tell him we're dead, of course."

"But—"

"Hurry," Keller interjected. "We've kept him waiting long enough."

Natalie sent a one-word reply: AIWA. It was the Arabic word for "yes." Instantly, the person at the other end of the exchange began working on a reply. It appeared a few seconds later. One word, Arabic script.

"What does it say?" asked Keller.

"Alhamdulillah. It means—"

"Thanks be to God."

"More or less."

"What it really means," said Keller, "is that we've got him."

"Or someone close to him."

"Good enough."

Keller rang Gabriel on the satellite phone and told him what had just transpired.

"You might have checked with me before sending that message."

"I didn't have time."

"Keep him talking."

"How?"

"Ask if he's hurt."

Keller told Natalie to send the message. A minute passed before the Samsung pinged with the reply.

"He's hurt," she said.

"Ask him if the others were killed in the drone strike," said Gabriel.

"You're pushing it," said Keller.

"Send the message, damn it."

Natalie did. The reply was instant.

"Many of the brothers were killed," she read.

"Ask him how many brothers are with him."

Natalie typed out the message and sent it.

"Two," she said a moment later.

"Are they hurt?"

Another exchange of messages.

"No."

"Does he need a doctor?"

"Easy," cautioned Keller.

"Send it," snapped Gabriel.

The wait for a response was nearly two minutes.

"Yes," said Natalie. "He needs one."

There was another silence on the line.

"We need to know where he's going," Gabriel said at last.

"Track the phone," replied Keller.

"If he turns it off, we'll lose him. You have to ask him."

Natalie typed out the message and sent it. The reply was vague.

AL RIAD. The house.

"We need more than that," said Gabriel.

"You can't ask him which house."

"Tell him you're sending Nazir to look after him until the doctor arrives."

"I hope you know what you're doing," said Keller.

"Send it."

Natalie did. Then she composed a second message and sent it

to Nazir Bensaïd's number. They had to wait five long minutes for their answer.

"We've got him!" said Natalie. "He's on his way."

Keller brought the satphone to his ear. "You still want us to go to Agadir?"

"Not all of you," answered Gabriel.

"Too bad about those guns."

"Any chance you can find them?"

"Yeah," said Keller. "I think I know where to look."

The next call to arrive at the Casablanca command post was from Adrian Carter.

"We had his phone for three or four minutes, but he went off the air again."

"Yes, I know."

"How?"

"He was talking to us."

"What?"

Gabriel explained.

"Any idea where the house is?"

"I didn't think it was a good idea to ask him. Besides, we have Nazir Bensaïd to show us the way."

"He's already on the move," said Carter.

"Where is he?"

"Leaving Fez and heading back to the Middle Atlas."

"Where he will tend to a wounded Saladin," said Gabriel, "until a doctor arrives."

"Are you thinking about making a house call?"

"Office style."

"I'm afraid you'll be on your own."

"Any chance we can borrow one of those drones for surveillance?"

"None whatsoever."

"When's your next satellite pass?"

Carter shouted the question to the officers gathered in the Black Hole. The answer came back a moment later.

"We'll have a bird over eastern Morocco at four a.m."

"Enjoy the show," said Gabriel.

"You're not thinking about going up there, are you?"

"I'm not leaving here without him, Adrian."

"It's the first part of that sentence that concerns me."

Gabriel rang off without another word and looked at Yaakov.

"We need to clean this place up and get moving."

Yaakov stood stock-still.

"You disagree with my decision?"

"No. It's just—"

"You're not worried about the damn jinns, are you?"

"We're not supposed to make noise at night."

Gabriel closed his laptop. "So we'll leave quietly. It's better that way."

Five minutes later the Moroccan armed forces and security services went on their highest state of alert. Nevertheless, in the confusion, they failed to take note of two small but significant movements of personnel and equipment. The first occurred on the outskirts of the village of Rissani, where a Jeep Cherokee and a Nissan Pathfinder paused briefly in the night at the intersection of two desert highways. There ensued a one-for-one exchange of passengers, a small bookish man for a tall lanky one.

Then the vehicles went their separate ways. The Jeep Cherokee headed west toward the sea; the Nissan, north toward the base of the Atlas Mountains. The passengers of the Cherokee knew what awaited them, but those riding in the Nissan were headed toward a more uncertain fate. They had in their possession two Beretta pistols, two Kalashnikov assault rifles, passports, credit cards, cash, cellular phones, and a satellite phone. More important, they had a phone that had been used briefly by Morocco's most prominent hashish producer. A phone, they hoped, that would lead them to Saladin.

The second movement took place some four hundred miles to the northwest in Casablanca, where two men slipped from a faded old villa, quietly, so as not to awaken the demons within, and loaded their bags into a rented Peugeot sedan. They drove along the empty boulevards of the old colonial section, past the tattered Art Nouveau buildings, and the modern apartment blocks of the newly rich, and the Bidon-villes of the wretchedly poor, until finally they reached the motorway. The younger of the two men handled the driving; the older passed the time by loading and reloading his Beretta pistol. He had no business being there, it was true. He was the chief now, and a chief had to know his place. Still, there was a first for everything.

He slipped the loaded gun into the waistband of his trousers at the small of his back, and checked his mobile phone. Then he stared out his window at the endless lights of Casablanca.

"What are you thinking?" asked the younger man.

"I'm thinking that you need to drive faster."

"I've never driven a chief before."

The older man smiled.

"Is that all you were thinking?"

"Why do you ask?"

"Because it looked to me as though you were pulling a trigger."

"Which hand?"

"Left," said the younger man. "It was definitely the left."

The older man looked out the window. "How many times?"

THE MIDDLE ATLAS MOUNTAINS, MOROCCO

The phone moved steadily south, across the lowlands around Fez, toward the slopes of the Middle Atlas. They could not be sure it was actually in the possession of Nazir Bensaïd. Now that the drones were gone, they had no eyes on the target, and neither the NSA nor Unit 8200 had been able to activate the phone's microphone or camera. For all they knew, the device was on the back of a flatbed truck, and Nazir Bensaïd was somewhere in the labyrinth of Fez's ancient medina.

It was half past one in the morning when the phone reached the Berber town of Imouzzer. Its pace of travel slowed as it moved along the town's main street. Gabriel, who was receiving updates from Adrian Carter, wondered whether the brass ring was already within his reach. There was much about a place like Imouzzer, he thought, for a fugitive to find appealing. It was small enough so that Westerners were easily visible, but sufficiently busy to allow a robed man to move about unnoticed. The uninhabited peaks of the Middle Atlas were close, should the fugitive feel the need to flee, and the delights of Fez were but an hour's car ride away. An image formed in Gabriel's mind—a tall, powerfully built man in a hooded djellaba, limping through the narrow alleys of the medina.

But at 1:35 a.m. the phone left Imouzzer and, increasing its pace, made for Ifrane, an artificial holiday town that looked as though it had been plucked from the Alps and dropped in North Africa. Once again, Gabriel allowed himself to wonder whether they were close. This time he dressed the prize in different clothing—trousers and a woolen sweater instead of a djellaba—and imagined him passing the winter after the attack on Washington in the comfort of a Swiss-style hotel. But when the phone departed Ifrane, Gabriel covered the image in a layer of obliterating paint and waited for the next update from Adrian Carter at the Black Hole.

"Faster," he said. "You have to drive faster."

"I'm driving as fast as I can," answered Yaakov.

"Not you," said Gabriel. "*Him*."

The next town on the phone's path was Azrou. There it turned onto the N13, the main highway linking the Middle Atlas Mountains with the Sahara, the same road on which Keller, Mikhail, Natalie, and Dina were now headed north. It passed through a chain of tiny Berber villages—Timahdite, Aït Oufella, Boulaajoul—before finally coming to rest a few hundred yards from the town of Zaida, under what circumstances they could only imagine. A house, a fortress, a camel-hair tent in an open field strewn with boulders. Ten interminable minutes elapsed before a text message appeared on Mohammad Bakkar's phone. Keller read it aloud to Gabriel.

"Nazir says the brother is very badly injured."

"What a shame."

"He says he needs a doctor soon. Otherwise, he might not live."

"The best possible outcome."

"You're not thinking about letting nature take its course?"

"Not for a minute," said Gabriel. "Tell him that the doctor is on his way. Tell him he's coming from Fez."

There was a moment of silence while Natalie composed the message in Arabic and sent it. A few seconds later Gabriel heard the ping of the reply.

"Alhamdulillah," said Keller.

"I couldn't agree more."

Gabriel heard another ping. "What does it say?"

"He wants to know where I am."

"I didn't realize you two were friends."

"He thinks I'm—"

"Yes, I know," said Gabriel. "Tell him it took you longer than expected to arrange transport. Tell him you'll be there in two hours, maybe less."

There was another silence while Natalie sent the message.

"Any reply?"

"No."

"Is he working on one?"

"Doesn't seem to be."

"Tell him you're concerned about the brother's safety."

A few seconds passed. Then Keller said, "Sent."

"Now ask him how many brothers are with him at the *riad*."

After another exchange of messages, Keller said, "Four."

"Ask him whether they have guns to protect themselves from the infidels."

A moment later they had their answer.

"Sounds to me as though they're well armed," said Keller. "Anything else you'd like to ask?"

"No more questions. The bird will be able to tell us everything else we need to know."

"Where are you now?"

Gabriel looked out the window at the darkened landscape. "Mars," he said gloomily. "You?"

"A little village called Kerrandou. It's about sixty or seventy miles from Zaida. If there are no more roadblocks, we'll be there in ninety minutes."

"We'll be right behind you."

Gabriel severed the connection and rang the Black Hole at Langley.

"We've got him," he told Adrian Carter.

"The bird will be overhead at four o'clock your time."

"You're sure?"

"Don't worry. It's a spy satellite," said Carter. "There's not a lot of unexpected traffic up there."

I t was a drab and dusty town of low brown buildings. The shops and cafés along the wide main street were tightly shuttered, and at that hour there was no sign of life except for three men waiting at a crumbling bus shelter. A Jeep Cherokee filled with Western faces was worthy of their undivided attention. Their dour expressions made it clear that outsiders were not welcome, especially at half past three in the morning.

"Looks like Saladin's kind of place," said Keller.

"Think they know about the tall Iraqi who's been living on the east side of town?" asked Mikhail.

"I doubt it."

"I wouldn't mind having a look at the property while we're passing through."

"Too risky. Better to wait for the bird."

Dina drove through the rest of the town without slowing and emerged into the bleak, treeless countryside. About a mile and a half north was a dirt road that led to a small lake, the kind of spot where a Moroccan family might spread a blanket on a cool autumn day and forget their troubles for a few hours. Dina switched off the engine while Keller rang Gabriel and told him where they could be found. A few minutes later they heard from Nazir Bensaïd via text. It seemed the brother's condition was worsening. When would the doctor arrive? Soon, Natalie assured him. Inshallah.

"Here they come," said Dina.

She flashed the headlights, and the approaching car turned off the highway and stopped. Keller and Natalie walked over and slid into the backseat. Keller checked the time on Mohammad Bakkar's phone. It was 3:45.

"Fancy meeting you here. How was the drive?"

Neither Gabriel nor Yaakov responded.

Keller stared out the window. "I wonder what's keeping Mohammad and that doctor."

"Maybe he had car trouble," suggested Gabriel.

"Or left leg trouble," quipped Keller. "Or maybe he's having trouble thinking straight."

He checked the phone again: *3:46 . . .*

"Think the Moroccans have found the camp yet?"

"I'd say so."

"Think they've identified any of the victims?"

"One or two."

"Pretty big story, don't you imagine? A major hashish producer and a French hotelier found dead together."

"Almost as big as a failed American drone strike on Moroccan soil."

"I wonder how long it will take to become public. Because if it does . . ."

Keller left the thought unfinished.

3:47 . . .

_____

Gabriel rang Carter at the stroke of four. Another ten minutes elapsed while the cameras and sensory devices of the satellite assessed the target.

"It's a walled compound. One substantial structure, two smaller outbuildings."

"How walled?"

"It's hard to tell how high it is, especially in darkness. You'll have to take a drive past the place or use your imagination."

"Is the gate open or closed?"

"Closed," said Carter. "And Nazir Bensaïd's Renault is definitely there."

"How many men?"

"Two outside, three inside. All in the primary structure. They're tightly grouped."

"Keeping watch over an injured man."

"Looks like it."

"Where are they in the house?"

"Second level, southeast corner."

"Facing Mecca."

"There's a lot of other heat in that room," said Carter. "Kyle thinks it's computer equipment."

"And heaven knows Kyle is never wrong."

"It's possible you've found the compound where he's been directing the attacks. The crown jewels of the network are liable to be on those computers."

"Are you suggesting we gather up as much as we can carry?"

"Might not be a bad idea."

"Is there anything else you can tell me?"

"Looks like he's got a couple of dogs inside the walls. Big ones," added Carter.

Gabriel swore softly. His fear of the canine was well known within the international brotherhood of spies.

"Sorry to be the bearer of bad news," said Carter sympathetically.

"What kind of self-respecting Muslim extremist would keep dogs in his home?"

"The kind who doesn't trust cats to warn him of an intrusion. And one more thing," said Carter. "The NSA has been listening in on the Moroccan police and military."

"And?"

"They know damn well that we carried out a drone strike on their soil last night. And they know that Mohammad Bakkar and Jean-Luc Martel are dead."

"How long before they go public?"

"If I had to guess, the Moroccan people will be hearing about this over their Froot Loops."

"Then maybe we should change the subject."

"We?"

"Let me know if there is any movement at the compound."

Gabriel hung up.

"Any problems?" asked Keller.

"Two dogs and a locked gate."

"Can't do much about the dogs, but the gate shouldn't be a problem."

Keller handed Mohammad Bakkar's phone to Natalie, who composed the message and sent it to Nazir Bensaïd inside the compound. The reply was a few seconds in coming.

"Done," she said.

Gabriel and Yaakov had carried more than just computers and secure communications equipment from the House of Spies in Casablanca. They had also taken two .45-caliber Jericho pistols and two Uzi Pro compact submachine guns. Gabriel gave Yaakov one of each, and Natalie an Uzi Pro. He kept only a Jericho for himself.

"The perfect self-defense weapon," said Keller.

"Also perfect for eliminating those who offer unwanted advice."

"I don't want to get in the middle of family business, but—"

"Then don't," said Gabriel.

Keller made a show of thought. "How many dogs are in that compound? Was it one or two?"

Gabriel said nothing.

"Let Mikhail and me handle it. Or better yet," said Keller, "let's send Yaakov in there alone. He looks like he's done this sort of thing a time or two."

Yaakov expertly rammed a magazine into the Uzi Pro and looked at Gabriel. "He has a point, boss."

"Not you, too."

"That satellite can tell us only so much. What it *can't* tell us is whether there are spider holes in the compound, or whether those boys are wearing explosive vests."

"Then we should assume they are."

Yaakov placed a hand on Gabriel's shoulder. "You're not some kid anymore. You're the chief now. Let the three of us take care of it. You stay here with—"

"With the women?"

"I didn't mean it like that," said Yaakov. "But someone needs to look after them."

"Dina was in the IDF, just like the rest of us. She can look after herself."

"But—"

"Duly noted, Yaakov. Are you going to drive, or should I handle it?"

Yaakov hesitated, then slid behind the wheel. Mikhail dropped into the front passenger seat, Gabriel and Keller into the back. Natalie watched as the car set off toward Zaida. Then she walked over to the Jeep Cherokee and climbed into the passenger seat. She placed the Uzi Pro on the floor between her feet and checked the time on Mohammad Bakkar's phone. It was 4:11.

"Maybe we should listen to the news."

Dina switched on the radio and searched the airwaves for something that sounded like a morning newscast. At the sound of a male voice, she stopped and looked at Natalie.

"He's reading verses from the Koran."

Dina rotated the tuner again. "Better?"

"Yes."

"What's she talking about?"

"The weather."

"What's the forecast?"

"Hot."

"I'll say."

Natalie laughed quietly. "Do you remember that day at Na-halal?" she asked after a moment. "The day I tried to say no to all this?"

Dina smiled at the memory. "And now look at you. You're one of us."

A truck passed on the highway. Then another. The stars in the eastern half of the sky were beginning to dim.

"What was he like?" asked Dina.

"Who?"

"Saladin."

"It doesn't matter." Natalie checked the time again. "In a few minutes, he'll be dead."

Like small villages the world over, Zaida was not by nature a late sleeper. One of the cafés on the main square was open for business, and a smoking Fez-bound coach was taking on passengers at the shelter opposite. The stench of diesel exhaust poured into the car as Yaakov, swerving to avoid a stray goat, drove past. His speed was ideal. Not too fast. More important, observed Gabriel, not too slow. One hand rested lightly on the wheel, the other lay motionless on the shift. By contrast, Mikhail was drumming his fingers on the center console. Keller, however, seemed entirely oblivious to what was about to occur. Indeed, were it not for the Kalashnikov lying across his thighs, he might have been a tourist on a sightseeing excursion in an exotic land.

"Can't you at least pretend to be a little worried?" said Gabriel.

"About what?"

"That gun, for one thing. It looks a museum piece."

"A damn fine weapon, the Kalashnikov. Besides, it worked just fine at the camp in the desert. Just ask your friend Dmitri Antonov. He'll tell you."

But Mikhail wasn't listening; he was still drumming his fingers on the console.

"Is there any way you can make him stop?" asked Keller.

"I've tried."

"Try harder."

Yaakov removed his right hand from the shift and placed it atop Mikhail's. The fingers went still.

"Much obliged," said Keller.

A few yards beyond the square the town dwindled. They crossed a dry creek bed and entered a nether region separating civilization and wilderness. A few broken buildings rose from the brown earth on both sides of the highway, and off to the east, an island in a sea of stones, was the compound. From a distance, it was impossible to tell what it was—a home, a factory, a secret government installation, the hiding place of the world's most dangerous terrorist. Its outer walls looked to be about ten or twelve feet high and were topped by spirals of concertina wire. The private track connecting it to the highway was unpaved, ensuring that any approaching vehicle would make a great deal of noise and raise a cloud of dust.

Gabriel brought a phone to his ear. It was connected to Adrian Carter at Langley.

"Can you see us?"

"You're hard to miss."

"Any change?"

"Two outside, three inside. They're in the same room. One of them hasn't moved in a while."

Gabriel lowered the phone. Yaakov was staring at him in the rearview mirror.

"Once we make the turn," he said, "we lose all element of surprise."

"But we're not going to surprise them, Yaakov. We're expected."

Yaakov guided the car onto the private road and started toward the compound.

"Switch on your high beams," instructed Gabriel.

Yaakov did as he was told, illuminating the harsh, rocky landscape with white light. "They see us now."

Gabriel raised a second phone to his ear, the one connected to Natalie, and told her to ring the doorbell.

Natalie had preloaded the text onto Mohammad Bakkar's phone. Now, on Gabriel's command, she thumbed it into the ether.

"Well?" he asked.

"He's working on the reply."

The message finally appeared.

"He says they'll open the gate."

"How nice of them. But tell them to hurry. The doctor is very anxious to see the brother."

Natalie sent the message on Bakkar's Samsung. Then she switched her own phone to speaker mode and waited for the sound of gunfire.

By then, Gabriel was already talking to Adrian Carter at Langley.

"Any change?"

"Two men getting ready to open the gate, one coming downstairs. Looks like he's carrying a gun."

"So much for Arab hospitality," said Gabriel, and lowered the phone.

They were about fifty yards from the compound and closing at a moderate speed. The headlamps now shone directly on the gate. It was a two-leaf swing model, stainless steel. A cloud of dust settled around them like fog as Yaakov slowed to a stop. For several seconds, nothing happened.

Gabriel raised the Langley phone to his ear. "What's going on?"

"Looks like they're unlocking it."

"Where's the third man?"

"Waiting outside the entrance of the house."

"And where's the entrance relative to us?"

"Your two o'clock."

Gabriel lowered the phone again as a crack appeared between the leaves of the gate. He relayed the satellite information to the other three men in the car and issued a terse set of instructions.

Keller frowned. "Mind saying that again in a language I can understand?"

Gabriel hadn't realized he was speaking in Hebrew.

All at once the gate began to swing away, drawn by two pairs of hands. Yaakov balanced the Uzi Pro atop the steering wheel and aimed at the pair of hands to the right. Mikhail leveled a Kalashnikov at the hands on the left.

"Never mind," said Keller. "No translation necessary."

At last, the gate was sufficiently open to accommodate a car. Two men, each cradling an automatic rifle, stepped into the breach and waved Yaakov into the compound. Instead, he unleashed a torrent of fire through the windscreen toward the man on the right. Mikhail, in the front passenger seat, squeezed off several rounds with the Kalashnikov toward the man on the left. Neither guard managed to fire a shot in return, but as Yaakov accelerated through the open gate, a gun opened up from the entrance of the main building. Mikhail answered through

the open front passenger window while Gabriel, directly behind him, fired off several rounds with the Jericho .45. Within
seconds, the gun in the entranceway fell silent.

Yaakov braked hard and rammed the shift into park while
Mikhail and Gabriel tumbled out of the car and started across
the outer yard of the compound. Mikhail quickly drew away
from Gabriel, and after a few paces Keller overtook him as well.
The two elite soldiers paused briefly at the entrance, next to the
body of the third gunman. Gabriel glanced down at the lifeless
face. It was Nazir Bensaïd.

Beyond the entrance was an ornate Moorish courtyard, blue
with moonlight, with cedar doors on all four sides. Keller and
Mikhail pivoted through the doorway on the right and crossed
a foyer to a stone flight of steps. Instantly, they were met
with automatic weapons fire from above. The two operatives
dived for cover, right and left, while Gabriel remained pinned
down outside in the courtyard. When the gunfire ceased, he
slipped into the foyer and sheltered next to Mikhail. Keller,
directly opposite, wedged his Kalashnikov into the stairwell
and blindly fired several shots into the darkness. Then Mikhail
did the same.

When they paused to reload, there was only silence from
above. Gabriel peered around the edge of the wall. The landing
at the top of the steps appeared empty, but in the darkness he
couldn't be sure. Finally, Keller and Mikhail mounted the first
step. At once, there was a piercing scream. A woman's scream,
thought Gabriel—two religiously significant Arabic words that
left little doubt as to what would occur next. He grabbed the
back of Mikhail's shirt and pulled with every bit of strength he
had left in his body while Keller hurled himself down the steps

toward safety. A second too late, the bomb exploded. Saladin, it seemed, had lost his sense of timing.

Gabriel was carrying two mobile phones in the pocket of his jacket, one connected to Adrian Carter, the other to Natalie and Dina. Carter and the rest of the officers gathered in the Black Hole had the advantage of the satellite's cameras and sensors, but Natalie and Dina had been privy only to the audio. The quality was muted. Even so, they had no trouble making out what was taking place inside the compound. A brief but intense firefight, a woman screaming "Allahu Akbar," the unmistakable sound of a bomb exploding. After that, there was only silence. Dina quickly started the engine. A moment later they were racing along the main street of Zaida. The little town in the shadow of the Middle Atlas Mountains was now wide awake.

The steps were strewn with the tattered remnants of a woman—smallish, about twenty or twenty-five, pretty once. Here a leg, here a portion of a torso, here a hand, the right, still clutching a detonator switch. The head had rolled to the bottom of the steps and come to rest at Gabriel's feet. He lifted the black veil from the face and saw a set of delicate features arranged in a mask of religious madness. The eyes were blue—the blue of a mountain lake. Was she a wife or concubine? Or a daughter perhaps? Or was she just another black widow, a lost girl to whom Saladin had strapped a bomb and an ideology of death?

Gabriel closed the blue eyes and covered the face, and followed Keller and Mikhail silently up the stairs. A Kalashnikov lay on the upper landing where it had fallen from the woman's hands, along with a magazine's worth of shell casings. To the right a hallway stretched into the darkness. At the end of it was a door—and behind the door, thought Gabriel, was a room at the southeast corner of the house. A room facing Mecca. A room where an injured man now lay alone with no one to protect him.

They picked their way carefully across the landing so as not to disturb the shell casings and moved silently along the corridor. When they reached the door, Keller tested the latch. It was locked. He exchanged a few quick hand signals with Mikhail and motioned for Gabriel to move away, but Gabriel quickly overruled him with a signal of his own. He was an operational chief, and he preferred to deal with his enemies at a meter rather than a mile.

Keller didn't argue, there wasn't time. Instead, he kicked down the door and then followed Gabriel and Mikhail inside. Saladin lay on a bare mattress in the darkest corner, his face lit by the glow of a mobile phone. Startled, he reached for the Kalashnikov at his side. Gabriel sprinted toward him, the Jericho in his outstretched hands, and fired eleven shots into Saladin's heart. Then he reached down and snatched up the fallen phone. It was vibrating with an incoming message.

INSHALLAH, IT WILL BE DONE . . .

Saladin had made his last stand not with a gun but with a Nokia 5 Android phone. There were more scattered around him, along with several Samsung Galaxies and iPhones, eight laptop computers, and dozens of flash drives. Mikhail and Keller quickly loaded the devices into a duffel bag while Gabriel snapped a photo of Saladin's lifeless face. It was not a trophy. He wanted to prove definitively that the monster was gone and thus deliver a body blow not only to the Islamic State but to the entire global jihadist movement.

Dina and Natalie were turning through the open gate of the compound when Gabriel, Mikhail, and Keller exited the house. Yaakov was digging another Nokia 5 from the pocket of Nazir Bensaïd. The rented Peugeot was not fit for the road, not with the blown-out windscreen and the bullet holes from stem to stern, so they all piled into the Jeep Cherokee instead. In total, from forceful entry to hasty departure, they were inside the compound for less than five minutes.

Evidently, the sound of the gunfire and the explosion had reached the center of Zaida. As they sped along the town's main street, they were met by a few stares, some curious, others manifestly hostile, but no one tried to stop them. It was not until they reached the tiny Berber hamlet of Aït Oufella, some ten miles down the mountain, that they spotted the first gendarmes coming up the valley.

The units swept past without slowing and continued on toward Zaida. In twenty minutes, perhaps less, they would enter the compound. And in a room on the second floor of the house they would find a large, powerfully built Arab lying alone, with eleven bullet holes in the front of his djellaba. Had he been capable of speech, he would have done so with a distinct Iraqi accent, and had he been ambulatory, he would have walked with a limp. He had lived a life of violence, and had died accordingly. But had he, in his final seconds, ordered another attack? One last curtain call.

Inshallah, it will be done . . .

It was possible the answer—along with other critical intelligence—resided somewhere in the mobile phones, computers, and flash drives they had taken from Saladin's room. Therefore, it was essential that the devices not end up in the hands of the Moroccans, who would be more interested in solving the riddle of a long and violent night than in preventing the next attack. Still, Gabriel decreed that theirs would not be a fighting retreat. There had been enough bloodshed already. And now that Saladin was dead, the Moroccans were less likely to throw a diplomatic temper tantrum or do something stupid, like prosecuting the chief of the Israeli secret intelligence service for murder.

It was approaching seven when they reached Fez. They headed north through the Rif Mountains, toward the Mediterranean coast. The bolt-hole was at El Jebha, but it could not be utilized until after dark, when it would be safe to bring the Zodiacs ashore. That meant an entire day, perhaps longer, would be lost before the technicians could begin scrubbing the phones and computers for intelligence. Gabriel decided they would leave Morocco by ferry instead. The port of Tangier was the most obvious choice. There were regular ferries to Spain, France, and even Italy. But to the east was a smaller port with service directly to the British overseas territory of Gibraltar. They boarded the twelve-fifteen with minutes to spare. Gabriel and Keller stood at the railing in sunlight, Keller smoking a cigarette, Gabriel holding a mobile phone, as the white limestone cliffs of Gibraltar's famous rock appeared before them.

"Home at last," said Keller.

But Gabriel wasn't listening; he was staring at the photo he had snapped of Saladin's lifeless face.

"Best picture he's ever taken," said Keller.

Gabriel permitted himself a brief smile. Then he fired the photo securely to Adrian Carter at Langley. Carter's reply was instant.

"What does it say?" asked Keller.

"Alhamdulillah."

Keller dropped his cigarette into the sea. "We'll see about that."

From Gibraltar's ferry terminal, it was only a short walk along Winston Churchill Avenue to the airport, where a chartered Falcon 2000 executive jet was waiting, courtesy of Her Majesty's

Secret Intelligence Service. Graham Seymour had stocked the plane with several bottles of excellent French champagne, but no one on board was in any mood for a celebration. Once the plane was airborne, they started switching on the captured phones and computers. All were locked, as were the flash drives.

It was late afternoon when they set down at London City Airport in the Docklands. Two vehicles were waiting, a panel van and a black Jaguar limousine. The van took Mikhail, Yaakov, Dina, and Natalie to Heathrow, where they would catch a late-departing flight for Ben Gurion. Gabriel and Keller rode in the Jaguar to Vauxhall Cross, along with the duffel bag.

They entered the building through the underground parking garage and carried the bag into Graham Seymour's office. Seymour had arrived from Washington a few hours earlier. He looked only slightly better than Gabriel and Keller.

"Amanda Wallace and I have agreed to a division of labor regarding the phones and computers. SIS will take half, and Five will get the rest. Our respective labs are fully staffed and ready to go."

"I'm surprised you were able to keep the Americans at bay," replied Gabriel.

"We weren't. The Agency and the FBI are sending liaison officers to look over our shoulders. In case you were wondering," added Seymour, "it was really him. The Agency confirmed it with an eight-point facial analysis." He offered a hand to Gabriel. "Honor is due. Congratulations, and thank you."

Gabriel reluctantly accepted Seymour's hand. "Don't thank me, Graham, thank *him*." He nodded toward Keller. "And

Olivia, of course. We would have never been able to get close to Saladin without her."

"The Royal Navy plucked her off that ersatz cargo ship of yours about an hour ago," said Seymour. "Needless to say, it is essential we keep her role a closely guarded secret."

"That might be difficult."

"Quite," said Seymour. "The Internet is already burning up with rumors that Saladin is dead. The White House is eager to make a formal announcement before the Moroccans beat them to the punch."

"When?"

"In time for the evening news. They were wondering whether the Office wanted any of the credit."

"God, no."

"They were hoping you would say that. The Moroccans will eventually get over an invasion of their sovereignty by the Americans, but the Israelis are another matter entirely."

"What about the British?"

"We're legally forbidden to take part in targeted killing operations. Therefore, we will say nothing." Seymour looked at Keller. "Even so, the debriefers are keen to have a word with you. The lawyers, too."

"That," said Keller, "would be a very bad idea."

"Were you the one who—"

"No," said Keller. "No such luck."

It was six that evening when the experts commenced work on the captured devices. MI5 was the first to break into a phone; MI6, a computer. As expected, all the documents were heavily encrypted. But by seven o'clock, technicians from both services were unbuttoning the documents at will and handing them off to the analytical teams to sift for vital clues. The first batch was low-grade stuff. But Gabriel and Keller, who were monitoring the search from Graham Seymour's office, warned against complacency. They had seen the look in Saladin's eyes as he was dispatching his final text.

At nine o'clock London time, the American president and CIA Director Morris Payne strode into the White House Briefing Room to announce that the ISIS terror mastermind known as Saladin had been killed overnight in a clandestine U.S. operation in the Middle Atlas Mountains of Morocco. It seemed his death was the result of a painstaking American effort to deliver justice to the man who had perpetrated the attack on Washington, and was evidence of the new administration's determination to wipe out radical Islamic terrorism once and for all. The Moroccans had known of the operation in advance and had provided valuable assistance, but otherwise it was an American undertaking from beginning to end. "And the results," boasted the president, "speak for themselves."

"No regrets?" asked Seymour.

"No," answered Gabriel. "I prefer to come and go without being seen."

When the president and his CIA director were finished, the reporters and the rented terrorism experts quickly tried to fill in the many gaps in the official account. Unfortunately for them, most of their information came directly from Adrian Carter and his staff, which meant little of it bore even a passing resemblance to the truth. By half past ten, Gabriel and Keller had had enough. Exhausted, they climbed into the Jaguar limousine and headed across the river to West London. Keller went to his opulent home in Kensington; Gabriel, to the old Office safe flat on Bayswater Road overlooking Hyde Park. Entering, he heard a woman singing softly to herself in Italian. He closed the door and smiled. Chiara always sang when she was happy.

W here are the children?"

"Who?"

"The children," Gabriel repeated deliberately. "Irene and Raphael. *Our* children."

"I left them with the Shamrons."

"You mean you left them with Gilah. Ari can barely look after himself."

"They'll be fine."

Gabriel accepted a glass of chilled Gavi and sat down on a stool at the kitchen counter. Chiara washed and dried a packet of mushrooms, and with a few deft movements of her knife reduced them to rows of perfect slices.

"Don't cook," said Gabriel. "It's too late to eat."

"It's *never* too late to eat, darling. Besides, you look like you can use some food." She wrinkled her nose. "And a shower."

"Hamid and Tarek said if I showered, I would disturb the jinns."

"Who are Hamid and Tarek?"

"Unwitting employees of Israeli intelligence."

"And the jinns?"

Gabriel explained.

"I wish I could have been there with you."

"I'm glad you weren't."

Chiara tossed the mushrooms into a sauté pan and a moment later the smell of warm olive oil filled the air. Gabriel drank some of the Gavi.

"How did you know we were coming to London?"

"A contact inside the Office."

"Does this contact of yours have a name?"

"He prefers to remain anonymous."

"Of course."

"He's a former chief. Very important." She gave the pan a shake, and the mushrooms began to sizzle. "When I heard you and the team were making a run for Gibraltar, I stowed away on a flight to London. Housekeeping was kind enough to put a few things in the fridge."

"Why didn't anyone tell the current chief about this?"

"I asked them not to. I wanted it to be a surprise." She smiled. "Didn't you notice my bodyguards down on Bayswater Road?"

"I was too tired to look."

"Your tradecraft is starting to slip, darling. They say it happens to those who spend too much time behind a desk."

"I doubt Saladin would agree with you."

"Really?" Chiara glanced at the television playing silently on the counter. "Because the BBC says it was all an American operation."

"The Americans," said Gabriel, "were very helpful. But we were the ones who got him, with significant help from Christopher Keller."

"And to think he tried to kill you once." She drank some of Gabriel's wine.

"How much did Uzi tell you about what happened?"

"Very little, actually. I know the drone strike didn't go as planned and that you managed to track Saladin to a compound up in the mountains. After that, things get a little fuzzy."

"For me, too," said Gabriel.

"Were you there?"

He hesitated, then nodded slowly.

"Were you the one who—"

"Does it matter?"

She said nothing.

"Yes," said Gabriel, "it was me. I was the one who killed him."

And then he told her the rest of it. The woman who had detonated herself on the stairwell. The roomful of phones and computers in which Saladin had spent his last hours. The final text message.

Inshallah, it will be done . . .

"It was probably just talk," said Chiara.

"From a man who nearly managed to smuggle a shipment of cesium chloride into France. Enough cesium chloride to build several dirty bombs. Bombs that would make the center of a city uninhabitable for years." He paused, then added, "You see my point."

Chiara waited until the mushrooms had shed their water before seasoning them with salt and pepper and freshly chopped thyme. Then she dropped several bundles of dried fettuccini into a pot of boiling water.

"How long are you planning to stay in London?" she asked.

"Until the British have finished scrubbing the phones and the computers we took from the compound."

"You're worried he's coming after us?"

"His first target was the Isaac Weinberg Center for the Study of Anti-Semitism in France. It's better for me to stay here while the intelligence is being processed. It's less likely that something will slip through the cracks."

"But no more heroics," she cautioned.

"No," said Gabriel. "I'm the chief now."

"You were the chief when you were in Morocco, too." She tested a strand of the fettuccini. Then she looked around the little kitchen and smiled. "You know, I've always loved this apartment. We've had good times here, Gabriel."

"And bad ones, too."

"We were married here. Do you remember?"

"It wasn't a real wedding."

"I thought it was." Her expression darkened. "I remember it all so clearly. It was the night before . . ."

Her voice trailed off. To the sauté pan she added wine and cream. Then she poured the mixture over the fettuccini and tossed in grated cheese. She prepared only a single portion and placed it before Gabriel. He plunged a fork into it and twirled.

"None for you?" he asked.

"Oh, no." Chiara glanced at her wristwatch. "It's much too late to eat."

Gabriel had used the safe flat so often that his clothing hung in the closet and his toiletries filled the bathroom cabinet. After finishing a second portion of the pasta, he showered and shaved and fell, exhausted, into bed next to Chiara. He had hoped his sleep would be dreamless, but that was not to be the case. He climbed an endless flight of steps that were drenched in blood and littered with the remains of a woman. And when he found the head and moved aside the veil, it was Chiara's face he saw.

Inshallah, it will be done . . .

Shortly before five o'clock, he awoke suddenly, as if startled by the sound of a bomb. It was only his mobile phone, which was shimmying across the surface of the bedside table. He brought it swiftly to his ear and listened in silence. Rising, he dressed in darkness. And to the darkness he returned.

68

THAMES HOUSE, LONDON

The Jaguar limousine was waiting downstairs on the Bayswater Road. It delivered Gabriel not to Vauxhall Cross but to Thames House, the headquarters of MI5. Miles Kent, the deputy director, escorted him quickly upstairs to Amanda Wallace's suite. She looked worn and tired, and was obviously under a great deal of stress. Graham Seymour was there, too, still dressed in the same suit he'd been wearing the night before, absent the club tie. Junior officers were rushing in and out of the room, and there was a secure videoconference up and running to Scotland Yard and Downing Street. The fact that they were gathered here instead of across the river could mean only one thing. Someone had found proof on Saladin's phones and computers that an attack was imminent. And London was once again the target.

"How long have you known?" asked Gabriel.

"We unearthed the first nugget around two o'clock this morning," said Seymour.

"Why didn't anyone tell me?"

"We thought you could use a bit of sleep. Besides, it's our problem, not yours."

"Where?"

"Westminster."

"When?"

"Later this morning," said Seymour. "We think around nine."

"What's the method of attack?"

"Suicide bomber."

"Do you know his identity?"

"We're still working on that."

"Just one? You're sure?"

"So it would seem."

"Why only one?"

Seymour handed Gabriel a stack of printouts. "Because one is all they need."

The text message had been dispatched at three fifteen the previous morning Morocco time, when the likely sender had been under emotional distress and in physical pain. As a result, it had lacked the network's normal secondary and tertiary encryption protocols, thus allowing an MI5 computer technician to unearth it from one of the phones taken from the Zaida compound. The language was coded but unmistakable. It was an order to carry out a martyrdom operation. There was no mention of a target, but the apparent haste with which the message was sent allowed the technician to find related communications and documents that made the objective of the attack, and the time it was to be carried out, abundantly clear. Numerous casing photos had been found, and even a document discussing prevailing winds and the likely dispersal pattern of the radiological material. The planners hoped, God willing, for an area of nuclear contamination stretching from Trafalgar Square to Thames House itself. MI5's own experts, who had studied similar scenarios, predicted that such an attack would render the seat of British power uninhabitable for months, if not years. The economic cost, not to mention the psychological toll, would be catastrophic.

The recipient of the message had been more cautious than the sender. Still, the sender's early mistake had effectively nullified the recipient's care. As a result, the MI5 technician had been able to locate the entire exchange of messages, along with a martyrdom video. The subject addressed the camera in a London accent, with his face concealed. MI5's linguistics experts reckoned he was from North London, that he was native born, and likely of Egyptian ancestry. With the help of GCHQ, Britain's signals intelligence service, MI5 was frantically comparing the man's voice to known Islamic radicals. What's more, MI5 and SO13, the Counter Terrorism Command of the Metropolitan Police, were monitoring known extremists and suspected members of ISIS. In short, the entire national security apparatus of the United Kingdom was in quiet but efficient panic mode.

By six o'clock, as the skies beyond Amanda's windows were beginning to brighten, all efforts to identify and locate the suspected suicide bomber had proven fruitless. Prime Minister Jonathan Lancaster, in the Cabinet Room at Number 10, convened a videoconference at half past. He opened it with a question no counterterrorism professional ever wanted to hear. "Should we cordon off Westminster and order an evacuation of the surrounding districts?" One by one, his senior ministers, civil servants, intelligence chiefs, and police commissioners gave their answers. Their recommendation was unanimous.

Close Westminster. Shut down all rail, bus, and commuter traffic into central London. Begin an orderly and thorough evacuation.

"And what if it's a hoax? Or a bluff? Or what if it's based on bad intelligence? We'll look like Chicken Little. And the next time we say the sky is falling, no one will believe us."

The intelligence, everyone agreed, was as good and timely as it gets. And they were rapidly running out of other options to prevent a monumental disaster.

The prime minister's eyes narrowed. "Is that you I see, Mr. Allon?"

"It is, Prime Minister."

"And what say you?"

"It's not my place, sir."

"Please don't stand on ceremony. You and I know each other too well for that. Besides, there isn't time."

"In my opinion," said Gabriel carefully, "it would be a mistake to order closures and evacuations."

"Why?"

"Because you'll lose your one and only chance to stop the attack."

"Which is?"

"You know the time and place it will occur. And if you try to cordon off the center of London, you'll incite mass panic, and the suicide bomber will simply choose a secondary target."

"Go on," instructed the prime minister.

"Keep the entrances to Westminster wide open. Place CBRN teams and undercover SCO19 firearms officers at strategic points around Parliament and Whitehall."

"Let him walk straight into a trap? Is that what you're saying?"

"Exactly, Prime Minister. He won't be hard to miss. He'll be overdressed for the summer weather, and the detonator will be visible in one of his hands. He'll probably be sweating with nerves and reciting prayers. He might even be suffering from radiation sickness. And when he walks past a Geiger counter," said Gabriel in conclusion, "he'll light it up. Just make sure the firearms officer who goes after him has the nerve and experience to do what's necessary."

"Any candidates?" asked the prime minister.

"Only two," said Gabriel.

69

PARLIAMENT SQUARE, LONDON

I think this is the beginning of a beautiful friendship."

"Or the end of one."

"Why are you always so fatalistic?" asked Keller. "We're not in the Sahara anymore. We're in the middle of London."

"Yes," said Gabriel, looking around. "What could possibly go wrong here?"

They were seated on a bench at the western edge of Parliament Square. It was a fine summer's morning, cool and soft, with a promise of rain later in the day. Directly behind them was the Supreme Court, the highest court in the realm. To their right were Westminster Abbey and the medieval St. Margaret's Church. And directly before them, across the green lawn of the square, was the Palace of Westminster. The clock in the iconic bell tower read five minutes to nine o'clock. Rush-hour traffic was flowing across Westminster Bridge and up and down Whitehall, past Her Majesty's Revenue and Customs, the Foreign and Commonwealth Office, the Ministry of Defense, and the entrance to Downing Street, official residence of the prime minister. Yes, thought Gabriel again. What could possibly go wrong?

He wore a radio earpiece in his right ear and a gun at the small of his back. The gun was a 9mm Glock 17, the standard-issue sidearm of SCO19, the tactical firearms unit of London's Metropolitan Police. The radio was connected to the Met's secure communications network. The head of SO15, the Counter Terrorism Command, was running the show, with assistance from Amanda Wallace of MI5. Thus far, they had identified two potential suspects approaching Westminster. One was coming across the bridge from Lambeth. The other was making his way along Victoria Street. In fact, at that very instant, he was walking past New Scotland Yard. Both men were carrying backpacks, hardly unusual in London, and both were Middle Eastern or South Asian in appearance, also not unusual. The man coming across the bridge had started his journey in the borough of Tower Hamlets in East London. The one walking past New Scotland Yard had come from the Edgware Road section of North London. He was warmly dressed and looked to be suffering from the flu.

"Sounds like our man," said Gabriel. "I'm betting on Edgware and influenza."

"We'll know in a minute." Keller was leafing through that morning's edition of the *Times*. It was filled with news of Saladin's death.

"Can't you at least—"

"What?"

"Never mind."

The man from Tower Hamlets had reached the Westminster side of the bridge. He passed a Caffè Nero coffeehouse and the entrance to the Westminster Tube stop. Then he passed an undercover CBRN team and two tactical firearms officers in plain clothes. No trace of radioactivity, no detonator in the hand, no sign of emotional distress. Wrong man. He crossed the street to Parliament Square and joined a small, sad protest having something to do with the war in Afghanistan. Was it still going on? Even Gabriel found it hard to imagine.

He turned his head a few degrees to the right to watch the second man—the man from the Edgware Road section of North London—walking along Broad Sanctuary, past the North Tower of the Abbey. Keller was pretending to read the sporting news.

"How does he look?"

"Sick as a dog."

"Something he ate?"

"Or something he's wearing. He looks like he would glow in the dark."

A CBRN team was on the north lawn of the Abbey, posing for photos like ordinary tourists, along with another SCO19 unit. The CBRN team had already begun to detect elevated levels of radiation, but as the man from Edgware approached, the levels spiked dramatically.

"Fucking Chernobyl," said Keller. "We've got him."

A commotion erupted over the radio, several voices shouting at once. Gabriel forced himself to look away.

"What are the odds?" he asked calmly.

"Of what?"

"That he chooses us?"

"I'd say they're getting better by the minute."

The man crossed Broad Sanctuary to the Supreme Court building and entered Parliament Square at the southwest corner. A few seconds later, sweating, lips moving, pale as death, he was approaching the bench on which Gabriel and Keller sat.

"Someone needs to put that poor bloke out of his misery," said Keller.

"Not without an order from the prime minister."

The man walked past the bench.

"What level of exposure did we just suffer?" asked Keller.

"Ten thousand X-rays."

"How many have you had?"

"Eleven thousand," said Gabriel. Then he said quietly, "Look at the left hand."

Keller did. It was clutching a detonator.

"Look at his thumb," said Gabriel. "He's already putting pressure on the trigger. Do you know what that means?"

"Yeah," said Keller. "It means he's got a dirty bomb with a dead man's switch."

Big Ben was tolling nine o'clock when the martyr-in-waiting reached the eastern flank of the square. He paused for a moment to watch the protest and, it seemed to Gabriel, to consider his options—the Palace of Westminster, which was directly before him, or Whitehall, which was to his left. The prime minister and his security aides were considering their options as well. At this point, there was only one. Someone had to grant the man the death he so badly wanted while someone else held his thumb tightly to the detonator switch. Otherwise, several people would die, and the seat of British power and history would be a radioactive wasteland for the foreseeable future.

At last, the martyr-in-waiting turned to the left toward Whitehall, with Gabriel and Keller trailing a few steps behind. A gentle breeze blew from the north directly into their faces—a breeze that would disperse the radioactivity all over Westminster and Victoria if the bomb detonated. The CBRN team that had been at Caffè Nero was now standing outside the Revenue and Customs building; their readings were off the charts as the man walked past them. It was all the proof the prime minister needed. "Take him down," he said, and the head of the Counter Terrorism Command repeated the order to Gabriel and Keller. Then he added quietly, "And may God be with you both."

But on whose side, thought Gabriel, was God on that morning? On the side of the fanatic with a weapon of mass destruction strapped to his body, or the two men who would try to prevent him from detonating it? The first move was Keller's to make. He had to seize the left hand of the martyr in an iron-lock grip before Gabriel fired the kill shot. Otherwise, the martyr's thumb would weaken on the detonator switch and the bomb would explode.

They passed the archway of King Charles Street and the entrance of the Foreign and Commonwealth Office. The traffic along Whitehall dwindled. Evidently, the police had blocked it off at Parliament Square to the south and Trafalgar Square to the north. The martyr-in-waiting seemed not to notice. He was walking toward destiny, walking toward death. Gabriel drew the Glock pistol from the small of his back and quickened his pace while Keller, a blur in his peripheral vision, drew a few deep breaths.

Before them, the sweating, radiation-sickened martyr passed unseeing through a knot of tourists and started toward the security gate of Downing Street, his apparent target. He slowed to a stop, however, when he saw the black-uniformed police officers standing on the pavement. At once, he noticed the peculiar absence of cars in the normally busy street. Then, turning, he saw the two men walking toward him, one with a gun in his hand. The eyes widened, the arms rose and stretched shoulder-width from each side.

Keller rushed forward while Gabriel raised the Glock. He waited until the instant Keller grabbed the bomber's left hand before squeezing the trigger. The first two shots obliterated the bomber's face. The rest he fired after the man was on the pavement. He fired until his gun was empty. He fired as though he were trying to drive the man deep underground and all the way to the gates of hell.

Suddenly, there were police and bomb-disposal technicians rushing toward them from all directions. A car pulled up in the street, the rear door opened. Gabriel hurled himself into the backseat, and into the arms of Chiara. The last thing he saw as the car drove away was Christopher Keller holding a dead man's thumb to a detonator switch.

Part Four

GALLERY OF MEMORIES

The evacuation of Westminster and Whitehall was far shorter in duration than Saladin might have hoped, but traumatic all the same. For nine long days, the beating heart of British politics, the religious and political epicenter of a once-glorious civilization and empire, was cordoned off from the rest of the realm and closed for business. The dead zone stretched from Trafalgar Square in the north to Milbank in the south, and eastward into Victoria to New Scotland Yard. The great ministries sat empty, as did the Houses of Parliament and Westminster Abbey. Prime Minister Lancaster and his staff left 10 Downing Street and relocated to an undisclosed country house. The Queen, against her wishes, was moved to Balmoral Castle in Scotland. Only the CBRN teams were allowed to enter the restricted area, and only for limited periods. They moved about the deserted streets and squares in their lime-green hazmat suits, sniffing the air for any lingering traces of radioactivity, while the mournful tolling of Big Ben marked the passage of time.

The reopening was a joyless affair. The prime minister and his wife, Diana, stole into Number 10 as though they were breaking into their own home, while up and down the length of Whitehall civil servants and permanent secretaries returned quietly to their desks. In the House of Commons there was a moment of silence; in the Abbey, a prayer service. London's mayor claimed the city would emerge stronger as a result of the near disaster, though he offered no explanation as to why that was the case. A headline of a leading conservative tabloid read WELCOME TO THE NEW NORMAL.

It was a Wednesday, which meant the prime minister was obliged to rise before the Commons at noon and field questions from the political opposition. They were deferential at first, but not for long. Mainly, they wanted to know how it was possible that, just six months after the devastating attack in the West End, ISIS had managed to smuggle the makings of a dirty bomb into the United Kingdom. And how, given the elevated threat level, the security services had been unable to identify the bomber before the morning of the planned attack. The prime minister was tempted to say that the near-impossible security situation confronting Britain was the result of mistakes made by a generation of leaders—mistakes that had turned the land of Shakespeare, Locke, Hume, and Burke into the world's preeminent center of Salafist-jihadi ideology. But he did not rise to the bait. "The enemy is determined," he declared, "but so are we."

"And the manner in which the suspect was neutralized?" wondered the MP from the Washwood Heath section of Birmingham, a heavily Muslim city in the British West Midlands that had produced numerous terrorists and plots.

"He wasn't a suspect," interjected the prime minister. "He was a terrorist armed with a bomb and several grams of radio-active cesium chloride."

"But was there really no other way to deal with him other than a cold-blooded execution?" the MP persisted.

"It was no such thing."

The stated position of Her Majesty's Government and New Scotland Yard was that the two men who prevented the terrorist from detonating his dirty bomb were members of Met's SCO19 special firearms division. The Met refused to make public their names. Nor did it agree to the media's request to release CCTV images of the operation. Somehow, there was only a single video of the incident, shot by an American tourist who happened to be standing at the security gate of Downing Street at nine o'clock. Out of focus and tremulous, it showed one man firing several rounds into the terrorist's head while another man held the detonator switch in the terrorist's left hand. The shooter immediately left the scene in the back of a car. As it raced up Whitehall, he could be seen embracing a woman in the backseat. His face was not visible, only a patch of gray, like a smudge of ash, at his left temple.

But it was his partner, the one who held the terrorist's thumb to the detonator for three hours while technicians disarmed the dirty bomb, who received most of the media's attention. Overnight, he became a national hero; he was the man who had selflessly risked his own life for Queen and country. But such stories rarely survive long—not in the graceless age of twenty-four-hour news and social media—and soon there appeared numerous stories calling into question his identity and affiliation. The *Independent* claimed he was a former member of the Special Air Service who had served notably in Northern Ireland and the first Iraq War. The *Guardian*, however, weighed in with a dubious claim that he was actually an officer of MI6. Lines had been blurred, the newspaper said, or perhaps even crossed. Graham Seymour took the unusual step of issuing a denial. Officers of the Secret Intelligence Service, he said, did not engage in law-enforcement activities, and few ever bothered to carry a firearm. "The allegation," he declared, "is laughable on its face."

Nearly lost in the finger-pointing was the fact that Saladin, the author of a transatlantic trail of bloodshed and broken buildings, was no more. At first, his legion of followers, including some who openly walked the streets of London, refused to believe he was really gone. Surely, they claimed, it was nothing more than a piece of black American propaganda designed to weaken ISIS's grip on a generation of young Islamic radicals. The photograph of Saladin's lifeless, retooled face didn't help matters, for it bore little resemblance to the original. But when ISIS confirmed his passing on one of its primary social media channels, even his most ardent supporters seemed to accept the fact he was truly gone. His closest lieutenants had no time to mourn; they were too busy dodging American bombs and missiles. London was the last straw. The final battle—the one ISIS hoped would lead to the return of the Mahdi and commence the countdown to the end of days—had begun.

But what were the exact circumstances of Saladin's death at the compound in the Middle Atlas Mountains of Morocco? The White House—and the president himself—gave several conflicting versions of the story. Complicating the issue further was a report from an independent Moroccan news site concerning three Toyota Land Cruisers found in the southeast corner of the country, not far from the sand sea at Erg Chebbi. One of the SUVs appeared to have crashed, but the other two were burned-out shells. The Web site claimed they were destroyed by an American Predator drone, a claim supported by an accompanying photograph of Hellfire missile fragments. The White House denied the report in the strongest possible language. So, too, did the government of Morocco. Then, for good measure, it shut down the Web site that had published the photos and tossed its editor in jail.

The allegation of an American drone strike on Moroccan soil ignited protests across the country, especially in the Bidonvilles where the ISIS recruiters plied their deadly trade. The unrest nearly overshadowed the brutal killing of Mohammad Bakkar, Morocco's largest producer of hashish, the self-proclaimed king of the Rif Mountains. The deplorable condition of the body, said the gendarmes, suggested Bakkar had been the target of a drug-related vendetta. Harder to explain was the fact that Jean-Luc Martel, the wildly successful French hotelier and restaurateur, had been found lying a few feet away, with two neat bullet holes in the face. The Moroccans were not terribly interested in trying to determine how Martel had met his fate or why; they wanted only to move the matter off their plate as quickly as possible. They delivered his body to the French Embassy, signed the necessary paperwork, and bid JLM a fond adieu.

In France, though, Jean-Luc Martel's violent end was an occasion for serious investigation, both by the press and the authorities, and no small amount of soul-searching. The circumstances surrounding his death suggested that the rumors about him had been true after all, that he was not a businessman with a golden touch but an international drug trafficker in disguise. As details found their way onto the pages of *Le Monde* and *Le Figaro*, once-promising political careers crumbled. The French president was forced to issue a statement of regret over his friendship with

Martel, as were the interior minister and half the members of the National Assembly. As usual, the French press approached the matter philosophically. Jean-Luc Martel was viewed as a metaphor for all that was ailing modern France. His sins were France's sins. He was evidence that something, somewhere, was amiss with the Fifth Republic.

Arrests soon followed, from the headquarters of JLM Enterprises in Geneva to the streets of Marseilles. His hotels were padlocked, his restaurants and retail outlets shuttered, his properties and bank accounts seized and frozen. In fact, the only thing the French government didn't lay claim to was his corpse, which languished for several days in a Paris morgue before a distant family member from his village in Provence finally requested it for burial. The funeral and graveside services were poorly attended. Notably absent was Olivia Watson, the beautiful former fashion model who was Martel's companion and business partner. All efforts to locate Miss Watson, by the French authorities and the media, were without success. Her gallery in Saint-Tropez remained closed for business, its display window overlooking the Place de l'Ormeau empty of paintings. The same was true of her clothing boutique on the rue Gambetta. The villa she shared with Martel appeared deserted. Curiously, so, too, did the garish palace on the opposite side of the bay.

But was there a connection between the death of Jean-Luc Martel and the killing of the ISIS terror mastermind known as Saladin? A connection other than a similar time and place? Even the most conspiratorially minded journalists thought it unlikely. Still, there were enough tenuous links to merit a second look, and look they did—from the West End of London, to the seventh arrondissement of Paris, to an empty art gallery in

Saint-Tropez, to a patch of blood-soaked pavement near the entrance of Downing Street. Reporters who specialized in matters related to security and intelligence thought they could detect a pattern. There was smoke, they said. And where there was smoke there was usually the prince of fire.

In time, even the most carefully woven lies unravel. All it takes is a loose thread. Or a man who feels compelled, for reasons of honor, or perhaps out of a sense of debt, to bring the truth to light. Not all of it, of course, for that would have been insecure. Only a small slice of it, enough to keep a promise. He gave the story to Samantha Cooke of London's *Telegraph*, who crashed it in time for the Sunday edition. Within hours, it had set four distant capitals ablaze. The Americans ridiculed the account as pure fantasy, and the reviews from the British and the French were only slightly less caustic. Only the Israelis refused to comment, but then that was their standard procedure when it came to intelligence operations. They had learned the hard way that it was better to say nothing at all than issue a denial no one would believe anyway. In this case, at least, their reputation was well deserved.

The officer at the center of the story was spotted at the weekly meeting of the prime minister's fractious cabinet and, later that evening, with his wife and two young children at Focaccia restaurant on Rabbi Akiva Street in Jerusalem. As for Olivia Watson, the former fashion model, gallerist, and not-quite wife of the disgraced Jean-Luc Martel, her whereabouts remained a mystery. A prominent French crime reporter wondered whether she was dead. And though the reporter had no way of knowing it, Olivia was wondering the very same thing.

WORMWOOD COTTAGE, DARTMOOR

They locked her away at Wormwood Cottage with only Miss Coventry the housekeeper for company and a couple of bodyguards to watch over her. And old Parish the caretaker, of course, but Parish kept his distance. He'd looked after all sorts during the many years he'd worked at the facility—defectors, traitors, blown field agents, even the odd Israeli—but there was something about the new arrival that rubbed him the wrong way. As usual, for reasons of security, Vauxhall Cross had withheld the guest's name. Even so, Parish knew exactly who she was. Hard not to; her face was splashed across the pages of every newspaper in the country. Her body, too, but only in the racier tabloids. She was the pretty girl from Norfolk who'd gone to America to become a fashion model. The girl who'd been mixed up with the Formula One drivers and the rock stars and the actors and that horrible drug dealer from the south of France. She was the one the French police were supposedly searching for high and low. She was JLM's girl.

She was a wreck the night she arrived and remained one for a long time after. Her blond hair hung long and limp, and in her blue Nordic eyes was a haunted look that told Parish she had seen something she should not have. Thin as a rail already, she lost weight. Miss Coventry tried to cook for her—proper English fare—but she turned up her nose at it. Mainly, she sat in her room upstairs, smoking one cigarette after the next and staring out at the bleak moorland. First thing each morning, Miss Coventry placed a stack of newspapers outside her door. Invariably, when she collected the papers later in the day, several pages would be torn out. And on the day her face appeared in the *Sun* beneath a deeply unflattering headline, the entire paper was ripped to ribbons. Only a photograph survived. It had been taken many years earlier, before the fall. Written across the forehead, in blood-red ink, were the words *JLM's Girl*.

"Serves her right to get mixed up with a drug dealer," said Parish judgmentally. "And a Frog drug dealer at that."

She had no clothing to speak of, only the clothes on her elegant back, so Miss Coventry offered to make a run to M&S to pick up a few things to tide her over. It was not what she was used to, mind you—she had her own clothing line, after all—but it was better than nothing. Much better, as it turned out. In fact, everything Miss Coventry selected looked as though it had been designed and tailored to fit her long, slender frame.

"What I wouldn't give to have a body like that for just five minutes."

"But look at what it's got her," murmured Parish.

"Yes, look."

By the end of the first week, the walls were beginning to close in on her. At Miss Coventry's suggestion, she went for a short walk across the moor, accompanied by a pair of bodyguards who looked far happier than normal. Afterward, she took a bit of sun in the garden. Once again, it was not what she was used to, the sun of Dartmoor being rather different than Saint-Tropez's, but it did wonders for her appearance. That evening she ate most of the lovely chicken pie Miss Coventry placed before her and then spent several hours in the sitting room watching the news on television. It was the night CNN broadcast the cell phone video shot by the American tourist outside Downing Street. When a grainy close-up appeared on the screen—a close-up of the officer who had held the terrorist's thumb to the detonator—she leapt suddenly to her feet.

"My God, that's him!"

"Who?" asked Miss Coventry.

"The man I met in France. He called himself Nicolas Carnot. But he's not a police officer. He's—"

"We do not speak of such things," said Miss Coventry, cutting her off. "Even in this house."

The beautiful blue eyes moved from the television screen to Miss Coventry's face. "You know him, too?" she asked.

"The man in the video? Oh, heavens no. How could I? I'm only the cook."

The next day she walked a little longer, and upon her return to Wormwood Cottage she asked to speak to someone in authority about the status of her case. Promises were made, she insisted. Assurances had been given. She insinuated they had come directly from "C" himself, a claim Parish found hard to believe. *As if "C" would ever trouble himself with the likes of her!* Miss Coventry, however, did not dismiss the idea out of hand. Like Parish, she had witnessed many peculiar events at the cottage, such as the night a rather notorious Israeli intelligence officer was handed a copy of a newspaper that declared he was dead.

An Israeli intelligence officer who, come to think of it, bore more than a passing resemblance to the man who'd fired several shots into the head of a terrorist on the pavements of Whitehall. No, thought Miss Coventry, it wasn't possible.

But even Miss Coventry, who occupied the lowliest rung on the ladder of Western intelligence, knew that it *was* possible. And so she was not at all surprised to find, on the front page of Sunday's edition of the *Telegraph* newspaper, a lengthy exposé regarding the operation that had led to the killing of the ISIS terror mastermind known as Saladin. It seemed Jean-Luc Martel, the now-deceased French drug trafficker and former companion of Wormwood Cottage's current occupant, was connected to the case after all. In fact, in the opinion of the *Telegraph*, he was the operation's unsung hero.

Miss Coventry placed the newspaper outside the woman's bedroom door, along with her coffee. And later that morning, while straightening the room, she found the article, intact and neatly clipped, resting on the bedside table. That evening, as a gale blew hard across Dartmoor, a man scaled the security gate without a sound and hiked up the gravel drive to the front door of the cottage. Entering, he wiped his feet and hung his sodden coat on the rack.

"What's for dinner?" he asked.

"Cottage pie," said Miss Coventry, smiling. "A nice cup of tea, Mr. Marlowe? Or would you like something stronger?"

She served them dinner at the little table in the alcove and then pulled on her raincoat and knotted a scarf beneath her chin. "You'll see to the dishes, won't you, Mr. Marlowe? And use soap this time, my love. It helps." A moment later the front door closed with a gentle thump and they were finally alone. Olivia smiled for the first time in many days.

"Mr. Marlowe?" she asked incredulously.

"I've grown rather fond of it."

"What's your first name?"

"Peter, apparently."

"It's not the name you were born with?"

He shook his head.

"And Nicolas Carnot?" she asked.

"He was just a part I played briefly to moderate acclaim."

"You played him well. Very well, actually."

"I take it you've met others like him."

"Jean-Luc seemed to attract them like flies." She studied Keller carefully. "So how did you do it? How did you get the part so right?"

"It's the little touches that count." He shrugged. "Hair, wardrobe, that sort of thing."

"Or maybe it's a part you've played before," suggested Olivia. "Maybe you simply reprised it."

"Your dinner is getting cold," said Keller evenly.

"I've never liked cottage pie. It reminds me of home," she said with a frown. "Of cold and rainy nights like this."

"They're not so bad."

She took an exploratory bite of the food.

"Well?" asked Keller.

"It's not like eating in the south of France, but I suppose it will do."

"Maybe this will help." Keller poured her a glass of Bordeaux.

She raised it to her lips. "This is definitely a first."

"What's that?"

"Having dinner with the man who killed my . . ."

She faltered. Even she seemed at a loss over how to refer to Jean-Luc Martel.

"You fooled him at first. But once you told him you were British, it didn't take him long to figure out who you really were. He said you were a former SAS officer who had spent several years hiding out on Corsica. He said you were a professional—"

"That's quite enough," interrupted Keller.

"I'm glad we cleared that up." After a silence she said, "We're not so different, you and I." "You're much more virtuous than I am."

She smiled. "You never judged me?"

"Never."

"And your Israeli friend?"

"People in glass houses."

"I saw him in that video," said Olivia. "You, too. He was the one who killed the dirty bomber. And you were the one who held on to the detonator. For three hours," she added softly. "It must have been awful."

Keller said nothing.

"No denials?"

"No."

"Why not?"

Why not, indeed? he thought. He watched the rain hurling itself against the windows of the snug little alcove.

Olivia drank some of the wine. "Did you have a chance to read the papers today?"

"Could you believe that story about Victoria Beckham in the *Mail*?"

"How about the one in the *Telegraph* about the killing of Saladin? The one about how Jean-Luc Martel helped British and Israeli intelligence penetrate Saladin's network and locate him in Morocco."

"Interesting reading," said Keller. "And true, for a change."

"Not all of it."

"Reporters," said Keller dismissively.

"I assume your Israeli friend was responsible."

"He usually is."

"Why did he do it? Why rehabilitate Jean-Luc's image after the way he acted at the camp in the Sahara?"

"Perhaps you didn't read the rest of the article," said Keller. "The part about how Jean-Luc's beautiful British girlfriend didn't know how he really made his money. The part about how the French authorities have no interest in investigating her in light of Jean-Luc's role in eliminating the world's most dangerous terrorist."

"I did read that part," she said.

"Then surely you realize he didn't do it for Jean-Luc's sake, he did it for yours. You're clean now, Olivia." Keller paused, then added, "You're restored."

"Just like you?"

"Much better, actually. You have your entire professional inventory of paintings plus the fifty million we gave you for the Basquiat and the Guston. Not to mention the loose change we found lying under the couch cushions in the gallery. The building alone is worth at least eight million. Needless to say," said Keller, "you're a very wealthy woman."

"With a blackened name."

"The *Telegraph* doesn't seem to think so. And neither will the rest of the London art world. Besides, they're nothing but a pack of thieves. You'll fit right in."

"A gallery?"

"That was the promise my friend made to you that afternoon at the villa in Ramatuelle," said Keller. "A blank canvas upon which to paint any picture you want. A life without Jean-Luc Martel."

"Without anyone," she said.

"Something tells me you'll have no shortage of suitors."

"Who would want to be with someone like me? I'm JLM's—"

"Eat," said Keller, cutting her off.

She tried another bite of the pie. "How long will I have to stay here?"

"Until Her Majesty's Secret Intelligence Service determines that it's safe for you to leave. Even then, it might be wise for you to retain the services of a professional security firm. They'll assign some nice ex-SAS lads to look after you, the kind Jean-Luc always hated."

"Any chance you can serve on my detail?"

"I'm afraid I have other commitments."

"So I'll never see you again?"

"It's probably better if you don't. It will help you forget the things you saw that night in Morocco."

"I don't want to forget. Not yet." She pushed away her plate and lit a cigarette. "What's your name?" she asked.

"Marlowe." And then, almost as an afterthought, Keller added, "Peter Marlowe."

"It sounds as though someone made it up."

"Someone did."

"Tell me your real name, Peter Marlowe. The name you were born with."

"I'm not allowed to."

She reached across the table and placed her hand atop Keller's. Quietly, she asked, "And are you allowed to stay here so I won't have to be all alone on this cold and dreary English night?"

Keller turned away from Olivia's blue eyes and watched the rain lashing against the windows.

"No," he said. "No such luck."

She had no plans for a splashy opening, but somehow, with the help of a hidden hand, or perhaps by magic, plans materialized. Indeed, no sooner had the sun set on the second Saturday in November than the art world and all its unclaimed baggage came flowing through her door. There were dealers and collectors and curators and critics. There were actors and directors from stage and screen, novelists, playwrights, poets, politicians, pop stars, a marquis who looked as though he'd just stepped off his yacht, and more models than anyone could count. Oliver Dimbleby pressed his gold-plated business card into the hand of any poor girl who happened to linger more than a second or two within his damp reach. Jeremy Crabbe, London's last faithful husband, seemed incapable of speech. Only Julian Isherwood managed to mind his manners. He planted his flag at the end of the courtesy bar, next to Amelia March of *ARTnews*. Amelia was gazing disapprovingly at Olivia Watson, who was posing for photographs in front of her Pollock, watched over by a couple of bodyguards.

"Worked out rather well for her in the end, don't you think?"

"How's that?" asked Isherwood.

"Gets herself involved with the biggest drug dealer in France, makes millions running a dirty gallery in Saint-Tropez, and now she's set up shop in St. James's, surrounded by you and Oliver and the rest of the Old Master fossils."

"And we are ever grateful she did," said Isherwood as he watched a gazelle-like girl float past his shoulder.

"You don't find any of it odd?"

"Unlike you, petal, I adore happy endings."

"I like mine with a grain of truth, and something about this doesn't add up. I'll have you know I intend to get to the bottom of it."

"Have another drink instead. Or better yet," said Isherwood, "have dinner with me."

"Oh, Julian." She pointed across the sea of heads, toward a tall, pale man standing a few feet from Olivia. "There's your old client, Dmitri Antonov."

"Ah, yes."

"Is that his wife?"

"Sophie," said Isherwood, nodding. "Lovely woman."

"That's not what I hear. And who's the one next to her?" she asked. "The dishy one who looks like another bodyguard."

"Name's Peter Marlowe."

"What's he do?"

"Couldn't say."

At half past eight Olivia took up a microphone and made a few remarks. She was pleased to be a part of the great London art world, she was happy to be home again. She made no mention of Jean-Luc Martel, the unsung hero of the hunt for the ISIS terror mastermind known as Saladin, and none of the reporters present, Amelia March included, bothered to ask her about JLM, either. She was free of him at last. It might as well have been stamped on her forehead.

At the stroke of nine the lights dimmed and the music started up and another wave of guests came squeezing through the door. Many were battle-scarred survivors of the blowouts at Villa Soleil. The ones who were busy being rich together. The ones with all the time in the world for everything. The Antonovs shook a few of the better hands before slipping into the back of their Maybach limousine, never to be seen again. Keller left a few minutes later, but not before pulling Olivia aside to offer his congratulations and bid her a good night. He thought she had never looked more beautiful.

"Do you like it?" she asked, beaming.

"The gallery?"

"No. The picture I painted on the blank canvas your friend gave me." She drew him close. "I want to see you," she whispered into his ear. "Whatever happened in your previous life, I promise I can make it all better."

Outside, it was beginning to rain. Keller snared a taxi in Pall Mall and rode it to his maisonette in Queen's Gate Terrace. After paying off the driver, he stood on the pavement for a long moment and scrutinized the blinds in his many windows. His instincts told him there was danger present. Turning, he crept silently down the steps to the lower entrance and drew the Walther PPK from the small of his back before unlocking the door. He entered his own home in a whirling blur, as he had entered the room in the southeast corner of the house in Zaida, and leveled his gun at the man seated calmly at the kitchen counter.

"Bastard," he said, lowering the weapon. "That one was close."

———

"You really have to stop doing this."

"Dropping in unannounced?"

"Breaking into my house. What would Mr. Marlowe's posh Kensington neighbors think if they heard gunfire?" Keller tossed his Crombie overcoat on the marble-topped island, where Gabriel, illuminated by the restrained recessed lighting, sat atop a stool. "You couldn't find anything to drink in my refrigerator?"

"Tea would be nice, thank you."

Keller frowned and filled the electric kettle with water. "What brings you to town?"

"A meeting at Vauxhall Cross."

"Why wasn't I on the guest list?"

"Need to know."

"What was the topic?"

"What part of need to know didn't you understand?"

"Do you want tea or not?"

"The meeting concerned certain suspicious activities related to the Iranian nuclear program."

"Imagine that."

"Hard to believe, I know."

"And the nature of these activities?"

"The Office is of the opinion that the Iranians are conducting weaponization research in North Korea. SIS concurs. It should," added Gabriel. "We're sharing the same source."

"Who is it?"

"Something tells me you'll know soon enough."

Keller opened one of the cabinets. "Darjeeling or Prince of Wales?"

"No Earl Grey?"

"Darjeeling it is." Keller dropped a teabag into a mug and waited for the water to boil. "You missed quite a party tonight."

"So I heard."

"Couldn't fit it into your busy schedule?"

"Didn't think it would be wise to show my face in a part of London where it is rather well known. Besides, I went to great effort to make Olivia presentable again. I didn't want to spoil my work."

"You removed the dirty varnish," said Keller. "Retouched the losses."

"In a manner of speaking."

"The article in the *Telegraph* was a lovely piece of work on your part. With one glaring exception," added Keller.

"What's that?"

"The heroic portrayal of Jean-Luc Martel."

"It was unavoidable."

"Are you forgetting he put a gun to Olivia's head?"

"I saw the whole thing."

"From the cheap seats."

Keller placed the mug of tea on the island. Gabriel left it untouched.

"Obviously," he said after a moment, "your feelings for Olivia are clouding your judgment."

"I have no feelings for her."

"Spare me, Mr. Marlowe. I happen to know that you were a frequent visitor to Wormwood Cottage during Olivia's stay there."

"Did Graham tell you that?"

"Actually, it was Miss Coventry. Furthermore," Gabriel sailed on, "it has come to my attention that you and Olivia shared an intimate moment tonight at the opening of her gallery."

"It wasn't intimate."

"Would you like to see the photograph?"

Keller wordlessly poured two fingers of whiskey into a cut-glass tumbler. Gabriel blew on his tea.

"Have I not been a good friend to you despite the unfortunate circumstances of our beginning? Have I not offered you sound advice? After all, if it wasn't for me you'd still be—"

"Your point?" interrupted Keller.

"Don't make the same mistake I made," said Gabriel. "Olivia knows more about you than any woman in the world other than that crazy fortune-teller on Corsica, and she's far too old for you. What's more, Vauxhall Cross has already rifled through all her dirty laundry, which means SIS won't stand in the way of your relationship. You were made for each other, Christopher. Grab on to her and never let go."

"Her past is—"

"Nothing compared to yours," said Gabriel. "And look how well you turned out."

Keller held out his hand.

"What?" asked Gabriel.

"Let me see it."

Gabriel handed his mobile phone across the countertop. "The happy couple," he said.

Keller looked at the photograph. It had been snapped from across the room while Olivia was whispering into his ear.

Whatever happened in your previous life, I promise I can make it all better . . .

"Who took it?"

"Julian," said Gabriel. "The true hero of the operation."

"Don't forget the Antonovs," said Keller.

"How could I?"

"They put in a brief appearance tonight, by the way. They actually looked happy for a change."

"You don't say."

"Think they're going to make it?"

"Yes," said Gabriel. "I think they might."

Which left one last loose thread. Not one, actually, but several hundred million. Not to mention a haunted house in the heart of old Casablanca, a lavish villa on France's Côte d'Azur, and a collection of paintings acquired under the expert eye of Julian Isherwood. The real estate was disposed of quietly and at a substantial loss, furnishings, caretakers, and jinns included. The paintings, as promised, found their way to Jerusalem, and onto the walls of the Israel Museum. The director wanted to call it the Dmitri and Sophie Antonov Collection. Gabriel, however, insisted the donation remain anonymous.

"But why?"

"Because Dmitri and Sophie don't really exist."

But the Antonovs' charity did not end there, for they had at their disposal a vast sum of money that had to go somewhere. Money they had borrowed, interest free, from the Butcher of Damascus. Money the Butcher had looted from his people be-fore gassing and bombing them, and dispersing them to refugee camps in Turkey, Jordan, and Lebanon. The Antonovs, through their representatives, donated countless millions to feed, clothe, house, and care for the medical needs of the displaced. They also pledged millions to build schools in the Palestinian territories— schools that did not teach children merely to hate—and to a facility in the Negev Desert that cared for severely disabled children, Jewish and Arab alike. Hadassah Medical Center received twenty million dollars to help construct a new suite of underground operating rooms. Another ten million went to the Bezalel Academy of Art and Design for new studio space and a scholarship program for promising Israeli artists from low-income families.

The largest portion of the Antonovs' fortune, however, would reside at the Bank of Israel, in an account controlled by the government agency headquartered in an anonymous office block on King Saul Boulevard. The amount was sufficiently large to see to all of life's little extras—assassinations, paid informants, defectors, false passports, safe houses, travel expenses, even an engagement party. Mikhail signed the last of the documents in Gabriel's office. In doing so, he laid Dmitri Antonov formally to rest.

"I'll miss him. He wasn't all bad, you know."

"For a Russian arms dealer," said Gabriel. "Did you bring the ring?"

Mikhail handed over the little velvet-covered box. Gabriel thumbed open the lid and frowned.

"What's wrong?"

"Is there a stone in there somewhere?"

"A carat and a half," protested Mikhail.

"It's not as nice as the one she was wearing in Saint-Tropez."

"That's true. But I don't have Dmitri's money."

No, thought Gabriel as he slipped the paperwork into his briefcase. Not anymore.

Chiara and the children were waiting downstairs in the parking garage, in the back of Gabriel's armored SUV. As they drove eastward across the Galilee, they were followed by a second SUV containing Uzi and Bella Navot, and a caravan of cars filled with more than two hundred members of the Office's analytical and operational staff. It was dark by the time they all reached Tiberias, but Shamron's villa, perched atop its escarpment overlooking the lake and the ancient battlefield, was ablaze with light. Mikhail and Natalie were the last to arrive. The ring sparkled on Natalie's left hand. Her eyes sparkled, too.

"It's much nicer than Sophie's, don't you think?"

"Oh, yes," said Gabriel hastily. "Much."

"Did you have anything to do with this?"

"Only by offering you a job no woman in her right mind would ever have taken."

"And now I'm one of you," she said, holding up the ring. "Till death do us part."

The occasion lacked the debauchery of the Antonovs' notorious parties at Villa Soleil, and for that everyone in attendance was grateful. Truth be told, none of them were real drinkers. Unlike their allies the British, they did not utilize heavy consumption of alcohol as part of their tradecraft. What's more, it was a school night, as they liked to say, and most would be back at their desks in the morning, save for Mikhail, who was leaving at dawn for an operation in Budapest. Office doctrine dictated he spend the night in a jump site in Tel Aviv. Gabriel and Yaakov Rossman, who was going with him, had granted Mikhail a reprieve.

Still, there was music and laughter and more food than anyone could possibly eat. Saladin, however, was not far from their thoughts. They spoke of him with respect and, even in death, with a trace of foreboding. Dina Sarid's dark prediction of the future—a future of endless cyberjihad—was coming to pass before their eyes. The caliphate of ISIS was slipping away. Too slowly, it was true, but it was dying nonetheless. But that did not mean the end of ISIS was at hand. In all likelihood, it would become just another Salafist-jihadi terrorist group, a first among equals with adherents around the globe who were willing to take up a knife or a bomb or an automobile in hatred's name. Saladin was now their patron saint. And thanks to the story in the *Telegraph*, the story Gabriel had planted, Israel and the Jews of the diaspora were their primary targets.

"It was," intoned Shamron, "a grave mistake on your part."

"It wasn't my first," answered Gabriel. "And I'm certain it won't be my last."

"I hope she was worth it."

"Olivia Watson? She was."

Shamron didn't appear convinced.

"Perhaps you merely used her as an excuse to justify that reckless leak to that British reporter friend of yours."

"Why would I have done something like that?"

"Maybe you wanted Saladin's followers to know that you were the one who killed him. Maybe," said Shamron, "you wanted to sign your name."

They had withdrawn from the party to Shamron's favorite

spot on the terrace. The lake shone silver in the moonlight, the skies above the Golan Heights flashed yellow and white with American ordnance. They were hitting targets all over Syria.

With his old Zippo lighter, Shamron ignited a cigarette. "Do they know what they're doing?"

"The Americans?"

Shamron nodded slowly.

"To be determined," said Gabriel.

"That doesn't sound hopeful."

"I've never cared for the word."

"Optimistic," suggested Shamron.

"There's little reason for it," said Gabriel. "Let's assume the Americans and their allies eventually defeat ISIS and roll back the caliphate. What then? Will Syria be put back together again? Will Iraq? Will the Americans stay this time to ensure the peace? Unlikely, which means there's going to be several million disaffected and disenfranchised Sunni Muslims living between the Tigris and the Euphrates. They will be a source of regional instability for generations to come."

"They were artificial countries to begin with, Iraq and Syria. Maybe it's time to draw new lines in the sand."

"Another failed Arab state in the making," said Gabriel. "Just what the Middle East needs."

"Perhaps now that Saladin is gone, they might actually stand a chance." Shamron gave Gabriel a sidelong look. "I must say, my son, you took the concept of operational chiefdom rather too far."

"You were the one who gave me that speech about walking and chewing gum at the same time."

"That didn't mean I wanted you to rush headlong into a

room and personally kill Saladin. What if he had been holding a gun instead of a cell phone?"

"The result would have been the same."

"I hope so."

"There's that word again."

Shamron smiled. "I *hope* you saved some of that money."

"The Butcher of Damascus," said Gabriel, "will be funding Office covert operations for many years to come."

"You gave an awful lot to help care for his victims."

"It will pay dividends down the road."

"Charity begins at home," said Shamron in disapproval.

"Is that a Corsican proverb?"

"Actually," said Shamron, "I'm fairly certain I coined it."

"One-fourth of the Syrian population is living outside Syria's borders," explained Gabriel. "And most are Sunni Muslims. Helping to care for them is smart policy."

"One-fourth," repeated Shamron, "and hundreds of thousands more are dead. And yet we are the ones the world blames for the suffering of the Arabs. As if the creation of a Palestinian state would magically solve all the many problems of the Arab world. The lack of education and jobs, the brutal dictators, the repression of women."

"It's a party, Ari. Try to enjoy yourself."

"There isn't time. Not for me at least." Shamron slowly crushed out his cigarette. "This horrible war in Syria should make it abundantly clear what would happen if our enemies ever managed to breach our defenses. If the Butcher of Damascus is willing to slaughter his own people, what would he do to ours? If ISIS is willing to kill other Muslims, what would they do if they could get their hands on the Jews?" He patted

Gabriel's knee paternally. "But these are your problems now, my son. Not mine."

They watched the light show in the sky, the former chief, the current chief, while behind them their friends and colleagues and loved ones forgot for a few moments the world of trouble that surrounded them.

"When I was a boy," said Shamron at last, "I used to have dreams."

"I had them, too," said Gabriel. "I still do."

The wind blew softly from the west, from the ancient battle-field of Hittin.

"Do you hear that?" asked Shamron.

"Hear what?"

"The clashing of the swords, the screams of the dying."

"No, Ari, I only hear the music."

"You're a lucky guy."

"Yes," said Gabriel. "I suppose I am."

House of Spies is a work of entertainment and should be read as nothing more. The names, characters, places, and incidents portrayed in the story are the product of the author's imagination or have been used fictitiously. Any resemblance to actual persons, living or dead, businesses, companies, events, or locales is entirely coincidental.

There are many graceful old buildings on the rue de Grenelle in Paris, entirely intact, but none house an elite counterterrorism unit of the DGSI called the Alpha Group, for no such unit exists. Also, one will search in vain for the headquarters of the Israeli secret intelligence service on King Saul Boulevard in Tel Aviv; it was moved long ago to a spot north of the city. The Liberty Crossing Intelligence Campus in McLean, Virginia— home of the National Counterterrorism Center and the Office of the Director of National Intelligence—was destroyed in a terrorist attack in *The Black Widow* but, fortunately, not in real life. Employees of the two agencies work day and night to keep the American homeland safe.

Gabriel Allon and his family do not reside at 16 Narkiss Street in Jerusalem, but occasionally they can be spotted at Focaccia or Mona, two of their favorite neighborhood restaurants. There are several art galleries in the *centre ville* of Saint-Tropez, some better than others, but none bear the name Olivia Watson. Nor will visitors to the St. James's section of London find an Old Master art gallery owned by anyone named Julian Isherwood, Oliver Dimbleby, or Roddy Hutchinson. The paintings referenced in *House of Spies* were quite obviously used fictitiously. The author has no comment on the manner in which they were acquired. Nor does he wish to imply that the murderous ruler of Syria maintains an account at the esteemed Bank of Panama.

The title of part 3 of *House of Spies* was suggested by a line from *The Sheltering Sky*, Paul Bowles's masterwork. The line also appears in the text of my novel, along with a portion of the subsequent sentence and one of Bowles's part titles. In addition, I borrowed iconography from Bowles—and poetry from Sting, also an admirer of *The Sheltering Sky*—in my depiction of Natalie Mizrahi's brief moonlit foray into the sand dunes of the Sahara. Obviously, Gabriel plundered F. Scott Fitzgerald's *The Great Gatsby* and *Tender Is the Night* when devising his operation, and it was more elegant as a result. Fans of the film version of *Dr. No* will doubtless recognize where Christopher Keller found his inspiration when describing the stopping power of a Walther PPK pistol.

I completed the first draft of *House of Spies*, with its depiction of two ISIS terrorist attacks in London, one successful, one foiled, on March 15, 2017. At 2:40 p.m. on March 22, Khalid Masood, a fifty-two-year-old convert to Islam, turned onto Westminster Bridge in a rented Hyundai. While crossing the Thames River at speeds reaching seventy-six miles per hour, he mowed down several helpless pedestrians on the southern pavement and then crashed the car into a railing in Bridge Street, outside the Houses of Parliament. There he stabbed to death forty-eight-year-old police constable Keith Palmer before being shot by an armed officer from the Metropolitan Police Service's close protection command. In all, the attack lasted eighty-two seconds. Six people died, including Masood, and more than fifty were wounded, some with catastrophic injuries.

The threat level at the time was "severe," meaning an attack was "highly likely." Four months earlier, however, Andrew Parker, director general of MI5, was even more blunt in his assessment. "There will be terrorist attacks in Britain," he told the *Guardian* newspaper. "It is an enduring threat and it's at least a generational challenge for us to deal with." ISIS's tactics differ from those of al-Qaeda. A suicide vest, a gun, a knife, an automobile, a truck: these are the weapons of the new jihadist terrorist. But ISIS has loftier ambitions. The group's external operations division is feverishly attempting to build a bomb that can be smuggled onto a commercial airliner without detection. And there is ample evidence to suggest ISIS has been trying to acquire the ingredients for a radiological dispersion device, or "dirty bomb."

With the caliphate of ISIS under siege from the United States and its coalition partners, the flow of foreign fighters from the West and other Middle Eastern countries has slowed to a trickle. Still, ISIS has proven adept at recruiting new members to its ranks. Oftentimes, they come with a criminal past. ISIS does not shun them. Quite the opposite: it is actively recruiting new members with criminal records, especially in Western Europe. "Sometimes people with the worst pasts create the best futures." So read a social media posting issued by Rayat al-Tawheed, a group of ISIS fighters from London. The message was clear. ISIS is willing to employ criminals to fulfill its dream of building a worldwide Islamic caliphate.

The nexus between crime and radical Islam is one of the most disturbing emerging trends confronting U.S. and Western European counterterrorism officials. Take, for example, the case of Abdelhamid Abaaoud, the presumed operational mastermind of ISIS's attack on Paris in November 2015. Born in Belgium and raised in the Molenbeek section of Brussels, he served terms in at least three prisons for assault and other crimes before joining ISIS. Salah Abdeslam, Abaaoud's accomplice and childhood friend, was also a petty criminal; in fact, they were once arrested together for breaking into a parking garage. Ibrahim El Bakraoui, who detonated a suicide bomb inside Brussels Airport in March 2016, fired on police with a Kalashnikov assault rifle during a 2010 attempted robbery of a currency exchange bureau. His younger brother, Khalid, who detonated a suicide device at a Brussels metro station, had a long criminal past that included convictions for several carjackings, a bank robbery, kidnapping, and weapons charges.

Numerous ISIS operatives have come from the world of illicit drugs, and ISIS has been linked to drug smuggling in the eastern Mediterranean almost since its inception. But there is now evidence to suggest that the group, with its finances under strain, is involved in North Africa's lucrative hashish trade. Not long after the fall of Muammar Gaddafi in Libya in 2011, Western European police noticed a sharp increase in the flow of hashish from Morocco, along with a change in the traditional smuggling route, with Libyan ports serving as the primary point of departure. Had ISIS, which had established a presence in post-

Gaddafi Libya, somehow attached itself to the hashish trade? European police couldn't say for certain. But they received a piece of welcome news in late 2016 when Moroccan authorities arrested Ziane Berhili, allegedly one of the world's largest producers of hashish. Berhili was the owner of a large dessert company in Morocco. But according to Italian authorities, he made most of his money by smuggling an estimated four hundred metric tons of hashish into Europe each year. The street value of those drugs would be somewhere in the neighborhood of $4 billion.

Morocco exports more than just drugs to Europe; it also exports terrorists. Abdelhamid Abaaoud, Salah Abdeslam, and Ibrahim and Khalid El Bakraoui have more in common than a criminal past. All are of Moroccan ethnicity. More than thirteen hundred Moroccans have joined ISIS, along with several hundred ethnic Moroccans from Western Europe, mainly from France, Belgium, and the Netherlands. During a research trip to Morocco in the winter of 2017, I saw a country on high alert. And with good reason. The chief of Morocco's counterterrorism service warned in April 2016 that his unit had broken up twenty-five ISIS plots in Morocco in the last year alone, one involving mustard gas. Morocco's vital tourism industry, which draws thousands of Westerners to the country each year, is a primary target.

Presumably, the United States and its partners will prevail in their campaign against ISIS in Iraq and Syria. But will the loss of the caliphate mean the end of ISIS-inspired or -directed terrorism? The answer is likely to be no. Already, the physical caliphate is being replaced by a digital one where virtual plotters recruit and plan in the security and anonymity of cyberspace. But the blood will flow in the real world, in the rail stations, airports, cafés, and theaters of the West. The global jihadist movement has proven itself uncannily adaptable. The West must adapt, too. And quickly. Otherwise, it will be left to ISIS and its inevitable offspring to determine the quality and security of our lives in "the new normal."

ACKNOWLEDGMENTS

I am enormously grateful for the love and support of my wife, Jamie Gangel, who helped with the conception of *House of Spies*, contributed numerous plot points, and skillfully edited my manuscript, which was completed only minutes before its deadline. My children, Lily and Nicholas, were a constant source of love and inspiration, especially during my research trip to Morocco, where they helped me chart the twists and turns of the novel's long climactic sequence.

I spoke to numerous spies, counterterrorism officials, and politicians involved in homeland security, and I will thank them now in anonymity, which is how they would prefer it. Louis Toscano, my dear friend and longtime editor, made countless improvements to the novel, large and small. Kathy Crosby, my eagle-eyed personal copy editor, made certain the text was free of typographical and grammatical errors. Any mistakes that slipped through their formidable gauntlet are mine, not theirs.

I consulted hundreds of books, newspaper and magazine articles, and Web sites while preparing this manuscript, far too many to name here. I would be remiss, however, if I did not mention *The Caliph's House* by Tahir Shah and *A House in Fez*

ACKNOWLEDGMENTS

by Suzanna Clarke. A special thanks to Michael Gendler, Linda Rappaport, Michael Rudell, and Eric Brown for their support and wise counsel.

The staffs of the Four Seasons Hotel in Casablanca and the Palais Faraj in Fez took wonderful care of us during our stay in Morocco, and our guides, M and S, gave us a glimpse of their remarkable country we will never forget. Stories of their travails against the jinns, told during a daylong drive through the snowy cedar forests of the Middle Atlas Mountains, found their way into my manuscript. So, too, did their generosity and kindness.

I am forever indebted to David Bull for his expert advice on all matters related to art and restoration. Each year, David grants me several hours of his valuable time to make certain my novels are free of errors. And for his punishment, he is now known throughout the art world as "the real Gabriel Allon." Finally, the inimitable Patrick Matthiesen took time out of a recent trip to America to regale me with stories of his experiences in a changing art market. Patrick's extraordinary Old Master gallery shares an address with the perpetually troubled establishment owned by the fictitious Julian Isherwood. Otherwise, they have in common only their deep love and knowledge of art, their sense of humor, and their humanity.